Young Lions Roar is dedicated to the memory of my
Great Uncle, Alec MacLennan, who served his country
in the Merchant Navy during the Second World War.

YOUNG LIONS ROAR

Andrew Mackay

Chapter One

"We don't stand a snowman's chance in the Sahara." Sam shook his head dejectedly as he peeked through the lace curtains from his first floor bedroom window.

"How many are heading your way?" Alan asked as he stood at the window next to Sam's.

"About a platoon of SS stormtroopers, and they look as mean as hell," Sam answered. "How many are heading your way?"

"About a platoon of SS stormtroopers and they also look as mean as hell," Alan echoed as he peered through the lace curtains at his window.

"Same here," Alice answered from the downstairs living room. "We're outnumbered and outgunned."

"So what else is new?" Sam guffawed grimly. "We're always outnumbered and outgunned, Alice." He carefully looked out of the window again. "The Huns are taking hostages. What's the current rate of exchange, Al?"

"One hundred hostages are to be executed for every German soldier that's killed," Alan answered.

"A platoon is walking up the street towards us and they're arresting all of the men from every house. They've just dragged Mr Cobb out of his front door." Alice's hand darted up to her mouth in concern as she gave a running commentary. "Oh no! Mrs Cobb is trying to stop them! Mrs Cobb! Don't do that! They'll-" Alice almost forgot herself and was on the verge of shouting a warning out of the window as a stormtrooper rifle butted Maria Cobb squarely in the face. There was a loud and sickening crack that echoed up the street as Maria collapsed like a sack of potatoes.

Edward Cobb moaned in despair as his wife lay in a motionless mound on the pavement. "Get your hands off me, you Nazi swine!" he shouted as he managed to momentarily twist free from the grip of the two stormtroopers who were holding him. He rushed over to the still form of his wife, carefully rolled her over onto her back and started to search for a pulse.

Alice watched as an SS officer walked over to Edward, pulled out his Luger pistol, cocked it, flicked off the safety catch and shot him twice in the back of the head. The Nazi side stepped nimbly out of the way as blood jetted from the back of Edward's head. Edward collapsed over Maria's body. The Cobb's two small children wailed inconsolably as they tried to pull their two dead parents to their feet.

Alice jammed her knuckles into her mouth and tears sprang to her eyes as she struggled to take in the scene of complete and utter horror that she had just witnessed. Lucy and Sophie Cobb had been turned into orphans in a matter of seconds. She had babysat the two Cobb girls on several occasions and knew the Cobb family well. Alice watched open mouthed as the SS officer pointed his pistol at the nearest crying child. Sophie screamed. Another SS officer batted the murderer's arm to the side just as he pulled the trigger. The round knocked a chunk of brick off the wall before ricocheting harmlessly into the air.

"What happened, Alice?" Sam asked from upstairs.

"They… they just murdered Edward and Maria Cobb," Alice said in shocked disbelief. "They were just about to kill Sophie and Lucy…" Alice's voice trailed off.

"Those murdering Nazi bastards!" Sam exploded in fury.

"They'll be here any minute," Alice continued as she wiped away her tears with the back of her hand. "If one of those dirty German swine sets one step inside the house then we open fire and kill as many as we can," she said, with steel in her voice.

6

"Killing's too good for those Nazi savages!" Alan said, with venom dripping.

Alice cocked her Schmessier submachine gun. " For mother and father, Edward and Maria Cobb and for all of the other poor souls who those murdering Nazis have killed. To hell with Ansett and keeping a low profile. Kill them all! Agreed?"

"Agreed," the boys answered as they cocked their machine guns in unison.

"Strength and honour, Sam. Strength and honour, Alan."

"Strength and honour, Alice," the boys chorused.

"You interfering old woman, Monat," the SS officer said with steam coming out of his ears. "You shouldn't have stopped me from shooting those two brats." He took out a cigarette from a silver case, tapped the end twice and lit it in order to calm his temper that was close to boiling point. He had never been so angry in his entire life. To have been humiliated in front of his own men, publicly manhandled by a brother SS officer no less. And all over the fate of a couple of English brats. What on earth was the world coming to?

"They were just children, Niebergall," Obersturmführer Hans Monat stuck resolutely to his guns. "You would have regretted it afterwards. We're not monsters."

Obersturmführer Martin Niebergall stopped walking so suddenly that Monat collided into the back of him. Niebergall turned around to face Monat, took out his wallet, flicked it open and shoved it roughly into Monat's face. "See these photos, Monat?" Niebergall stabbed the photos rapidly with his forefinger as he bared his teeth only inches from Monat's face.

Monat grimaced in disgust as spittle landed on his nose.

"These are my nephew and niece, Kurt and Heidi," Niebergall continued.

Monat found it hard to resist the urge to automatically recoil as Niebergall's garlic sausage breath assaulted his nostrils.

"Aren't they beautiful?"

Monat nodded again. He had absolutely no idea where Niebergall was going with this.

"They're my sister's children. Sabine's children. They're German children. Aryan children. Those brats," Niebergall gestured down the street with a contemptuous flick of his fingers, "those brats are English. They're not children. They're one step above Jewish untermenschen scum. They're the enemy and don't you forget it. I would kill those two brats with as little thought as I would stub out this cigarette." Niebergall dropped his cigarette on the floor and ground it out with the heel of his boot. "Or crush a cockroach. Try and stop me from carrying out my duties again and I'll shoot you like the cowardly English-loving dog that you are."

"Achtung!" Niebergall thumped the door with the heel of his hand. "Raus! Raus! Schnell! Schnell!"

The door opened to reveal a strikingly beautiful young woman. Niebergall was stunned and could not help staring. A genuine English rose. The evening had suddenly become more interesting. Who said that you could not mix business with pleasure? "Good evening, fräulein... are your parents at home?"

"My parents are both dead. You hanged them both from the Town Hall balcony."

"I'm sorry to hear that, fräulein, but I'm sure that you don't blame me personally..."

"As a matter of fact I do," Alice interrupted defiantly. "You Nazis are all equally to blame."

"I admire your spirit, fräulein." Niebergall bowed and clicked his heels in genuine admiration. "Are you alone?"

"Yes."

"Sehr gut. I'm going to have to teach this young lady some manners, boys," Niebergall said over his shoulder in German.

His stormtroopers laughed and nodded their heads with grim amusement. "It's much more enjoyable if they put up a fight, sir!"

Niebergall laughed. "Is that a fact, Hotz? Well, since you're such a Casanova you can have sloppy seconds as a reward for your advice."

"Thank you, sir! Much appreciated."

"Don't say I'm not good to you! Any of you boys not a double veteran yet?" Niebergall asked.

"Me, sir." A young soldier shyly raised his hand like a schoolboy. "Von Choltitz, sir."

"Tonight's your lucky night, my boy, and with such a beauty as well. You go last. You know what to do afterwards, von Choltitz?"

"Jawohl, sir! Thank you, sir!"

"Right boys, in you come. You know the drill: search the house from top to bottom," Niebergall ordered. "I don't want any nasty surprises like two big brothers hiding in a bedroom waiting to batter my brains out with a cricket bat."

"Yes, sir!" the soldiers answered in chorus. The stormtroopers streamed past him with practised ease and started mounting the staircase.

"Now, fräulein," Niebergall turned to Alice and pinched the pressure point above her elbow with a practised vice-like grip, "if you would be so kind as to show me to the nearest bedroom. I would like to sample firsthand some of your famous English hospitality…"

Two prolonged bursts of Schmessier submachine

gun fire interrupted his sentence. Niebergall turned around in time to see two young men at the top of the stairs fire a full magazine, sending his stormtroopers tumbling to the bottom of the stairs to lie in a bloody heap.

Niebergall looked at the scene in open-mouthed horror.

"You were going to let von Choltitz rape me and then kill me?" Alice asked with fire and fury in her eyes.

The blood drained from Niebergall's face. "Wait a minute, I…!"

Alice hit Niebergall right between the eyes with the butt of her Schmessier and he dropped like a felled tree.

"Goodnight, Vienna."

"Did you hear that, sir? Schmessier submachine gun fire! It sounds as if Obersturmführer Niebergall's patrol may be in trouble, sir." The SS sergeant gestured over his shoulder.

"Oh, I wouldn't trouble yourself, Scharführer," Obersturmführer Monat said casually as he examined his dirty fingernails with deliberate nonchalance. "Obersturmführer Niebergall is a big boy: I'm sure that he can take care of himself. He and his boys are due a spot of weekend leave. They've probably found some English girls who may be rather reluctant to join their party. I'm sure that the good Obersturmführer is merely trying to convince the girls of the error of their ways. A machine gun can be a very persuasive incentive to cooperate."

The scharführer chuckled. "Boys will be boys, eh, sir?"

"My thoughts exactly, Scharführer," Monat nodded. "After all, we wouldn't want to try and stop the Obersturmführer from carrying out his duties, would we?"

"Wakey, wakey, Fritz, rise and shine."

Niebergall spluttered and shook his head as another bucket of water was thrown over him. He slowly opened his eyes. He felt as his eyelids and eyelashes were glued together. He had a cracking headache. He felt as if someone had stabbed him between the eyes with a red-hot poker. The first thing that he noticed was that two people were sitting on what appeared to be milking stools in front of him. The second thing that he noticed was that he was tied up in a spread-eagled position. The third thing that he noticed was that he was completely and utterly butt naked.

"Good morning, Niebergall," Alice said.

Niebergall was too petrified to answer.

"What's the matter? Cat got your tongue?" Alice turned to her companion. "And this Nazi was going to teach me some manners. Talk about the pot calling the kettle black."

Her companion chuckled good-naturedly. "Hello, Fritz. My name is Archie Leon."

Niebergall was gradually becoming aware that he was in a large concrete block building with a curved corrugated iron roof. He was also aware that he was lying propped up on a pile of straw on the floor so that he could see his interrogators. He was also aware that the straw was soiled with a matted mixture of urine, vomit and excrement. His own corrupt bodily fluids.

"I'm going to tell you three things, Fritz, that I want you to remember, so pay attention. The first thing is that I'm a pig farmer." Leon held up his fingers as he counted.

Niebergall looked at Leon in blank bewilderment.

"Contrary to what most people think, the domestic pig, or to use its Latin name, the Sus Scrofa, is a very intelligent and adaptable animal. Pigs are omnivores rather than herbivores. They will eat just about anything including grass, vegetables, plants, snakes and lizards and so on and so on. You name it, they'll eat it. I bet you didn't know that, did you, Fritz?" Leon flashed a full set of gum-lined hyena like teeth.

Niebergall shook his head. "No, Mr Leon, I didn't know that."

"I didn't think so, Martin. But please, call me Archie. You don't mind me calling you Martin, do you? After all, I feel like I know you so well already."

"You can call me Susan if it makes you happy, Mr… Archie."

Leon slapped his thigh and chuckled. "I like this man, Miss Roberts. I know that he's a murdering Nazi bastard, but he's got guts and guts go a long way. Talk about laughing in the face of death." Leon shook his head in admiration.

"Yes, Mr Leon. I'm glad I wore my corset this morning or I fear that my sides would split from laughing so much," Alice said dryly.

"Now, now, Miss Roberts, we must always keep our sense of humour," Leon scolded jokingly with a wagging finger. "The second thing I want you to remember is that although I give the impression that I am a salt of the earth country bumpkin, I like to flatter myself that I am a bon viveur and a raconteur and I am, in my own small way, a patron of the arts. Did you know that I co-sponsored the recent Cambridge production of my favourite musical, Sweeney Todd?"

"The demon barber of Fleet Street?" Niebergall had seen the production himself with some fellow officers. In fact he had seen it twice as the horror story appealed to his morbid and macabre sense of humour.

Leon slapped his thigh again. "The very same! You see, Miss Roberts? Martin is not a complete and utter philistine! There's hope for the boy yet! He is not completely beyond redemption!"

Niebergall allowed a glimmer of a smile to ghost across his lips for the first time. What did the 'Escape and Evasion' manual suggest? Try to build up a rapport with your captor? Well, he was certainly well on his way to doing that.

Leon threw a handful of shiny pieces of metal onto Niebergall's lap. They looked strangely familiar but Niebergall couldn't identify them.

"What were their names again, Miss Roberts?" Leon asked rhetorically.

"Hotz, von Choltitz. Sound familiar, Niebergall? Rapists one and all. Those are fillings, Niebergall," Alice explained. "Those are all that the pigs left of your men..."

Niebergall recoiled in disgust as he unsuccessfully tried to heave the grisly mementoes off his lap.

"The third thing that you must remember is that Edward Cobb, the man that you murdered yesterday, was my brother in law," Leon's face was as cold as that of an iceberg. "And Maria Cobb was my sister."

Niebergall vomited violently.

"The only difference between what happened to your men and what is about to happen to you, Niebergall, is that your men were already dead when my pigs ate them, where as you will be very much alive..." Leon let the full horror of his words sink in.

Niebergall's bowels erupted in a tidal wave of faeces.

"The pigs are going to eat you alive, Niebergall..."

"No! For the love of God...!"

"I'd like to promise you that it will be a quick and painless death, but that would be a complete and utter lie so I won't..."

"No, please...!"

"You will probably still be alive as they eat your balls and intestines..."

"Nein! Nein! Bitte... bitte...!" Niebergall pleaded desperately through tear-filled eyes as he struggled futilely against the heavy chains that secured him to the floor.

"And then the cherry on the cake, so to speak, is that after the pigs have eaten you we are going to slaughter them and sell the bacon, ham, pork chops and pork pies to your countrymen..."

"How could you lose a whole patrol?" Sturmbannführer Norbert Ulrich shook his head in disbelief, as he leaned on his clench-fisted knuckles on his desk.

"Strictly speaking, they weren't my patrol, sir," Obersturmführer Monat stood at a rigid position of attention looking at a portrait of Adolf Hitler above Ulrich's head. "Obersturmführer Niebergall was in command of the patrol and he asked me to accompany him..."

"On whose orders?" Ulrich interrupted.

"Sir?" Monat asked in genuine confusion. "I'm afraid that I don't understand..."

"Who gave Niebergall the orders to take an entire neighbourhood hostage?" Ulrich asked with mounting impatience and anger.

"Well, it's standard procedure to take one hundred civilians into protective custody every time one of our men is murdered, sir... I just assumed..."

"When you "assume" something you make an ass out of you and me."

"I'm sorry, sir...?"

"Never mind, Monat," Ulrich waved his hand dismissively. Pearls before swine, he thought to himself.

"You didn't give any such order, sir?"

"No, Obersturmführer Monat, I most certainly did not."

"Ah…"

"Yes, Monat. 'Ah…' The penny drops," Ulrich said menacingly. "Obersturmführer Niebergall was carrying out an independent Search and Destroy mission in revenge for the deaths of most of his platoon who were killed in the St George's Day Massacre. Do you agree with my assessment of the situation so far?"

"Yes, sir…"

"And you were naïve and stupid enough to go along with his one-man vigilante operation without making sure that he had the necessary authorisation?" Ulrich asked rhetorically.

"Yes, sir,"

Ulrich unscrewed the cap of his bottle of Whyte and Mackay whiskey, slowly poured himself a dram, and swung idly from side to side in his padded leather chair. "Whatever am I going to do with you, Monat?"

Ulrich watched as Monat gulped. He was certain that Monat's throat would be as dry as the Sahara desert.

" I mean, technically speaking you haven't exactly disobeyed an order as you were not in fact given any order… technically speaking…"

Ulrich looked up at Monat who had resumed his position of staring at the picture of the Führer. He watched as a bead of sweat slowly ran down Monat's face from his temple to his chin. Ulrich smiled as he imagined how sweaty the palms of Monat's hands must be, as he deliberately made him squirm and suffer…

"On the other hand, I don't want a loose cannon under my command waging a one-man war on his own…"

"If you give me another chance I promise that I won't disappoint you, sir," Monat blurted out before he could stop himself.

Ulrich paused dramatically.

"You better not, Monat, or I will have you shipped back to garrison duty in Berlin so fast that it will make your head swim. Understand?"

"Yes, sir!"

"I sincerely hope so for your own sake. Don't give me cause to regret my decision to give you a second chance. Return to your duties, Obersturmführer Monat. Dismissed!"

"Yes, sir! I won't let you down, sir! Heil Hitler!"

"Heil Hitler!"

Ulrich chuckled to himself, shook his head in amusement and took another sip of whiskey as he watched Monat virtually float out of his office with relief. Ulrich patted his stomach. All of this empire building had made him feel rather peckish. He reached for another one of the exceedingly good pork pies that were arranged in a pyramid on a plate on his desk. He must remember to pass his recommendations through Alice to the farm butcher who made them.

"Mission accomplished?" Sam asked as his sister walked through the front door.

"Mission accomplished," Alice said as she slumped down wearily on top of a sofa.

"Did he talk?" Alan asked.

"Niebergall? Well, he knew that he was going to die, but we gave him the chance to die hard or to die easy. What choice do you think he made?"

"To die easy," Alan answered.

"Of course he did," Alice nodded. "As would any of us in a similar situation."

"I know that I would," Sam agreed. "I'd give both of you up to the Gestapo as soon as they allowed a pig to start tickling my toes."

"Well, let's just be grateful that the Gestapo haven't stumbled across that particular torture technique. As for Niebergall, he sang like a canary," Alice chuckled as she slung her legs over the arm of the settee. "At the end he would have admitted that he wore lady's underwear."

"Did he say anything interesting?" Alan continued.

"Yes, he did." Alice sat bolt upright, suddenly deadly serious. "We've got to let Edinburgh know right away."

"Percy has informed us that the 'Triple S' has started carrying out intensive Brigade scale river crossing exercises at the mouth of the Great Ouse River where it meets the Wash at King's Lynn," Brigadier John Daylesford said as he passed the decoded message to Peter Ansett.

"How many independent sources have confirmed the report, sir?" Ansett asked as he read the message.

"Two." Daylesford answered as he folded up the message. "From an SS Obersturmführer in the Fifth SS Regiment and the Sturmbannführer in acting command of all SS forces in Hereward."

"From Ulrich? From 'The Cat?'" Ansett asked with raised eyebrows.

"Yes," Daylesford confirmed in confused surprise. "You sound as if you know him."

"I do," Ansett nodded. "He basically stopped a mob of SS thugs from beating me to death when I was a prisoner in SS torture cells."

"By Jove!" Daylesford exclaimed. "That was lucky!"

"You could say that I owe him my life... in fact, I'm not exactly sure whose side he's batting for." Ansett furrowed his eyebrows as he spoke his thoughts aloud. "It could very well be ours."

17

"Don't let your personal feelings cloud your judgement, Peter," Daylesford warned. "In this game, all suspects are guilty until proven innocent; don't forget that he's the enemy until proven otherwise."

"Yes, sir," Ansett said formally. "So it looks like the invasion is coming?"

"I'm afraid so," Daylesford nodded sombrely. "The evidence points to a river crossing over the River Tweed at Berwick- upon-Tweed."

"The question is: when?"

"Yes. That's the six million dollar question. Peter, send a message to Percy to find out where and when the invasion will take place."

"Yes, sir."

Daylesford stood up, flattened down his trousers, straightened his tunic and put on his cap. "I'm off to tell Winston."

"Will we be ready for them when they come, sir?" Ansett asked.

"We'd better be," Daylesford replied grimly.

Chapter Two

David Mitchell cannonballed into his big brother with such force and velocity that he almost knocked him off his feet.

"Whoa! Easy tiger!" Alan said with a smile as he gave his little brother a gigantic bear hug.

"Where have you been, Al? I've been worried sick!" David asked as he wiped away tears of joy with the back of his hands. "I thought that you were dead!"

"What do you mean?" Alan asked with genuine bewilderment. "I stayed with Sam and Alice during the Easter holidays. You know that, Davie, just as you stayed with the Millers."

"Yes, but after the St George's Day Massacre and the destruction of the Specials I thought that you and Sam were dead. You could have phoned to let me know that you were all right!"

"The destruction of the Specials? What on earth are you talking about?" Alan asked.

"After the Specials and the Police opened fire on the SS the Huns killed them all, even the wounded, and refused to take prisoners," David explained.

Alan's face drained of all colour and he turned as pale as the wall that he leaned against. "Are they still hunting down all of the surviving Specials?" he asked as he tried to figure out how he could warn Sam. He felt sick as he realised that the Germans could have already arrested Sam and could already be on their way to arrest him.

"That's unlikely, Al," David shook his head. "If they haven't arrested you already then I think that it's unlikely that they still intend to arrest you in the future."

"Why do you think that?"

"Because the Records Room in Police Headquarters

containing the names, addresses and personal details of both the Police and Specials burnt down last night. I think that you and Sam are safe, big brother." David put his hand on Alan's shoulders.

"Thanks, Davie." Alan put his hand on top of his brother's and gave him a squeeze.

David paused before he spoke. "Al, Mr Ansett is missing."

"Really?" Alan found it difficult to act as if he was surprised. He was certain that his little brother would not be fooled by his amateur dramatics.

David nodded his head. "Yes. That's why I guess that we're here." David stretched both of his arms wide. "The whole of Cromwell House is gathered here, Al... at least, what's left of it. The word on the grapevine is that Ashworth is coming to speak to us."

"I see." Alan noticed for the first time that several familiar faces were missing.

"Fatty Arbuckle, George West and Del Boy Blake are all missing."

"They were probably killed in the crossfire. Has anyone checked in the morgue? Ah, here's movement..."

Harold Ashworth, the Rector of St John's Academy, swept imperiously into the Cromwell Junior Common Room with a dramatic swish of his gown. A slim tweed-suited young man, who was similarly clad in a cape, followed him. Ashworth strode purposefully to the bay window end of the room and turned around to face the housemates. He planted his legs apart and placed both of his clenched fists on his hips. The House Matron, Mrs Abby Burgess, stood beside him.

"Boys, as you have no doubt realised, Mr Ansett is missing, as are many of your schoolmates, both in this house and in the wider school community. The Germans have not yet allowed access to the morgue, which is full to the point of overflowing. However, I have visited Hereward Hospital to search for your friends. Unfortunately, the vast majority of the missing have not been found, and it is my sad duty to inform you that they most likely never will be, and are probably dead."

Most of the boys burst out crying and Alan knew that it was futile to fight the flood of tears that ran freely down his face. He put his arm around his brother and gave him a tight squeeze. One of Davie's young friends came up to the two brothers and Alan gathered him into the group hug. Another of Davie's mates joined them, until all of the Cromwell boys were joined together in a giant circle of grief like a team talk before a rugby match. Mrs Burgess walked amongst the boys offering an ample bosom to cry on.

Ashworth waited for the crying to die down and for the boys to look up before he continued. "It is my pleasure to introduce Mr John Baldwin. Although I wish that I was doing so under more pleasant circumstances. Mr Baldwin completed his teacher training at Cambridge University last year and is an Old Boy. In fact, he was House Captain of Cromwell from 1935 until 1936. He will replace Mr Ansett as Principal Teacher of Geography and he will perform the duties of acting House Master of Cromwell House until Captain Mason recovers and is able to take over as permanent House Master of Cromwell…"

"Excuse me, sir," Alan interrupted. "I didn't quite catch you. Did you say that Captain Mason was going to take over as permanent House Master of Cromwell?"

"Yes, I did, Mitchell, and I would ask you to be so kind as not to interrupt in the future."

"Sorry, sir." Alan dipped his head in apology.

"Why do you ask?"

"Well, I thought that the SS killed all of the

Specials, sir."

"But you're a Special and the SS didn't kill you."

"Yes, sir." There was no denying it.

"Captain Mason also survived and is recovering from his war wounds at Hereward Hospital." Ashworth started to leave and then stopped in his tracks. "In fact, come to think of it, both you, Captain Mason and young Sam Roberts all survived not only the destruction of the Specials but also the destruction of the Hereward Home Guard as well."

"Yes, sir."

"It seems that the fates of yourself, Roberts and Captain Mason are inextricably linked."

Alan's heart was beating so hard that he thought that if he opened his mouth to answer his heart would literally leap out of his mouth. Alan said nothing as Ashworth left the room, leaving Baldwin in charge.

Alan was too preoccupied with deep thought to notice the new housemaster examining him with keen interest.

"Good afternoon, ma'am," the boys said in unison.

"Good afternoon, boys," the Hereward Hospital receptionist answered, "What can I do for you?"

"We were wondering if it might be possible to pay Captain Mason a visit," Alan asked.

"You're two of his students?"

The boys nodded.

The receptionist checked her notes and shook her head. "I'm sorry, boys, but Captain Mason is in no fit state to receive visitors and probably will not be for many days, if not weeks, to come."

"How is he?" Sam asked.

"Frankly, it's an absolute miracle that he's still alive. He had a thick King James I Bible in his tunic pocket and the book absorbed most of the impact of the bullets. The bullets didn't even penetrate his skin, although he did break a few ribs and he has some pretty impressive nasty purple bruises on his chest. He also has a hairline fracture as a result of striking his head hard against the floor when he fell. He is also suffering from cracking headaches and he slips in and out of consciousness…"

"But he'll live?" Sam interrupted abruptly.

"Oh yes, he'll live all right, but it will be many months before he's fully recovered."

Sam slammed a fist into the palm of his hand and swore under his breath; which was rather a strange reaction, the receptionist thought.

"Would it be possible for us to leave these flowers for him?" Alan asked, flashing his most charming boyish smile, holding up a bouquet that he'd stolen from the cemetery on the way to the hospital.

"Yes, of course. You can leave them in a vase on the table outside his room."

"Where is it, ma'am?"

"Room one hundred and one on the first floor." The receptionist pointed to the staircase. "You can't miss it."

"Thank you, ma'am. You've been very helpful," Alan said as he touched the peak of his school cap.

"My pleasure, boys. Glad to have been of assistance," the receptionist answered with a smile.

Sam mumbled something that sounded vaguely grateful under his breath.

Wasn't the taller of the two young men a queer kettle of fish? the receptionist thought to herself as they both disappeared up the stairs.

"What the hell's the matter with you, Sam?" Alan hissed angrily as they mounted the stairs two at a time. "Are you trying to get us killed?"

23

"I can't believe the bastard's still alive. I shot him twice at point-blank range." Sam mimicked the action with his two top right hand fingers.

"Mason was lucky, that's all."

"Mason has the luck of the devil." Sam shook his head in frustration. "First Fairfax then St George's Day. Well this time the treacherous bastard won't get away. This time I'll finish what I started..."

The boys stopped suddenly in their tracks, as if they had run into a brick wall. Two armed men stood outside room one hundred and one at a rigid position of attention. As they spotted the two boys, the two guards came to the en guard position with their bayonet fixed rifles held in out in front of them. "Halt! Who goes there? Friend or foe?" the leader challenged.

"Friends! Easy, boys!" Alan said with his palms held up in front of him. "We come in peace!"

"At ease!" the leader said. The two guards cradled their weapons in their hands as the two boys walked up to them.

"Who are you men?" Sam asked as he tried to identify the guards' black battle dress uniforms. "You're not Police or Specials..."

"We're certainly not Specials, mate," the younger guard answered. "The Specials have been disbanded across the whole of the country as a result of this St George's Day Massacre of yours. Or haven't you heard? You probably don't get word as quickly, being way out here in the sticks," the young man said in a broad cockney accent.

"So what are you then?" Sam tapped the elder guard's armband with genuine curiosity.

"We're Fascist Militia, son," the older guard replied.

Sam reacted as if he had been slapped in the face. He whipped his hand away from the armband as if he had been burnt.

The older Fascist pointed at the initials on his armband BUFM. "British Union of Fascist Militia," he said proudly as he puffed out his be medalled chest.

"Prime Minister Joyce has sent us up here from London to take care of your Jewish Bolshevik terrorist problem, innit?" the young militiaman explained.

"Prime Minister Joyce?" Alan asked in confusion.

"Crikey, you country bumpkins are ignorant!" the young Fascist guffawed. "Don't you know anything?"

"Deputy Prime Minister Joyce has taken over as PM following the recent murder of Prime Minister Mosley," the older militiaman explained. "God rest his soul." He crossed himself solemnly.

An Irish-American Nazi as Prime Minister? Alan could still remember the ridiculous broadcasts that Joyce had made from Berlin during the War. He always began his broadcasts with "This is Germany calling..." and spoke with a terrible hammy put-on upper class accent... Lord Haw Haw.... they used to laugh at him, and now he was Prime Minister? There was definitely something rotten in the state of Denmark.

"That's... an interesting development," Alan managed to say with a weak smile.

"But why are you here?" Sam asked.

"We're here to guard Golden Boy," the young Fascist gestured over his shoulder at the room behind him. "He's become a regular pin-up poster boy for the Party."

"But why?" Sam persisted. "He's not even a member of the BUF."

"That's a mere technicality, son." The older militiaman tapped his nose confidentially. "I've known Wily Willy since the early street fighting days of the Party when we used to fight the Jews and the Reds in the East End. The new Prime Minister is a master propaganda artist. He would make Goebbels look like a beginner. By the time that he's finished with Captain Mason the whole country will believe that the first words to come out of the good captain's mouth were 'Sieg Heil' instead of 'Mummy!'"

The younger militiaman laughed uproariously at the older man's words as if it was the funniest joke that he'd ever heard.

Alan could only smile weakly.

"Captain Mason is our trump card because he is the only British survivor of the Massacre..." the older Fascist continued.

We'll soon see about that, Sam thought to himself.

The two figures crept quietly through the sleeping streets of Hereward, keeping closely to the shadows. They were dressed entirely in black, from their balaclavas to their black plimsolls. Their faces were camouflaged with black shoe polish and their Schmessier submachine guns had black material wrapped around them to disguise their shape and also to prevent their weapons from giving away any tell-tale shine. They wore black gloves and moved like shadows through the night towards their target.

They stopped at the corner before the building and watched the two lorries that were parked in front of the hospital. They knew that the one on the left contained an Army guard unit, whilst the one on the right contained an SS guard unit. The men in black knew from earlier observation that each unit consisted of an under strength squad of eight men commanded by an NCO with a junior NCO as second-in-command. The black figures knew that the Army and the SS had divided their responsibilities so that two Wehrmacht soldiers patrolled the outside of the hospital in pairs and two stormtroopers patrolled the inside of the hospital in pairs. Each guard duty lasted two hours. Both guard units had been on duty since six pm and they were due to be relieved at six am. The time was now three am in the morning, which meant that the guards currently on patrol were now on their second stint of sentry duty, and had probably had little sleep since their first patrol. They would be tired, bored and fed up and the only thing on their mind would be getting back to the lorries and hitting the sack in their sleeping bags. The men in black also knew that the guards as a whole would rather be somewhere else, and considered the entire duty to be a complete and utter waste of time. Their comrades were busy enjoying the May Day Bank Holiday and were no doubt tucked up snugly in bed with their English girlfriends, enjoying their weekend leave whilst they were stuck on this chicken shit detail. In military terms both the Army and SS guards had low morale and were somewhat less than diligent in their attitude towards the carrying out of their duties.

The men in black were determined to capitalise on the guards' carelessness and lack of attention and dedication to detail.

The black figures gave the Army sentries a one hundred feet head start, before they carefully and cautiously followed them on their patrol around the outside of the hospital. When the two shadows reached the Emergency Exit at the back of the building they silently climbed three flights of stairs to the top floor. They slowly opened the Emergency Exit door and both slipped through. They were at the end of a short corridor with three rooms to the left of them - the drug store, the linen store and the cleaning store - and two toilets to the right of them, male and female. Directly in front of them was the main staircase and a pair of lifts. The men in black slowly crept to the end of the short corridor and carefully looked around the corners to the left and right. There was nobody in sight. The black figures knew from earlier reconnaissance that the ward on the left was full of Wehrmacht wounded whilst the ward on the right was full of SS wounded. The vast majority of the German wounded had been injured in the recent fighting on St George's Day. There were no SS guards visible. Nor did there appear to be any medical staff on duty.

One of the dark figures breathed a huge sigh of relief. "There's no one here. That makes things a whole lot easier," he whispered to his companion.

"I guess that the doctors and nurses don't consider looking after wounded Nazis to be a top priority." Truth be told, the medical staff were also probably working with a skeleton crew as a result of the public holiday. "We need to be quick before the SS guards turn up on their patrol."

The first figure nodded his head in the darkness. "Let's do this. Strength and honour."

"Strength and honour." Both figures shook hands.

The first man slowly took off his rucksack and placed it on the floor. He loosened the drawstring and took out a large box-shaped object that he put down silently. He slowly unwound the thick towel that he had wrapped around the jerrycan. He unscrewed the cap and instinctively screwed up his nose at the sudden release of petrol fumes. The man picked up the petrol can and carefully poured some underneath the door of the drug store. He continued pouring and left a stream from the drug store to the linen store and on to the cleaning store. He poured the remains of the petrol can underneath the linen store and the cleaning store. The two figures retraced their steps to the Emergency Exit and stepped through the door onto the Emergency Exit stairs. The last man through took a box of matches out of his trouser pocket, extracted a match, lit it and set fire to the petrol-soaked towel that he was holding in his hand. The towel instantly caught on fire and the man threw the burning material into the middle of the petrol-soaked floor. The entire floor erupted in flames and the arsonists had barely descended to the second floor when the whole of the drug store erupted with a massive explosion as the fire reached the ether and oxygen bottles stacked on the floor inside.

"Put your hand on your heart and tell me that you had absolutely nothing to do with it!" Alice repeatedly stabbed her forefinger at her brother.

Sam held up his hands in defence. "I tell you, sis, that I had absolutely nothing to do with it. I was a surprised as you were." Sam looked out of their living room window at the tall column of smoke that still came from the hospital.

"I don't believe you!" Alice shouted angrily. "You and Alan are in this up to your eyeballs!"

"I swear to you, Alice, that it has absolutely nothing to do with us," Alan insisted.

Alice turned to her brother. "Swear on mother and father's grave, Sam, that you had absolutely nothing to do with the fire at the hospital last night, and I'll believe you," Alice demanded.

"You're not serious, Alice," Sam shook his head with furrowed eyebrows.

"I'm deadly serious, Sam," Alice answered coldly. "Swear on Mother and Father's grave."

"Sis, I..."

"Swear it!"

"All right, all right," Sam surrendered. "I swear on Mother and Father's grave that I had absolutely nothing to do with the fire at the hospital last night."

"Alan?"

"I swear on the life of my father and mother that I had nothing to do with the fire at the hospital last night."

"Because if the Germans believe for one moment that the fire was anything other than an accident, if they even suspect that it was a partisan attack, then they will execute the hostages that they captured the other night without hesitation and without mercy," Alice explained with passion in her voice. She looked at both of the boys in turn to make sure that the weight of her words sunk in. "They will kill our friends and our neighbours. People that we know and whom we grew up with…"

"Okay, sis!" Sam lost his temper. "We get the point! The Huns will kill the hostages if they think that the fire was a Resistance attack."

"I sincerely hope that you do get the point, Sam, because you have displayed pyromaniac tendencies in the past, so forgive me if I find it hard to believe that you have not been playing with fire again."

Sam said nothing. What could he say? Everything that his sister had said was true.

Alice breathed out a huge sigh. "Okay. I believe you both. Although God knows why I should." Alice shook her head. "You two are as trustworthy as a nest of vipers."

The two boys looked sheepish because they knew that Alice's words were true.

"So if it wasn't you, who was it?" Alice asked.

"Maybe it was an accident?" Alan said.

"If it sounds too good to be true then it usually isn't, Al," Sam said.

Alice nodded in agreement. "You know what this means, don't you?" Alice asked rhetorically.

"Yes," Alan answered. "There's another Stay Behind Unit operating in Hereward."

"Well, if they're an SBU, why didn't they help us with the assassination attack on Kaiser Eddie then?" Sam asked angrily. "God knows we could have done with their help. Robinson and Napoleon's commandos could still be alive."

Alan shrugged his shoulders. "Maybe they were ordered not to. Maybe they knew nothing about it. Who knows? Maybe they're a sleeper cell and they're being saved for something else. Something bigger."

"'Something bigger?'" Sam asked. "What could possibly be bigger than an assassination attempt against the Puppet King?"

"I don't know," Alan answered. "But I guess that we're going to find out..."

"So let me get this straight," General Major Christian von Schnakenberg said as he toyed with a glass of whiskey, swishing the amber liquid from side to side in its crystal tumbler. "Both the Police and the Fire Brigade are maintaining that it was a tragic accident caused by an electrical fault..."

"Yes, sir," Oberleutnant Nicky Alfonin answered. "Hereward Hospital was built at the beginning of the Victorian era about one hundred years ago and the maintenance records confirm that the entire electrical wiring system was due to be replaced..."

"Don't tell me, let me guess," von Schnakenberg interrupted. "The upgrade was delayed due to the war."

"Yes, sir," Alfonin nodded as he consulted the notes in his open folder.

"How very convenient." Von Schnakenberg took a sip of his whiskey and poured some for his adjutant. "But none of our men were injured?"

"No, sir," Alfonin answered as he took a drink. "For whatever reason the fire seemed to spread towards the SS ward as opposed to the Army ward, and our guard were on the ball and were able to evacuate all of our wounded using the fire escape at the Army end of the ward, without loss."

"And SS casualties?"

"Thirty-one killed, sir."

"Mein Gott!" Von Schnakenberg spilled his whiskey.

"The fire escape collapsed as the SS sentries were evacuating the wounded. The entire guard unit were killed…"

"Any civilian casualties?" von Schnakenberg interrupted as he mopped up the spillage with a tissue.

"Yes, sir." Alfonin consulted his notes again. "No civilian patients, but a nurse, a doctor and a fireman were killed trying to rescue the SS wounded." Alfonin closed the folder. "The Police are insistent that it was nothing more sinister than a tragic accident and are not treating the fire as a suspicious incident."

"A tragic accident indeed." Von Schnakenberg pointed his captured British Army officer's swagger stick at Alfonin. "Of course the police are not treating the fire as a suspicious incident, because if they said that the fire had been deliberately caused by an arson attack than the SS would execute hundreds, if not thousands, of Hereward hostages." Von Schnakenberg took a swig of his whiskey. "I tell you this, Nicky - if the SS have even the smallest sneaking suspicion that their wounded were burnt to death as a result of a Resistance attack then they will exact a swift and bloody revenge which will be ruthless and completely without mercy."

Chapter Three

"Yes please, Auntie Monique." Anne Mair smiled up at her auntie as Monique speared another two sausages from the frying pan and placed them on Anne's plate.

"There you go, my dear, eat up. There's plenty more where they came from, don't you worry." Monique Roos looked down at her niece and smiled warmly at her. She found it hard to believe that the last time Anne had sat at the table she had been accompanied by her mother, Sarah and by her father, Davie, Monique's younger brother. And now both of her parents were dead, murdered by the SS. Davie had died as a result of the horrific wounds that he had suffered at the hands of SS torturers, and Sarah had been hung in the Town Square on the day of the Hereward Cathedral Hangings. Anne had come to live with them on their farm in the small village of Frampton-on-the-Ouse which was located on the outskirts of Hereward, not far from the recently fire-damaged hospital.

"Let me hold Harry whilst you get your coat on, Emily," Anne offered as the family got ready to go to church. Her cousin Emily handed over her baby boy to Anne. Harry cooed with delight as his Auntie Anne blew cool air through the seven-month-old's wispy hair. Emily had moved from Hereward to Frampton to live with her parents when Harry had been born as she was finding it increasingly difficult to cope since her husband Archie, a fighter pilot in the RAF, had been shot down and killed in the recent Battle of Britain. Emily had always had a very close relationship with her younger cousin and thought of Anne as the younger sister that she never had. It was a real comfort for them both to be living under the same roof.

The family walked down the farm lane on their regular route to the Frampton Church of England village church and were joined on the way by other villagers. Monique's husband, Victor, was painfully aware that the churchgoers were overwhelmingly made up of women, children and older men such as himself. The only young men in the village were a few disabled veterans who were wheeled along on wheelchairs or who propelled themselves through the village streets on crutches. The wounded had all been crippled in the War. Victor's eyes filled up with tears as he thought of his only son, Paul, Emily's younger brother, who had been a Merchant Seaman and had been lost at sea when German U-boats had sunk his ship, 'The Russell.'

"Morning, Vicar." Roos shook Bill Ritchie's hand as the Vicar greeted him on the church steps. "Nice day for it."

"Morning, Vic. May I have a moment of your time?" Ritchie gestured with an open palm to the side of the door.

"Certainly, Bill." Roos stepped to the side as the Vicar welcomed the rest of the family as they entered the church.

"How is she, Victor?" Ritchie asked with concern.

"Anne?" Roos answered. "As well as can be expected, under the circumstances."

"She's lost both her parents in a matter of days, Vic, which is a heavy burden for anyone to carry, never mind a seventeen year old girl..."

"Yes it is..."

"But she could not be in safer hands, Vic, and if anyone can pull her through, you can."

"Thanks, Bill... that means a lot to me."

A pause. "And how's Monique bearing up? Any word about Paul?"

"Absolutely nothing." Roos shook his head in despair. "There were very few survivors from 'The Russell' and none of them knew what had happened to

34

Paul. We can only assume the worst and presume that Paul is dead."

"Your family has been particularly badly hit by the War, Vic." Ritchie said sympathetically. "First Paul, then Archie. Now Davie and Sarah…"

"Our family has been no more badly hit than any other family in Britain, Bill." Roos said stoically. "We just have to grin and bear it just like in the last war. Slowly but surely we'll grind the bastards down. As long as Churchill and the King keep fighting up in Scotland, there's always hope."

Ritchie straightened up to a position of attention. "That's the spirit! Once a Fusilier always a Fusilier! Strength and honour, Vic." Ritchie reached out his hand.

"Strength and honour, Bill." Victor clasped his old friend's hand in a firm handshake.

The sound of lorries entering Frampton Village Square and stopping at the foot of the church steps caused the congregation to stop singing. The thick oak door opened and the parishioners collectively gasped in horror as an SS officer strode confidently down the aisle towards the pulpit, slapping his leather gloves in his hand as he approached the vicar. The congregation's reaction to the German was as severe as if Satan himself had made an appearance and desecrated the holy ground of the church. When he reached the pulpit, the SS officer turned around and flashed a smile that revealed a set of dazzling dentures that would have made a Hollywood star green with envy.

"Judging by your reaction to my entrance I'll wager that it's been many a year since an enemy soldier has corrupted your church with his presence. Possibly the first since the Norman Conquest? Don't worry." He chuckled good-humouredly, "I won't take it personally." He waited in vain for a response from the congregation. "Ladies and Gentlemen, boys and girls, my dear Vicar," the SS Obersturmführer continued in perfect English without a hint of a guttural German accent. He bowed to Ritchie before turning back to face the congregation. "There is absolutely no cause for alarm. I must apologise for this unseemly intrusion, but I'm afraid that duty calls even on a Sunday." The Obersturmführer clicked his jack booted heels together like a Prussian fencing instructor. "We are searching for Jewish Bolshevik terrorists who cowardly attacked a Red Cross convoy carrying British refugees to a resettlement camp. I'm afraid that I'm going to have to ask you to show me your identification cards so that we can make sure that the terrorists are not cunningly hiding amongst the good people of Frampton..."

Mumbling and grumbling came from the congregation at this inconvenience. Interrupting a church service? Were there no depths to which the Germans would not sink?

"So I'd like all of the men and all boys over the age of fourteen to accompany me outside to the village square and I would like all the women and children to remain here in the church where your ID cards will be checked separately..."

The men and older boys stood up and put their Sunday best jackets on. "This should only take a minute, dear," Roos said to Monique as he kissed her on the cheek. "I'll see you soon, girls," he said to Emily and Anne. "I'll be back before you can say blackberry pie."

"Blackberry pie," Anne said automatically.

"Maybe not that quick, but pretty quick," Roos chuckled as he adjusted his hat at a jaunty angle.

"Come back quickly, Daddy," Emily said as she hugged Harry closer to her.

"You too, Vicar," the Oberstürmfuhrer insisted. "It's a sad sign of the times that even a man of the cloth is not above suspicion."

Ritchie shrugged his shoulders, put on his grey suit jacket and walked down the aisle past Roos.

"Don't worry. Nothing's going to happen. Even the Germans wouldn't harm a vicar," Roos assured his family. "This is a routine ID check, that's all."

"Your father is absolutely right, fräulein," The SS officer said, making the family jump with surprise. He had walked so silently in his patent leather jackboots that they had not heard him approaching. "There is absolutely nothing to worry about. This is nothing but a routine ID check. Sir?" The Obersturmführer gestured with a bow and an outstretched arm towards the door.

Roos was the last man to leave.

As the SS officer reached the door he turned around to face the women and children. "Don't worry," he assured the worried faces, "it will all be over soon." He clicked his heels, bowed graciously and closed the door behind him. He turned to face the stormtrooper guarding the door. "Lock the door," he ordered curtly.

The loud staccato burst of continuous machine gun fire made the congregation jump and set off a cacophony of crying, shouting and screaming.

"What's happening?" Emily shouted as Harry started wailing in her arms.

"They're killing all of the men!" a woman shouted in horror as she looked outside through a stained glass window by the door. There was a burst of machine gun fire and the glass shattered as the woman fell backwards and lay sprawled on the floor with a line of bloody bullet holes stitched across the front of her dress.

The door burst open and half a dozen stormtroopers

entered and fired a full magazine of machine gun bullets at point-blank range into the defenceless crowd, knocking down women and children like dominoes.

"Take cover behind the pulpit!" Monique ordered as each soldier threw a grenade into the church. The family covered their ears as the bombs exploded, setting off half a dozen fires and filling the church with thick acrid smoke.

Monique watched with mounting horror as a continuous chain of stormtroopers filed into the church and threw chairs, tables and anything made of wood onto the pile of bodies of the people that the Nazis had already murdered.

"They're going to burn down the church!" Monique realised. "Quickly! Head for the vestry! There's a window that we can escape through to the cemetery and the river. Follow me," she ordered.

Monique started to crawl on her hands and knees towards the vestry at the back of the church, and Anne and Emily followed her. The young mother was finding the crawling difficult as she was carrying Harry with one hand and supporting their combined weights with the other hand. Smoke continued to rise towards the roof, and the fires were crackling with greater force and fury as they spread though out the church. Stormtroopers positioned at the door continued to periodically fire bursts of bullets into any areas where they thought any survivors might be hiding. The sound of people crying, shouting, screaming and begging for help and mercy was swiftly becoming overwhelmed by the cracking sound of the wooden rafters and furniture breaking as the fire consumed them.

Monique crawled through the door to the vestry, stood up and climbed onto a table positioned under the window. She looked away and shielded her face with one hand and smashed the window with her other elbow, sending the shattered glass flying onto the ground outside.

"You first, Anne," Monique ordered. "Be careful of the drop; it's quite a distance, it's almost three yards."

Anne quickly climbed onto the table and nimbly climbed through the window. She lowered herself as far as she could before she fell onto the ground outside, landing on all fours like a cat.

"I'll go next and then you climb onto the table and lower Harry to me, Emily. Then you follow, all right?"

"Yes, mum," Emily answered.

Monique climbed through the window, lowered herself and dropped onto the ground outside, where she landed with surprising agility.

"All right, Emily. Climb onto the table and pass Harry through the window."

Emily face appeared at the window and she had already passed Harry through the window, before she recoiled in shock and horror as she realised how far the drop was to the ground outside.

"Drop Harry, Emily!" Monique ordered. "We'll catch him!"

"What?" Emily asked in disbelief. "Drop my baby? Are you crazy?"

"We can't reach him, Emily," Anne explained. "The window is too high off the ground and we're not tall enough. Drop Harry, Emily. We'll catch him, I promise."

"No!" Emily protested through tear-filled eyes as she hugged Harry tightly to her chest. "You'll miss catching him and he'll be killed!"

A burst of machine gun fire.

"Save Harry, Mummy!" Emily's face disappeared from the window as she threw Harry out of the window with her last ounce of strength.

Monique caught Harry squarely in both of her arms

and planted a great big kiss on his sooty forehead through tear-filled eyes.

Another burst of machine gun fire.

Monique crumpled in a heap to the ground. Anne spun around to see a Nazi standing less than fifty yards away; she reacted instinctively and ran full pelt for the river that she knew ran parallel alongside the cemetery wall. She cleared the wall with a perfect hurdle jump that would have made her athletics coach proud, took half a dozen steps, and then dived into the swiftly flowing River Ouse.

Obersturmführer Heinrich Koch smiled with paternal pleasure as he listened to his boys belting out the rousing verses of the popular marching song 'We march against England.' "The men more than compensate for their lack of skill with their enthusiasm, Reinhard."

"Oh, I don't know, sir," Scharführer Reinhard Frank replied, "They're not that bad: they have no trouble singing the right notes..."

"They just have trouble singing them in the right order!" Koch completed the joke as the whole car dissolved into fits of laughter.

Koch jolted forwards in his seat as his driver suddenly slammed on the brakes in an emergency stop.

"What the hell, Ley?" Koch said in anger as he rubbed his bruised chest.

"The road is blocked, sir," Ley explained patiently.

"What is it this time?" Koch said. He slammed the seat in frustration with his fist as he stood up in the back of the car to see over the head of his driver. "Cows? Sheep?"

"No, sir," Ley replied. "Pigs."

"Pigs?" Koch shielded his eyes to see more clearly. The convoy was driving west back towards their barracks in Hereward and his vision was obscured by the glare of the setting sun. "Well, I don't care whether they're pigs, cows, sheep or a herd of buffalo, Ley - get them the hell out of the way!" Koch ordered angrily.

Ley beeped the horn three times and then got out of the car. "You there, get your pigs the hell out of the way! Raus! Raus! Schnell! Schnell!" Ley shouted at the farmer and waved his arms towards the pigs to shoo them out of the way.

"Now, now, temper, temper," the farmer replied.

The burst of Schmessier machine gun bullets drilled a line of bloody holes into Ley's chest, caught Koch in the stomach, and took off the top of Frank's head, exposing his brains.

Two MG 42 machine guns opened fire on the two lorries from the side of the road, raking each lorry from front to back methodically once, twice, three times.

When the screaming had finally stopped and had been replaced by moans, the farmer blew three short sharp blasts on his whistle.

The MG 42 machine guns immediately stopped firing.

A figure rapidly ran towards the rear of the last lorry, fired a burst of machine gun rounds into the back, threw in a hand grenade, and took cover. After the hand grenade had exploded, he opened the driver's door and fired a burst of bullets into the cab. The man then moved onto the front lorry and repeated the procedure.

"Clear!" the figure shouted.

The farmer blew a long, loud whistle blast. The MG 42 machine gun crews leaped up from their ambush positions and ran towards the convoy with their weapons in the ready position, prepared to fire at a moment's notice. The ambush had been executed so efficiently and effectively that the Nazis had not had the opportunity to fire back a single round in reply.

"Re-org," the farmer ordered. "Check the enemy

dead."

"Any survivors?" Alice asked as she approached Leon with her finger on the trigger of her Schmessier.

"I don't know: your brother is just checking," Leon replied. "Sam, remember to take care of the wounded."

Two double taps. "Taking care of the wounded right now," Sam announced. He emerged from the back of the rear lorry with his Luger pistol still smoking in his hand. "Two of them survived the MG 42s, my Schmessier, and a hand grenade. Lucky bastards," Sam shook his head in awe and wonder. "Miracles will never cease to amaze me."

"When I said 'take care of the wounded', Sam, two bullets in the brain was not exactly what I had in mind," Leon said dryly.

"Christ!" Sam said in exasperation. "How was I to know? What the hell do we need prisoners for? If I wanted to look after Nazis rather than kill them then I would've become a nurse!"

"We need prisoners to interrogate to find out what the hell happened in Frampton, Sam," Alice explained slowly. "Next time, maybe I should draw you a diagram," she continued sarcastically. Alice suddenly grabbed her little brother in a headlock and knuckled his head roughly.

"Ow! That hurts! Get your cotton-picking hands off me, sis!" Sam protested.

"Hey! We've got a live one here!" Alan shouted from the front of the convoy.

The ambushers ran to the front with their weapons at the ready.

"Who is it?" Sam asked.

"An Obersturmführer," Alan answered. "He's been shot in the stomach. I don't think that he's going to live very long…"

"You're bloody right he's not going to live very

42

long!" Alice interrupted angrily. "Anne said that an SS Obersturmführer was in charge. I bet that this is the bastard who gave the orders!" Alice raised her Schmessier machine gun to her shoulder and squeezed the trigger.

Leon batted her weapon out of the way just as she opened fire, and the rounds flew harmlessly into the air.

"What the hell did you do that for?" Alice demanded angrily. "The bastard deserves to die a thousand deaths!"

"And he will, Alice, he will," Leon said. "But first of all we need to find out what the hell happened in Frampton - as you explained earlier, do you remember? So calm down."

"All right, all right," Alice agreed grudgingly as she flicked on her safety catch and took her finger off the trigger.

Leon turned to face the ashen-faced Obersturmführer who was bleeding his life away on the back car seat. "Now listen up, Fritz, and listen well. You're dying and there's nothing that can be done to stop that, but we can ease your suffering so that you die quickly and relatively painlessly, or we can increase your suffering so that you die slowly and painfully. Do you understand?"

Koch nodded his head through gritted teeth.

"Why Frampton?"

"Why not?" Koch smiled, revealing blood-soaked teeth.

"What had the people of Frampton ever done to you, you murdering Nazi bastard?" Alice lunged at him and had to be held back by Leon and his two sons.

"Alice, please!" Leon urged. "Control yourself!"

Alice reluctantly relented, and stopped struggling. "All right! I won't kill him... yet."

"Frampton was the nearest village to the hospital,"

the Nazi explained. "They were simply in the wrong place at the wrong time."

"But the villagers were completely innocent!" Alice exclaimed in exasperation. "And the Police said that the fire was an accident!"

Koch shrugged his shoulders nonchalantly. "Whether the fire was an accident or was started on purpose is of no consequence…"

"What do you mean?" Leon asked.

"Germans died so British people had to die…"

"Even if they were completely innocent and had nothing to do with it?"

Koch gave a crooked smile. "An eye for an eye, a tooth for a tooth, as the good book says." He chuckled and coughed up a globule of blood.

"You're damn right," Alice said. A single pistol shot rang out, and Koch slumped forwards in his seat with a surprised expression on his face.

"So Koch didn't mention a damn thing to you?" Sturmbannführer Ulrich demanded as he leaned on his desk, resting his weight on both sets of knuckles. Ulrich's face was scarlet with anger.

"Koch did say that he was going to teach the British a lesson that they would never forget, but he didn't give any specific details, sir," Obersturmführer Monat replied.

"Did he say who gave him the order to carry out the operation, Monat?"

Monat shook his head. "No, Sir. Technically, Koch and his platoon were off duty and were actually on weekend leave…"

"So Koch decided to carry out a one-man vigilante mission." Ulrich shook his head in disbelief. "Don't tell me, in revenge for the deaths of our wounded in the Hereward Hospital fire?"

Monat's silence answered the question.

"And Niebergall carried out his revenge attack as payback for the Saint George's Day Massacre? And now both of them are dead along with all of their men. No doubt they were killed in turn by the Resistance in revenge for their attacks against British civilians, and so it goes on and on ad infinitum. What a bloody waste of lives." Ulrich shook his head in frustration. "You would have thought that the stupid bastards would have learnt something by now."

A pregnant pause. "Permission to speak, sir?" Monat asked awkwardly.

"Permission granted, Monat," Ulrich replied. "Feel free to speak frankly."

"I... I don't know quite how to put this, sir..." Monat stumbled.

"Come on, man. Out with it. I'm a big boy. I can take it."

Monat coughed and straightened even further to a more rigid position of attention. "There is a general feeling that you're in over your head and that you don't have a firm enough grip of the situation and don't know how to deal with the British or the Resistance," Monat blurted out. "Sir." The young German officer clicked his heels together and bowed his head in submission as he waited for the inevitable storm which was about to burst over him.

Ulrich stared at Monat for a second, before he exploded with a full-throated belly-aching laugh. Monat was caught completely off-guard as his commanding officer rocked backwards and forwards in his chair. Monat looked as if he was about to suffer a heart attack. "My dear Monat, do you think that this comes as a complete surprise to me? Six months ago I was the same rank as you. I was an Obersturmführer in command of a platoon of thirty men and now I'm a

Sturmbannführer in command of a brigade - a brigade, Monat, of approximately three thousand men. Of course I'm in over my head!" Ulrich wiped away tears of laughter from his eyes with one hand as he continued, "No one is more aware of that than yours truly. Talk about stating the bloody obvious! I know more than anyone that I was promoted to fill dead man's shoes and that it is purely as result of luck and being in the right place at the right time that I am here where I am today, the youngest Sturmbannführer in the entire SS."

Monat was rendered speechless by such a frank response. "I... I don't know what to say, sir."

Ulrich waved his hand dismissively. "It's all right, Monat, you don't have to say anything. I know that many people consider me to be too soft to deal with the situation because I happen to think that the right way to win the loyalty of the British is not necessarily by executing innocent hostages or by reducing entire villages to nothing but rubble and ashes."

"And what is the right way, sir?" Monat was genuinely intrigued.

"By winning their hearts and minds and by convincing them that National Socialism is a superior method of government to democracy."

"Oh..."

Ulrich waved his hand in the air dismissively. "Anyway, it's all academic now. My command of the brigade was only ever going to be temporary." Ulrich chuckled. "You can't have a twenty-three-year-old running an entire brigade permanently!"

"I... I don't understand, sir..."

"Berlin is sending someone over to take the situation in hand, Monat." Ulrich glanced down at the name written on his notepad. "Brigadeführer Fritz Herold."

Ulrich enjoyed watching the colour drain from Monat's face.

"Brigadeführer Herold, sir?"

"Yes, Monat." Ulrich smiled wickedly. "The Butcher of Birmingham himself."

Monat gulped.

"He will make Brigadeführer Schuster seem like the Virgin Mary in comparison. God save us all." Ulrich took a gulp of whiskey.

"Amen to that."

"I am known as a brutal dog," Brigadeführer Fritz Herold announced to the assembled SS officers of his new Brigade. "That is why the Führer chose me to take command of all SS forces in Hereward." Herold gazed across the sea of faces who were hanging on his every word. "Let me make one thing perfectly clear, gentlemen: our mission is to suck from Britain all the good that we can get hold of without consideration of the feelings or the property of the British. We will accomplish this mission with or without the co-operation of Prime Minister Joyce's Government of National Unity," Herold said scornfully. "Personally, I have little time for traitors who sell out their country. I have far more respect for Churchill up in Scotland. He hasn't sold out his country for pieces of silver. If Joyce doesn't cooperate he will simply be replaced with someone who does, such as a Petain-like figure in France or a Quisling-type character in Norway, or the British Government will be done away with completely and we will rule directly such as we already do with Bohemia Moravia. In order to achieve this mission I expect from you the utmost severity towards the British population: the Führer has ordered the complete and utter annihilation of all British men, women and children who oppose us, without pity or mercy. Only in this way can we achieve security in Britain and protect our Western flank against an American attack in the future."

There was a murmur of agreement from the assembled SS officers.

"I have organised this demonstration for the benefit of our British subjects so that they understand that we are deadly serious in our determination to destroy all of our enemies." Herold turned to an SS officer standing by his side. "Proceed, Hauptsturmführer."

"Jawohl, Brigadeführer." The SS captain turned to face his stormtroopers. "Feur!"

Half a dozen MG 42 machine guns opened fire at the rate of one thousand five hundred rounds per minute at the one hundred male hostages who had been captured during Niebergall's raid. They fell into the open grave that they had been forced to dig before Herold's speech.

Herold walked up to the edge of the grave and spat into the mess of torn and mangled men. "Don't mess with the SS," he said. Herold turned on his heels and walked away without a backwards glance.

Chapter Four

"Was it worth it?" Alice asked through tear-filled eyes as she looked out of her bedroom window at the deserted neighbourhood street.

"It's not a case of whether or not it was worth it..." Alan explained.

"The SS would have killed the hostages anyway, sis, and there is absolutely nothing that we could have done to prevent that from happening," Sam said.

"The execution of the hostages had nothing to do with us killing Koch and Niebergall, Alice," Alan continued. "The hostages were executed in revenge for the Saint George's Day Massacre."

"So is this all there is then?" Alice asked dejectedly. "We kill them and they kill us until the bitter end?"

"Yes," Alan nodded his head.

"Until when?"

"Until we capture Berlin and conquer Germany and Hitler and all of the other Nazi bastards are dead."

"Or until we're dead."

"Yes," Alan answered resolutely with his head held high. "Until we're dead and they prise our weapons from our cold and stiff bodies, and not one moment before. Strength and honour, my friends."

"Strength and honour, Al," Alice and Sam chorused.

Alan first spotted her when he was waiting outside the main school building to go to Morning Assembly.

"Who is she?" Alan asked Sam.

"Who?"

"That girl over there," Alan gestured with his chin. She was tall and slim and she was about Alan's height. She had shiny raven black hair that fell in flowing locks to her shoulders, long eyelashes, deep brown eyes and olive skin. She was the most exquisite creature that

Alan had seen in his life and he could not keep his eyes off her.

Sam turned around, spotted her and shrugged his shoulders. "Oh, Alice mentioned that a new girl was starting school today and since Alice is a prefect she's been asked to be her Guardian Angel and look after her. Alice said that she was Italian or Portuguese or something, but I can't remember."

"Fat lot of use you are, Sam!" Alan said with frustration.

"All right, Casanova, if you're so keen why don't you go and say hello to her?" Sam suggested.

"No, I can't do that!" Alan protested as he stole another furtive glance at her.

"Come on, Al! Put your money where your mouth is!" Sam urged. "Walk over there and introduce yourself. I dare you, I double dare you!"

Alan shook his head in surrender.

"I don't understand you, Al!" Sam was exasperated. "You will quite happily shoot it out with a section of SS stormtroopers at twenty paces, but you're too scared to talk to a girl that you fancy!"

"I don't... this is different, Sam," Alan explained weakly.

"Bah!" Sam said with feigned disgust. "A little less conversation and a little more action is what's called for, I think." Sam looked at her again and gave a low wolf whistle. "Come to think of it, Al, she is a stunner. If you're too scared to have a go then perhaps I will..." he teased.

"Don't you dare, Sam! I saw her first!" Alan's eyes flared.

"All's fair in love and war, chum," Sam said with a wicked grin on his face.

Alan thumped Sam on the arm.

"Ow!" Sam rubbed his arm tenderly. "That hurt, you

bugger! You know that I'm only joking."

"You better be joking, Sam! She's mine," Alan threatened with a growl in his throat.

"Well, I'll believe it when I see it," Sam said as he punched his friend on the shoulder. "But you better be quick, Al: you've got competition." Sam pointed with his chin at another group of boys who were checking out the new girl's form.

Alan looked at the mysterious girl again and his heart skipped a beat as they locked eyes for several seconds, before they both looked away.

After Assembly, Alan saw the mystery girl speaking to Alice and couldn't believe his eyes when she put her hand on Alice's shoulder, turned her around and pointed at ...him! Before he had time to compose himself, mystery girl and Alice were walking towards him.

"Alan, may I introduce Aurora. Aurora, may I introduce Alan," Alice announced.

"I asked Alice to introduce me to you, Alan," Aurora explained pointedly.

Without any further ado, Alice spun on her heels and walked away.

"Alice, where are you going?" Alan asked desperately. He felt like a shipwrecked sailor watching his rescue ship sail off into the distance.

"I'm leaving you two to get acquainted," Alice replied with a beaming smile over her shoulder.

"But I...!" Alan protested with a raised hand.

Alice rushed back and planted a big kiss on Alan's cheek. "Just be yourself, Al," she whispered in his ear. "You'll be fine." And then she was gone.

"Hello... Aurora," Alan said bashfully. "Pleased to meet you."

"Pleased to meet you, Alan," Aurora replied with a

mischievous sparkle in her eyes. She was enjoying the effect that her presence and her earlier comment were having on Alan. The pair shook hands.

Alan jolted as if a bolt of lightning had hit him.

"What the... what the hell was that?" Alan asked in confusion. "Did you feel it?" Alan's pulse rate was suddenly racing at a rapid rate of knots and his heart was pounding so hard that it threatened to burst out of his chest.

"I... I certainly did, Alan," Aurora replied breathlessly. She was flustered and the tips of her fingers were tingling. "I think it is what you refer to in English as... chemistry." She could feel the endorphins surging through her body as if she had overdosed by drinking a massive cup of chocolate caliente. Aurora was grateful that her olive skin helped to disguise her flushed complexion.

"So... what brings you to England?" Alan asked awkwardly as he tried to take slow regular breaths in order to slow down his heart rate.

"My father is the Military Attaché at the Spanish Consulate here in Hereward. We only arrived at the weekend and we're still unpacking." Aurora tried to recover her composure.

"Spanish Consulate?" Alan was confused. "Why on earth does Spain want to have a consulate in Hereward?"

"Franco wants to have a consulate where ever there is a seat of power. Hereward is going to be Hitler's Official Residence is in Britain, so Franco wants to have his eyes and ears open where the action is," Aurora explained.

Alan noticed that Aurora referred to Franco by his name and did not use the more respectful Caudillo. In Occupied Britain you could often tell what a person's attitude was towards the Government of National Unity by paying particular attention when they talked about Joyce or Mosley: did they refer to the puppet prime ministers by name, or did they use the more respectful Leader?

"Everyone is opening consulates here in Hereward," Aurora continued, "the Italians, the Portuguese and so on."

All the Nazi's Fascist fellow travellers, Alan thought to himself.

"We also have the embassy in London, of course, and also an embassy in Harrogate where the British Government is based..."

"Where the puppet British Government is based, Aurora," Alan interrupted abruptly. "Forgive me for correcting you, Aurora, but making that mistake in less forgiving company could get you into a lot of trouble..."

"What kind of company, Alan? What kind of trouble?"

"The wrong kind of company," Alan said sternly. "The kind of company who shoot first and ask questions later. The kind of trouble where you're likely to end up lying face down in a ditch with a bullet hole in the back of your head and your brains scattered all over the pavement."

A pregnant pause. "Thank you for giving me such valuable advice, Alan." Aurora bowed slightly.

"Well... I'd hate to see anything happen to you," Alan said without thinking.

"Why, Alan?" Aurora asked mischievously. "After all, I'm only an enemy alien and we've only just met," Aurora said coquettishly.

"As far as I know, Spain and Britain are not at war, Aurora; and you're a guest in my country and it is my duty to protect you against all enemies," Alan replied seriously.

Aurora laughed at Alan's gallantry. "Against all enemies?" she teased.

"Against all enemies." Alan nodded resolutely.

"You're serious?" Aurora asked with raised eyebrows.

"I'm deadly serious, Aurora," Alan replied with menace. "In fact, I've never been more serious in my life. I will defend you against all enemies, both British and German."

"But the British are your friends, they are your people." Aurora was confused.

Alan shook his head. "Not all of them. There's something that you must understand, Aurora. We're in the middle of a civil war. Britain is not at peace. The smoke has hardly cleared from the battlefields in Spain. You should know what a civil war is like."

"Yes, I know what civil war is like, Alan," Aurora said bitterly. "Father against son, brother against brother. God forbid that it should ever happen here."

Alan shook his head sadly. "It's too late for that, Aurora; it's already started. This war will not be over until Britain is united and free from Fascists and Nazis and Hitler and his band of bastards are dead and buried," Alan said with venom in his voice. "Until that day I'll decide who the enemy is, Aurora, and I'll fight them by whatever means are necessary." He thought for a moment before he spoke again. "Why did you want to meet me?" Alan asked bashfully.

Aurora shrugged her shoulders. "I was curious, Alan. I looked at you and I saw you looking at me and I liked what I saw. So I told Alice that I wanted to meet you and here we are," Aurora explained. "I had no idea that she was a special friend of yours... an ex-girlfriend, perhaps?" Aurora asked as she remembered Alice's kiss on Alan's cheek.

Alan laughed and shook his head. "You couldn't be

further from the truth, Aurora. Alice is my best friend's big sister."

"Your best friend?"

"Yes. Sam Roberts. We're practically brothers."

"Ah! I see," Aurora breathed a sigh of relief. "So you do not have a girlfriend?" Aurora asked as she twisted a lock of her raven-coloured hair around her little finger.

"Me? Have a girlfriend?" Alan guffawed. "I've never had a girlfriend."

"We'll soon see about that," Aurora said with a twinkle in her eye.

Major Juan Mendoza walked arm in arm with his daughter through the streets of Hereward, without a care in the world.

"So, Aurora, my little butterfly," Mendoza said, "tell me about your first week at school. Have you made any new friends?"

"Yes, Papa!" Aurora answered. "They are all very nice and friendly."

"Muy bien." Mendoza patted Aurora's arm.

"English, please, Papa!" Aurora scolded.

"Yes, of course, my butterfly. Sorry. Very good!"

"And I've met a boy!" Aurora announced proudly.

Mendoza was so shocked that he nearly walked into a lamp post.

"A... a boy?" Mendoza was at a complete loss for words. He had known that one day this day would come and he had been confident that he would be ready for it, but he had not expected this day to come... so soon. "What do you mean, Aurora? A boy? You're too young! I forbid it!"

Aurora laughed. "What do you mean 'you forbid it', Papa?"

"Well," Mendoza fumbled and stumbled, "I'm your

father and I expressly forbid it and that's my last word on the matter."

"You forbid me to have any male friends, Papa?"

"No, my little butterfly." Mendoza was confused. "Of course I don't forbid you to have any male friends - in fact you must have male friends…" …to defend you against other males who want to become your boyfriend. Oh, why didn't Aurora have any big brothers to protect her?

"But that's all Alan is, Papa," Aurora explained. "A friend." For now, Aurora thought to herself.

"Alan?" Mendoza practised pronouncing the name. "So he's not your boyfriend, he's just a friend?"

"I never said that he was my boyfriend, Papa. I said that he was my friend and that's all." Aurora looped her arm through her father's once more and patted his hand. "Besides, I'm only fifteen, Papa. As you said, I'm far too young to have a boyfriend."

"Well, in that case of course you can have a boy friend, I mean a boy who is a friend… a friend who is a boy…"

Aurora patted her father's hand again. "It's all right, Papa. I know exactly what you mean."

With that misunderstanding successfully straightened out, the happy pair continued on their way.

"So tell me about this male friend of yours, Aurora. Alan, is it? Perhaps we should invite him around for lunch some day?"

"Oh, Papa! That would be wonderful!" Aurora hugged her father and jumped up and planted a big kiss on his cheek. "You won't regret it! I promise!"

Mendoza was so relieved that he and Aurora had managed to clear up the confusion that he did not notice that someone was watching.

Scharführer Lothar Kophamel apologised profusely for

his clumsiness as the attractive waitress knelt down to pick up the pieces of the broken pint glass. "I'm sorry for my butterfingers, fräulein," Kophamel said as the bartender approached with a mop and bucket. He put some more money on the pub counter and then walked outside to double-check what he had seen. Yes, Kophamel nodded, it was definitely him.

Kophamel was so shaken that as he walked off to report the news, he did not notice that he was being followed.

"Are you sure, Lothar? Are you one hundred percent sure that it was him that you saw?" Hauptsturmführer Manfred von Stein asked.

"I am one hundred percent sure, sir," Kophamel replied. "How could I forget? His face is the first thing that I see in the morning and the last thing that I see at night." Kophamel tapped his temples three times. "I... I still have nightmares, sir."

"It's all right, my old friend. So do I," von Stein admitted as he rubbed his forehead. "What have you found out about him?"

Kophamel consulted his notebook. "I found out that his name is indeed Juan Mendoza, sir, of the Spanish Foreign Legión, but he is now a major now, sir, not a captain. Mendoza is the Spanish Military Attaché based at the new Spanish Consulate here in Hereward."

"Mein Gott!" Von Stein slammed a fist into his other hand. "That's just our damned luck!"

Kophamel's brows furrowed in confusion. "I don't understand, sir. You still want to kill him?"

"Of course I still want to kill him, Lothar!" von Stein exploded. "After what he did, I want to kill him, his wife, his children, his parents and everyone who knows him! I even want to kill his dog if he has one! Mendoza deserves to die a thousand deaths!" he

57

continued furiously. "The problem is that the Spanish must never suspect that it was Germans that killed him. The Führer wants Franco to give permission for German forces to cross Spain to attack Gibraltar, and if they have even the slightest suspicion that Germans murdered their Military Attaché in Hereward then there will be absolutely no way that they will give permission, and that will also sink any chance of Spain entering the war on our side," von Stein explained. "We will have to be very careful."

"We could make it look like the Resistance murdered him, sir," Kophamel suggested with raised eyebrows.

"Excellent idea, Lothar!" Von Stein slammed his fist into his hand. "We can kill two birds with one stone! Franco will be absolutely furious! He may well declare war on Churchill and the Free North there and then!" von Stein continued with a twinkle in his eye. He was practically frothing at the mouth in his enthusiasm. "At the very least he will give permission for our troops to cross Spain to attack the British and he may very well join in the attack with Spanish troops!" Von Stein stared off into the distance as if he could see the events unfold in the future as he had foreseen, planned and predicted.

Kophamel paused before he spoke again. "Sir, there's something else. The icing on the cake, so to speak."

"What is it, Lothar?" Von Stein's ears pricked up like a cat's.

"Remember that you said that you wanted to kill Mendoza, his family and everyone who knew him?"

"Yes," von Stein replied. "What of it?"

Kophamel's mouth widened like a jackal to reveal a set of gum-lined teeth.

"Mendoza has a daughter, sir…"

"Are you sure, Francisco? Are you one hundred per cent sure that it was him that you saw?" Major Mendoza asked.

"I am one hundred percent sure, sir." Sergeant Francisco Borghese answered. "How could I forget? I still remember the sick and twisted expression on his face when he tortured that Red prisoner for fun." Borghese shook his head in disgust as he remembered. "A look of pure sadistic delight. Besides, how could I forget such a face? That scar that stretches from his mouth to his ear is unmistakable."

Mendoza nodded his head as he agreed. "What I don't understand is how did the bastard survive?" He shook his head in amazement. "We must have fired a whole magazine at them."

"Luck of the devil, sir," Borghese answered. "The question is: did anyone else survive? There was an oberleutnant in command with Scar Face, sir, and he probably was in charge of about ten men…"

"A standard infantry squad," Mendoza interrupted.

"Yes, sir," Borghese agreed. "Although he may have lost a few men in the fighting before the murder."

"So there may well have been a dozen Nazis in total, but certainly no more than that." Mendoza was thinking aloud.

"Yes, sir."

"But how many survivors, Francisco? Two? Three? Perhaps more."

"I would say certainly no more than three, sir. Surely our shooting can't be that bad? After all, we shot them at point-blank range."

Mendoza shook his head in disgust. "Apparently our marksmanship is not all that it's cracked up to be." He drummed his fingers on his desk as he spoke. "We need to spend more time on the firing range."

Borghese came to a position of attention. "Your orders, sir?"

"Kill Scar Face and every one he comes into regular contact with. Let's finish off these Nazi murderers once and for all."

"But why did you want to meet me specifically, Aurora?" Alan asked as they walked through the park,

"Because of the way that you looked at me."

"I don't understand," Alan was perplexed. "I'm sure that you've noticed that your arrival has stirred up a hornet's nest. Boys are hovering around you like bees around honey."

Aurora laughed. "How very gallant, Alan! Yes, of course, I've noticed. But you are different; your eyes are different."

"What do you mean, Aurora?"

"Your eyes have seen things that your average fifteen year old boy hasn't," Aurora explained.

Alan stopped walking as if he had rammed into a brick wall. "Aurora... you have no idea," Alan searched for words. "I have seen things... I have done things which would give you nightmares. If I told you about the things that I have done you would run a mile and you would never talk to me again. You would not want to know me."

Aurora tenderly took both of Alan's hands in her own. "Trust me, Alan. Let me help you fight your demons."

"There he is, Carlos," Sergeant Borghese said under his breath. "Let's go."

Borghese flicked his cigarette on to the pavement and ground it out with the heel of his boot. He didn't want Scar Face to be able to spot the telltale light of the lit cigarette.

"Where do you think he's going, Jefe?" Corporal Carlos Ramirez asked him, "the pub?"

Borghese nodded "Probably the 'Chicken and Egg', which is the SS pub, or if the Virgin Mary is smiling on us he'll head for the 'King Alfred Hotel'."

"Why is the King Alfred Hotel better?"

"Because the King Alfred is neutral territory," Borghese answered. "The SS, the Army, the Luftwaffe and even Navy officers and NCOs use it if any of them happen to be in town. It has dozens of bedrooms and many Germans use it for dirty weekends with their British girlfriends."

Ramirez gave an appreciative wolf whistle. "But how does that help us, Jefe?"

"Because it's also open to Government of National Unity personnel, British Union of Fascists members, and, crucially for us: friendly governments."

"Ah, I see," Ramirez smiled cunningly. "So no one should bat an eyelid when we turn up. "

"I certainly hope not, because we are probably the least Aryan-looking people in the entire town, if not the whole of England."

Ramirez laughed at Borghese's dark humour as he looked at his own short-sleeved arm, that had been tanned the colour of mahogany by years under the Moroccan sun.

"Let's just hope that our Identification Cards don't let us down..." Borghese thought aloud.

"Fernando used to be a forger before he joined the Legión, Jefe," Ramirez replied confidently. "He's world class."

Borghese guffawed. "Fernando can't be that world class, Carlos, or he wouldn't have joined the Legión to escape from the Police. And I notice that he didn't travel up with the rest of you from London."

"Major de Rivera couldn't spare any more men,

Sergeant," Ramirez explained. "He said that it would have left him with too few Legiónaries to defend the Embassy against an attack by the Reds." Old habits died hard with Ramirez. As far as he was concerned, any enemies of Spain were dirty, stinking Communist vermin, whatever their nationality. Ramirez straightened up. "Fernando won't let us down," he said resolutely.

"Fernando better not, Carlos, or we'll be chopped up like sliced chorizo before you can say seafood paella," Borghese joked grimly.

Borghese and Ramirez reached the King Alfred Hotel shortly after Scharführer Kophamel and his three comrades. About a dozen assorted Germans with their British girlfriends separated the Spaniards from their target. Borghese casually glanced behind him, and was reassured to see two more members of his hit team join the queue. About a dozen people also separated the other two assassins from Borghese. The queue was lengthening rapidly. Borghese looked to the front and paid close attention to the sentries guarding the entrance; the guards consisted of a squad of Army Military Policemen led by a Sergeant Major. Borghese was relieved to notice that the MPs were giving the Identification Cards no more than the most cursory of inspections. Borghese guessed that such was the length of the quickly growing queue that the Hauptwachtmeister had ordered his MPs to process as many thirsty military personnel and their girlfriends as quickly as possible.

Borghese reached the front of the queue.

"Identification Card, please, sir," The MP Sergeant-Major requested.

Borghese realised that since he was wearing civilian clothes the MP Hauptwachtmeister had no idea what rank he was. The German had obviously decided that it was more diplomatic to play it safe by referring to everyone in mufti as "Sir" rather than run the risk of offending someone important. Borghese handed over his ID card.

"Bolivian eh, sir?" the MP asked as he examined the ID card. "Como estas, señor?" the Sergeant Major asked with a South American Spanish accent.

"Ah... muy bien, gracias." Borghese was momentarily taken by surprise.

"You speak Spanish, Hauptwachtmeister?" he asked in Spanish.

The MP laughed. "I certainly do, sir!" he continued in Bolivian Spanish. "I immigrated to Bolivia after the War when I saw an advertisement for military advisers. After the War, Germany was a complete and utter mess and you couldn't get a job for love of money. So I spent nearly twenty years in Bolivia and I only returned to Germany when this war started. Happiest years of my life, sir! I fully intend to return when this blasted war is over. My wife and kids are still over there. I must say that it's a surprise to meet a fellow Bolivian here. What brings you to Hereward, sir, if you don't mind me asking?"

"I'm... I'm with the consulate..." Borghese thought quickly on his feet.

"The consulate?" The Sergeant Major was confused. "I didn't know that Bolivia had a consulate here."

"Ah no, Hauptwachtmeister, you're correct." A thin film of sweat broke out on Borghese's forehead. "We don't have a consulate here... Bolivia is too small a country. But we do have a Representative at the Spanish Consulate. Yours truly."

"I see." The MP smiled.

Borghese breathed a silent sigh of relief.

"And how is La Paz, sir? Have they finished

restoring the Cathedral yet?"

"Well, La Paz is... La Paz," Borghese said with a weak smile. "And as for the Cathedral? I'm afraid that I don't know. It's been many years since I've visited La Paz, or Bolivia for that matter..."

"And your accent, sir. You don't have a Bolivian accent. You speak more like a Spaniard than a Bolivian..."

"As I said, Hauptwachtmeister, I've spent many years abroad in the Diplomatic Service," Borghese said with a false smile fixed on his face. "Listen, I don't mean to be rude. I've enjoyed talking with a fellow Bolivian..."

The MP laughed.

"But my compadre and I have been looking forward to this drink for a long time, and..."

"Of course, sir! My humble apologies. I didn't mean to detain you." The Sergeant Major stood aside and waved them through.

"Nice to meet you, Hauptwachtmeister...?"

The Sergeant Major came to a position of attention. "Hauptwachtmeister Bratge, sir. Jakob Bratge." He clicked his heels and bowed. "At your service, sir."

"Delighted to meet you, Hauptwachtmeister Bratge," Borghese said as he shook the MP's hand.

"The pleasure's all mine, sir," the Sergeant Major replied with a firm handshake as he waved Borghese and Ramirez through.

"Maybe we'll see each other again," Borghese said over his shoulder as he waved goodbye.

"I guarantee that, sir."

"Do you think that he suspects anything, Jefe?" Ramirez asked with concern as he put his hand on his holster under his leather jacket.

"I don't know, Carlos," Borghese said as he chewed

his lip. "If the Virgin Mary is smiling on us then we may have gotten away with it by the skin of our teeth. If not...?"

"Madre Dios!" Ramirez swore. "Now I know why I hate cops so much!"

"But I tell you what, Carlos," Borghese continued. "Even if we've gotten away with it, they certainly won't." He pointed outside to the other two members of the assassination squad who were swiftly approaching the front of the queue where the Sergeant Major was waiting. "I don't mean to be rude; the boys are born killers and I'd sooner have them beside me in a fight than anyone else, but they're hardly the sharpest knives in the drawer. That bloody cop will have them confessing to being Spanish hitmen before they have time to sing 'The song of the Legiónary.'" Borghese shook his head. "Two pairs of South Americans on the same night are too much of a coincidence."

Borghese walked outside, where he swiftly caught the eye of his other two hitmen. Borghese shook his head from side to side, and the two would-be assassins immediately left the queue and wandered off as if they were looking for a less busy venue.

Borghese breathed a giant sigh of relief and walked back in to rendezvous with Ramirez.

"It's just you and me now, Carlos," Borghese said grimly. "Are you ready for this?"

"I was born ready, Jefe," Ramirez said brazenly.

Borghese laughed and clapped Ramirez on the shoulder. "I knew that I could count on you, Carlos!"

Ramirez flashed his set of pearly whites. "Two's company and four's a crowd, Jefe. Besides, Antonio and Enrique are rotten shots. They'd just slow us down."

Borghese was too busy laughing to notice Hauptwachtmeister Bratge turn around and stare after them as they walked towards the bar.

Chapter Five

The Battle of the Ebro River, Catalonia, Spain, August 1938.

El Bonito lowered his binoculars and spoke in a low voice to his Runner. "Bob, pass the word along: stand to, the Fascists are massing for a new attack, everyone is to open fire with everything that we've got when I give the order by whistle blast, and not a moment before. Understood?"

"Yes, boss. Understood," Bob replied with a smile, before he took off as fast as his young legs could carry him, running down the zigzag network of trenches.

Captain Juan Mendoza shouted at the top of his voice "Viva España! Viva la Legión!" He blew his whistle and clambered out of his foxhole with his pistol in his hand. Three companies of the XVIIth Bandera of the Spanish Foreign Legión followed Mendoza over the top and repeated the slogan that echoed around the valley. The Moorish troops advancing on the Bandera's left flank joined in the general cacophony with high-pitched battle cries that were designed to unnerve and intimidate their Republican opponents. The Legiónaries advanced rapidly up Dead Man's Hill, that had been given its nick name as a result of the Nationalist's repeated failed attempts to capture the hill from their Republican enemies. The hill was literally strewn with a carpet of Legiónary and Moor corpses and it was almost possible to walk all the way to the top on bodies without one's feet touching the stony ground.

"Right on cue," Mendoza said, as he heard a barrage of shells fired by a German Condor Legión Artillery Battery fly over head to crash onto the Republican trenches.

"Take cover!" El Bonito shouted as the shells landed on the Republican position. He dived to the ground of the trench and covered his head with his hands as a shell exploded a dozen yards away, collapsing a bunker and burying its occupants alive inside. Shells continued to land in front of, behind and on top of the Republican position, until the artillery barrage suddenly stopped. El Bonito heard another whistle blast and loud cheering from nearby, which could only mean one thing.

"Stand to!" El Bonito rushed to the trench firing step, hoisted himself up, and shouted "Battalion! One hundred! To the front! Rapid fire!"

The British Battalion's six surviving Maxim machine guns and five hundred assorted rifles opened fire at virtually point-blank range into the shocked and surprised Legiónaries and Moors, who had optimistically expected the German artillery barrage to have destroyed the British Battalion's trenches and to have swept their Republican enemies from the summit of the hill. The machine guns cut huge swathes through the ranks of the advancing Nationalists, and the Legiónaries and Moors fell as if a giant scythe wielded by the Grim Reaper himself had cut them down. Within a few minutes the six hundred attacking Nationalists had been reduced to half that number and fled in a confused rabble like rabbits with their tails between their legs, abandoning their weapons and their wounded in their desperation to get back to their lines and find safety. The Republican machine guns offered no mercy and continued to fire at the retreating troops without respite, with rounds striking the Nationalists at ranges of up to eight hundred yards.

"Come on, boys! We've got them on the run! After

them!" a British volunteer shouted.

He was answered with a ragged cheer as dozens of volunteers climbed out of their trenches and poured over the top, pursuing the fleeing Nationalist troops.

"No! Come back, you idiots!" El Bonito shouted desperately. "You'll be caught out in the open with no cover!"

"Come on, boss!" Bob his young runner urged, "We've got them on the run! We can chase them back to Morocco!"

"No, Bob!" El Bonito shouted in vain. "Come back!"

But Bob had already disappeared. Bob Robinson was only sixteen and had run away from home in Liverpool to join the International Brigade. He was frequently teased for his useful exuberance and impulsive behaviour, and was acting true to form.

"It's no use, Jefe. You're wasting your breath." Ramón, the British Battalion's Spanish Republican liaison officer said. "Your men smell victory and they think that the battle is won."

El Bonito shook his head in despair. "The bloody fools. Once the Fascists get back to their foxholes they'll be able to open fire on them with their machine guns and their artillery."

Mendoza had only just managed to reach the relative safety of the Nationalist lines and had barely caught his breath when he saw dozens of Republican soldiers streaming over No Man's Land in hot pursuit.

"Legiónaries! One hundred metres! To your front! Rapid fire!" Mendoza ordered.

His surviving Legiónaries fired a ragged salvo that succeeded in dropping a dozen or so Republican soldiers. The remaining volunteers took cover and started to open fire on the Nationalist positions.

However, most of the Legiónaries had managed to find fox-holes, and the Republicans were sheltered from fire and from view by the stony ground, covered in thick cactus, which concealed many dips and ditches. The fire fight was threatening to settle into an inconclusive stalemate when the guns of the German Condor Legión decided to join in and began to fire shells into No Man's Land. The artillery intervention tipped the balance and the volunteers started to rise up and retreat back to their positions at the top of the hill. The Legiónaries stood up in their fox hills and cheered whenever an artillery shell found its target and blew up a band of Republican soldiers.

A volunteer scrambled over the top of the trench and landed in a tangled heap on the bottom of the trench.

"Paddy, did you see Bob?" El Bonito asked.

"No, boss," a soldier answered in a broad Irish brogue. "I didn't see him."

Another soldier appeared over the parapet and plummeted to the bottom of the trench.

"Fred, have you seen Bob?" El Bonito asked anxiously.

"No, boss, I…" Fred began to answer, when a terrible wailing sound began to echo from the Nationalist position at the bottom of the valley to the Republican position at the summit of the hill. The hair on the back of El Bonito's neck stood on end and he felt a cold hand squeeze his heart as he listened to the tortured sound of a soul in agony.

"What the… what the hell is that?" Fred asked, as the blood drained from his face.

El Bonito carefully climbed the firing step, raised his binoculars to his eyes and looked over the edge of the trench.

A figure stumbled across No Man's Land with his

arms stretched in front of him, crying and sobbing inconsolably. The man turned and for a fleeting moment, El Bonito saw his face. The man's face was covered in blood and he gave a yelp of pain as he tripped and fell into a shell crater.

"What... who is it, boss?" Fred asked, with his hand to his mouth.

El Bonito answered as if he was in a trance. "It's... it's Bob..." he answered as tears streamed down his face. "They've blinded him..."

"What?"

"They've gouged out his eyes..."

Fred gave a cry of horror. He rushed over to El Bonito, snatched the binoculars from his hand and leaped onto the firing step. He searched No Man's Land and found Bob as he finally managed to scramble out of the shell crater. A mop of gore-matted hair hung down over Bob's eyeless sockets that were still leaking blood which ran in streams down his blood and dirt-encrusted face.

"Those bloody bastards!" Fred said with fury.

"He was the same age as my kid brother..." El Bonito said with tear-filled eyes.

There was a sudden shot, and Bob collapsed onto the ground for the last time with a bloody hole between his eyes.

"What the...?" Fred said in confusion. He turned around to see Ramón holding the battalion's sole sniper rifle with the smoke still coming from the end of the barrel.

"You bloody bastard, Ramón!" Fred was as angry as a berserker. "What did you do that for? You killed him! We could have saved him!"

"No, Fred, you could not have," Ramón said slowly as he shook his head. "That's what the Moors wanted. You would have gone out to save him and they would have killed you, or they would have captured you and you would have suffered the same fate as poor Bob, or worse."

"Worse? What could possibly be worse than being blinded?" Fred asked incredulously.

"Being castrated," Ramón answered matter-of-factly. "Losing your manhood." He shrugged. "I saw it in Morocco in 1921 when the Moorish rebels castrated some of our men who were captured at the Battle of Anual."

"That doesn't change anything, Ramón, you're still a murderer." Fred raised his rifle, flicked off the safety catch and pulled the trigger, just as El Bonito rifle butted him in the back of the head. Fred collapsed like a sack of potatoes and the round thudded harmlessly into the back of the trench wall.

"Thanks, Jefe," Ramón said with relief.

"Don't mention it," El Bonito said graciously. "You'd do the same for me, Ramón. Besides, you did the right thing. Fred lost his head. So did I for a moment back there... Hello? What's going on?"

El Bonito mounted the firing step and peered over the edge as he heard the stirring lyrics of the Republican anthem the 'Internationale' floating over the valley.

"What is it? What can you see?" Ramón asked.

El Bonito's brows furrowed in confusion. "There are about fifty or so volunteers walking up the valley towards our position, and they're singing and waving their rifles above their heads."

"And the Fascists are not opening fire?" Ramón asked.

"No, they're not," El Bonito confirmed. "Maybe our boys have arranged a cease-fire with them in order to bury the dead; it's not the first time that it's happened. The same thing happened at the Battle of Jarama last year." El Bonito shrugged and scratched his head. "I don't know: perhaps our men are returning to our lines to grab stretchers to collect our wounded and spades to bury the dead..."

"Anyway, let's welcome them back, Jefe!" Ramón said cheerfully. "God knows that we could do with some good news around here."

"It's working, Jefe."

"Don't count your chickens yet, Francisco," Mendoza replied. "The Reds may still see through your cunning plan, and if that happens we'll be cut to pieces."

"What should we do, Captain?" Corporal Borghese asked.

"Keep singing, Francisco!"

"They're nearly here, Ramón." El Bonito lowered his binoculars as the returning volunteers steadily approached the Republican trenches. "Have you managed to gather up any stretchers or spades?"

"Yes, Jefe," Ramón answered. "But it's not much. It's nearly dusk and we don't have much time to collect our dead and wounded. How's Fred?" Ramón pointed with his chin.

El Bonito chuckled. "Well, put it this way: he's going to wake up with one hell of a headache."

Ramón laughed.

"One other thing, Ramón; if I were you I'd watch your back from now on when Fred's around. He and Bob were close. Fred looked after him like a younger brother."

"And I'd advise you to grow a pair of eyes in the back of your head as well, Jefe," Ramón advised. "Fred doesn't particularly strike me as the forgiving type."

El Bonito nodded in agreement. "Hello? What's

this?" His brows furrowed in confusion. "They've stopped singing... what's going on?"

"Grenades!" Mendoza shouted.

In a split second each of the fifty returning "volunteers" threw two grenades in quick succession into the Republican positions. The bombs exploded amongst the unsuspecting British volunteers, who were caught completely unawares.

"Viva la Legión! Viva España!" Mendoza shouted, and jumped into the nearest trench with a pistol in one hand and a bayonet in another. He shot a dazed and confused volunteer twice in the stomach before burying his bayonet in the chest of another other Republican soldier, who died with a look of utter surprise and confusion on his face. "Legiónaries, spread out down the length of the trench!" Mendoza ordered. "Capture the machine guns! Kill all of the Reds!"

The Legiónaries cheered and flowed through the trench like an unstoppable flash flood, shooting and bayoneting all of the volunteers that they could find without mercy.

"The Fascists are in the trenches!" El Bonito shouted in horror. "We've got to clear them out before they get reinforcements!"

Ramón cocked his rifle and flicked off the safety catch. "I'm with you, Jefe!"

"Follow me!" El Bonito ordered as he cocked his pistol and took out a grenade from his pocket.

"Fire the Verey pistol, Corporal!" Mendoza ordered.

"Yes, sir!" Borghese pointed the pistol straight up in the air and pulled the trigger. The flare shot straight up and exploded in a shower of green lights. A cheer erupted from the Nationalist trenches as hundreds of

Legiónaries and Moor Regulares poured out of their fox-holes like an army of ants and swarmed over No Man's Land, running as fast as they could towards the Republican lines.

"Keep fighting, men!" Mendoza urged. "Reinforcements are coming!"

"Grenade!" El Bonito threw a grenade around the corner of the trench, that exploded seconds before Ramón threw another. El Bonito ran around the corner before the dust had settled and shot two wounded Legiónaries in quick succession. He stuffed his still-smoking pistol back in his holster and picked up one of the dead Legiónaries' rifles. Ramón swapped his rifle for the other dead Legiónnaire's Star 9 millimetre submachine gun.

"I've always wanted one of these..." Ramón said with childish joy as he stroked the barrel with appreciation.

At that moment two Moor Regulares leaped into the trench behind them. Ramón spun around, pulled the trigger, and dropped the Regulares with a short burst.

"We've got to get out of here, Jefe! They're all around us!" Ramón urged.

El Bonito nodded. "We'll retreat to the second line of trenches and then we'll counter attack..." He raised his whistle to his lips and blew three short blasts, signalling the withdrawal.

"Hande hoch!" a guttural voice suddenly ordered.

"Too late, Jefe." Ramón said in despair as he raised his hands in surrender.

El Bonito's shoulders slumped in defeat as he wearily lifted up his arms.

"For you the war is over, Tommy," the voice announced triumphantly in heavily-accented English. "Slowly lower your weapons and take three steps

75

backwards."

The two Republicans did as they were told.

"Sehr gut."

The two men didn't see the rifles that butted them in the back of their heads.

The high-pitched scream stopped Mendoza in his tracks and sent him and Borghese doubling back along the trench in the opposite direction. Moaning and sobbing followed another ear- piercing scream.

"Those bloody Moors..." Mendoza swore. "Their bloody officers are just as cold-blooded and cruel as they are..."

Mendoza rounded the corner in time to see an SS Corporal stand up with an expression of sheer sadistic delight and satisfaction on his face.

"What have you got there, Rottenführer?" Mendoza asked coldly.

The stormtrooper held a bloody dagger in one hand and waved what looked like a bloody piece of meat in the air with the other hand. "Hello? Hello? Sorry, I can't hear you!"

The remaining half a dozen SS troopers collapsed into fits of raucous laughter. The SS Corporal had a scar that stretched from his mouth to his jawline that twitched when he laughed. A Republican volunteer lay curled up on the ground with two hands wrapped around his head, vainly trying to staunch the flow of blood that streamed down his face in a never-ending flood.

"These evil Nazi bastards cut off Fred's ears!" Another Republican prisoner spat blood out of his mouth in furious accusation.

"Shut up, you Red bastard! You're next!" The Rottenführer pointed his finger angrily. "And maybe I won't stop at cutting off your ears! Remember what the

Moors did to your friend!"

"This is completely unacceptable," Mendoza said forcefully. "These men are prisoners of war and should be treated as such according to the Geneva Convention."

"What men, Captain?" the Rottenführer asked mockingly. "I don't see any prisoners of war, I only see Jewish Bolshevik scum. Pick him up."

Two stormtroopers hauled the dazed and disfigured prisoner to his feet and, ignoring his howls of pain, pulled his bloody hands behind his back.

"This is what I think of your precious Geneva Convention, Captain." Before Mendoza could protest, the Rottenführer dragged his dagger across the throat of the helpless prisoner. An arc of blood spurted from the dying man's throat like a geyser and formed a rapidly growing pool on the floor of the dusty trench.

Mendoza gazed unblinking in total and utter shock and horror.

"Now I'm going to kill the other two prisoners, Captain." The Rottenführer advanced towards the two helpless prisoners. "And you're going to watch me do it… sir."

"For God's sake, stop him, Captain! I beg you!"

"Captain Mendoza! For the love of God and for the honour of Spain and the Legión - stop this Nazi murderer!"

The mention of his name snapped Mendoza out of his stupor. He looked at the third Republican prisoner who had appealed to him in his native Spanish.

"Obersturmführer, for the last time, I advise you to order your man to stop or I will be forced to stop you," Mendoza threatened menacingly.

"Captain Mendoza, these dirty Red bastards killed four of my men today and they deserve everything that they've got coming to them. However, we're not going to blind them like your Moorish friends: we Germans are not barbarians. Rottenführer?" the SS Lieutenant in command of the Condor Legión detachment said.

"Yes, sir?"

"I order you to cut the throats of these two Red untermensch bastards. I want to hear them squeal like pigs before they die."

"With pleasure, sir." The Rottenführer advanced menacingly towards the two helpless prisoners with a predator's smile on his lips as two pairs of SS troopers held the prisoner's arms firmly behind them.

"I warned you, Obersturmführer."

"Oh yeah? Who's going to stop me? You and whose army?" the SS officer asked arrogantly.

"Me and my army," Mendoza replied. "A mí la Legión!"

Thirty pairs of arms cocked their weapons and flicked off their safety catches.

The stormtroopers looked up and saw Legiónaries standing on the parapet of the trench both to the front and behind them. The Germans were completely surrounded. A pungent stench of faeces drifted through the air as the Obersturmführer realised that more than a few of his men had lost control of their bodily functions.

"Come, come, Captain," The SS officer backtracked desperately. "Let's not be too hasty. Don't do something that you'll regret later. Let's be reasonable. After all we are allies, and these prisoners are nothing but dirty Reds..."

"These dirty Reds are Spanish prisoners. They are Franco's prisoners, they are my prisoners and they are certainly not your prisoners, you murdering Nazi bastards!"

"Captain, please...!"

"No second chances, Adolf. Legiónaries!"

The Legiónaries all raised their weapons to their firing positions.

"No…!"

"Open fire!"

The Legiónaries shot the stormtroopers at point-blank range and did not stop firing until their magazines were completely empty. The Nazis collapsed like a stack of cards and lay in a steaming bloody heap on the ground.

"Cease fire!" Mendoza ordered. "Well done, Legiónaries! You have performed your duties efficiently and with dedication. The execution of these Nazis was regrettable, but was necessary in order to uphold the honour of Spain and of the Legión. Viva la Legión! Viva España!"

"Viva la Legión! Viva España!" The Legiónaries repeated the motto with gusto.

"Now reorganise the captured position: distribute any remaining ammunition, gather any useful weapons and supplies from the Reds and from our own dead and wounded, take care of our injured men, guard any prisoners, and prepare for an immediate Red counterattack."

"Yes, Captain!" The Legiónaries chorused.

"Corporal Borghese?"

"Stay with me and take care of any wounded Germans," Mendoza ordered.

"With pleasure, sir." Borghese smiled as he slung his rifle and took his pistol out from his holster.

Mendoza holstered his own pistol and walked up to the Republican prisoner who had addressed him by name in Spanish.

"Hello, Ramón."

"Hello, Juan."

El Bonito's jaw dropped as the men embraced in a bear hug.

Chapter Six

"Would someone mind telling me what the hell is going on?" El Bonito asked in wide-eyed confusion.

Ramón wiped tears from his face as he turned around to face his commander. "I'm sorry, Jefe. How rude of me not to introduce you properly. This is my big brother, Juan."

"Your big brother is a Fascist?" El Bonito blurted out without thinking before he could stop himself. He had wondered why Ramón was so reluctant to talk about this family. And now he knew.

Ramón's back visibly stiffened as he answered El Bonito's question. "Juan is not a Fascist, Jefe; he is as much of a Spanish patriot as I am. We have agreed to disagree about the best way to serve Spain's interests. And if you were any other man I would challenge you to a duel for insulting my family's honour."

Juan laughed at his younger brother's old-fashioned notions of chivalry and honour. "That won't be necessary, little brother. I wouldn't expect a foreigner to understand…"

"And what's that supposed to mean, Captain Mendoza?" El Bonito interrupted angrily. "I'm an educated man and I've been here since July '36. I think that I've got a pretty good idea of what we're fighting for and what we're fighting against."

Mendoza sighed in resignation. "What you are fighting for and what you are fighting against may not necessarily be the same as what we are fighting for," - Mendoza pointed to his brother and himself - "and what we are fighting against."

"Well, perhaps you could enlighten me, Captain. What are you fighting for and against?" El Bonito asked as he folded his arms. "I'm all ears and I don't think that I'll be going anywhere in a hurry."

"It's complicated..."

"Are you fighting for this?" El Bonito pointed at Fred's mutilated corpse. "Are you fighting for them?" He pointed at the dead Nazis. "For the right to torture, mutilate and murder helpless captured prisoners of war?"

"No!" Mendoza answered angrily. "I am not fighting for those Nazi bastards! What that Nazi bastard did was utterly barbaric and was beyond the pale. I don't approve of the way that some of our own Moor Regulares treat their prisoners either. However, we needed weapons and ammunition and tanks and aeroplanes to fight against the Reds. After all, you had Soviet Communist help."

"I see. Beggars can't be choosers, eh?" El Bonito said provocatively.

"The enemy of my enemy is my friend, Jefe." Ramón tried valiantly to defend his big brother's motives.

"Christ, Ramón! Whose side are you on?" El Bonito accused.

"I'm on the side of truth and justice and democracy and I'm against lies, injustice and Fascism!" Ramón replied angrily.

"God help you if England ever suffers a civil war, señor," Mendoza said wearily. "I wouldn't wish that on my worst enemy: you may not find it so easy to decide whose side to fight on when your countrymen are at each other's throats."

"Don't worry, Captain. I assure you that I will know whose side to fight on," El Bonito replied defiantly.

"Captain Mendoza!" Borghese ran up to him with a smoking pistol in his hand.

"Yes, what is it, Corporal?"

"The Reds are counterattacking, sir! With more than thirty tanks and supporting infantry!"

Mendoza suddenly became aware of the ominous clanking noise made by the caterpillar treads of dozens of tanks steadily approaching the captured Republican trenches. He carefully climbed the rear of the trench and cautiously peered over the edge through his binoculars. "Madre Dios! Soviet tanks, and we don't have a single anti tank rifle in the entire battalion!" He turned to face Borghese. "What's the condition of the captured Maxim machine guns? And do we have radio contact with the Condor Legión Artillery Battery?"

Borghese shook his head. "It's no use, sir. Most of the Maxims were damaged beyond repair in our attack and the radio was riddled with bullets, so we have no way of contacting the battery to request a fire mission. We have absolutely nothing to stop the attack. The Reds will roll over us any minute, Captain."

Mendoza swore again. "You're absolutely right. We'll have to retreat and hope that the Red tanks follow us to within range of our own artillery." Mendoza turned to face his younger brother. "Ramón, I want you and Trotsky here to remain in the trenches. I'm not going to take you prisoner: you're free."

"Juan... Juan, I don't know what to say..." Ramón said as his eyes filled up with tears.

"You are going to lose the war, Ramón. Resistance is futile. Promise me that you'll get away safely to France or England."

"I... we won't lose, Juan! We are going to win! We won't surrender!" Ramón protested.

Mendoza shook his head in frustration "Promise me that you'll escape when the time comes, or I swear to God I will take you back to our lines with me right now!"

"All right! I promise that when... if we lose, I will escape..."

"And take Stalin here with you!"

"Captain Mendoza!" Borghese interrupted. "You need to signal the order to withdraw right now, sir! We have to leave! The Reds are almost on top of us!"

Mendoza took out his pistol, mounted the firing step at the front of the trench, and blew his whistle three times to signal the withdrawal.

"Captain Mendoza?" El Bonito said.

Mendoza turned around.

"I just wanted to say thank you for saving us."

Mendoza nodded. "Just look after my little brother for me; that will be thanks enough, señor…?"

"My name is -"

"El Bonito," Ramón interrupted, "the men call him El Bonito."

Mendoza looked at the British volunteer's sun-bleached blonde hair, tanned high cheek-boned face and bright shining blue eyes, and nodded his head with an amused grin on his face. "El Bonito…. The Pretty One?"

Ramón laughed. "El Bonito is widely acknowledged to be the most handsome man in the Battalion!"

El Bonito blushed through his dirty blood and dust-encrusted face. "Shut up, Ramón! I could have you shot!" he joked.

Mendoza laughed and straightened up to a position of attention. "Adios, amigos!"

"Adios!" the two Republicans replied.

"Ramón, I'll tell mother and father that you're alive and kicking!"

Ramón nodded. "Juan, give my love to Aurora!"

"Viva España!" both of the brothers chorused.

"Take care, little brother!" Mendoza executed a perfect parade ground salute, and disappeared over the top.

Hospital, Madrid, Spain, September 1938.

"I don't understand, sir," Obersturmführer Manfred von Stein said with furrowed brows as he sat up in his hospital bed. "I identified the killer as Captain Mendoza of the Spanish Foreign Legión..."

"You're the one who doesn't understand, Obersturmführer," the SS Colonel interrupted. "Mendoza is connected directly to Franco. Franco used to be in command of the Spanish Foreign Legión and he identified Mendoza early on as a rising star and he has followed and furthered Mendoza's meteoric career path with fatherly interest. Mendoza is the highest decorated junior officer in the Nationalist forces, and he is also married to a woman who is the daughter of one of the top men in the Falange Party and who is also a close personal friend of Franco."

"Christ almighty!" Von Stein swore in frustration.

"Forgive me if I'm wrong, sir," Rottenführer Lothar Kophamel said, "but if I understand you correctly, what you're saying is that Mendoza is untouchable?"

The Standartenführer nodded his head. "I'm afraid that's exactly what I'm saying, Rottenführer. You are not to take any action against Mendoza..."

"Even though he murdered my men?" Von Stein interrupted.

"Yes, von Stein!" The SS Colonel exploded in rage at the impertinent interruption. "For the love of God, don't you understand? The Führer himself has been made aware of this incident and his express orders are that you are not to take any action against Mendoza; and furthermore you are expressly forbidden from mentioning this incident ever again, whether in public or in private, upon pain of death. Do you understand?"

"Yes, sir!" the two wounded SS troopers chorused.

"This is the last time that you will ever mention the name Mendoza and if you ever say his name again -

whether in company, alone, together, or even in your sleep - I will hear of it and you will find yourself in front of a firing squad so fast that your feet will not touch the ground. Do I make myself clear?" the SS Colonel thundered.

"Yes, sir!"

"Good. I hope so, gentlemen, for both of your sakes and also for the sake of your families. You realise that the Gestapo will be censoring all of the mail that you send and receive from now on until doomsday. God forgive you if there is even the slightest hint of anything untoward having occurred here in Spain. Your families will end up in a concentration camp so fast that it will make their heads spin."

The two wounded SS troopers gulped.

The Standartenführer reckoned that he had made his point. The blood had drained from the faces of the two stormtroopers as they realised that they had placed their families in serious harm's way. The future health and prosperity of their loved ones depended on the men's ability to ignore the fact that, although a serious injustice had been committed, they were not permitted to seek vengeance for the murder of their men. "Gentlemen, I know that this is not fair, I know that this is a bitter pill to swallow. Believe me that I would like nothing better than to provide you with the services of a squad of the meanest, toughest hombres in the SS in order to hunt down and execute this Mendoza bastard, but I can't. The Führer has expressly forbidden it. This War is bigger than me, and it is bigger than you. We will need the goodwill, support and possibly alliance of Spain in the coming war against our enemies, and nothing and no one will be allowed to jeopardise that relationship, even the cold-blooded massacre of our men by a treacherous Spanish captain. I'm sorry, gentlemen, but that is the world of Real Politick."

The two wounded SS troopers nodded slowly. They could not trust themselves to speak.

"Get well soon, men. The Führer needs all of her sons fit and ready for the forthcoming struggle."

"Thank you, sir."

The SS Colonel headed for the door. "Oh and one more thing, boys. If I hear even a whisper of the name Mendoza any time in the foreseeable future I will track you down and kill you myself. Do I make myself clear?"

"Crystal clear, sir," von Stein replied.

"Good." The Standartenführer smiled. "I'm glad that we understand each other. And then I will track down and kill your parents, your wives and girlfriends, your children, your friends and anyone who has ever met you. I will even kill your pets, boys; and if you doubt my word you only have to mention my name to your SS comrades and they will tell you that Standartenführer Fritz Herold is a brutal dog and that my word is my bond and I am not to be tested. Comprendes?"

"Yes, Standartenführer."

"Good." Herold gave a crocodile smile. "So it ends here: not a peep." He put a single finger to his lips. "Adios, compadres."

"Adios, Jefe," von Stein and Kophamel chorused.

Herold left.

The King Alfred Hotel, Hereward, May 1941

"There he goes, Carlos. After him," Sergeant Francisco Borghese ordered.

Borghese and Corporal Carlos Ramirez stood up and casually followed Scar Face out of the room as he walked tipsily towards the toilets. They hung back as the German disappeared into the Gents. The Spaniards quickly looked behind them to check that they were not being followed. They swiftly drew their pistols from their holsters, cocked the weapons, flicked off the safety catch and tucked the pistols beneath their belts, placing the weapons in the small of their backs.

"Jefe?" Ramirez pointed at a sign.

Borghese smiled and nodded. "Bueno."

Ramirez picked up the "Out of order" sign and placed it on the toilet door handle. Borghese swung the door open and stepped inside the Gents, followed closely by Ramirez.

"Where the hell is he?" Borghese asked in frustration. The German was nowhere to be seen.

"Good evening, gentlemen. Have you come to join the party?" a voice asked good-naturedly in German.

The Spaniards looked towards the end of the toilets. Five assorted SS Non Commissioned Officers stood in a circle, having a chat.

"It looks like a God damned town hall meeting," Ramirez hissed out of the corner of this breath. "What do we do now, Jefe?"

"Follow my lead, Carlos," Borghese whispered. "Buenas noches, señor. Lo siento, no entiendo." Borghese bowed graciously.

"What did he say?" one of the SS NCOs asked.

"He said that he doesn't understand," the first stormtrooper replied.

"Stupid Spanish bastards," another NCO sneered. "We had to hold their hands and teach them how to tie their shoelaces and wipe their arses in Spain."

The other stormtroopers laughed.

"The Nationalists wouldn't have stood a chance against the Reds without our help," the same NCO continued.

"Imagine coming to England without being able to speak German?" another stormtrooper added. "I bet the stupid bastards don't know how to speak English either. German will soon become the official language of Spain unless Franco pulls his finger out of his arse and starts doing as the Führer tells him."

The other NCO s all laughed.

Borghese coughed. "Gentlemen, remember that I told you that I don't understand German?"

"Yes…" the first stormtrooper replied with a confused look on his face as he realised that the words were German.

"Well, I lied…"

The blood drained from the NCO's face. " No…!"

"Viva la Legión! Viva España!"

Borghese and Ramirez whipped their pistols out from under their jackets and fired the entire clip of rounds at virtually point-blank range into the startled Nazis. The Germans collapsed in a bloody heap on the floor.

"Magazine!" both of the Spaniards shouted in unison to warn their companion that they had run out of rounds. They reached into their pockets to find another fresh magazine.

At that precise moment Scar Face burst through the cubicle door like a battering ram, executed a perfect forward roll and recovered into a crouching position, firing his Luger 9 millimetre pistol as he manoeuvred. The first two rounds blew off the top of Ramirez's head, the second two rounds missed, and the third two rounds thudded into Borghese's stomach.

Scar Face stood up and, still breathing heavily, stood in triumph over Borghese. The Spaniard clutched his stomach as he lay in the foetal position, vainly trying to staunch the flow of blood through his rapidly weakening fingers.

"Scar Face…" Borghese smiled through his gritted teeth.

"Rottenführer Lothar Kophamel of the 4th SS Infantry Regiment, at your service." Kophamel bowed.

"I… I wondered what your name was… and now I know," Borghese said as he coughed up a globule of blood.

"And I don't know your name."

"Sergeant Francisco Borghese of the XVII Bandera of the Spanish Foreign Legión," he hissed though pain-filled lips.

Kophamel shook his head "You stupid bastard, Borghese. I was onto you as soon as you spoke Spanish. You should have kept your mouth shut."

"My friends always tell me that I talk too much…" Borghese joked at his own expense.

"And here you lie with your guts falling out and your blood flowing out onto a cold English toilet floor…"

"We all have to die, Kophamel. I would rather die here with my face to the enemy than in my bed, drowning in a sea of my own shit."

"Spare me the sentimental bullshit, Borghese. Believe me; I've heard it all before." Kophamel shook his head dismissively. "Why did you and Billy the Kid here try to kill me?" Kophamel asked.

Borghese spat out a globule of blood that landed on Kophamel's shoe. The Nazi kicked the Spaniard in the stomach as if he was kicking a football, and Borghese moaned in pain.

"It doesn't matter, Borghese. I already know: Mendoza ordered you to kill me, didn't he?"

Kophamel saw a flicker of fear in Borghese's eyes.

"Ah yes, Sergeant. I can see that it's true. Mendoza did send you to kill me."

"It's Major Mendoza to you, you murdering Nazi bastard!"

Borghese suffered another painful kick to the

stomach as a reward for his defiance.

Kophamel tutted and shook his head slowly. "You know, it's a crying shame that you tried to kill me, because when I discovered that Major Mendoza was the Spanish Military Attaché in Hereward I told Hauptsturmführer von Stein. However, he didn't want to exact any revenge because he's a bit of a soft touch. He was all for letting sleeping dogs lie. But I'm afraid that now you have left me with little choice but to kill Mendoza and his daughter."

Kophamel was pleased to see Borghese stiffen at the mention of Mendoza's daughter.

"Pretty little thing, isn't she? Aurora, isn't it? Shame to let such a pretty girl go to waste. I'll probably have some fun with her first before I throw her to the wolves. Some of my men are not double veterans yet."

Borghese suddenly started laughing, which was the exact opposite reaction to the one that Kophamel had expected.

"What are you laughing about, Borghese? You are about to die."

"So are you, Kophamel…" Borghese smiled.

"What… what do you mean?"

"Look inside the briefcase…"

Kophamel opened the briefcase that Borghese had been carrying. The blood drained rapidly from the Nazi's face. "Oh shit."

The massive explosion instantly killed Kophamel and the dying Borghese, and ripped apart Ramirez and the bodies of the five SS stormtroopers. The force of the blast was so powerful that it destroyed the concrete pillars in the toilets that supported the three floors above. The rooms situated directly above the toilets plummeted to the ground in a massive cloud of smoke and dust, and the impact killed and wounded the occupants of the dozen or so bedrooms.

"I'm glad to see that you're alive and kicking and in one piece, Hauptwachtmeister Bratge," General-Major Christian von Schnakenberg said with a smile as he welcomed Bratge into his office.

"Well, I'm alive, sir, but I'm not so sure about kicking," Sergeant Major Jakob Bratge replied jovially.

"So, Hauptwachtmeister, what's your appreciation of the King Alfred Hotel incident?" von Schnakenberg asked as he steepled his fingers on his desk.

"Well, sir, the Fire Brigade said that the explosion was caused by a bomb, and their conclusion has been confirmed by our own Army engineers."

"No attempt to blame the deaths on faulty wiring this time?"

"No, sir. Not this time." Bratge shook his head.

"Casualties?"

"The hospital took delivery of twelve casualties, sir. The bodies of two SS officers, one Army officer, one Navy officer and four women. One SS officer, one Army officer and two women were wounded and are presently in Intensive Care. It's touch and go whether they'll make it or not, sir."

"Six dead and another six who may well also die," von Schnakenberg said grimly. "Quite a butcher's bill. Anything else that I should know about?"

"Yes, sir." Bratge nodded his head. "Our sources have informed us that another six SS NCOs are missing and their bodies have not been found."

Von Schnakenberg did not delve any further into the identity of "our sources". He knew that there were Army spies buried deep in the SS, just as he was fully aware that their brothers in arms also had spies in the Army and most probably in his own Brigade.

"The missing men were in the hotel?"

"Yes, sir. Our sources report that at the moment of the explosion they were all in the toilet."

"In the toilet?" Von Schnakenberg asked incredulously. "All at the same time? What were they all doing? I know that the SS are great fans of the Spartans, but is this not taking their love of all things Greek a bit far?"

Bratge examined his notes carefully. "Our sources do not give any indication that the missing men are suspected homosexuals, sir..."

"I'm only joking, Bratge!" Von Schnakenberg shook his head in wonder at the Sergeant Major's gullibility.

Bratge blushed in embarrassment. "There's something else, sir..."

"What is it?" Von Schnakenberg was intrigued. "Don't keep me in suspense, Jakob."

"Two men entered the hotel claiming to be Bolivians, sir, but they weren't; they were Spaniards."

"How do you know that they were Spaniards, Hauptwachtmeister? Did they have the appropriate IDs?"

"Their IDs appeared to be genuine, sir. But I don't know. I have no idea what genuine Bolivian ID papers look like. But the men were definitely not Bolivian, sir. I don't know if you know this, sir, but I trained the Bolivian Army for twenty years. I know what a Bolivian sounds like and they weren't Bolivian, sir. They spoke Spanish like Spaniards."

"Did you check with the Spanish Consulate here in Hereward? Did they tell you that any of their people were missing?"

"I did check with the Consulate, sir. None of their people are missing and, furthermore, there are no Bolivian Representatives there. The two men were lying, sir."

"Curiouser and curiouser, Sergeant Major. So there

are two Spaniards pretending to be Bolivians on the loose in Hereward."

"That's not all, sir," Bratge added. "There were two more of the leader's men waiting in the queue to enter the hotel. The leader signalled them to leave the queue, which they did. I think that he suspected that I was onto him. I ordered two of my men to follow them at a distance. They reported that the two men went through the motions of looking for another pub to go to, but they didn't actually enter any of them even though several of them were not full. After thirty minutes the two men returned to the King Alfred and they waited outside."

"Where did they go after that?"

"I don't know, sir." Bratge shrugged his shoulders. "In the confusion following the explosion my men lost track of them, and they disappeared."

"I see, Bratge," Von Schnakenberg nodded and pointed his finger at the Sergeant Major. "Find them, Hauptwachtmeister. There can't be that many swarthy-looking Spanish looking types walking around Hereward. Find them and bring them here personally. I want to find out at first hand why a Spanish hit team has come to Hereward."

"Jawohl, General-Major von Schnakenberg." Bratge saluted, executed a perfect about turn, and marched smartly out of the office. At last, he thought to himself, the kid gloves are off.

Chapter Seven

"They're not coming, Miguel. Sergeant Borghese and Carlos are dead."

"They're not dead! The sergeant and Carlos are alive!" Miguel threw his hat across the room in frustration. "We just need to give them more time."

"More time?" Private Alfonso de Cervantes asked incredulously. "More time to do what, Miguel? The dead need no more time. Borghese and Carlos are buried five metres under the rubble of the hotel!"

"It's Sergeant Borghese to you, you disrespectful bastard!" Corporal Miguel Pizarro slapped Alfonso backhanded across the face, sending him flying across the room.

De Cervantes lay sprawled on the floor in an untidy heap. He slowly raised himself onto his elbows and rubbed his red cheekbone tenderly with one hand. "Corporal Pizarro, whether you like it or not, Sergeant Borghese and Carlos are dead. It's time that we decided what the hell we should do."

Pizarro sighed as if he was breathing his last breath and his shoulders slumped and sagged like a tired old man's. "I know, Alfonso. You're right. Sergeant Borghese and Carlos are dead. The question is: what do we do now?"

"We find out if Sergeant Borghese and Carlos completed the mission and Scar Face is dead. If he is then we go home, and if he isn't dead then we find him and we kill him," Alfonso said, with steel in his voice.

Pizarro straightened up in his chair and seemed to grow six inches. "Spoken like a true Legiónary, Alfonso! I knew that I could count on you!"

"I'm with you until the end, Jefe!"

"That's my boy." Pizarro had recovered his resolve. "Here's what we'll do: we'll stay here in the safe house and observe the SS Barracks from this window. We'll be able to see who enters and who leaves the barracks. Sooner or later Scar Face will come out for air, and when he does we will kill him and avenge the deaths of Sergeant Borghese and Carlos. Understood?"

"Understood, Jefe," De Cervantes answered. "However, I have one question, Corporal: how long do we stay here before we decide that Sergeant Borghese and Carlos must have completed their mission and killed him?"

Pizarro thought for a moment. "One week, Alfonso? How does that sound?"

De Cervantes nodded. "Sounds fine, Jefe. How long will our sentry duties be?"

"Six hours on, six hours off, from six am until midnight." Pizarro answered. "How does that sound, Alfonso?"

De Cervantes nodded his head. "Sounds good, Jefe."

A pregnant pause. "Alfonso?"

"Yes, Jefe?"

"I'm sorry that I hit you. It was wrong and I shouldn't have struck you. It was bang out of order and I humbly apologise." Pizarro bowed his head.

De Cervantes laughed jovially. "Forget about it, Jefe. It's no more than I deserved. Viva La Legión! Viva España!"

"Viva la Legión! Viva España!" Pizarro chorused.

"And that was the last time that you saw Lothar, Andreas? When he went to the toilets?" Hauptsturmführer von Stein asked the three SS sergeants standing in front of him.

"Yes, sir," Scharführer Andreas Schmitt answered. "Lothar went to the toilet and then the bomb blew up…"

"It's just a case of damn bad luck, sir." Another SS

95

sergeant shook his head with resignation. "If he hadn't needed to take a piss at that precise moment he would have stayed in the bar with us, and he would have survived."

Von Stein shook his head sadly. "Bad luck had nothing to do with it, Walter; Lothar was murdered."

Scharführer Walter Hausser laughed. "With all due respect, sir, I doubt if the Resistance targeted Lothar specifically. The partisans killed Lothar because he was German, sir. If I had gone to take a piss at that time then the bomb would have killed me. It wasn't personal. It's just politics." Hausser shrugged his shoulders philosophically. "He was simply in the wrong place at the wrong time."

"When your time's up, your time's up, sir. It's time for you to go and there's nothing that you can do about it," the third SS sergeant said matter-of-factly.

Von Stein shook his head again. "I wish that you and Walter were right, Geyr, I really do. I also wish that Lothar had been killed randomly by the Resistance, but I'm afraid that it's not as simple as that."

"What do you mean, sir?" Schmitt asked.

"Lothar was assassinated by a Spanish Hit Team," von Stein answered.

"What?" Hausser said incredulously.

"I don't understand, sir," Scharführer Geyr von Berlichingen said. "You're saying that the Spanish killed him, and not the Resistance?"

"Correct, Geyr." Von Stein nodded. "Lothar was murdered by members of the Spanish Foreign Legión. Spanish Legiónaries planted the bomb which killed Lothar and the others and I will be their next target, unless you help me to stop them first."

"Yes, sir, of course we'll help. That goes without saying, sir," Schmitt answered. "All for one and one for all."

"We're with you all the way, sir," Hausser added.

"To the death, Hauptsturmführer," von Berlichingen said resolutely, as he clicked his heels together and bowed.

"Good, I knew that I could count on you."

"So what's this all about, sir?" Von Berlichingen asked.

" I'm going to tell you a story, gentlemen, but before I do, you must swear that you will not repeat what I am about to tell you to another living soul; because if you do and word gets out, I'll be shot in front of a firing squad quicker than you can say 'ready, aim, fire!'"

"We swear it, sir," the three sergeants chorused.

"Bueno." Von Stein nodded his head. "The story begins in Spain during the Civil War..."

"What's the matter, Aurora? You seem worried about something. You hardly said a word during the whole lesson." Alan asked as he tenderly wrapped an arm around his girlfriend's shoulders. He had waited until everyone had left the Geography classroom before he had approached her.

"I am worried, Alan," Aurora nodded as she wiped away tears from her red-rimmed eyes with a damp handkerchief. "Papa and I are in terrible danger."

"Why? What's happened?" Alan asked with concern.

"Sergeant Borghese and three of papa's men are missing. Francisco was papa's bodyguard. Papa thinks that they've been killed by the SS."

"What?" Alan asked incredulously. "By the SS? I thought that the Spanish and the Germans are friends. What happened?"

"I don't know the exact details, Alan. But something happened in Spain during the war. Papa stopped the SS from executing some captured Republican prisoners, there was a gunfight, and papa thinks that the SS survivors of the gun fight somehow followed him to Hereward and are trying to kill him."

"Bloody hell!" Alan exclaimed.

"The problem is that with Francisco dead, papa and I are on our own. The Spanish Embassy in London cannot spare the Legiónaries to come up here and protect us. Papa says that if they sent up another four men it would leave the Embassy exposed and vulnerable to Resistance attack. We will have to wait for reinforcements to leave Spain and arrive in London before the Embassy can send us any replacements."

"But that could take days or even weeks, Aurora," Alan said.

Aurora nodded as she rested her head on Alan's shoulder. "I know, Alan, and until then it is just papa and me. Papa has given me this to protect myself." She took a Luger 9 millimetre pistol out of her school bag and showed it to Alan.

"For God's sake, Aurora! Put it away!" Alan said in horror. "We're in a classroom! If any one sees us we will be in a world of trouble!"

"I'm sorry, Alan." Aurora burst out crying as she put it away. "I wasn't thinking."

"It's all right, Aurora." Alan tenderly kissed her fore head. "It's me who should apologise. I shouldn't have shouted at you like that. You are under a terrific amount of stress and strain. Here, let me show you where to hide it. Stand up."

Alan turned Aurora around, pulled up the back of her shirt and tucked the pistol underneath the waistband of her skirt, where it rested in the small of her back.

"There. Now you can grab it in a hurry if you have to instead of rummaging around, searching the depths of your school bag for your pistol."

"How do you know all of this, Alan?" Aurora asked

with furrowed brows.

Alan shrugged his shoulders dismissively. "I just know things. Listen, Aurora, you are not alone, so you don't have to worry: I will protect you."

"Against the SS?"

"Aurora." Alan faced his girlfriend and put his hands on both of her shoulders "I've killed more Germans than you've had hot dinners."

Aurora's eyes widened in amazement.

"I will protect you against the SS, against the Army, the Fascist Militia, Uncle Joe Cobley, and against anyone else who tries to mess with us," Alan promised. "And not just I; Sam will protect you too."

"Sam? Is he like you? Is he not scared of the Germans either?"

"Sam?" Alan laughed. "Sam eats Germans for breakfast, lunch and dinner. Sam would like nothing better than to help a damsel in distress and in the process pin some more Nazi scalps to his totem pole."

Aurora laughed and her eyes sparkled with newfound hope.

"So don't worry, Aurora: Sam and I'll look after you and if a dirty, stinking Nazi even looks sideways at you it will be the last thing that he ever does, and he will rue the day that he was born."

"I feel more confident already." Aurora looped her arm with Alan's. "With my two knights in shining armour, my two paladins to protect me."

"That's my girl." Alan smiled.

The couple were unaware that someone stood outside the class room door, eavesdropping with interest.

"There they are, Hans. Come on, let's go. Let's follow them."

"How do you know that it's them, Christian? They

could be anyone."

"Open your eyes, Hans. Look at the way that they're dressed. They are too well-dressed and they look too well-fed to be English. And if they were German then they would be in uniform. Look at their suntans. They certainly didn't get them in rain drenched England, did they?"

"I suppose not, Christian. But still, shouldn't we contact Sergeant Major Bratge and wait for reinforcements, as we've been ordered? He was very clear about his instructions: these men are armed and dangerous."

Christian guffawed. "We're armed and dangerous, Hans! The Spaniards should be worried about us, not us about them. And as for contacting Bratge? I don't know about you but I haven't seen a phone box recently that works, and if we waste time looking for one these killers will escape and we'll be back where we started. Look, Hans, if we arrest these two then we'll be home in time for beer and medals."

"I'm not sure, Christian… maybe we should still try and find a phone and wait for reinforcements…"

"For God's sake, Hans!" Christian was exasperated and rapidly running out of patience with his cautious companion. "What did I just tell you? If we do that, then the Spaniards will be long gone! What about using your initiative? Come on; are you a man or a mouse? If we pull this off, then we'll probably get promoted."

"And if we don't?"

Christian shrugged his shoulders nonchalantly. "Then we'll be dead and none of this will matter."

"All right, Christian. Fair enough. You've convinced me. Come on, let's go and arrest these two hitmen."

The two young Army Military Policemen quickened up their pace to catch up with the two Spaniards who had disappeared around the corner in front of them.

"We're being followed, Alfonso. The Germans are onto us," Corporal Miguel Pizarro said as the Spaniards rounded the corner.

"I know, Jefe," Private Alfonso de Cervantes replied. "What are we going to do? Do we fight, or do we flee?"

Pizarro looked at de Cervantes as if the private had just insulted his mother. "We're Legiónaries, Alfonso. We always fight and we never flee. I would have thought that after five years in the Legión you would know that by now."

"It was a rhetorical question, Jefe."

"I don't give a damn if it was rhetorical, Miguel: it was stupid." Pizarro's eyes expertly scanned the ground around him. "Quick. In here," he ordered.

De Cervantes followed him into the narrow alleyway.

"Silencers," Pizarro instructed as he drew his pistol from the small of his back and screwed on the silencer attachment. De Cervantes did the same.

"Ready, Miguel?" Pizarro asked.

"I was born ready, Jefe."

"Bueno." Pizarro nodded "Then let's do this and then get the hell out of Hereward."

"Viva la Legión! Viva España!" De Cervantes answered.

"Where the hell are they?" Hans asked in surprise as the two MPs rounded the corner. The Spaniards were nowhere to be seen.

"Quick," Christian replied. "Let's pick up the pace. They can't be too far ahead." He drew his pistol from his holster as he started to walk faster. Hans did the same.

As they walked past a narrow alley, the two

Spaniards quickly stepped out and shot the two MPs in the back at virtually point-blank range. The Germans were dead before their bodies hit the ground. The Legiónaries fired another two rounds into the back of their heads to make doubly sure that the MPs were dead. They then dragged the two bodies into the depths of the narrow alley and dumped them in the corner, unscrewed their silencers, replaced their pistols, and left without saying a word.

"Sturmbannführer Ulrich, why is the Army searching for two Spaniards on the loose in Hereward?" Brigadeführer Herold asked, as he leaned on his desk with steepled fingers.

Ulrich's raised eyebrows betrayed his shock at Herold's question. "I didn't... I didn't know that you knew about that, sir. How did you...?"

Herold waved his hand dismissively. "Don't look so surprised, Ulrich: I have my sources, just as you have yours. Why is the Army searching for two Spaniards?"

"The Army thinks that these two Spaniards are responsible for the bomb explosion at the King Alfred Hotel, sir," Ulrich answered.

Now it was time for Herold to raise his eyebrows in surprise. "The Army thinks that the Spanish bombed the hotel? I thought that we and the Spanish were friends. After all that we've done for them? The ungrateful bastards!" Herold shook his head.

"No, sir. Not the Spanish, but two Spaniards," Ulrich answered. "There is a significant difference, sir."

"So the Wehrmacht thinks that this might be a bomb attack which was carried out by Republican die-hards who escaped to Britain during or after the Civil War?"

Ulrich nodded. "I assume so, sir."

Herold wagged his index finger at Ulrich. "Don't assume anything, Ulrich." Herold thought for a moment before continuing. "What are the names and ranks of our men who were killed in the bomb attack, Sturmbannführer?"

Ulrich looked at the list of names in his hand. "Hauptsturmführer Abetz, Hauptsturmführer Zimmermann, Obersturmführer Bayerlein…"

"Wait a minute, Ulrich," Herold interrupted. "I thought that only two SS officers were killed in the attack?"

Ulrich glanced down at this notes and nodded. "Hauptsturmführer Zimmermann died of his wounds this morning, sir."

"Bloody Spanish bastards!" Herold snarled. "Continue, Sturmbannführer."

"Scharführers Witzleben, Dannhauser, Unger, Dollmann, Tresckow and Kophamel were also killed, sir…"

"Kophamel?" Herold suddenly sat up in his chair as if he had been hit by a bolt of lightning.

"Sir?" Ulrich asked in confusion.

"Uh, nothing, Ulrich," Herold shook his head. "I just had a sudden thought. I want to see the service records of all of our dead men, and I particularly want to know if any of them served in Spain with the Condor Legión."

"Yes, sir." Ulrich snapped his folder shut.

"I also want to know the names and service record of all the personnel at the Spanish Consulate, particularly the name of their Military Attaché."

Ulrich shook his head. "Finding out the names of all of the personnel should be relatively simple, sir. However, finding out their service records may be more difficult…"

"I don't want to hear any excuses, Ulrich. Just do it, and I want it done yesterday!" Herold shouted. "Is that understood?"

"Yes, sir."

"I hope so, Sturmbannführer. For your sake." Herold pointed his finger at Ulrich. "Because your record so far in command of Hereward has failed to impress me, and you are one whisker away from being sent back to Berlin in disgrace. Dismissed."

"Heil Hitler!" Ulrich saluted.

"Heil Hitler!"

"Two of my MPs are missing, sir, Privates Marlene and Schwarzkopf. They failed to return from their patrol today," Sergeant Major Bratge reported as he stood at a position of attention.

"What do you think has happened to them, Sergeant Major?" General-Major Christian von Schnakenberg asked him.

"Well, I don't think that they've deserted, sir," Bratge replied. "They only joined the unit recently and they were both as keen as mustard and desperately trying to impress, especially young Schwarzkopf, sir."

"So do you think that they tried to arrest your two Spanish hitmen?" von Schnakenberg asked.

Bratge nodded. "That's exactly what I think happened, sir. They spotted the assassins and decided that the two of them were up to the job of arresting them without calling for reinforcements, despite the fact that they were expressly ordered to do so. They bit off more than they could chew and as a result of their overconfidence they are no doubt dead and lying in a ditch somewhere." Bratge shrugged his shoulders in resignation.

"Ah, the folly of youth," von Schnakenberg commented. "When you're young you think that you are indestructible and that you can do anything."

"Marlene and Schwarzkopf found out the hard way that their appraisal of their own abilities was hopelessly optimistic."

"Anyway, we can't let this situation continue, Sergeant Major. This is Hereward, not Chicago, and I will not allow a pair of Spanish hit men to run around like they own the place. I want these two men found and brought back to me alive."

Bratge scratched his head. "That's going to be difficult, sir. I'm undermanned as it is. Looking for these two will be like looking for a needle in a haystack. I need more men, sir."

"Brigadeführer Herold has offered us the services of his SS military policemen," von Schnakenberg said. "I haven't accepted his offer yet and I would rather not, as I simply do not trust those Nazi bastards. However, needs must: do you need the men?"

"Yes, sir," Bratge replied. "I need all the help that I can get, sir. The more the merrier."

"All right then," von Schnakenberg nodded. "I'll contact Brigadeführer Herold and gratefully accept his kind offer. You'll get your extra manpower."

"Thank you, sir." Bratge bowed. "One more thing, sir."

"Yes, what is it, Sergeant Major?"

"Are you sure that you want both hitmen taken alive, sir, or will one suffice?"

Von Schnakenberg thought for a moment before replying. "On second thoughts, one will suffice, Sergeant Major," von Schnakenberg replied. "You can feed the other one alive to the swans on the River Ouse for all I care."

"Very good, sir." Bratge saluted.

"Carry on, Sergeant Major. Dismissed!"

"Sir, I have the service records of all of our men who were killed in the hotel bombing," Sturmbannführer Ulrich announced.

"Carry on, Sturmbannführer," Brigadeführer Herold ordered.

"Very good, sir." Ulrich clicked his heels. "All of the officers and men fought during the invasion of Britain and also the invasion of France, sir. Hauptsturmführer Abetz and Scharführers Witzleben, Dollmann, Unger and Kophamel all served in Spain with the Condor Legión..."

"What is the name of the Spanish Military Attaché?" Herold interrupted abruptly.

Ulrich looked at his notes before he replied. "Major Mendoza, sir. Major Juan Mendoza of the XVIIth Bandera of the Spanish Foreign Legión, sir." Ulrich continued to read his notes and blew a wolf whistle. "Franco's poster boy, sir. He was awarded the Laureate Cross of Saint Ferdinand, Spain's highest military medal for gallantry during the civil war, and he is a genuine war hero. He is married to the daughter of a very prominent Falange Government Minster and by all accounts he has a shining and glittering military, and probably political, career ahead of him, sir. Mendoza will probably end up as a general."

"Not if I can help it," Herold hissed to himself under his breath.

"Halt! Hande hoch!" The order echoed over the cobble stoned market square.

The two men who were the object of the order looked at each other in confusion and slowly raised their hands above their heads.

"Turn around with your hands above your heads!" the heavily German-accented voice ordered in English.

The men did as they were told.

"Good! Now, kneel...!"

The double shot interrupted the German Military Police sergeant's orders.

"Berger! What the hell do you think you're doing?" The MP sergeant barked.

"I thought... I thought he was going for his gun," Berger replied.

"Berger, you bloody idiot! Both of his hands were up! How the hell could he be going for his gun? Hauptwachtmeister Bratge gave express orders that the suspects were to be captured alive!" the sergeant shouted in anger.

"Yes, Sergeant Schulenburg, I'm sorry, Sergeant Schulenburg..."

Berger was still apologising when Schulenburg's head disappeared in a spray of blood, bones and brains.

Berger looked up as the surviving Spaniard fired another two shots. The German ducked as the rounds ricocheted off the stonework above his head. Berger snapped off two rounds to keep the Spaniard's head down as he took cover. The German leaped behind a pillar and waited for the Spaniard to return fire. Nothing happened. Berger cautiously peered around the pillar, and saw the second Spaniard lying flat on his back. The German carefully approached the fallen man as he lay on his back in a pool of blood. There were two bloody holes in his stomach.

"Mio Dio... mio Dio..." the Spaniard moaned between groans. His hands vainly tried to staunch the bleeding. "Bagnata... bagnata." His hands looked as if they had been dipped in a bucket of blood.

Berger's eyes welled up with tears. He had recently been posted to England and he had never seen a dead body before, and he had certainly never shot and killed anyone before. The German whipped a field dressing out of his jacket and applied it to the Spaniard's stomach wound. "Perdone, amigo..." Berger desperately tried to remember a few words of his schoolboy Spanish to comfort the dying man. "I didn't mean to kill you."

The Spaniard's eyes blinked in obvious confusion "No... no... no..."

"It's all right, amigo. Help will be here any minute."

"No soni di España... soni di Italia... soni di Italia... no soni di España..."

Berger's face drained of blood as he picked up the dying man's dog tags.

Gian Lorenzo Bruno. Sergeant. 24860143. 2nd Bersaglieri Regiment. Berger hurriedly ran over to the other dead man. Cesare Galilei. 2484104. Major. 2nd Bersaglieri Regiment.

Berger stood up on unsteady legs and he staggered over in a daze to the decapitated corpse of Sergeant Schulenburg. He looked down at the body of his sergeant, the man who had welcomed him to the unit and who had looked after him and had treated him like a son. Sergeant Schulenburg was his friend. And now he was dead as a result of Berger's stupidity and two innocent men also lay dead, killed by Berger's own hand. Berger stood up as his mind raced into the future: court martial and inevitable punishment, disgrace both for him and his regiment, shame and humiliation for his family, never mind the diplomatic fallout between Germany and Italy. Berger experienced a Saint Paul on his road to Damascus-like epiphany, and suddenly realised what he had to do to right the wrongs that he was responsible for. He walked over to Bruno and knelt down. "I'm sorry, comrade." Berger shook his head through tear-filled eyes as he gathered his strength to do what he had to do. He swiftly put one hand over the dying Italian's mouth and pinched his nostrils closed with his other hand. He ignored the man's feeble attempts to fight him off. When the Italian was dead Berger picked up the dead man's pistol, put it back in the Italian's hand, put the pistol to his own heart, and pulled the trigger.

"What a bloody mess." General-major von Schnakenberg threw the report across his desk in disgust.

"Yes, sir." Sergeant Major Bratge bent over to pick up the report which he had written and had landed at his feet. He understood von Schnakenberg's frustration.

Von Schnakenberg swivelled his chair and looked out of the window. "And of course the Italians are screaming blue murder and demanding their pound of flesh in compensation. God knows what we will have to give them to quieten them down. Tanks, aeroplanes, weapons which we can ill-afford to give them since we invaded Yugoslavia and Greece last month. We're going to need all of the weapons and equipment that we can get hold of for when we invade Russia."

"Russia, sir?" Bratge asked with raised eyebrows.

"Oh yes, Bratge. Russia. Come on, it was only a matter of time. Surely you saw it coming, Hauptwachtmeister? You didn't really think that Hitler would honour the Non-Aggression Treaty which we signed with the Reds?"

Bratge shook his head. "Of course I didn't think that the Führer would honour the agreement which we signed with the Reds, sir; I just didn't think that we would break it so soon. After all, we haven't won the war in the West yet, sir. Churchill is still holding up north in Scotland. Is it wise to attack Russia whilst we are still fighting in the Balkans, North Africa and in Britain, sir?"

Von Schnakenberg nodded. "I fully understood your concerns, Bratge, and I have discussed this precise issue on many occasions with my colleagues. I also think that we may have bitten off more than we can chew but 'ours not to reason why', Sergeant Major."

"It's the 'ours but to do or die' that I object to, sir. If I'm to do or die I at least like to know that there's a reasonable chance of success before I put my neck on the line."

"You're familiar with the works of Tennyson, Hauptwachtmeister? You're a poetry fan?" Von Schnakenberg swivelled around to face his Sergeant Major.

"I may only be a humble policeman, sir, but I am not a complete philistine."

Von Schnakenberg laughed. "Touché, my dear Bratge."

"It's just that I was at Verdun in the last war, sir: I am painfully aware of what it is like to feel that the High Command are squandering our lives and throwing us away like so much confetti. I'm not prepared to go through that again and I'm not prepared for my men to go through that again either, sir. Once is quite enough for several lifetimes."

Von Schnakenberg nodded sombrely. "I couldn't agree with you more, Hauptwachtmeister, and I salute the sacrifices that you and your comrades made on that bloody battlefield for the Fatherland."

Bratge bowed. "Thank you, sir."

"Now, onto the matter in hand: we may not be able to influence what's going on in headquarters in Berlin, but we can bloody well influence what goes on in Hereward." The general pointed at Bratge. "I want the two Spaniards found and I want them found today. Not tomorrow, not next week. Today. Do you understand?"

"Yes, sir!" Bratge came to a position of attention.

"And Bratge?"

"Yes, sir?"

"I've changed my mind: I want them dead or alive. I'm tired of pussyfooting around. Let's show them that we mean business. Hereward is my town, not the SS's, not the Resistance, and certainly not the Spaniard's. Comprendes?"

"Si, Jefe!"

"Bueno. Dismissed!"

"Repeat your orders, Sturmbannführer Ulrich," Brigadeführer Herold ordered.

"My mission is to capture the two Spaniards and if that is not possible then I am to kill them." Ulrich stated. "On no account am I to allow the Army to capture the two Spaniards alive."

Herold stood directly in front of Ulrich, eyeball to eyeball. "Very good, Sturmbannführer." Herold walked back to his desk.

A moment's hesitation. "Sir, may I ask…"

"No you bloody well may not, Ulrich! This is not a bloody trade union meeting!" Herold slammed both of his hands on the tabletop.

"Sir, it would just make it easier to…" Ulrich persisted.

"Ulrich, on a need-to-know basis, you don't need to know a God damned thing! You will carry out your orders, Sturmbannführer, or I will find someone who is capable of following my orders without questioning my authority!" Herold's face was scarlet with barely-contained rage, and he looked as if he was about to burst a blood vessel.

"Yes, Brigadeführer." Ulrich clicked his heels together and bowed in submission. "Of course I will carry out your orders, sir, without question. I was out of line, sir, and it won't happen again."

"You're damn right it was out of line, Ulrich and if it happens again I will have you shot," Herold threatened. "I know that you're known as 'The Cat' but I doubt that you'd be able to survive a firing squad at point-blank range."

"Yes, sir." Ulrich bowed again.

Herold swivelled his chair and looked out of the window.

Ulrich coughed. "I have one more question, sir."

"It better be a good one, Ulrich, you've nearly used up all of your nine lives."

"What do I do if the Wehrmacht refuse to hand over their prisoners to me?"

Silence.

Herold swivelled his chair to look out of the window again. "Use your initiative, Ulrich," Herold said over his shoulder. "After all, that's what you're paid for, isn't it?"

Chapter Eight

"This is the Military Police! You are completely surrounded! Come out with your hands up!" Hauptwachtmeister Bratge ordered through his loud hailer.

"Sweet Mary, Jesus and Joseph!" Corporal Miguel Pizarro exclaimed as he leapt out of bed. "It's the pigs! How the hell did they sneak up on us like that? Didn't you spot them, Alfonso?"

Private Alfonso de Cervantes rubbed his eyes blearily and shrugged his shoulders. "I'm sorry, Jefe. I fell asleep," he said, shamefaced.

"You fell asleep?" Pizarro's eyes blazed. "You stupid bastard, we may be soon be sleeping forever because of you!" The corporal grabbed his Schmessier submachine gun from his bedside table.

"I'm sorry, Jefe: it won't happen again."

"You're damn right it won't happen again, because soon we'll be dead." Pizarro slowly crawled on his hands and knees towards the window and carefully looked over the window ledge. He didn't like what he saw. Two lorries were parked across the road immediately opposite the entrance to the Spaniard's terraced apartment block, and they provided protection to the twenty or so MPs who sheltered behind them. Pizarro cautiously looked up and down the length and breadth of the street. A lorry with another squad of a dozen or so men blocked each end of the street.

"How the hell did they find us, Jefe?" De Cervantes asked, as he stuffed extra magazines of ammunition and as many grenades as he could possibly carry into his trouser and jacket pockets.

"How the hell should I know?" Pizarro replied angrily. "Wait a minute..." He slowly raised his head and looked down at their car that was parked just outside the entrance to the apartment block. The car which they had intended to use that very morning to drive back to London, "Christ... I don't believe it."

"What is it?"

"Diplomatic plates..." Pizarro replied in disgust. "Our Bolivian ID cards might have been perfect, but we forgot to replace our Spanish diplomatic number plates for Bolivian ones."

"Christ almighty...!"

"The Germans must have driven around the town searching for us and spotted our Spanish number plates."

A pause to reflect. "What now, Jefe?"

"What now, Alfonzo?" Pizarro smiled. "What else? We fight! To the death! Viva la Legión! Viva España!" The corporal smashed the window with the barrel of his Schmessier 9 millimetre submachine gun and fired a burst of bullets at the nearest bunch of MPs, whilst de Cervantes copied him.

Bratge ducked as the bullets shattered the window of the lorry cab door, sending shards of sharp glass flying through the air in every direction. The man standing beside Bratge yelped as razor-sharp fragments impaled themselves in his body, and he frantically and futilely clawed at his face as he tried to find and remove the shards with his hook-like fingers. He was still trying to take out the pieces of broken glass when the next burst of machine gun fire cut him down.

Bratge ducked again as two objects landed with an ominous thud in the open topped lorry. "Grenade!" he shouted. The force of the explosion killed and wounded the half a dozen or so MPs standing behind the lorry. Bratge looked down at the bloody and broken bodies of his men in horror, and knew that most of them would not get up again. Bratge looked at his surviving MPs who were cowering on the ground, taking shelter behind the other lorry. "Get up, you bastards! Start firing at the windows!" Bratge kicked the nearest soldier in the ass and physically pulled the others to their feet. "Open fire! Open fire!" he shouted frantically.

"More of the same, I think, Alfonso."
"Very good, Jefe."

Another two grenades flew through the air and landed in the second open-topped lorry. The explosion knocked the surviving MPs down like skittles and they lay in an untidy heap on the pavement, twitching and moaning.

"Christ!" Ulrich exclaimed in his disbelief as he lowered his binoculars."They've wiped out the MPs..."

"What are we going to do, sir?" the sergeant who was second in command of the squad asked.

"We're going to reinforce the MP's position, Scharführer Gersdorff. The MPs are combat ineffective," Ulrich answered as he looked at the shattered and torn bodies that were still smoking. "We can't do anything here, Scharführer. The Spaniards are bound to make a break for it any second. That's what I'd do if I was them."

"What about Obersturmführer Monat, sir?" Gersdorff pointed at the lorry that was blocking the opposite end of the street.

"We'll go first, and then we'll cover Obersturmführer Monat when he moves," Ulrich answered. "I'll go first with half the squad and you cover me, Scharführer, and then you come to my position and I'll cover you. Understood? "

"Understood, Sturmbannführer."

"Very well." Ulrich smiled and squeezed

Gersdorff's shoulder. "Pass the word, Scharführer. First five men, forward on my command."

"Alfonso, I think that we've wiped out the pigs!" Pizarro shouted.

De Cervantes nodded. "What's the plan, Jefe?"

"We burst out of the front door all guns blazing, get in the car, and get the hell out of Hereward. How does that sound?"

De Cervantes grinned. "Sounds good to me, Jefe."

Pizarro paused. "Alfonso, we can't let them take us alive. The Gestapo…"

"I understand, Jefe," De Cervantes interrupted. "They would torture us and connect us to Major Mendoza."

Pizarro nodded. "Are you ready?"

De Cervantes grinned. "I was born ready."

"Forward!" Ulrich ordered.

Five stormtroopers followed hot on Ulrich's heels as the Sturmbannführer sprinted the one hundred metres to the MP's position. Gersdorff's remaining five SS soldiers provided covering fire and shot at the apartment windows on the second floor where the Spaniards had been sheltering.

At that precise moment the two Spaniards burst out of the front door of the apartment block and almost collided with the running stormtroopers. Pizarro and De Cervantes were the first to recover and opened fire at almost point-blank range with their Schmessiers, and cut down three of the surprised Germans before they had time to react. Ulrich opened fire with his machine gun and drilled a neat line of holes across Pizarro's front. De Cervantes continued running to the car door, but when he realised that Pizarro had been shot he turned around and was shot in the stomach by one of the surviving stormtroopers.

"Cease fire!" Ulrich ordered.

The two surviving SS troopers pointed their weapons at the wounded Spaniards.

De Cervantes slowly crawled on his stomach towards Pizarro, leaving a trail of blood on the road like a wounded snail.

Ulrich turned around as he heard Gersdorff and the rest of the squad run up to his position. "Check the Spaniards, Scharführer," Ulrich ordered. "Remember our orders: we want them alive if possible."

"Yes, sir."

"Obersturmführer Monat?" Ulrich shouted.

"Yes, sir?" Monat replied from the second road block.

"Check the MPs for survivors, and get some ambulances."

"Yes, sir."

"Alfonso... Alfonso..." Pizarro rasped through blood-clenched teeth.

"Ycs, Jefe," De Cervantes replied as he coughed up a globule of blood. "I'm here."

"Remember what we talked about?"

"Yes, Jefe," De Cervantes nodded.

"Good man." Pizarro smiled through a mouthful of blood. "It's been a pleasure and a privilege, Alfonzo..."

"The pleasure has been all mine, Miguel."

"Are you ready?"

De Cervantes smiled. "Like I've always told you, Jefe: I was born ready."

"All right, Pedro," Gersdorff said as he aimed his machine gun at the two wounded Spaniards. "Hang on;

you're going to be okay. Help is on its way."

"Hey, Adolf," De Cervantes said. "I've got a present for you. Come over here."

Gersdorff was intrigued as he knelt down beside the dying Spaniard. "What is it, Pedro?"

De Cervantes put something in Gersdorff's hand and wrapped the German's fingers around it. The Spaniard grasped Pizarro's bloody hands in his own, and they shouted together in unison at the top of their voices, "Viva La Legión! Viva España!"

Gersdorff opened his fingers. "Oh shit."

Gersdorff barely had time to recognise that he was holding a grenade-pin in his hand when the bomb exploded. The blast instantly killed Gersdorff and De Cervantes and also detonated the half a dozen grenades that the Spaniard had been carrying in his jacket and trouser pockets. The secondary blasts also set off the grenades that Pizarro had been carrying in his pockets. The resulting explosion sent shrapnel flying in every direction and killed and wounded everyone standing within a radius of one hundred metres of the blast.

When the smoke and dust had finally settled, Hauptwachtmeister Bratge emerged phoenix-like from the bodies of his dead and dying MPs. His uniform was ripped and torn and was hanging off him in shredded strips of material. His helmet had been blasted off his head and blood was streaming down his dirt-encrusted face. Bratge walked as if he was in a trance and he stumbled from blackened body to blackened body searching for survivors, to no avail. All of the twenty or so SS stormtroopers were dead. They had gathered around the wounded Spaniards and they had all been killed in the initial blast when De Cervantes's grenades had exploded. Bratge reached the spot where the two

Spaniards had been lying. There was absolutely nothing left of their bodies except a giant black smear on the road. They had been completely vaporised when the ten grenades that they had been carrying had exploded, and there wasn't enough left of their bodies to fill a shoebox.

A wounded MP stumbled up to Bratge. He was cradling a broken arm with his good hand. His mouth was opening and closing, but Bratge could not hear what he was saying. Slowly the ringing in his ears subsided, and the fog in Bratge's head lifted.

"What now, Hauptwachtmeister?" the young MP asked. "What do we do now?"

Bratge put a reassuring hand on the soldier's shoulder. "Check for survivors, Nietzsche, and administer immediate first aid; if any of our men are walking wounded then tell one of them to go and fetch help; find an ambulance."

"Yes, Hauptwachtmeister," the MP nodded.

"If you find any other walking wounded, tell them to go to headquarters and tell a forensic team to get here on the double."

"Yes, sir." The MP hobbled away to begin searching for survivors.

Bratge looked at the scene of utter death and destruction. It was like something out of a painting by Hieronymus Bosch: all of the cars surrounding the blast sight were on fire and were lying on their sides as if they had been knocked over by the hand of an angry giant. Charred carcasses of smoking and bleeding meat lay as far as the eye could see in various conditions of carbonisation, depending on how close the soldiers had been standing when the grenades had exploded. At least twenty and possibly closer to thirty German soldiers had either been killed or wounded in the gunfight and

119

in the grenade explosions - and all for what? In order to capture two Spaniards. Bratge winced as he shook his head in frustration. He could not even be one hundred percent certain that the two suspects were actually Spaniards and he was no closer to discovering why they had tried to blow up the King Alfred Hotel. It was all idle speculation. Bratge suddenly stopped in his tracks. Something was embedded in the wall by the entrance to the Spaniard's apartment block. Bratge found himself drawn towards the flashing and twinkling object as if he was a moth drawn to a flame. He touched the object, and quickly snatched his fingers away and stuck them in his mouth. The object was red-hot. Bratge tore a strip of material from his ripped and ragged uniform and wrapped a length of cloth around his fingers. He grasped the end of the object and slowly but surely pulled it out of the stonework where it had been impaled. A smile broke out over Bratge's cracked and bloody lips as he examined the bent, burnt and twisted piece of metal. "The plot thickens," he said to himself.

"I've got to hand it to you, Sturmbannführer: you fully deserve your nickname of The Cat." Brigadeführer Herold shook his head in awe and amazement. "I don't know how you do it, Ulrich."

"Just lucky, I guess, Brigadeführer." Ulrich shrugged his shoulders bashfully. He winced as a sharp jab of pain stabbed through his bandaged head. He had suffered concussion when the force of the grenade explosions had thrown him like a rag doll against a brick wall. Only the fact that he been wearing his helmet had prevented him from suffering severe brain damage. The helmet may well have saved his life.

"And as for you, Obersturmführer Monat; if I was a betting man I'd wager good money that if you had not been with The Cat here you would be a dead man now, and you would be lying alongside the bodies of your unfortunate soldiers in the morgue."

"I don't doubt it for a second, sir," Monat agreed from his bed, where he also sat with a bandage wrapped around his head.

"I'm sorry that I wasn't able to capture the suspects alive, sir," Ulrich apologised with a bowed head.

Herold waved his hand dismissively. "Don't worry about it, Sturmbannführer: the important thing is that you didn't let the army capture them either."

"So what happens now, sir?" Ulrich asked.

"Well the trail has run cold: the army has no proof that the bombers were Spanish and there is no connection between the bombers, the Spanish and our men."

"So... who do we say was to blame for the bombing of the Hotel, sir?"

Herold shrugged his shoulders as if he hadn't really thought about it. "The Resistance, of course. In fact I only issued orders this morning for the arrest and execution of two hundred hostages," Herold said matter-of-factly.

"Two hundred hostages, sir?" Ulrich repeated in horror.

Herold put his hands up in mock protest. "I know, Ulrich, I know. The present rate of exchange is that we execute one hundred hostages for every German soldier who is killed, but twenty of our men were killed and twenty Wehrmacht soldiers were killed and wounded. That makes forty German casualties, and if you do the maths you will soon calculate that that means four thousand Hereward hostages should be executed." Herold laughed. "There are simply not enough hostages available! After all, I don't want to depopulate the whole of Hereward. The Führer wants a living, breathing town when he comes to visit. Who would do all of the work for us if we kill all of the people? So I thought that as a compromise I would execute two hundred hostages in exchange for the deaths of our men." Herold shrugged his shoulders again indifferently and scratched his head. "I don't know; maybe I'm going soft in my old age. I'm going to leave the Army to deal with the issue of their dead and wounded as they see fit."

Herold looked at Ulrich, who looked as if he had just been told that his mother had died. "You disagree, Sturmbannführer? You think that we should go ahead and execute four thousand hostages?"

"No, sir," Ulrich shook his head. "It's just that we know that the Resistance didn't blow up the hotel. The Spanish did it."

"Spaniards did it, as you said before, not the Spanish. And anyway, that is all speculation, Sturmbannführer. Fascists or Republicans, official or unofficial, political or personal, none of that matters now. All that matters if that this bomb explosion gives us an ideal opportunity, excuse and reason to tighten the screws on the English and remind them once again who's boss." Herold mimicked screwing on the lid of a jar with his hands.

Ulrich was speechless with rage and fury, but was compos mentis enough to realise that on this occasion discretion was the better part of valour.

"I thought it rather fitting that I should use men from your regiment to carry out the arrest and executions, Ulrich." Herold smiled a crocodile smile.

"Thank you, sir. It's an honour, Brigadeführer," Ulrich replied haltingly.

"Good." Herold slapped his hands on his knees and stood up. "Then that's settled then. Get well soon, boys. I need both of you in tip-top condition for the invasion of Scotland."

122

"So it's coming then, sir?" Monat's eyes lit up with boyish enthusiasm. "We're finally going to finish off Churchill once and for all?"

"Yes, Obersturmführer: it's coming sooner than you think. So get well soon. Germany needs all of her sons fit and well for the coming struggle." Herold pointed both of his forefingers at his two wounded officers.

"Yes, sir!" both men answered in unison.

"Heil Hitler!" Herold saluted. "Anything you need, boys, tell the sentries, all right?"

"Yes, sir, thank you, sir. Heil Hitler!" Ulrich replied.

Herold left the room.

Monat thumped his chest with like a gorilla. "The invasion of Scotland! About bloody time! What do you think about that, Sturmbannführer?"

"What do I think, Monat?" Ulrich looked at him blankly. "The wheel turns…"

Chapter Nine

"Alan can help us, Papa," Aurora said earnestly.

"Alan?" Major Mendoza shook his head. "Alan is just a child, Aurora. How on earth can he help us?"

"Alan is... well, Alan is... experienced, Papa," Aurora said cryptically.

"You mean that he's killed Germans before?" Mendoza asked bluntly.

"Well, I..."

"Aurora, my butterfly, virtually every male over the age of fourteen who lives in Hereward was in the Home Guard and fought the Germans during the invasion, or if they were too old then they fought them in the last war. Every Tom, Dick and Harry in Hereward has killed Germans." Mendoza was busy stripping, cleaning and oiling his Luger pistol.

Aurora said nothing.

"Or is it something else? Is Alan in the Resistance?"

Aurora blushed.

"It's all right, Aurora." Mendoza put down his pistol and ruffled his daughter's hair affectionately. "It's all right, don't worry, my butterfly. I'm not going to turn Alan in to the Germans. God knows we need all of the help that we can get."

"So Sergeant Borghese and the others are all dead?" Aurora asked through tear-filled eyes.

"Yes, my sweet," Mendoza nodded his head. "I'm afraid that Francisco and the other Legiónaries are all dead."

"How can you be so sure, Papa?"

"You know about the gun fight and the explosion on Queen Alexandra Street?"

"Yes, Papa, of course. The firing woke me up in the morning just as it woke up half of Hereward. But the Germans blamed the fighting on the Resistance."

"Yes, of course they did. But it wasn't the Resistance; it was Francisco's men."

"Do you know the names of the dead Legiónaries, Papa?"

Mendoza shook his head. "No, I don't, my little butterfly. All I know is that the embassy sent up three Legiónaries who were all from the XVIIth Bandera, my old regiment."

"Do you think that the Germans know that the dead men were Legiónaries?"

"I sincerely hope not, Aurora, or else we are in even worse trouble and we may have to leave Hereward in a hurry. It will be some time before the embassy can send reinforcements to protect us."

"Alan will be able to help us escape, Papa," Aurora asserted confidently.

"Really? You have a lot of confidence in this boy, Aurora," Mendoza said with raised eyebrows.

"You would understand if you met him, Papa."

"Then perhaps I shall, perhaps I shall..." Mendoza said thoughtfully.

"The suspects were from the XVIIth Bandera of the Spanish Foreign Legión, sir," Hauptwachtmeister Bratge stated confidently.

"You seem very sure of yourself, Hauptwachtmeister. How do you know?" General-Major von Schnakenberg asked curiously.

"Because I found this, sir." Bratge stepped forward and placed an object on von Schnakenberg's desk.

Von Schnakenberg picked up the torn and jagged object and read aloud the writing engraved on the metal: Miguel Pizarro, Corporal, 880427, XVIIth Bandera, Legión Extranjero. The Spanish Foreign Legión. Von Schnakenberg looked up at Bratge with awe and wonder. "How the hell did you find this dog

125

tag in that fiery inferno, Hauptwachtmeister? Queen Alexandra Street looked like an abattoir."

Bratge shrugged his shoulders and winced as a sharp stab of pain lanced across his shoulder blades. He had still not fully recovered from the Spanish grenade blasts. "I just got lucky I guess, sir." Bratge smiled.

"Well, I'm very impressed, Hauptwachtmeister, but what does it all mean?"

"Well, I checked the service records of all the men who were killed or wounded in the King Alfred Hotel bomb, sir, and Hauptsturmführer Abetz and Scharführers Witzleben, Dollmann, Unger and Kophamel of the SS all served in Spain with the Condor Legión during the civil war - but only Kophamel had any contact with the XVIIth Bandera. They both fought in the Battle of the Ebro River, sir, in Catalonia in '38."

"The Legiónaries are tough hombres, Hauptwachtmeister." Von Schnakenberg nodded his head. "I served alongside them with the Condor Legión during the Battle for Madrid."

"That's not all, sir," Bratge continued. "Kophamel's present company commander, Hauptsturmführer Manfred von Stein, was his platoon commander at the Battle of the River Ebro and both men were wounded. Von Stein's entire unit was wiped out in the battle, sir."

Von Schnakenberg's brows furrowed in confusion. "That's odd, Hauptwachtmeister - apart from the air crew, the role of the Condor Legión was largely advisory, not combative. It was very unusual for German personnel to take part in actual fighting."

"Well, the records show that von Stein's entire unit was wiped out, and von Stein and Kophamel suffered very severe injuries and were lucky to escape with their lives, sir."

Von Schnakenberg nodded his head.

"There's something else, sir." Bratge examined his notes. "The Spanish Military Attaché here in Hereward, Major Juan Mendoza, is also from the XVIIth Bandera and served as a Captain at the Battle of the River Ebro..."

"Don't tell me, Hauptwachtmeister: Corporal Pizarro served under Mendoza at the Battle..."

"As did the two other Legiónaries that the Spanish Embassy has notified are missing from their London embassy guard; Privates De Cervantes and Ramirez. Also, Mendoza's personal bodyguard Sergeant Borghese is missing, sir, and the good Major has made an urgent request for Legiónaries to be dispatched as soon as is humanely possible to reinforce the consulate guard."

"So Mendoza is in it up to his neck as well, then?"

"It looks like it, sir," Bratge answered with a nod.

"What a bloody mess." Von Schnakenberg swivelled his chair and looked out of the window. "There's some sort of vendetta going on in Hereward, Hauptwachtmeister, and unfortunately the army seems to be stuck in the middle of it. The Spanish always did like a blood feud. Well, I want to find out what the bloody hell it's all about, and I want to stop it. I don't want the Spanish and the SS as well as us and the Resistance fighting it out in the streets of Hereward."

Bratge coughed into his hand. "Sir, should we inform our SS colleagues of our findings?"

Von Schnakenberg swivelled his chair back to face Bratge and thought for a moment before answering. "No. I don't think so, Hauptwachtmeister. I don't think that it's necessary to involve our SS brethren at this stage. I think that it's for the best if we keep this information to ourselves for the moment, don't you?"

"Yes, sir."

"Keep digging, Hauptwachtmeister. I want more

dirt. But a job well done so far. I'm very impressed. Dismissed!"

Bratge saluted, about turned, and marched smartly out of von Schnakenberg's office.

"Are you sure that this is a good idea, Al?" Sam asked with concern. "Have you really thought this through? Because if you're wrong, then we're going to find ourselves in a whole world of trouble."

Alan shrugged his shoulders as he started to strip and clean his Luger pistol. "Aurora is already in a world of trouble, Sam. She needs my help and that's all there is to it. She and Major Mendoza are all alone here in Hereward and it may be many days or even weeks before reinforcements arrive. In the meantime she and her father are in mortal danger from the SS so I'm going to help them." Alan looked at his friend and put his hand on Sam's shoulder. "We've been best mates for a long time, Sam, and if you don't think that Aurora's worth the risk then I understand. No hard feelings. You just walk away and I'll protect her by myself."

"No hard feelings?" Sam guffawed. "I can just walk away?" Sam shook his head. "If I refused to help you and Mendoza and Aurora were killed by the Germans you would never forgive me, and you would certainly never let me forget until the day that I died!" Sam laughed easily and clapped Alan on the shoulder. "Of course Aurora's worth the risk, Al! Did you ever truly doubt that I would help you?"

"Of course not," Alan admitted with a cheeky smile. "But I thought that I should at least go through the motions of giving you a choice."

Sam playfully ruffled his best friend's hair. "You sly dog! Can you imagine what would happen to me if Alice found out that I'd refused to help you, and that

I'd let you go off by yourself and you had gotten yourself killed?"

"The thought had crossed my mind," Alan admitted. "Your life would not have been worth living."

Sam shivered at the thought of it. "You're damn right. The very idea of it brings me out in a cold sweat!"

"I would rather face an entire Panzer division by myself than suffer the wrath of Alice! Anyway, Sam, I knew that you could never resist coming to the rescue of a damsel in distress!"

"You're right, Al. You know me too well. However, I hope that you are aware that if Mendoza betrays us to the Germans, Alice and Mr Leon will feed him to the pigs so quickly that he won't have time to say 'adios' to his daughter. Aurora will still end up an orphan either by our hand or by the Germans."

Alan smiled and shook his head. "Major Mendoza will not betray us to the Germans, Sam. He is a Spanish Legiónary and he is a man of honour."

"As long as you're confident, Al, then that's good enough for me." Sam slapped his thighs with both hands and stood up with a mischievous grin on his face.

"So when arc you going to meet the mysterious Major Mendoza?"

"Major Mendoza has invited me to his official residence for tea and crumpets at two o'clock this afternoon."

Sam nodded his head with approval. "How very civilised. Does Edinburgh know that you're making contact with the Spanish Military Attaché in Hereward with the intention of establishing an anti German unofficial Anglo-Spanish alliance?" Sam asked in a mocking tone, with raised eyebrows.

Alan shook his head as he loaded his Luger pistol with a full magazine of rounds. "No, Sam. I thought that on a need-to-know basis Edinburgh doesn't need to know." Alan slipped the pistol under the back of his shirt, where it rested underneath the waistband of his trousers.

Sam nodded his head. "Wise decision, Al. Those old women up in Edinburgh probably wouldn't agree and would order you to break off all contact with Mendoza and throw Aurora to the SS wolves."

"That's precisely what I thought, Sam, and I'm not prepared to do that."

"Neither am I," Sam said resolutely. "I was getting bored sitting around waiting for orders, anyway. I think that it's time for some independent action: let the chaos and carnage begin!"

"Major Mendoza, your Spanish guests are here," Mrs Purlieu announced as she peered through the front door spy hole.

"Already?" Mendoza said as he folded up the Sunday Times newspaper that he was reading in the living room. "That was quick and unusually efficient. I wasn't expecting the Legiónaries to arrive for at least another week. I would have expected Major de Rivera to have phoned me." Mendoza shrugged as he walked towards the front door. "Oh well, maybe Antonio meant to give me a pleasant surprise. Mrs Purlieu, could you let in our visitors, please, and then go and find Aurora and tell her that our guests have arrived? She's probably in her bedroom."

"Certainly, Major." The house keeper paused as she opened the front door. "Although I must say, Major, that your Legiónaries don't look particularly Spanish..."

"What... what do you mean, Mrs Purlieu?" Mendoza asked as an alarm bell began to ring in the back of his head.

"Well, Major, when my Tom - God rest his soul -

returned from a tour of duty from India, he was tanned as brown as a Bengal Lancer. Your guests look as if they've lived their entire lives in England..."

"...Or in Germany," a guttural voice interrupted.

Mendoza ran into the entrance hall just in time to see one of his 'Legiónaries' shoot his housekeeper straight between the eyes with a silencer-attached Luger pistol.

The killer turned to face Mendoza and pointed his still smoking pistol straight at the centre of the Spaniard's forehead. "Major Mendoza, I presume?"

Mendoza regained consciousness when the third bucket of water was thrown over his head. He slowly opened one of his eyes and saw a tall man standing in front of him, holding a bucket and looking like a lion watching wounded prey. Mendoza tried to open his other eye but found that he couldn't. Judging by the painful throbbing behind the shut eye, Mendoza guessed that the eye was glued shut with dried blood.

The man with the bucket bent down, gripped Mendoza by a mop of blood-matted hair and painfully wrenched his head up to look into the wounded Spaniard's face. A sharp burst of pain shot through Mendoza's head like a shooting star, and the Spaniard thought that he would pass out again.

"Ah, you're awake, Major. That's good to see because this wouldn't be half as much fun if you were asleep..."

"...Or if you were dead," another voice interrupted.

"Yes, or if you were dead," the first voice continued. "Thank you, Walter."

So two Germans, Mendoza thought to himself. The Spaniard slowly started to check his body for injuries, flexing and unflexing his toes.

"Forgive me, Major. How remiss of me: I believe

that introductions are in order. I am Scharführer Andreas Schmitt of the 4th SS Infantry Regiment." Schmitt bowed. "And this is Scharführer Walter Hauser, also of the 4th SS Infantry Regiment."

"At your service, Major." Hauser clicked his heels behind Mendoza's back.

"Major Juan Mendoza, XVIIth Bandera, Spanish Foreign Legión," Mendoza rasped painfully through broken lips. He slowly circled his ankles and put pressure on his feet. Bueno. He thought that he could stand.

Schmitt laughed and shook his head with amusement. "It's not necessary for you to introduce yourself."

"We know who you are, Major Mendoza," Hauser added.

So it's personal then, Mendoza thought to himself. These were Scar Face's friends out to avenge their fallen comrade. The Germans were definitely going to kill him then, or else they would not have given their names. Mendoza slowly flexed and unflexed his fingers. His wrists were bound to the arms of a chair. The fog in his head gradually lifted. Aurora. Aurora! His heart suddenly leapt. Had he managed to warn her before the Germans had overpowered him? Had she managed to get away?

"Aurora. That's who you're wondering about, isn't it?" Schmitt asked.

Mendoza's wrists strained in vain against his restraints. "If you've hurt her, I'll..."

"You'll do what exactly, Major?" Schmitt interrupted mockingly. "You'll break free of your bonds, overpower Scharführer Hauser and kill me?"

"Something like that..." Mendoza rasped through a blood-soaked mouth. The Spaniard glanced quickly at the clock above Schmitt's head. A quarter to two.

Bueno.

Schmitt waved his hand dismissively. "It's all right, Mendoza: it's perfectly understandable. After all, you are her father." Schmitt walked closer to Mendoza. "You're perfectly entitled to threaten and rant and rave as much as you want. It's your prerogative. If it makes you feel any better - 'yes' you did try to warn her, but 'no' you were not successful, and 'yes' we've captured her."

"You bloody bastards! If you've laid one dirty finger on her I'll..."

Hauser interrupted Mendoza with a vicious crack of his Luger pistol butt on the back of the Spaniard's head. Mendoza lurched forwards in his chair and was only prevented from toppling over by the two ropes which bound his wrists to the arms of the chair.

"Walter, what the hell did you do that for?" Schmitt asked as he looked at Mendoza's slumped and unconscious form. "We were just getting to the good bit where we tell him what we're all going to do to his daughter!"

"I'm sorry, Andreas." Hauser shrugged. "But all of his empty threats were starting to do my head in. Let's just get Geyr to bring in the bitch and get this over and done with. I want to get back to the barracks in time for dinner. It's a hog roast tonight with all of the trimmings, and it's my favourite. If we're late then those greedy bastards in the 5th SS will eat everything and we'll be left with nothing but pig fat."

Schmitt shrugged his shoulders. "All right, fine. Ruin my fun, you rotten spoilsport. The trouble with you, Walter, is that you're always thinking with your stomach."

"The trouble with you, Andreas, is that you're always thinking with 'little Andreas' instead of your stomach!"

"Hey, not so much of the 'little,' Walter, you cheeky bastard! Geyr!" Schmitt shouted. "Bring in the bitch!"

Alan looked at his watch for the tenth time in as many minutes as he walked along at a brisk pace.

"All I'm saying, Al, is that you might consider offering some conditions," Sam suggested as he struggled to keep up with his friend's quick march.

"For the last time, Sam, no," Alan said angrily. "I am not going to bargain with Major Mendoza over the life of his daughter. I will protect Aurora and her father unequivocally, without conditions."

"It's just that if you tell Edinburgh that you are protecting them in exchange for intelligence then it might sweeten them, that's all," Sam persisted.

Alan stopped walking and turned to face Sam with his hands knuckled on his hips. "Sam, protecting Aurora and Major Mendoza is not a means to achieve the end of gathering intelligence: it is an end in itself. Edinburgh will just have to like it or lump it. Anyway, Edinburgh is not going to find out unless you tell them." Alan stormed off in a fury.

"Oh, j'accuse! J'accuse!" Sam pointed a stabbing finger at Alan's back as he ran to catch up. "I like that, Al! I like that! That's rich after all that we've been through. To accuse me of base treachery!" Sam stood with his arms folded and his brows furrowed in the huff.

Alan wrapped an arm around his friend's neck. "Oh, Sam, of course I'm only joking! I know that you would never give the game away!" Alan playfully knuckled Sam's hair. "I would rather have no-one else beside me in a fight."

"Do you mean that?" Sam rubbed his head with a frown on his face.

"Of course!" Alan punched Sam playfully on the

arm.

"All right." Sam nodded his head. "As long as we're clear, then. Let's discover what the good Major Mendoza has to say then."

"Papa! Papa! What have they done to you?" Aurora tried to break free from her captor's grasp but the German's grip was too tight.

The German laughed. "Easy, tiger!" von Berlichingen said as he tightened his grip on Aurora's wrists.

"You dirty German bastards! If you've hurt him, I'll...!"

Von Berlichingen viciously slapped Aurora across the face with a ferocious forehand. Aurora was only prevented from collapsing by the fact that the German held onto one of her wrists with a painful vicelike grip.

"You'll do what?" Von Berlichingen sneered into Aurora's sobbing face as she knelt on the floor. The German lifted up his hand for another slap.

Aurora raised one hand to defend herself. A tear rolled down Aurora's face as she shook her head and bit her lip in order to stifle a reply.

"I didn't think so." Von Berlichingen slowly lowered his hand and flexed his fingers.

"Oh, Geyr! You're so masterful!" Schmitt said in a falsetto voice.

"You certainly have a way with the ladies, Geyr!" Hauser said.

"Casanova, eat your heart out!" Von Berlichingen said. "Treat them mean and keep them keen, that's what I say, gentlemen." All three Germans laughed uproariously.

Aurora tenderly touched her bruised cheekbone with a shaking hand.

Mendoza gritted his teeth in pain and fury and kept

his eyes welded shut. Surely it must be ten to two by now. His only hope was that Alan would be a stereotypical British stickler for timing and would not be late. Mendoza did not know how long he would be able to hold on. He had to prolong Schmitt's monologuing and buy some time.

"You've got a right little wildcat there, Geyr!" Hauser said with a smile.

Von Berlichingen shrugged his shoulders. "I like it when they struggle: it makes it more of a challenge."

"She's got spirit, I'll say that for the little Spanish bitch," Schmitt said as he took a sip of wine from a glass on the dining room table. The German smacked his lips with appreciation and then held the wine glass up to the sunlight and swilled the red liquid around. "I must say that Major Mendoza has very good taste. My compliments to the host, sir." Schmitt bowed to the Spaniard and then tutted in annoyance. "I forgot: the bastard's unconscious again. Honestly, no staying power." Schmitt shook his head in disappointment. "I thought that the Legiónaries were tougher than that. I guess that I was mistaken."

Von Berlichingen guffawed. "Andreas, why do you act so surprised? We have consistently overestimated the fighting capabilities of our enemies: first the Poles, then the French and the British, and now the Spanish. Why are you so surprised? These untermensch bastards are simply no match for a Third Reich fighting man. I have no doubt that the Russkis will prove to be as useless a pile of shit as the rest of them when the time comes to invade."

Schmitt shrugged his shoulders. "Of course you're right, Geyr."

Hauser coughed. "Another bucket of water, Andreas?" He suggested.

"Good idea, Walter," Schmitt agreed with a nod. "If

you would be so kind to do the honours?"

"Certainly." Hauser disappeared.

"Pull the bitch to her feet, Geyr," Schmitt ordered.

Von Berlichingen roughly pulled the sobbing Aurora to her feet.

Hauser reappeared with a bucket of water and Schmitt swiftly threw the contents over Mendoza. After two more buckets had left the Spaniard thoroughly drenched, Hauser roughly wrenched the semi-conscious Mendoza's head back.

"Wakey, wakey, Major," Hauser said.

"Aurora…" Mendoza said through blood-cracked lips and a foggy daze of pain.

"Papa!" Aurora struggled to break free again. "Papa! What have they done to you?"

"Nothing, my butterfly…" Mendoza reassured his daughter as he painfully coughed up and spat out a globule of blood.

"At least nothing compared to what is going to happen to you, you Spanish bitch," Hauser threatened nastily.

"Your wings are going to be well and truly clipped, my little señorita. You'll never fly again," von Berlichingen added menacingly.

"Now, now, gentlemen." Schmitt smiled like a crocodile. "Promises, promises. Geyr, bring Aurora over here, please."

Von Berlichingen dragged the struggling girl over to where Schmitt stood behind the dining table. Schmitt swiftly punched Aurora in the base of her stomach and, as the girl doubled over, struggling for air, he turned her around and pushed her face down over the dining room table. Von Berlichingen stepped to the front of the table and grabbed hold of both of Aurora's wrists and pulled her arms out as far as they would stretch. It was obvious that the two Germans had carried out this manoeuvre many times before.

"What… what are you doing?" Mendoza asked as his eyes bulged with horror as he realised what was about to happen.

"Come, come, Major," Schmitt said with genuine astonishment. "Don't play the innocent with me; surely you've been to war before?" The German took off his belt and holster and laid it on the dining room table in front of him.

"Don't you dare lay a finger on her, Schmitt! Or I swear to God you will wish that you'd never been born!" Mendoza struggled against his rope bonds.

The three Germans all broke out into fits of belly-aching laughter.

Schmitt wiped tears of laughter away from his eyes with the back of his hand and shook his head with amazement at the Spaniard's brave, but futile words of defiance. "Now I'm going to rape your daughter, Mendoza and you're going to watch me…"

"No!" Mendoza moaned like a wounded animal.

"Papa! Please save me!" Aurora begged through tears.

"Aurora! Hold on, my sweet! Be strong!" Mendoza urged.

"…Then Geyr and Walter will do the same, and then I'm going to cut her pretty little throat with this bayonet."

Mendoza groaned and slumped in his chair. His shoulders sagged and he appeared to have given up all hope of release or rescue.

Schmitt held up his bayonet and the blade twinkled in the sunlight as he slowly twirled it around. "And there will be absolutely nothing that you can do to stop me."

"Papa!" Aurora sobbed.

"…And then I'm going to kill you, Mendoza, with

the same knife." Schmitt stuck the bayonet into the dining table top. "And the cherry on the cake will be that we will leave a note claiming that you were executed by a British Resistance Death Squad. Franco will demand retribution for the cold-blooded murder of a favourite son…"

"Oh yes, Major: we know that you are Franco's Golden Boy," Hauser added contemptuously. "Correction: you were Franco's Golden Boy. The dead are no one's favourites."

"Franco will also demand retribution for the rape and murder of a child," von Berlichingen continued. "The much-loved granddaughter of a powerful Government Minister no less. What's the going rate of exchange, Andreas?"

"Oh, I think that the deaths of two hundred innocent Hereward hostages would be a fair punishment for the murders of these two Spanish celebrities, don't you think, Geyr?"

"I think so, Andreas."

"Enough talking." Schmitt bared his teeth and grinned like a jackal.

"Geyr, hold on tight. Aurora, brace yourself - this is going to hurt you more than it's going to hurt me."

"Papa!" Aurora screamed as Schmitt roughly pushed her skirt above her waist and brutally ripped off her underwear. "Do something! Stop them! Don't let them hurt me!" Aurora begged through tear-filled eyes.

"I can't, Aurora." Mendoza shook his head with hopeless frustration. "Be strong, Aurora and hold on. It will be over soon."

"Knowing Andreas it will be over very soon," Hauser said with a smile.

"I'd say three minutes should do the trick. What do you think, Romeo?" Geyr asked Schmitt.

"Oi! You cheeky bastards! Shut up! You'll put me

off my stride!" Schmitt shouted jokingly at his two comrades. "And as for you, Mendoza, I want you to remember that all of this is happening - the rape and murder of your daughter, and your own death - because you wouldn't let Kophamel kill a bunch of useless Red prisoners." Schmitt shook his head in disgust as he unbuttoned his trousers. "All of this was so easily avoidable."

Mendoza looked at the clock above the German's head. It was five minutes to two. For God's sake, Alan, be early for once in your life.

"Who said a soldier's lot is not a happy one?" Schmitt said as he brutally thrusted.

As Aurora screamed out in pain and agony, Mendoza shook his head in despair as a large tear fell from his bloodstained face onto the floor. It was too late. By the time that Alan arrived, both he and Aurora would be dead.

Chapter Ten

Alan looked at his watch. "Look: two o'clock. Bang on time." Alan headed up the garden path towards the front door.

Sam grabbed Alan's arm. "Al, wait - look at the door."

Alan stopped dead in his tracks and followed Sam's gaze. The front door was slightly ajar and Alan could see some dark liquid slowly spreading in an ever-widening pool on the tiled floor. And he could see something else: a hand.

Alan nodded in recognition of the changed situation. "Silencers. Make ready," he ordered.

Both of the boys quickly looked behind them and checked that the coast was clear. They swiftly extracted their Luger pistols from beneath their trouser waistbands and screwed on a silencer attachment. The boys cocked their weapons and flicked off the safety catches.

"Ready," both boys said softly.

"Cover me," Alan ordered as he raised the pistol to the firing position and used his left hand to help steady the weapon.

"Right behind you, Al," Sam said as he adopted a similar position.

Alan slowly approached the open door and silently pushed it open far enough to give him enough room to squeeze through. He entered and carefully stepped over the body lying in the hall. Alan breathed a sigh of relief as he realised that although the body was female, it wasn't Aurora. "Must be Mrs Purlieu, the housekeeper," Alan explained.

Sam nodded. "What's that sound?"

A rhythmic crying and sobbing sound of someone in acute pain and distress was echoing from further down the corridor.

Alan's face turned white. "Aurora," he whispered as he quickened up his step, and Sam following close on his heels.

Alan came to the end of the corridor and carefully peeked around the corner. He was at the entrance to the dining room. He was facing the back of a tall-backed chair and he could see the back of a man's head. Each of the man's arms was tied to an arm of the chair with a length of rope against which the man struggled futilely in impotent fury. Major Mendoza. Another man stood to the right of the Major; he had his left arm wrapped around Mendoza's neck and he held a pistol in his right hand that he held loosely against the right hand side of his body. He was not expecting any trouble and was obviously enjoying the horror show, squeezing Mendoza's neck from time to time and laughing uproariously. Alan looked beyond the chair to the dining room table. He saw the back of another man pulling Aurora's arms out over the table. His pistol was still in his holster. The top half of Aurora's body was stretched over the table and her eyes were squeezed shut with pain. Two streams of tears ran down her face in a continuous flow. The rapist stood directly behind her. The two men shouted out filthy obscenities and laughed at each other's jokes as the rape continued. The rapist had placed his belt and holster that still contained his pistol on the dining room table.

Alan stepped back and allowed Sam to have a look.

"Right, Al, this is the plan: we'll both go around the corner all guns blazing. I'll kill the German standing by the Major and you kill the one holding Aurora by the arms. I'll free the Major and arm him. You cover the rapist and free Aurora and then Aurora and the Major will decide what to do with the rapist. Agreed?"

"Agreed."

" Are you ready?"

"Yes." Alan smiled resolutely. "Strength and honour, Sam."

"Strength and honour, Al."

Schmitt opened his eyes just in time to see Hauser's head explode in a crimson shower of blood, bones and brains. The dead German fell forwards like a timbering tree. At the same time two massive holes appeared in von Berlichingen's chest, and the German fell forwards and lay slumped on the dining room table with his eyes open and a confused look of surprise on his face.

"Was ist...?" Schmitt said as two schoolboys armed with pistols suddenly appeared in front of him. One of the boys pointed his pistol at Schmitt's chest with a look of such pure hatred and rage on his face that the rapist's state of arousal faded and wilted at an astronomical rate. Schmitt hastily withdrew from the body of the child that he had been raping.

"Aurora, Aurora, are you all right?" Alan asked as he briefly took his eyes off the rapist.

"Alan, Alan... is that you?" Aurora asked weakly.

"Yes, my love, it's me. You're safe now," Alan reassured her. "Can you walk?"

"Yes, I can," Aurora replied. "Papa?"

"Yes, my butterfly," Mendoza replied. "I'm all right. Alan's brave young friend...?"

"Sam, Major Mendoza." Sam bowed.

Mendoza returned the bow. "Sam has freed me."

"As for you, you dirty, murdering, child rapist. What are we going to do with you?" Alan pointed his pistol straight at Schmitt's face.

"Now, Al. I know that you're mad as hell, but let's not be too hasty." Sam said with upturned palms. "We could squeeze some valuable information out of him.

Major Mendoza, what do you think?"

"What do you mean by 'valuable information,' Sam?" Mendoza asked as he rubbed his wrists that had been rubbed raw and bloody by the ropes. "If you're part of the Resistance then I don't want to know anything about it. Aurora and I are in as much trouble with the Germans as it is, and…"

The sudden gunshot and Schmitt's scream cut through the conversation. The rapist lay doubled up on the floor in the foetal position with his eyes screwed tightly together in agony and his two hands clutched together between his legs, trying in vain to staunch a steady stream of blood which flowed down his legs from his groin and formed an ever increasing pool on the floor.

Aurora stood in front of him with a still smoking pistol in her hand. Schmitt's pistol that she had picked up from the dining room table. "I don't want information," she said through gritted teeth. "I just want revenge. I want this dirty, murdering, child raping bastard to suffer as I have suffered." Aurora spat on the German's face which was screwed tight in absolute agony. "As Mrs Purlieu suffered."

"That's good enough for me." Alan nodded grimly. "Major Mendoza, do you have a telephone?"

"Yes, I do. Why?"

"Because I know someone who is an expert in the twin arts of making stinking Nazis suffer a slow and agonisingly excruciating death, and also of extracting information as efficiently and effectively as possible." Alan explained.

"We can kill two birds with one stone and also dispose of the bodies without fuss."

"Mr Leon?" Sam asked.

"Just the man," Alan replied.

"Then be my guest." Mendoza showed the way with

an outstretched arm to his study and a telephone.

"What's all this I hear about you missing three of your men, Hauptsturmführer von Stein?" Brigadeführer Herold asked.

"Three scharführers in my company did not return from their weekend passes to London, sir," von Stein explained from a position of attention as he stood in front of Herold's desk.

"What do you think has happened to them?" Herold asked with steepled fingers.

"I don't know, sir." Von Stein shrugged his shoulders. "I know the men well, sir. We've served together since Poland and it's highly unlikely that they've gone AWOL and it's extremely unlikely that they've deserted. I mean where would they desert to? It's virtually impossible to make it to Ireland. I think that the Resistance in London must have killed them, sir."

"The usual suspects, eh, Hauptsturmführer?" Herold said as he swivelled his chair from side to side. "Well you've lost four sergeants from your company in a matter of weeks, von Stein - that's pretty damned careless of you, don't you think?"

Von Stein's cheeks coloured at the criticism. "With all due respect, sir, what my men do when they are off duty is no concern of mine. They're not children, they're grown men, and it is certainly not my responsibility to..."

Herold slammed both his palms onto the top of his desk. "What your men do is always your responsibility, von Stein, whether they are on or off duty!" Herold shouted angrily. "The realisation of that responsibility is what separates a good officer from a bad officer. You are a father to your men, von Stein, and they are your children. Don't you forget it!"

145

"Yes, sir," von Stein answered with lowered head. He felt suitably chastised.

"Good." Herold stood up and straightened out his tunic. "I sincerely hope so, von Stein, both for your sake and more importantly for the sake of your men. You're a good officer, Hauptsturmführer."

"Thank you, sir." Von Stein acknowledged the compliment with bowed head.

"Your men admire and respect you, von Stein." Herold started to pace around his office. "It may surprise you, Hauptsturmführer, that despite my reputation as a ruthless bastard, the morale, wellbeing and spiritual welfare of the men under my command is, and always will be, my number one priority. The word on the street is that the men of your company would follow you to the gates of hell itself."

"Thank you, sir." Von Stein blushed with pride. "Charlie Company is indeed a band of brothers, sir."

Herold stopped pacing for a moment. "And therein lies the problem, von Stein…"

Von Stein gulped nervously. His throat felt as dry as a dead man's armpit.

"You are aware of the Queen Alexandra Road explosion?" Herold asked.

"Yes, sir," von Stein nodded. "My company took the hostages into protective custody, sir."

"And carried out the executions?"

"As per your orders, sir," von Stein confirmed. "Two hundred hostages were executed as punishment for the Resistance attack which killed and wounded over twenty of our men, sir."

"Except that the Resistance didn't kill our men, Hauptsturmführer."

"The Resistance didn't kill our men?" Von Stein asked with raised eyebrows. "I… I'm afraid that I don't follow, sir. Then who killed our men, sir?"

"Spaniards." Herold answered grimly.

"The Spanish?" Von Stein appeared to be absolutely flabbergasted. "I thought that we and the Spanish were friends, sir! After all that we did for them in the Civil War..."

Herold shook his head. "Not the Spanish, von Stein. Spaniards - there is a significant difference."

"Republican diehards, sir?"

"Perhaps..." Herold stopped pacing and looked directly into von Stein's eyes. "And you know nothing about it?"

Von Stein looked as surprised as if Herold had asked him if he had killed his own men personally. "No... no, sir. How could I, sir?"

Herold continued to look directly at von Stein. "Mendoza's men were responsible for the King Alfred Hotel bombing, the Queen Alexandra Road attack and were probably also responsible for the disappearance of your three scharführers. I'm afraid that your three scharführers probably never even made it out of Hereward and their bodies are probably lying in some forgotten ditch somewhere."

"What? How? Mendoza is here in Hereward?"

Herold nodded. "Major Mendoza is the Military Attaché at the Spanish Consulate in Hereward." Herold watched von Stein's reaction.

"Mein Gott, sir." Von Stein's eyes bulged with shock. "What a bloody mess..."

"I think that Kophamel told his three mates about what happened in Spain and when he was killed your Three Musketeers decided to carry out a revenge attack..."

"Kophamel!" Von Stein punched a fist into an open palm. "That bloody idiot." Von Stein shook his head in despair. "I told him to forget about Mendoza or else it would eat him up like a cancer. He always was a hothead."

"Wise words, Hauptsturmführer." Herold nodded. "Kophamel should have followed your advice."

"So what now, sir?" Von Stein asked. "Is that the end of it? Will the Spaniards be satisfied that honour has been served?"

"I hope so, von Stein, for your sake and for the sake of the Triple S Brigade and German forces in Hereward in general," Herold said grimly.

"What do you mean, sir?"

Herold handed him an envelope. It was addressed to: "Brigadeführer Fritz Herold, Commanding Officer of the Triple S Brigade." Von Stein opened the envelope, extracted the note, and read the typed writing: Any attack carried out against Lieutenant-Colonel Juan Mendoza or his daughter Aurora will be interpreted as a declaration of War against the XVIIth Bandera, the Spanish Foreign Legión, and Spain. Hauptsturmführer Manfred von Stein will be held personally responsible for the safety of the Colonel and his daughter and should any harm befall Lieutenant-Colonel Mendoza or his daughter Aurora, Hauptsturmführer von Stein will be punished accordingly.

Von Stein turned as white as a sheet. "Surely... surely this is a joke, sir?" Von Stein smiled weakly. "I would have thought that the Spanish Foreign Legión in Britain consisted of Major Mendoza and no more than a platoon of embassy guards in London, sir."

Herold shook his head sadly. "I wish that that was true, Hauptsturmführer. That was certainly the case until fairly recently, but by the end of next week the situation will have completely changed."

"I'm... I'm afraid that I don't understand, sir." Von Stein's brows furrowed in confusion.

"I'm going to tell you this now, von Stein, because

this information directly concerns you. The rest of the Brigade will find out soon enough." Herold took a deep breath before continuing. "The 6th SS Infantry Regiment is being redeployed from Britain to Poland and will leave Hereward at the end of next week."

"But... but that will leave us seriously under strength, sir," von Stein protested. "And what of our invasion of Scotland? We will barely be able to keep a lid on Partisan activities in Cambridgeshire with two regiments, never mind invade the Free North."

Herold nodded his head in agreement. "I know, Hauptsturmführer, but it's ours not to reason why. The Führer in his wisdom has decided that the 6th SS is better deployed on anti-Partisan duties in Poland. However, every cloud has a silver lining as they say, and the powers-that-be have decided that this redeployment provides a marvellous opportunity for our fellow Fascist brothers in Arms to show their support in the common struggle against Churchill's Jewish Bolshevik clique of war mongering terrorists."

"Don't tell me, sir," von Stein said. "Franco has offered the services of the XVIIth Bandera?"

Herold nodded grimly. "Spain and Great Britain are not technically at war so the Caudillo can not officially offer the services of the Spanish Foreign Legión, so the XVIIth Bandera has been disbanded and reformed as the 1st LVE Infantry Regiment, or the 1st Spanish Volunteer Legión Infantry Regiment..."

"You say tomato, I say tomato..." Von Stein shrugged his shoulders with weary resignation.

"Incidentally, Marshall Petain has also offered the services of a military unit - the 1st LVF Infantry Regiment or the 1st French Volunteer Legion Infantry Regiment - to take part in the invasion of Scotland."

Von Stein snorted contemptuously. "It didn't take long for the French to change their spots. What is the price of French support, sir?"

"I don't know." Herold shrugged his shoulders. "At the very least, the transfer of sovereignty of the Channel Islands."

"And I would imagine that the Spanish will want our help to recover Gibraltar, sir," von Stein said.

"If I was a betting man then I'd put good money on it," Herold agreed. "The 1st LVE will take up quarters in Hereward by the end of next week, and together with the 4th and 5th SS Infantry Regiments will form a brigade under my command."

"So... what happens to me, sir?" Von Stein asked nervously.

"Absolutely nothing, von Stein," Herold answered. "As far as I am concerned and as far as you are concerned, this incident is dead and buried. I don't want to hear another word about a vendetta or a blood feud. This incident is finished. Finito. If I hear that Colonel Mendoza has tripped over a cobblestone and has fallen over and bruised his knee, you will find yourself face down in a ditch beside your three scharführers with a bullet in the back of your head before you can say 'please, sir, it wasn't me,' and I'll be the one with my finger on the trigger. Do you understand?"

"Yes, sir." Von Stein stood at a ramrod straight position of attention.

"Hauptsturmführer von Stein, I've decided to give you the benefit of the doubt about the deaths of your three scharführers. I'm willing to publicly acknowledge that the Resistance killed them and I am willing to privately accept that Kophamel led them astray and put the idea of vendetta into their heads, and not you. But - so help me God - if I find out that you put thoughts of revenge into the minds of your men and that you were responsible for their deaths then I will hunt you down like a dog and kill you without a moment's hesitation. Do you understand?"

"Yes, sir."

"I cannot afford to have a civil war going on in the streets of Hereward, von Stein," Herold explained, "with Legiónaries and my stormtroopers fighting each other instead of the British. Of course I would prefer to have the 6th SS instead of the Spaniards, but they've been sent to Poland and there's absolutely no point crying over spilt milk. I have to welcome the 1st LVE as brothers in arms and weld them together with the 4th and 5th SS to form a team. I cannot form a team based on trust and mutual respect and support if my men are constantly looking over their shoulder worrying that they might be shot in the back because of a private blood feud between two allied officers. Do you understand?"

"Yes, sir."

"Good." Herold stopped pacing around the room, straightened his tunic, and sat down behind his desk. "By the way, von Stein, did you notice how the XVIIth Bandera's warning notice referred to Mendoza?"

"No, sir." Von Stein was too dazed and confused to notice very much.

"It referred to Lieutenant-Colonel Mendoza: he's been promoted. Mendoza is the new commanding officer of the 1st LVE Infantry Regiment."

Von Stein rocked back on his heels as if he had been slapped in the face.

"And a word of warning, Hauptsturmführer: four of Mendoza's Legiónaries managed to kill and wound approximately fifty SS and Wehrmacht soldiers," Herold said. "Mendoza will now be in command of approximately five hundred Legiónaries based in Hereward. My advice would be to stay well clear of him. Dismissed!"

"How are you, Aurora? How do you feel?" Alan asked as he kissed his girlfriend on her forehead and sat on a chair beside Aurora's bed. He picked up Aurora's hand and held it tenderly.

"I'm drugged up to my eye balls, Alan," Aurora replied with a croaky voice as she carefully moved the morphine drip that was attached to the back of her hand. "I'm attached to a catheter which is not very comfortable and the painkillers make me feel nauseous. I feel like I'm going to be sick all of the time." Aurora pointed to the tin bowl that sat on her bedside table. "I haven't eaten for twenty-four hours and I haven't had anything to drink either. My throat feels very dry."

Alan gently kissed Aurora's hand. "I'm sure that you'll be able to eat and drink very soon. How are your scars?"

"The doctors say that the tears are healing and that the stitches are doing a good job. However, I'm confined to my bed for a week and I'm not allowed to walk in case it rips the stitches."

"Good." Alan nodded as he patted Aurora's hand. "That's a good idea. It sounds as if you're in safe hands."

"Yes, I am," Aurora agreed. "I am in very safe hands. The doctors and nurses have been very kind to me, despite the fact that I'm an enemy alien," Aurora said bitterly.

Alan smiled. "Now that's not true, my love and you know it. You are the victim of a terrible crime. Nationality has got nothing to do with your treatment and the doctors and nurses would treat you the same if you were German. You are a human being and that's the end of it. A person's nationality is nothing more than an accident of birth. You no more chose to be Spanish than I chose to be English. And anyway, Spain and Britain are not at war…"

"Yet," Aurora interrupted sadly.

"Oh, Aurora, that's a very pessimistic thing to say," Alan teased playfully.

Aurora shook her head. "I'm afraid that I'm not just being pessimistic, Alan. Papa told me that his regiment, the XVIIth Bandera of the Foreign Legión, has been disbanded and has been reformed as the 1st Spanish Volunteer Legión Infantry Regiment, and will arrive in Hereward by the end of next week."

Alan's eyes were widened in shock. "Bloody hell! But why are they here?"

"To take part in the invasion of Scotland, of course! And papa has been promoted to Lieutenant-Colonel to lead them."

"Remind me to congratulate your father on his promotion, Aurora," Alan said sarcastically.

"It's not his fault, Alan!" Aurora protested passionately. "He does not want to fight against the British!"

"It looks as if he won't have any choice, Aurora," Alan said bitterly.

Aurora did not persist in defending her father, because she knew that what Alan had said was true.

Alan decided to change the subject; he had not come to the hospital to argue with his girlfriend. "At least the damage is not permanent, my love, and you will recover."

Aurora nodded. "You are right, Alan: the doctors have said that I will still be able to have children." Aurora paused. "The physical scars will heal, but the emotional scars will never heal," Aurora said sadly.

"What… what do you mean, Aurora?" Alan asked.

"That animal raped me, Alan!" Aurora shouted angrily. "That Nazi bastard raped me and destroyed my virginity. A woman's virginity is a gift that she should only give to a man that she loves, and that rapist destroyed that gift." A large tear slowly trickled down Aurora's cheek. "I wanted to give my virginity to the man that I love, Alan. I wanted to give my virginity to you and now I will never be able to."

"I... I'm sorry, Aurora," Alan said with tear filled eyes. "I... I don't know what to say."

"You don't have to say anything, Alan. Just hold me."

Chapter Eleven

"How is Mendoza's daughter, Hauptwachtmeister Bratge? Her name's Aurora, isn't it?" General-Major von Schnakenberg asked with concern.

"Yes, sir. Aurora's recovering in hospital, sir," Bratge replied as he stood at a position of attention in front of von Schnakenberg's desk. "But she's lucky to be alive, sir. Those animals really tried to hurt her. Fortunately the damage isn't permanent and she will be able to have children in the future."

Von Schnakenberg shook his head in disgust. "Bloody animals, raping a child. Some people have absolutely no morals. How old is Aurora?"

Bratge consulted his notes. "She's fourteen, sir."

"Bastards.Well, I hope the Police catch the swine. Has Mendoza identified the rapists?"

Bratge shook his head. "No, sir. Both she and Major - sorry, Lieutenant-Colonel Mendoza - told the Police that they were unable to identify the rapists. They said that they had never seen them before."

"Were they able to identify the nationality of the rapists?"

"They said that the rapists were British, sir," Bratge replied.

"How convenient." Von Schnakenberg swirled his whiskey filled crystal tumbler.

"Both of the rapists were shot from behind in the head and one of them was also shot twice from behind in the back. Their heads were virtually blown apart because they were shot at virtually point-blank range and their faces were unrecognisable, sir."

"How did Mendoza manage to shoot them? I presume that he was tied up when they were raping his daughter?" Von Schnakenberg asked.

Bratge nodded. "Yes he was, sir. However, Mendoza

155

said that the two rapists had obviously never been Boy Scouts and they couldn't tie knots for love of money. They were too busy concentrating on raping Aurora to notice that Mendoza had slowly but surely been unloosening his ropes."

"How did he manage to get a weapon?"

"Mendoza said that he had a Luger pistol taped underneath the seat of his chair for emergency use."

"How very cloak and dagger," von Schnakenberg said. "What do you think, Hauptwachtmeister? Is his story plausible?"

Bratge shook his head. "Mendoza has obviously never read any Sherlock Holmes novels, sir. His story has more holes in it than a chunk of Swiss cheese. These rapists must have been professionals to force entry to the house, kill the housekeeper and overpower Mendoza, sir, a man who has been a soldier for the last twenty years and no doubt must know a thing or two about close quarter and hand-to-hand unarmed combat. It seems likely that the rapists have done this sort of thing before, sir. Perhaps they were serial rapists. It certainly seems like a professional job. I'm certain that they would know how to tie good, strong, solid knots of rope. They had also beaten Mendoza pretty badly and he was concussed and he had lost a lot of blood by the time that the Police brought him to the hospital. One of his eyes was more or less glued shut with dried blood."

"So how did Mendoza manage to escape from his ropes unnoticed, find and make ready his weapon, and aim and fire four well-aimed rounds whilst he was concussed, with one eye glued shut with blood, and kill the rapists?" von Schnakenberg asked.

"That's the six million Mark question, sir." Bratge smiled. "I don't think Mendoza did free himself, sir. I don't think that he was in any fit state to shoot those two men. I think that Mendoza was rescued by someone who shot the two rapists and then untied and released him."

"But by whom?" von Schnakenberg asked. "The XVIIth Bandera - sorry, the 1st LVE - doesn't arrive in Hereward until the end of next week and I thought that the Spanish Embassy wasn't able to send any reinforcements to Mendoza."

"Perhaps his rescuers were British, sir."

"British?" Von Schnakenberg raised his eyebrows. "Mendoza has hardly lived in Hereward for a month, Hauptwachtmeister. He would barely have found the time to get to know the town. Where would he have found the time to get to know a local with a gun?" Von Schnakenberg paused with thought for a moment. "Do you have any suspects, Hauptwachtmeister?"

Bratge shook his head. "No, sir. I have absolutely no idea who freed Mendoza and killed the two rapists."

"So the trail runs cold yet again. How bloody frustrating, Hauptwachtmeister." Von Schnakenberg shook his head.

Bratge flashed his set of pearly whites. "Not quite, sir."

"Oh, what do you mean?" Von Schnakenberg sat up in his seat with renewed interest.

Bratge passed von Schnakenberg an A4-sized brown manila envelope.

"What's this, Hauptwachtmeister?" Von Schnakenberg asked with raised eyebrows.

"An early Christmas present, sir," Bratge replied mysteriously.

Von Schnakenberg impatiently tore open the envelope. Six black and white photographs fell out onto the desk. Von Schnakenberg picked up the first photo. He looked at it in confusion. "What the hell is this? A letter?"

Bratge nodded as he enjoyed the air of suspense.

157

"Yes, sir. It's the letter 'A' written in gothic script. It was found tattooed on the underside of the left arm by the armpit of one of the rapists."

Von Schnakenberg picked up another photo with mounting excitement. "Another letter A tattooed on the underside of the left arm by the armpit?"

"Yes, sir." Bratge could not resist smiling. "Blood groups."

Von Schnakenberg picked up the other four photos in quick succession. 'My honour is my loyalty?' "

"Yes, sir. Both mottoes were tattooed onto the upper right arm of both of the rapists."

"And a Death's Head skull and cross bones with the stylised runes underneath."

"Yes, sir. Tattooed onto the upper left arm of both men, which would suggest that they went to the same tattoo artist."

"SS" von Schnakenberg looked like a cat that had got the cream.

"Elementary, my dear Watson. It's standard SS procedure to tattoo all stormtroopers with their blood group in case the soldier is wounded and requires a blood transfusion." Bratge smiled in triumph.

"So the SS are raping children now. Why does that not surprise me?" Von Schnakenberg shook his head with disgust. "No doubt they would have killed Mendoza's daughter afterwards and made Mendoza watch before they killed him as well."

"Probably, sir."

Von Schnakenberg's face darkened with barely suppressed fury and rage.

"The SS have no honour, they have no code. They blacken the name of the German armed forces and their despicable actions tarnish us all with the same brush," von Schnakenberg said, with venom in his voice. In an instant the anger and hatred vanished from von

Schnakenberg's face as if a shadow had lifted. He smiled at the Sergeant Major and shook his head in awe and wonder. "I've got to hand it to you though, Hauptwachtmeister, what an amazing piece of detective work. I would not be surprised if you start another career in the Police when this War is over, Bratge. Detective Inspector Bratge of Scotland Yard," von Schnakenberg chuckled.

Bratge's chest puffed out with pride as he replied, "I have seriously thought about it, sir."

"How did you find out all of this information?" von Schnakenberg asked curiously.

Bratge shrugged his shoulders modestly. "I have a contact at the Police station in Hereward, sir. It's amazing the way that a couple of bottles of schnapps can help loosen tongues."

"And the photographs?"

"I suggested that the Police photographer take those, sir. The photos cost me three bottles of schnapps."

Von Schnakenberg thought for a moment. "Do the Police know that the rapists are SS stormtroopers?"

"Yes, sir. And they also know the names of the rapists."

"Mein Gott!" Von Schnakenberg sat up straight with surprise. "How on earth did they find that out?"

"The Second in Command of the 4th SS Infantry Regiment requested that the Police help in the search for three scharführers from the regiment who had left Hereward to go on weekend leave to London but who had not returned…"

"The 4th SS? But isn't that Sturmbannführer Ulrich's regiment?"

Bratge nodded. "Yes, sir. Sturmbannführer Ulrich is the second in command…"

"Does he have his sticky little paws in everything?" von Schnakenberg interrupted. "Wasn't he involved in the Queen Alexandra Road bombing?"

"Yes, sir. He was virtually the only sole survivor."

"No wonder that he's known as The Cat." Von Schnakenberg shook his head in amazement.

"It's standard procedure for both ourselves and the SS to ask the Police to assist in the search for missing personnel, sir."

Von Schnakenberg nodded in confirmation of the familiar fact, and took a drink of his whiskey.

"The three missing scharführers were called Hauser, Berlichingen and Schmitt, sir. Both Hauser and Berlichingen had A blood groups and Schmitt has a B blood group. All three men were platoon sergeants in Hauptsturmführer von Stein's company, sir, along with Scharführer Kophamel who was killed in the King Alfred Hotel bombing."

"So the vendetta continues. A plague upon both their houses!" Von Schnakenberg slapped his desk with the palms of both of his hands in frustration. "For bringing such death and destruction to my city!" Von Schnakenberg stood up and started to pace around his office.

Bratge did not react to the General-Major's uncharacteristic loss of self control.

"Hauser and Berlichingen were the two dead rapists, Hauptwachtmeister Bratge. The question is: where is Schmitt?"

"Aurora! It's so good to see you. But I didn't expect to see you out and about so soon." Sam gave Aurora the gentlest of hugs and kissed her delicately on both cheeks.

"It's good to see you as well, Sam." Aurora held onto Sam's forearms in order to steady herself.

"How do you feel?" Sam asked with concern.

"It's good to be up on my feet again. As you know, I

was consigned to my bed in the hospital for a week."

"Yes, I know. Remember when I came to visit you? You had been in for a few days."

Aurora held a hand up to her forehead. "Ah, yes. I forgot." Aurora smiled. "I must be losing my marbles in my old age."

"Either that or you were still pumped high on morphine."

Aurora laughed. "Yes, that as well. I feel like a Chinese opium addict. I'm still on painkillers four times a day. Listen, Sam, do you mind if we find somewhere private where we can sit down and talk? It's just that I find it painful to stand for long periods of time."

"Of course, Aurora. Here." Sam guided Aurora over to a bench and supported her as they sat down.

"Does it still hurt?" Sam asked.

Aurora nodded as she laid her hand on top of Sam's. "Yes, it does. I can only walk very slowly and I have to sleep lying very still on my back. The doctors warned me that I had to be aware that my stitches could still rip if I walk too fast and that my scar could still separate." Aurora paused. "That Nazi really hurt me, Sam."

Sam's face turned crimson with rage. "I swear as God as my witness, Aurora, that we will pay those murdering Nazi bastards back for all of the crimes that they have committed against us. We will make each and every one of those swine rue the day that they were born."

"You really hate the Germans, don't you, Sam?"

Sam nodded. "The Germans murdered my mother and my father. The Germans made me and Alice orphans. I hate the Germans when I wake up in the morning and I hate them when I go to sleep. I even hate the Germans in my dreams." Sam paused. "Hatred is all I have left now, Aurora."

161

"That is sad, Sam." Aurora looked Sam directly in the eyes. "And what of love, Sam? Is there any room for love?"

Sam straightened up. "I love my God, my King and my country. And I love my friends and family. But hatred is a stronger emotion than love: hatred makes me feel alive and gives me the motivation to keep fighting rather than surrender."

Aurora nodded in understanding. "I hate the Germans as well, Sam, for what they did to me, what they did to Spain and also for what they continue to do to Britain." Aurora paused. "Will you help me when I decide to exact my revenge on them?"

"Of course, Aurora." Sam's eyes lit up with excitement. "What do you have in mind?"

"I don't know yet." Aurora replied as she patted Sam's hand. "But I'll think of something. Revenge is a dish best served cold."

Brigadeführer Herold stood at the front of the stage, gripping a captured British Army officer's swagger stick in both of his hands. "Gentlemen, I invited you all here today because I have a very important announcement to make." The assembled officers of the Triple S brigade were sitting on the edges of their seats with excitement. "Der Tag has finally arrived. Operation Thor - the invasion of Scotland - will take place on June 22nd in exactly one month's time." An electric current of excitement surged through the officers as they heard the news and made them sit ramrod straight in their chairs as if they had been hit by a bolt of lightning. Herold waited patiently for his officers to calm down and settle themselves before he continued. "As you know, gentlemen, our mission was to carry out a river crossing and capture the town of Berwick-upon-Tweed. That mission has now changed and will no longer be carried out by our Brigade. That mission has been re-tasked to our brothers in arms in Hereward, General-Major von Schnakenberg's Brigade." There was a murmur of discontent from the assembled officers. The Triple S thought that an evil stepsister was a more accurate description of their Wehrmacht fellow occupiers than brothers in arms. "Our new mission is to capture and hold until relieved two bridges over the Beattie Canal and the Auchterlonie River, and also the village of Robinson." Herold walked over to the rear of the stage and pulled a large piece of black material that concealed the back wall. The black sheet floated to the floor of the stage, revealing a massive five metre by five metre map of the Scottish-English border from the west to the east coast. There was a sharp intake of breath from the officers as they marvelled at the impressive detail of the map, which had been painstakingly and patiently copied and enlarged by the Brigade's own cartographers from the Engineering unit.

"As you can see, there are only two roads which are capable of carrying our panzers - the Carlisle to Gretna road on the west coast which leads onto Glasgow, and the Newcastle to Berwick-upon-Tweed road on the east coast which leads on to Edinburgh. Both of these roads are double carriageway. There are another half a dozen or so roads that also cross over the border, but they are all single track and are completely unsuitable for our panzers. So it is of absolutely vital importance that we capture these roads. If we do not capture and hold onto these roads then the entire invasion will fail. However, we are not concerned with the ways and means that our comrades on the west coast will utilise to capture their targets. Nor are we concerned with the methods that General-Major von Schnakenberg will use to capture Berwick-upon-Tweed. Any questions so far, gentlemen?"

Sturmbannführer Ulrich raised his right hand.

"Yes, Sturmbannführer Ulrich?"

"Forgive me if I have misunderstood, sir, but does this mean that we have to wait for General-Major von Schnakenberg's Brigade to capture Berwick-upon-Tweed before we can carry out our mission?"

There was muffled grumbling from the assembled officers.

"No, Sturmbannführer," Herold replied with a smile.

"No, sir? Then I fail to see how we can capture our targets, sir." Ulrich sat back in his chair with his arms folded in frustration.

"It's simple, Sturmbannführer: we fly in," Herold replied with a smile.

A ripple of excitement ran through the officers like a Mexican wave.

"Gentlemen, gentlemen, if I can have your attention please…" Herold waited until the talking had ceased. "As you already know, the 7th Fliegerdivision were redeployed from England to Greece at the end of April and have since spearheaded the airborne assault on Crete. The battle is carrying on as we speak and the fate of the struggle very much hangs in the balance, although I am sure that German arms will eventually prevail…" There were shouts of "Hear, hear!" from the assembled officers. "The original plan had been to redeploy the paratroopers back to England to take part in the invasion of Scotland but it has now been decided that there simply isn't enough time. As a result, there is not a single paratrooper in the whole of England or Wales."

Herold enjoyed looking out over the furrowed faces in the crowd. He knew that his officers were all thinking the same thing: That's all very interesting, but what's that got to do with us?

164

"However, carrying out an airborne assault behind enemy lines in order to capture vital strategic targets is an absolutely essential component of the plan. The simple problem is that we do not have any airborne forces in England, but the solution is equally simple: we will create them. I am proud to announce that the Triple S brigade is going to become an airborne brigade - henceforth we will be known as the 1st SS Airborne Brigade of the 1st SS Airborne Division. We will capture our targets by glider and by parachutes!"

For a moment there was a delayed reaction from the officers before the news properly sunk in; then to a man they all leapt to their feet and started whooping and hollering, shaking each other's hands, slapping each other on the back, giving each other bear hugs and throwing their hats in the air. The officers knew what the new title would mean: the very word "Airborne" would raise them to another level and would separate them from the run-of-the-mill SS units. The 1st SS Airborne Brigade would from now on be recognised as an elite unit, handpicked and chosen by Reich Marshall Himmler and the Führer themselves to spearhead the invasion of Scotland in a do-or-die mission. None of the officers could envisage anything other than a future full of honour, glory and prestige.

When the excitement had finally died down, another officer raised his hand.

"Yes, Hauptsturmführer von Stein?" Herold said.

"There is one thing that I am unclear about, sir..." von Stein began.

"Yes, what is it?"

"A brigade usually consists of three battalions, sir, but since the 6th SS redeployed to Poland the Brigade only consists of two battalions, the 4th and the 5th SS. We are seriously under strength, sir."

Herold looked at von Stein for a second before he

replied. "That is why I have invited their replacements to join us at this briefing. Gentlemen, I have the pleasure and the privilege to present to you the senior officers of the 1st Spanish Volunteer Legión!"

Von Stein's face suddenly drained of all colour. If he had been standing up his legs would have given way, and he would have collapsed to the ground.

Lieutenant-Colonel Mendoza dramatically pushed open the theatre's double doors and walked down the aisles to the front by the stage. He was followed by his second-in-command, Major Primo Astray, and the four captains commanding Mendoza's four companies. The Spaniards sat in the front row of seats to the left of the aisle.

"Let us welcome our new comrades with our traditional Triple S Brigade hospitality," Herold announced.

Herold's words were met with a stony silence. The stormtrooper officers had all lost comrades as a result of the King Alfred Hotel and Queen Alexandra Road bombings, and although the deaths had been officially blamed on diehard Spanish Republicans and not on Spanish Foreign Legiónaries the thought of working with - never mind fighting alongside - any Spaniards of whatever political creed or colour left a sour taste in the SS officers' mouths. The Germans looked as if they had just discovered a piece of dog shit smeared onto the bottom of their jackboots.

For their part, if looks could kill, all of the Germans would have instantly dropped dead as if they had been cut down with one fell sweep of the Grim Reaper's scythe. The Spaniards all knew about the rape and attempted murder of their commanding officers' daughter, Aurora, and looked forward to exacting divine retribution and holy vengeance on the SS for their despicable and dastardly assault on a their CO's defenceless young daughter. Major Astray had personally written the letter to Herold asking him to pass on the warning to von Stein that he would be held personally responsible if Mendoza so much as cut his chin whilst shaving, and would suffer swift and ruthless punishment as a direct consequence. Astray smiled to himself as he thought how ironic it was that the same Brigadeführer Herold was now welcoming the 1st LVE as fraternal Fascist comrades.

Herold chose to ignore his officer's somewhat less than cordial welcome to the new arrivals. "Now, gentlemen, I am sure that there will be sufficient time and opportunity in the future for us to get to know each other a little better. After all, we are comrades-in-arms now. Let's continue with the briefing…"

"Gentlemen, that concludes the briefing. Thank you for your patience. Colonel Mendoza, if you would be so kind as to leave first…"

"Thank you, Brigadeführer Herold." Mendoza stood up and gave an impeccable parade ground salute.

Herold responded with an outstretched "Heil Hitler!"

As Mendoza and his men stood up to leave, Herold turned around to give instructions to the stage crew to tidy up.

"These stupid Spanish bastards have come here to learn how to fight. I swear that these dirty dagoes wouldn't know how to wipe their own arses if we didn't teach them how to do it first," an SS Hauptsturmführer sitting on the third row said in a stage whisper, loud enough for his comrades sitting on the same row and the Spaniards walking by to hear it. His fellow officers sniggered like naughty schoolboys in agreement.

Mendoza winced as he heard the words, but chose to

ignore it and continued walking.

However, one of his men chose not to. Quick as a flash, Captain Enrique Mazzoli grabbed the stormtrooper by his lapels and hauled him to his feet. Mazzoli drew his bayonet and held it against the German's throat.

"Choose your next words wisely, German. They could well be your last."

Another Spanish officer put his hand on his comrade's shoulder and said matter-of-factly, "I would advise you to do as he says, Adolf. My friend here has killed more Germans then you have had hot dinners…"

"Except they were all Communists. I've never killed a Nazi before, although there's always a first time for everything," Mazzoli said menacingly.

"What the bloody hell is going on here?" Herold roared as he leaped off the stage and rushed to separate Mazzoli and the SS officer.

"The Hauptsturmführer expressed the opinion that us 'stupid Spanish bastards' had come to England to learn how to fight, Brigadeführer Herold." Mendoza explained in fluent German. "My Captain here was merely demonstrating that the Hauptsturmführer was gravely mistaken in his appreciation of our fighting abilities: we 'dirty dagoes,' as your officer so eloquently called us, do not need to be taught how to 'wipe our own arses', nor do we need to be taught how to fight," Mendoza explained drolly.

Herold looked at the hapless and helpless SS officer with such intense fury and anger that the unfortunate stormtrooper visibly shrunk before his eyes.

"I apologise for this insult, Colonel. It won't happen again." Herold bowed and clicked his jack-booted heels.

"Your apology is not necessary, Brigadeführer. However, it is unfortunate that our relations have got

168

off to such an inauspicious start on our first day together," Mendoza replied. "Captain?"

"Yes, sir?" Mazzoli replied.

"Release Big Mouth here."

"Yes, sir." Mazzoli let go off the German, who promptly collapsed to the ground.

"Brigadeführer." Mendoza saluted again.

"Colonel." Herold returned the salute.

Mendoza led his men out of the theatre.

Herold looked with contempt at the heap of humanity lying on the ground.

"Get up, Hauptsturmführer!" Herold hissed. "On your feet! You're an officer in the SS! Act like one!"

"Yes, sir. I'm sorry, sir. It won't happen again, sir."

"You're damn right it won't." Herold took out his Luger pistol, cocked it, flicked off the safety catch, and shot the startled officer right between the eyes. The Hauptsturmführer died with a look of complete and utter bewilderment and incomprehension on his face.

The SS officers remained rooted to the spot like statues, their mouths hanging open in shock and surprise as they watched a rapidly-spreading pool of blood seep out from underneath the dead man's body.

"Nothing and no one is going to be allowed to jeopardise the success of this mission! No-one!" Herold bellowed at the top of his voice as he waved his weapon around.

The stormtroopers were too dazed to reply.

"No one!" Herold repeated. "Do I make myself clear?" Herold haphazardly pointed his pistol at the nearest officer.

"Yes, Brigadeführer," his men answered lamely.

"I can't hear you! Do I make myself clear?" Herold shouted.

"Yes, Brigadeführer!" His officers shouted in unison.

"Good." Herold nodded his head as he flicked on the safety catch, made safe his Luger and holstered the weapon. "I sincerely hope so, gentlemen, because if I hear of anyone else being a big mouth, if I hear of anyone else speaking before they stop to think, I will find you and shoot you myself. Sturmbannführer Ulrich?"

"Yes, sir." Ulrich saluted.

Herold casually returned the salute. "Is this worthless piece of shit one of yours?"

"Yes, sir," Ulrich nodded. "Hauptsturmführer Krauss commanded - sorry, Brigadeführer, used to command - Bravo Company, sir."

"Well, you need a new Company Commander. See that Krauss is sent home with the next shipment of bodies to Germany."

"Cause of death, sir?"

Herold thought for a moment before replying. "The usual reason will suffice, Sturmbannführer: partisan attack."

"Very good, sir." Ulrich saluted and clicked his heels together like a Prussian Drill Sergeant.

"And Sturmbannführer Ulrich?"

"Yes, sir?"

"Arrange for a crate of Whyte and Mackay whiskey to be sent to Colonel Mendoza by way of an apology."

"Very good, sir." Ulrich saluted again.

"Dismissed." As his officers filed out of the theatre, Herold walked over to Krauss's body. He looked at the corpse for a second before he spat on Krauss's face.

"That's the last time that you screw up one of my morning briefings, you stupid loud mouthed bastard."

Chapter Twelve

"But, Papa, I don't understand. How can you fight for the Nazis after all that they have done to us?" Aurora asked her father with tears in her eyes.

"Aurora, I am not fighting for the Germans, I am fighting with them. The Caudillo has ordered me to take part in the invasion of Scotland. I am a professional soldier, Aurora. I have no choice, I have to obey my orders," Mendoza explained gently.

"Why can't you refuse?"

"Because I would be shot, Aurora!" Mendoza reacted with wide eyed horror as if his daughter had asked him to commit suicide.

"Then why can't you resign?" Aurora persisted.

"Resign? Resign, Aurora? What would I do? Work as a baker? Work as a butcher? I am a professional soldier, Aurora. I joined the Army when I was eighteen, I have been fighting my whole life, and I don't know how to do anything else except fight."

"And kill," Aurora accused bluntly.

"Yes, and kill," Mendoza admitted.

"The problem is that you've been fighting and killing the wrong enemy, Papa."

Mendoza bristled and sat up straighter in his chair. "I fight and I kill who ever I've been ordered to, Aurora, whether it's rebellious Moroccans or Spanish Reds, who also are the enemies of Spain..."

"Whoever you have been ordered to kill as the enemies of Spain? The British are not the enemies of Spain, Papa. You are not a robot and you are not a slave. You have a conscience, Papa. You are made of flesh and blood, you have free will, and you are not obliged to follow an illegal and immoral order," Aurora insisted.

"My conscience is clear," Mendoza said stiffly. "I

am a professional soldier and I do not have the freedom of will to pick and choose which orders I decide to follow. I am obliged to follow the legal orders of my superior officer, whether I personally consider those orders to be morally justifiable or not."

"Except this time you have been ordered to fight and kill the British, Papa," Aurora interrupted. "The British are our friends. Two British boys saved my life and they saved your life."

"I know that, Aurora!" Mendoza snapped as he slapped the top of the table in frustration. "Do you think that I don't know that? Every second of every day I think about what happened. The memory of that day is seared onto the surface of my eyeballs. I even see the images when my eyes are shut. Every night I have nightmares and I wake up in a cold sweat with horror at the injuries that those Nazi animals inflicted on you. Every day I light a candle and thank the Blessed Virgin that you ignored my orders not to start going out with Alan!" Mendoza continued angrily.

"Alan and Sam saved our lives, Aurora; they saved the life of my only child. The debt of gratitude which I owe the boys is so massive that it would take me several lifetimes to repay it." Mendoza suddenly stopped talking as if he had run out of energy. He was physically as well as emotionally drained and exhausted and he was breathing heavily. After several seconds Mendoza gathered his thoughts, and sighed wearily before he answered, "Believe me, my sweet, it gives me no pleasure that I have been ordered to fight against the British..."

"Then why are you going to do it, Papa?" Aurora persisted. "I thought that the enemy of my enemy is my friend. Those Nazi animals raped me, Papa, and they were going to kill me, but Alan and Sam stopped them. The Nazis are the boys' enemies; does that not make

172

them our enemies as well? The Nazis murdered Sam's parents, one of his brothers is missing and has probably been killed, and his other two brothers are still fighting the Nazis. Surely, the most effective way for us to start repaying our debt to the two boys is to join them in the fight against the Nazis instead of joining the Nazis in their fight against the boys?"

Mendoza did not answer. There was no way that he could argue against his daughter's logic.

"But the Spanish people will suffer if I switch sides and fight against the Germans, Aurora. The Germans will think that we are filthy turncoats and traitors. At the very least they will cut off food supplies and at the very worst they may decide to invade us after they have finished off the British." Mendoza bit his fist in horror as he contemplated the terrible consequences of any attempt to switch sides. He stared off into the distance as he imagined the sight of hundreds of thousands of German jackboots trampling over the sacred soil of his beloved Fatherland.

"The trouble is that you think too much about the welfare of the Spanish people and not enough about the honour of Spain," Aurora said wearily. "Honour demands that a son of Spain avenges the rape of a daughter of Spain at the hands of the Germans. The Spanish people are made of sterner stuff than you think, Papa: they will understand."

After a few seconds thought and reflection Mendoza gently placed his hand on top of his daughter's hand. "I must... I must think about it, Aurora." Mendoza smiled weakly.

"Very well." Aurora slid her hand out from underneath her father's. "I will leave you to think about it, Papa."

Aurora stood up, straightened her skirt and bowed formally. Mendoza nodded. He was already deep in thought as he seriously considered his options. If Mendoza was not willing to take action to restore his daughter's honour, the honour of the Mendoza family and the honour of Spain, then she would.

Lieutenant-Colonel Nicholas Griffiths VC played with the wax-tipped ends of his bushy moustache as he listened to the briefing continue. He looked across the row of chairs and he was pleased to see that his officers were as rapt with excitement as he was. They were hanging on the Brigadier's every word. Griffiths smiled at his men the way that a father would smile at his children. Yes, he considered the young officers to be his sons. Although they had only been together as a unit for a short time he thought of his men as being part of his family, and not just the officers - the rank and file as well. They were young and (for the most part) fit and healthy, they were as keen as mustard, and literally chafing at the bit to be let loose at the enemy. Yes, there was a definite buzz in the air. Griffiths gripped his swagger stick tighter. He could feel a tingling in his spine and the hair on the back of his neck was standing on edge. He tried to remember the last time that he had felt that way. Griffiths remembered that when he was a schoolboy at St John's he used to feel the same excitement and sense of anticipation before a cross-country run, or before a swimming race, or before a rugby match. He remembered that he used to feel that way when he was a student at St Catherine's College, Cambridge and he was about to take part in a rowing race against their arch-rivals, Oxford. He reminisced fondly as he remembered the day that he had been awarded a Blue in recognition of his achievements and prowess as a rower. Griffiths looked across at his officers again. Some of them were barely old enough to have graduated from varsity and he knew for a fact that some of them had only just done so when this unnecessary war had started. Griffiths shook his head sadly as he thought about how many of his fine young men would not live to see the end of the War. It was all such a damn shame and such a tragic waste of life.

His mind drifted back to the last war where he had started as a young Second Lieutenant in the local regiment, The Royal Regiment of Fens Fusiliers, the RRiFFs. Griffiths had served throughout the war and had survived without a scratch. He puffed out his chest with pride as he looked down at the ribbon medals pinned to the chest of his black Battle Dress. He remembered the day when he had been awarded the Victoria Cross by the King himself when Griffiths was a captain serving on the Western Front. He had risked life and limb to rescue a dozen of his men who had been seriously wounded during the Battle of the Somme and who were lying in No Man's Land bleeding to death. Griffiths could not abandon his men to their fate and had picked each of them up in a fireman's lift, and had carried them back to an Emergency Aid Station one at a time.

A file of faces seemed to cross before his eyes as he remembered his closest comrades in arms:- Mason, Hook, Witherspoon and Ansett. They had all been in the War right from the beginning and they had all survived more all less intact, physically if not emotionally. Griffiths checked himself. Apart from Mason. His good friend Ted Mason had been killed in a German artillery barrage as he tended the wounded in an Army Hospital behind the front lines. Yes, they had had their differences since the War, but they had been political differences of opinion, not personal differences. Their differences had not prevented them from remaining friends, even if relationships had at times become strained. Griffiths shook his head sadly.

Yes, he would have liked to have seen more of his friends but had not been able to since the start of the new War and the recent unpleasantness. Now all of them were dead. They had all been killed since the Invasion. Griffiths shook his head bitterly.

Griffiths remembered the private talk that he had had with the Prime Minister only a month or so before. He had known the PM for years and had previously been in command of his personal bodyguard. The PM had emphasised that it was absolutely essential that his unit put up a good show in the fighting which was to come. Griffiths' unit was an experimental unit and had only been established and armed with great reluctance by the powers that be after relentless pressure from the PM It was vital that his unit gave a good account of itself and proved its worth. If Griffiths was successful, then those in power would agree to the raising of more and more similar units. The floodgates would be well and truly opened and Griffiths might well find himself in command of a brigade, or perhaps even a division. Griffith's eyes clouded over as he daydreamed. Brigadier Griffiths... General Griffiths! Why not? Griffiths chuckled to himself. He had to admit, it did have a certain ring to it.

Griffiths glanced over at his officers again. They were so focused on listening to the briefing that they had not noticed that their Colonel was looking at them. Captain, no sorry, Major Mason, had proven himself in the late unpleasantness in the fighting against the Germans. Griffiths smiled to himself. How ironic it was that he now found himself serving with another Mason, the son of his old friend, Ted Mason, whom he had served with more than twenty-five years ago. Griffiths was sure that his old friend was looking down on them both from heaven with a smile on his lips. As for the other officers, all of them apart from Captain John

176

Baldwin were either ex-military and had served in either the last War or this one, or were veterans from the old Party street-fighting days. Griffiths looked at Baldwin again. He was an unknown commodity and his only 'military experience' had been service for three years in the Cambridge University Officer Training Corps. However, beggars couldn't be choosers and Griffiths realised that in the present climate and under the current conditions he couldn't afford to be too fussy. And anyway, Baldwin was a Cambridge graduate and although he was not a member of Cats and had been a member of an inferior college, Magdalene, Baldwin was still a varsity man.

Griffiths turned his attention back to the briefing and the matter in hand. Operation Thor, the long-awaited-for invasion of Scotland. Griffiths glanced at his officers once more and nodded to himself. Yes, he was confident that the 1st Battalion of the British Union of Fascists Militia would deliver a bloody blow against Churchill and the rest of his Jew-loving Bolshevik war-mongering clique, and they would bring this unhappy and unnecessary civil war to an end once and for all.

"Welcome home, sir," Alan smiled. " It's good to have you back."

"Thank you, Alan," Peter Mason replied. "It's good to be back."

Sam and Alan had waited at the end of the German lesson to welcome their old teacher back to St John's. The boys leaned against their school desks as they spoke to Mason.

"How do you feel, sir?" Sam asked.

"Rather delicate," Mason replied as he tenderly rubbed his chest.

So you bloody well should feel, Sam thought to himself. I shot you twice in the chest at point blank range, you treacherous bastard. It's a bloody miracle that you're still alive.

Mason had been busy rubbing the blackboard whilst the rest of the students had been filing out of the classroom. He had not noticed that Sam had quickly looked up and down the corridor before he had silently closed the classroom door.

"What happened, sir?" Alan asked.

"The doctors told me that I had been shot twice in the chest," Mason replied.

"Where, sir?" Alan asked.

"Here and here." Mason lowered his head and pointed at the two entry wounds with his index finger. As he displayed his war wounds, Alan sat down on a chair. Sam stood up and casually walked over to where Alan was sitting, and stood behind his seated friend. Sam put his right hand behind his back and silently extracted his Luger pistol from where it was concealed behind his trouser waistband. He held the weapon behind his back with his forefinger lying alongside the trigger guard. He reached into his left side blazer pocket with his left hand, and took out a silencer attachment. Sam put his left hand behind his back and expertly screwed the silencer onto the end of the Luger barrel. He coughed loudly as he cocked the weapon and flicked off the safety catch.

"Excuse me, Al. Do you have a tissue?" Sam asked.

"Sorry, Sam. I don't," Alan replied as he looked over his shoulder. Alan now knew that Sam was ready. Alan turned back to face Mason. "Sir, do you know who shot you?"

Mason shook his head. "The last thing that I remember is the bomb going off in the Square," Mason answered grimly. "The next thing I remember is regaining consciousness in Great Ormond Street Hospital in London."

178

"Great Ormond Street Hospital? I thought that Great Ormond Street was a children's hospital, sir?" Alan asked with furrowed brows.

"It was, Alan," Mason confirmed. "It was a children's hospital until the Germans commandeered it for the use of sick and wounded German soldiers."

"So where do sick and wounded British children go to now, sir?" Alan asked.

Mason shrugged his shoulders. "I don't know, Alan."

"Bloody Huns," Sam swore with venom in his voice. "Yet another reason to hate the bastards. Pardon my French, sir."

Mason shook his head. "There's absolutely no need to apologise, Sam. I understand why you hate them. You have more reason to hate them then most, but German surgeons saved my life, Sam," Mason said. "So I'm sure that you'll understand if I don't join you in your condemnation of them."

Sam bit his lip in order to stifle a reply that would be sure to give the game away.

"So you have absolutely no idea who shot you, sir?" Alan asked again.

"No, Alan." Now it was time for Mason to furrow his brows. "Why are you so interested to know?"

Alan shrugged his shoulders. "No particular reason, sir, I'm just interested. It's not every day that you meet someone who has escaped certain death."

Mason smiled. Boys will be boys, he thought to himself with amusement. They would always be interested in death and destruction and blood and gore. "I don't know who shot me, but the doctors did say an interesting thing."

"What's that, sir?" Sam asked as a bead of sweat ran down his temple.

"I was shot at point blank range, which means that

179

the shooters were within a few yards from me and yet I made no attempt to draw my revolver. The doctors think that I must have known the attackers and, more than that, I must have trusted the attackers."

"And yet you have no idea who these attackers might have been?" Alan asked.

Mason smiled. "Alan, I have been a teacher at St John's for ten years and I live in the town. Hereward is my home. I know a lot of people in Hereward and I have a lot of friends here. The shooters might have been regulars in my local pub; they could be present or ex-pupils; they could even have been Specials. Who knows? You boys could have shot me for all I know. God knows, I've given you just cause to do so after all of these years of teaching you French and German."

The colour drained from Sam's face, and he started to raise his pistol.

Mason suddenly burst out laughing.

"What... what is it, sir?" Alan asked with a nervous smile on his face.

"I'm only joking, boys!" Mason was laughing so hard that tears were streaming down his face. "Of course I don't think that you boys shot me! But the look on your faces! Sam, you look as if you've seen a ghost!"

Sam laughed weakly. "When... when I saw you here today, sir, for a moment I did think that I'd seen a ghost. The last time that I heard anything about you was that you were in intensive care with a serious chest wound."

"Yet here I am." Mason stretched out his arms with a smile.

"Yet here you are, sir," Alan said.

"Like Lazarus back from the dead."

The boys did not reply. Sam silently flicked on the safety catch. He coughed loudly as he uncocked his

180

pistol. Sam swore under his breath.

"Are you all right, Sam?" Mason asked with concern.

"Sudden twinge in my back, sir," Sam explained as he rubbed it. "Old war wound. Do you mind if I sit down?"

"No, of course not, Sam. Please do."

As Sam sat down he quickly placed the Luger behind his back beneath his trouser waistband.

"Talking of war wounds," Mason started, "what happened to you two on the day of the St George's Day Massacre?"

"We had to shoot our way out, sir." Alan replied matter of factly. "After the bomb explosion and the assassination of the King and Queen everyone went crazy, sir. The SS started shooting at us, and we and the Police returned fire."

"So the SS started it?" Mason asked.

"Of course, sir!" Alan replied, "You're not suggesting that we started the shoot out? That would be like signing our own death warrant! As it was, the Army turned up and prevented us from wiping out the SS. The Army gave us no quarter and killed all of the Police and the Specials."

"So how did you boys escape?"

Alan shrugged his shoulders. "We had to fight our way out, sir." Alan shook his head as he remembered the horrific scenes of chaos and carnage. "It was absolutely terrible, sir. There were men and women and children screaming and running all over the place trying to escape, and we were shooting at the Huns and they were shooting at us. There was blood and bodies everywhere, sir."

"Don't worry, sir. We didn't kill any people; only Germans," Sam explained matter of factly.

"I see," Mason nodded his head grimly. "You boys

seem to have a knack of getting into and getting out of trouble."

"As do you, sir." Alan smiled.

"You know what they say, boys…"

"What's that, sir?"

"The devil looks after his own."

Alan stood up. "Thank you for your time, sir. It was good to talk to you and it's good to have you back, sir."

Sam repeated his friend's sentiments and the boys started walking towards the door.

"And boys?"

"Yes, sir?"

"If I do suddenly remember who shot me, you can rest assured that you two will be the first to know."

"What happened in there, Sam?" Alan asked as they walked down the street. "You looked flustered."

"That's because I was flustered." Sam stopped walking and grabbed his friend's forearm. "Listen, Al: I dropped a bullet on the floor of Mason's classroom."

"You did what?" Alan's eyes bulged wide open with horror.

"It happened when I was uncocking my Luger. I had my hands behind my back, and I couldn't see what I was doing. I tried to catch the round as it ejected but my hands were slippery, and I couldn't hold the bullet and I dropped it on the floor," Sam explained with a staccato-style delivery.

"Bloody hell!" Alan said. He looked up and down the street to check if anyone was close enough to listen to their conversation. "Did you try and look for it?"

"Of course I did! I'm not a complete idiot!" Sam was exasperated. "That's why I sat down, but I couldn't see it. The round must've rolled under a cupboard or something. I couldn't see it anywhere."

"Then I hope to God Mason hasn't seen it yet,

because if he's found it we will soon be in a world of hurt," Alan was thinking aloud.

"All the more reason to kill the treacherous bastard now," Sam said grimly.

"Not yet, Sam." Alan put his hand on his friend's forearm. "Mason might be useful."

"Useful? Useful for what? " Sam guffawed. "Useful to whom?" Sam continued angrily "The only people who that dirty traitor has been useful to are the Germans. I say that we go back to his classroom now, kill him, and get the whole thing over and done with. We can't afford to run the risk of him remembering that it was me that shot him one month ago."

"I think that we should ask Edinburgh what they want us to do. If they order us to kill him then we'll do what they say without any delay, but if they order us to leave him alone for the time being as a possible source of information then we follow our orders. Agreed?"

Sam nodded his head reluctantly. "Agreed. But as soon as we get even the slightest hint or the merest suspicion that he has recovered his memory, we kill him immediately. Agreed?"

"Agreed," Alan replied. "But first things first: we need to find the lost bullet."

"When?"

"Tonight."

Chapter Thirteen

"Bloody hell, Al!" Sam swore angrily. "This is a complete waste of time. I can't see a bloody thing."

"Keep searching, Sam. It's bound to be here somewhere," Alan urged.

The two boys continued searching on their hands and knees for the missing bullet. They each gripped a small torch in their teeth as they looked for the lost round in the pitch black classroom.

After a few more minutes Sam stopped crawling and took the torch out of his mouth. "It's no use, Al. We'll never find it. I told you that this was a stupid idea."

"Stupid idea?" Alan said. "You were the stupid idiot who dropped it in the first place. I don't remember you coming up with any cunning plans!" Alan hissed angrily.

"I suggested that we should wait until the morning..."

"And do what?" Alan interrupted. "We don't have German tomorrow so we can't look for the bullet during a lesson. What possible reason could we give to Mason to come back here and search his classroom? You dropped a pen or pencil that must have rolled underneath a cupboard? He would never believe that we would come back to the class room to search for something so small and insignificant."

"So what shall we do?" Sam said. "We're not going to find the missing round scrambling around the class room floor in the dark."

Alan shrugged his shoulders. "I guess that we'll just have to hope that Mason hasn't found it...."

"But if he has then we'll be up shit creek without a paddle. One word to his Gestapo friends and they'll be pulling out our fingernails before we can say blueberry pie."

184

Alan nodded his head grimly. "Then we have no alternative. If we can't find the evidence then we will have to destroy the evidence."

"What do you have in mind?"

After Alan told him, Sam smiled like a werewolf flashing his fangs.

Mason poked through the burnt remains of his classroom with a stick. The Nissan hut that had housed two German language classrooms and a languages resources store cupboard had been completely burnt to the ground. All that remained were the twisted metal frameworks of the wooden desks.

Alan and Sam stood at the edge of the ruins. "What happened, sir?" Alan asked.

"Ten years of work and resources up in smoke. Completely ruined...completely wasted..." Mason seemed to be mumbling to himself in a trance. When he turned to answer Alan's question, he looked as if he was about to announce a death in the family. "Arson, faulty wiring, someone throwing a still glowing cigarette stub into the litter bin; the Fire Brigade aren't sure of the cause yet, and perhaps never will be."

"Damned bad luck, sir." Sam shrugged his shoulders with his hands buried deep in his pockets.

"Is it bad luck though?" Mason asked rhetorically. "It seems too much of a coincidence that on the very day that I return to work my class room burns down. If you notice, none of the other classrooms have burnt down." Mason gestured towards the other Nissan huts. They had been temporarily erected when the Germans had commandeered the use of some of the school buildings in order to transform part of St John's into Hitler's official residence in Britain.

"With all due respect, sir. I think that you're being paranoid. Why would anyone want to destroy your life's work? You're a well liked and respected teacher at St John's, sir," Alan said reassuringly.

Mason smiled. "That's very kind of you, Alan, it really is, but many people have a reason to dislike me or even hate me. Many people will not forgive or forget the fact that I was an inspector in the Specials."

"But we were in the Specials as well, sir, and we did our duty before that in the Home Guard. No one has attempted to attack us. No one can accuse you of not having done your duty, sir," Alan maintained.

"And anyway, sir, our remit in the Specials was to help the Police. Our role was strictly to do with civil affairs, not political affairs. We were never ordered to fight against the Resistance and if we were I'm confident that most, if not all of us would have resigned, sir," Sam said.

"Oh, the innocence of youth. What I would give to be young again and look at life through rose tinted spectacles." Mason chuckled. "You don't consider guarding Kaiser Eddie and the Wicked Witch of the West to be a political job, Sam? I'm afraid that you're being rather naïve." Mason smiled.

Sam shrugged his shoulders nonchalantly. "That may be so, sir; but anyway, the Specials have been disbanded, so it's all water under the bridge now," Sam said as he crossed his arms.

Mason sighed wearily as he surveyed the wreckage of his classroom. Charred pieces of paper were scattered across the school grounds as far as the eye could see.

"What we've got to do is to get this country back on its feet again. Stability is what we need." Mason punched his right fist into the palm of his left hand as he spoke. "It is absolutely essential that we strengthen the forces of Law and Order so that we can prevent further acts of wanton vandalism and anarchy from occurring in the future. The surest way to do that is get the Germans out of the country…"

"I second that!" Alan echoed enthusiastically.

"Hear! Hear, sir!" Sam clapped. Maybe Mason had decided to return to the light side of the struggle?

" …And the most effective way to do that is to deal once and fall with Churchill and his mob of war-mongering gangsters - and to that end I've joined the Fascist Militia…"

"You've done what?" Alan reacted as if he'd been slapped in the face.

"Join the bloody Fascists? Joyce's stool pigeons? Now people really will think that you're a traitor!" Sam shook his head in disbelief at Mason's barefaced and blatant treachery.

Mason held up his hands to mollify the boys. "Now, Sam, Alan, I know what you're thinking, but I've given this a lot of thought and I honestly think that the best way to get the Germans out of our country is to end this disastrous civil war one way or another. Prime Minister Joyce will extend the rule of the Government of National Unity throughout the whole country, and once the Germans are convinced of our sincere commitment to the New Order they will leave…"

"And you call me naïve!" Sam's eyes were blazing with fury. "The only way to 'get the Huns to leave' is to physically kick them out of the country! You should be joining up with the partisans not joining up with the Fascists!"

Mason hurriedly looked over both of his shoulders to see if anyone was listening. "Be quiet, Sam!" Mason warned. "Such talk of treason will get you shot!"

"Treason?" Sam spat the word out in disbelief. "Treason against whom? I'm not committing treason, you are!"

Mason opened his mouth to answer. After a

moment's hesitation he put his right hand into his pocket and pulled out a small see through plastic packet. The boys were too far away to see what it was.

"Do you know what this is, boys?" Mason asked.

The colour suddenly drained from the boys' faces as they recognised the object. "A... a bullet, sir?" Alan answered gingerly.

Mason nodded. "Well observed, Alan. And do you know what kind of bullet it is... Sam?"

Sam looked like a rabbit that had been caught in the headlamps of a speeding car. "A bullet from a... from a gun, sir?" He could hardly trust himself to think, never mind speak.

"Sherlock Holmes, eat your heart out! Come on, Sam. You can do better than that!" Mason was enjoying the game, playing with the boys as a cat plays with a mouse.

"A .303 round, sir?" Sam answered.

Mason shook his head. "No, not a British .303 round, Sam. A German 9 millimetre round."

A bead of sweat ran down Sam's temple. Alan's mouth had suddenly become as dry as a dead man's armpit.

"The first question is: where did I find it?"

The boys didn't answer.

"I was marking some exercise books and I dropped my pen." Mason explained. "I dropped my pen and when I looked underneath my desk it had disappeared. You know how precious a commodity good pens are in the present situation and I was damned if I was going to lose it, so I got down on my hands and knees in order to look for it. I noticed that the floor of the classroom is not completely flat and the floor has a slope. My pen had rolled under a nearby cupboard, and when I found it I also found this live round." Mason took the bullet out of the plastic packet and carefully held it using only his thumb and forefinger to hold the bottom and top of the round respectively.

The boys looked at the bullet as if they had never seen one before.

"The second question is: who does it belong to?" Mason waved the round in front of the boys' faces.

"It probably belongs to one of the boys in one of your German classes, sir," Alan answered. "A lot of the lads collect military equipment…"

"You know, sir, boys will be boys." Sam laughed uneasily. "The bullet has probably been there for weeks, if not months, sir."

Mason shook his head. "Oh, I don't think so, Sam. There was no dust on the round, and in fact the round was covered in a thin film of lubricating oil. If the bullet had been under the cupboard for weeks it would have been absolutely coated in dust. Oh no, I don't think that the round had been down there for months, or even weeks. I know that we can't get good help these days, but I'm sure that even our cleaners would've spotted it. No, I think that the bullet has been there a mere matter of days. In fact, the round may have rolled under the cupboard yesterday during your lesson, for all I know." Mason smiled like an assassin as he looked at both of the boys in turn.

Mason paused before he spoke again. "The third question is: how did this 'military equipment enthusiast' acquire a live German round? The Germans don't exactly hand them out on request. Correct me if I'm wrong, but I'm pretty certain that the penalty for being found with live German ammunition is death." Mason paused to let the weight of his words sink in, before he continued. "What did this War junkie have to do in order to obtain this live round?" Mason waved the bullet around again mere inches away from the boys' noses. It was so close that they could smell the oil on the round's casing.

The boys could not think of a rational explanation that would not arouse suspicion.

"You'll notice how carefully I'm holding the bullet: I daresay that it would be reasonably simple to lift a fingerprint from the casing. I am sure that my colleagues in the Gestapo would be all too happy to oblige a request from a fellow Fascist to investigate a possible lead to the Resistance. All they would have to do is to fingerprint all of the students who regularly use this classroom. Then Bob's your uncle, Fanny's your aunt. I'm sure that a short visit to Gestapo headquarters would soon loosen the tongue of even the most reluctant suspect, what do you boys think?"

Sam and Alan looked as if they were about to faint.

Mason carefully put the bullet back into the plastic packet and put it back into his tweed jacket pocket. He gave the bulge a couple of pats and looked at the boys once more. "Of course it doesn't have to come to that, does it, boys?"

None of the boys answered.

"I mean I may be a traitor," he looked directly at Sam, "but I'm not a complete bastard. I mean they are my students, after all. I don't want to see one of my boys hauled before the Gestapo and subjected to their rather medieval interrogation techniques any more than you do. I mean, for one thing, can you imagine the letters of complaint that we would get from the parents? What ever happened to little Johnny's fingernails? Why can't he write any more? Why can't he walk anymore? Why can't he talk anymore?" Mason looked at the boys before he continued. "It would be a public relations disaster for the school, which would be sure to adversely affect our admission numbers. In the present financial situation we've got to pay close attention to our marketing, don't we? After all, I don't want to bite the hand that feeds me, so for the sake of the school I'm willing to forget about the mysterious bullet... for now."

The boys could not help breathe a massive sigh of relief. Mason had them both over a barrel, and both he and the boys knew it.

"On one condition," Mason continued menacingly.

Mason gave both of the boys a piece of A4 sized paper.

"What's... what's this, sir?" Alan asked.

Sam recoiled in horror. "It's a bloody application form to join the Fascist Militia!" Sam shook the piece of paper in front of Mason's face. "If you think for one moment that you can blackmail me into...!"

Alan snatched the piece of paper out of Sam's hand. "The two application forms will be on your desk first thing tomorrow morning, sir."

"Hey, give that back!" Sam protested as he futilely tried to grab the application form from Alan.

Alan had to physically drag Sam kicking and screaming away from their teacher.

"They'd better be, Alan," Mason warned. "I'd hate to be the bearer of bad news. I don't want to have to write to your parents in Hong Kong in order to tell them that their son and heir had been arrested by the Gestapo."

"I'll kill him, I'll kill, him!" Sam punched his hand in frustration as tears rolled down his face.

"Yes, Sam." Alan put his hand on his friend's shoulder. "We both will. But first of all we have to get authorisation from Edinburgh. Agreed?"

"Yes, and then we kill him," Sam nodded his head as he wiped the tears away from his face with the back of his hand. "When?"

"After Edinburgh gives us the green light.

191

Tomorrow."

"I don't believe it. Edinburgh must be out of their minds." Sam made no attempt to disguise his disgust and he dropped the piece of paper on the floor as if it was cursed.

Alan bent down to pick it up. He carefully read the message and then he read it again to make sure that he hadn't made any errors. "I don't believe it," he said as he shook his head in horror. "This must be a mistake."

"I'm afraid that there's no mistake, Alan. I've checked the message twice," Alice said with her finger hovering above the Morse code key. "Do you want me to send a reply?"

"Not yet please, Alice," Alan replied. "I want to take some time to think about our response."

"Well, I'll tell you one thing for free, I'm not bloody well doing it! They can take their bloody orders and shove it where the sun don't shine!" Sam said stubbornly with his arms folded in frustration and anger. "Mason is a dead man and that's the end of it! And as for joining the Militia, I'd rather die a thousand deaths than join that viper's nest of traitors!"

Alan read the message again:

DO NOT KILL MORGANA STOP JOIN THE MILITIA STOP GATHER INTELLIGENCE STOP NAMES OF RECRUITS AND DATE OF INVASION STOP SABOTAGE FROM WITHIN STOP ACKNOWLEDGE STOP

Alan shook his head in disbelief at the order. "They must be mad. It must be all of that whiskey that they've been drinking up in Scotland. It must have gone to their heads and scrambled their brains. What the hell are we going to do?"

192

"It's simple, Al: we kill Mason and we don't join the bloody Militia," Sam answered.

Alan shook his head. "Believe me that I'd like nothing better than to put a bullet into that dirty traitor's rotten and twisted heart, but we can't disobey direct orders, Sam. We can't go off the reservation. Edinburgh can't afford to let us go rogue on a oneway do-it-yourself vigilante mission."

"What would they do about it, Al - kill us?" Sam guffawed.

Alice nodded her head. "You may well laugh, Sam, but it wouldn't surprise me. Edinburgh ordered the execution of Kaiser Eddie and Simpson without any hesitation, the King's own brother and his own sister-in-law; what makes you think that they would not order the execution of a couple of disobedient school boys?" Alice asked grimly. "After all, we may not be the only Active Service Unit in Hereward. Remember the Hereward Hospital fire? You boys said that the fire wasn't your handiwork."

"It wasn't us, sis," Sam maintained.

"It's all right, I believe you," Alice laughed.

"So what do we do now?" Alan asked.

"You boys go off and play with your guns. I'll think of something," Alice answered.

"Sam's not going to join your Fascists, sir." Alan announced the following day.

"What? I don't believe it!" Mason bared his teeth in anger. "The nerve of the boy! Has he forgotten about our deal?" He took the plastic packet out of his pocket and dangled the bullet in front of Alan's face.

Alan shrugged his shoulders, which only seemed to make Mason even madder. "Sam doesn't care, sir. You've got to remember that the Nazis murdered both his father and his mother. The SS hung them both from the Town Hall balcony."

"I know that, Alan, but doesn't he realise that he doesn't have a choice?"

"We all have a choice, sir, whatever we do," Alan maintained resolutely. "The Nazis murdered his parents and they would turn in their graves if Sam joined your Fascists. He absolutely refuses to work for the Nazis, sir."

Mason sighed wearily. "They are not 'my Fascists,' Alan. I am not a Fascist and I have never considered myself to be a Fascist. I simply think that the BUF at this moment in time represents the best chance of restoring law and order to our damaged and destroyed country. Can Sam not see that?" Mason shook his head with frustration. "This is the only way that we can bring peace to our country. Sam would not be working for the Germans; he would merely be working with the Germans."

Alan shrugged his shoulders dismissively. "You say tomato, Sam says tomato, sir."

"Can he not see that the only way to bring this civil war to an end is for one side to beat the other?"

Alan nodded. "Yes, sir, he does; but Sam thinks that you've joined the wrong side, sir. The side of the traitors instead of the patriots."

"So it's like that, is it?" Mason said angrily. "It's that simple, eh? You're either a traitor or a patriot. And what does that make you, Alan?"

Alan shrugged his shoulders with disconcerting nonchalance. "I'm neither, sir. I'm a pragmatist. I was on the losing side at Fairfax and I can't say that I enjoyed it. Being massacred was not a particularly pleasurable experience either, and I don't care to repeat it. I don't want to be on the losing side again."

"So you don't think Churchill can win the War?" Mason asked with a twinkle in his eyes. At last, progress.

Alan's eyebrows rose up at the temerity of the question. "I don't see how he can, sir. Not with the whole of Europe stacked against him. Spanish Fascist volunteers and Italian troops have already arrived to take part in the invasion of Scotland. I wouldn't be surprised if French Fascist volunteers are also on the way. They'll all want a piece of the pie when Hitler carves up our Empire."

Mason shook his head. " That's where you're wrong, Sam: the Führer has promised the Prime Minister that if British troops take part in the invasion of Scotland then he will guarantee that no British territory will be handed over to any other countries…"

"Apart from former German territories…" Alan interrupted.

"Well, yes, of course," Mason coughed into his hand. "It seems only fair and reasonable that former German colonies stolen from her at the end of the First World War should be restored to her. Even Lloyd George, in retrospect, thought that the terms of the Treaty of Versailles were too harsh towards Germany."

"So Germany won't touch the British Empire apart from former German territory, sir?"

"Scout's honour, Alan," Mason promised.

Alan thought for a moment before answering. "Well, if it's good enough for you, then it's good enough for me, sir." Alan flashed his most charming schoolboy smile.

"Glad to have you on board." Mason smiled. "Has Sam considered the consequences of his decision?"

Alan laughed. "That's strange, sir, because Sam asked me to ask you the very same question."

Chapter Fourteen

"Section at fifty yards, to your front, rapid FIRE!"

There was a sudden salvo of shots that shredded the targets.

After about forty-five seconds there was a shouted chorus of "Magazine!" as the marksmen ran out of rounds and changed their magazines.

Leon checked his watch and after another fifteen or so seconds he shouted, "Cease fire! Apply safety catches! Make safe!" There was a sound of bolts being drawn back as the marksmen ejected any spare rounds, which they caught in their hands. The three assistants standing behind the marksmen knelt down and examined the rifle chambers that were all now empty of rounds. Each of the assistants raised their right hands and shouted, "Clear!"

Leon nodded his head. "Excellent! Stand up! Examine the targets!"

The three marksmen leapt to their feet, placed their rifles on the ground, and started to walk towards their targets.

"When the Kaiser's Army first encountered the British Expeditionary Force in Belgium, they were horrified to discover that the BEF was armed with hundreds of machine guns. They came to that conclusion because the BEF mowed the Huns down by the hundred and by the thousands. Except that the Huns were wrong: the BEF was not armed with hundreds of machine guns, they were armed with tens of thousands of these." Leon held up a rifle, "A .303 Lee Enfield rifle, the standard issue rifle of the British Army. The reason why the Huns thought that we were armed with hundreds of machine guns was because our marksmanship was so accurate and because the British soldier is trained to fire fifteen rounds per minute. We

196

fired so accurately and so fast that the Huns thought that we were armed with machine guns, but we weren't, we were armed with the humble rifle." Leon puffed out his chest with pride. "I know because I was there."

The marksmen and their assistants had stopped walking in order to listen to Leon's story.

"And that's why we're here, Mr Leon," Anne Mair said. "So that you can teach us how to kill Huns as quickly as possible by the hundred and by the thousand."

"That's my girl, Anne." Leon smiled. "And God willing, we will."

Leon examined each of the targets in turn. He and his two sons had built three scarecrows, which were all now dressed as German soldiers. Leon, Bob and Russ had chosen the most rough and ragged sets of uniform that they could salvage from the collection of clothes that they had stripped from the bodies of the dead Germans that they had killed in the previous six weeks. The boys had even managed to find a few dented helmets, which had definitely seen better days. However, the helmets did complete the look and when they were placed on top of the heads at a rakish angle they did give the scarecrows an extra degree of authenticity and a certain je ne sais quoi.

Leon nodded his head in admiration. "Not bad, not bad at all. Actually quite good." He looked at Anne. "A three inch group at fifty yards. Where did you learn to shoot?"

Anne's face beamed with pride. "On my uncle's farm, Mr Leon, in Frampton before the... before the..." Anne's eyes welled up with tears.

Leon put a fatherly arm around her shoulders and gave her a hug. "It's all right, Anne, it's all right. It's good to cry, let it all out."

"I'm all right, Mr Leon." Anne wiped her eyes with

the back of her hand. "I'm all right. Really I am. It's just that sometimes I feel so weak and helpless. I really want to hurt those Nazi bastards!" Anne punched a fist into the palm of her hand.

"I promise you, Anne, as God is my witness, that we will pay those murdering Nazi bastards back for all of the pain and suffering that they have inflicted on you and on all of our people."

Anne nodded in agreement as Bob Leon walked over to comfort her.

Leon examined the next target with awe and wonder. "Now this, now this is really astounding!" Leon's eyes bulged in amazement. "A two inch group at fifty yards. Where did you learn to shoot, Aurora?"

Aurora Mendoza smiled like a cat that had got the cream. "On my grandfather's estate, Mr Leon, before the Civil War."

"Well, this is really very impressive." Leon fingered the bullet holes in the scarecrow's uniform again. "Well, done, keep it up."

Leon walked over to the third target. He smiled to himself and chuckled. "Alice, I take it that you did not have the chance to practise either on your uncle's farm or on your grandfather's estate?"

"Mr Leon, has no one ever told you that sarcasm is the lowest form of wit?" Alice asked.

Leon laughed again and shook his head in amusement. "Several times, Alice. I'm afraid that we're going to have to work on your marksmanship." Leon looked at the target again. There were only five bullet holes and they were scattered randomly all over the scarecrow from his helmet to his jackboots.

"Practise makes perfect," Alice said.

"That's the spirit, Alice! Now, let's move on to practising with the Schmessier submachine gun..."

"Father!" Russ Leon burst into the shed which

served as a makeshift shooting range. "There's a German patrol coming! They must've heard the shots!"

"Strength?" Leon asked as made his rifle ready, ramming his bolt forward and forcing a round into the chamber.

"One patrol car with a lorry, father," Russ replied.

"Christ!" Leon swore. "There may be as many as a full platoon…"

"Or as few as a squad," Alan interrupted.

"Let's hope that it's the latter, then!" Leon said grimly. "You know the drill, people! To your positions!"

Leon hurriedly walked over to his son and put his hand on his shoulder. "Now Russ, it is absolutely vital that you lure them all into the shed at the same time. Because if they split up and search the farm separately then there's absolutely no chance that we'll be able to kill them all. We have to kill them all at once or else they'll hunt us down like dogs."

"How will I manage to lure them all into the shed?" Russ asked anxiously.

Leon's eyes lit up as he found a sudden source of inspiration. "This is how…"

Obersturmführer Monat stepped out of the car as his driver applied the hand brake. A young man wearing mud and dirt-stained dungarees stood in front of him. Monat's lips curled up in distaste and his nostrils flared instinctively as the smell of pig shit hit him like a tidal wave. He hurriedly extracted a handkerchief from his pocket and held it to his nose to disguise the noxious aroma. He realised with revulsion that the young farmer's filthy dungarees were probably encrusted with pig shit as well.

"Good morning, Obersturmführer. What can I do for you, sir?" The young man asked cheerily as he wiped his dirty hands on his dung stained dungarees. He watched a sergeant and driver get out of the patrol car and stand behind the officer.

Monat was pleasantly surprised to discover that the young man spoke surprisingly good schoolboy German. It just proved that appearances could be deceptive. "Just a routine patrol, young man." Monat smiled as he answered. "And your name is…?"

"Leon, Obersturmführer. Russell Leon, sir," Russ answered as the soldiers piled out of the back of the lorry.

"Not the Leon of 'Leon's Organic Pig Farm?'" Monat asked with raised eyebrows.

"The very same, sir," Russ answered. He watched a squad of ten SS stormtroopers assemble in two ranks behind their officer.

Monat was amused to see that the young man had puffed out his chest with pride as he answered. "And you are Leon?"

"No, sir." Russ laughed. "That's my father, Obersturmführer." Thirteen Nazis in total.

"And where is your father, Russell?"

"Call me 'Russ,' sir." Russ smiled. "All of my friends do."

"All right… Russ. Where is your father?"

"He's somewhere on the farm, sir. He's probably in the shed." Russ pointed over his shoulder. Seven inside the shed, plus me. Eight in total.

Monat turned around to look at his assembled men. "Scharführer Blucher, where the bloody hell is Scharführer von Clausewitz? I thought that he was right behind us."

Blucher turned around and looked back up the road which led out of the farm. He turned back to face Monat and shrugged his shoulders. "Von Clausewitz was right behind us, sir. Maybe his lorry had a flat tyre.

I'm sure that he'll catch up with us very soon."

Russ's German wasn't fluent enough to understand everything that Monat had said to Blucher.

"Oh well, we'll just have to make do without him. I'm sure that we have enough men to search this farm for hidden caches of Resistance weapons." Monat turned around to face the young farmer. "We're going to search the farm, Russ. Just a routine search. Nothing to worry about. We'll be gone before you know it." Monat turned and barked an order over his shoulder.

Russ's eyes suddenly lit up with inspiration. "Sir, would you like a personal tour? Would you like to find out where the pies come from? Would you like to see the pigs?"

Not really, Monat thought to himself.

"I'm sure that my father would be able to offer mate's rates, sir." Russ snapped to a position of attention. "I would like to offer you and your men pork pies at cost price, sir."

"That's very kind of you, Russ," Monat smiled.

"It would be a pleasure and a privilege, sir." Russ bowed.

"All right." Monat barked another order over his shoulder at his men.

Russ smiled as he saw the stormtroopers sling their rifles over their shoulders. They weren't expecting any trouble.

"Lay on, MacDuff." Monat gestured towards the shed with his hand.

"You're a fan of Shakespeare, I see, sir," Russ said as he led the way.

Monat laughed. "Schoolboy English lessons. And I see that you've had some military training?" Monat asked casually.

Russ laughed. "Hardly, sir. Officer's Training Corps at St John's, sir…"

201

"And Home Guard as well, no doubt?" Monat asked rhetorically.

"Every male around here with a pulse has served in the Home Guard, sir."

"Fair enough." Monat shrugged his shoulders nonchalantly. Never the less, it was still worth filing away that particular piece of news for future reference. You could never tell when tit bits of information could come in useful. "And you must tell me, Russ, what is the secret of your exceedingly good pork pies?"

Russ put his filthy fore finger to his lips. "Trade secret, sir. I could tell you but then I'd have to kill you."

Monat laughed.

"Here we are, sir. The shed." Russ opened the door for Monat. "After you, sir. My father will be inside."

"Thank you, Russ." Monat turned around to face his soldiers. "I hope that you've brought your wallets, men. Scharführer von Clausewitz and his men will be green with envy when we return home with the pies."

Monat's men cheered and started to extract their wallets from their battle dress trouser pockets. They thanked Russ and followed their officer into the shed.

Scharführer von Clausewitz was at that very moment effing and jeffing and cursing to high heaven. His lorry had indeed suffered a punctured tyre as Blucher had predicted. However, when the driver had fetched the spare tyre he had discovered that the 'spare' also had a puncture. The lorry must have suffered a punctured tyre in the past and when the puncture had been replaced with the spare tyre the punctured tyre had not been replaced with a new one. Von Clausewitz cursed the powers that be again. They had decided that, rather than having a designated lorry for each unit, patrols had to make do with whichever one was available. What that meant was that the unit that used the lorry did not care what condition they left it in when they returned it, as long as the lorry was in a satisfactory state when they themselves used it. An abdication of responsibility.

Von Clausewitz looked at his wristwatch. He knew exactly where he was as he had driven down this road many times in the past; he was about a kilometre and a half from the farm or a fifteen minutes' walk. He knew that he had to get to Obersturmführer Monat as quickly as possible because if he did not then it might jeopardise the success of the mission. Von Clausewitz also knew that Monat would also probably tear strips off him for not having checked that the lorry had had a spare tyre. He was not looking forward to that.

"Come on, lads!" Von Clausewitz shouted over his shoulder. "This isn't a Sunday school outing! Put your back into it!"

He was answered with a dramatic chorus of groans.

"It's rather dark and gloomy in here, Russ. I can't see your father. Where did you say that he is?" Monat asked.

Russ followed the last soldier into the shed and closed the door. "He's probably at the far end, sir."

Monat started walking.

"Obersturmführer, do you still want to know what the secret ingredient in our pies is?"

"Yes," Monat answered as a sudden tingling began at the back of his spine.

"You!" Russ suddenly dropped to the ground.

"Open fire!" a voice ordered.

Three MG42 machine guns opened fire at point-blank range and caught the Germans in a cross fire. The bullets scythed into the bunched up stormtroopers and cut them down like sheaves of corn. The Nazis died with a look of utter shock and surprise on their faces. None of them even had a chance to unsling their weapons, never mind cock them and return fire. Most of them were still holding their open wallets when they died. Torn and tattered banknotes were scattered all over the bloody shed floor.

"Cease fire!" Leon bellowed. "Sam and Alan, take care of any wounded."

Sam flashed a wolflike grin and climbed over the hay bale wall that ran down the entire length of the shed. The wall was two bales high and two bales thick and had proved to be a crude, but effective, bulletproof barrier. The wall had also helped to prevent some of the sound of the shooting from escaping from the shed. Not enough of the sound, apparently. What other reasonable explanation could there be for the sudden arrival of the German patrol? An identical hay bale wall also ran down the length of the other parallel wall and a six hay bale high, three hay bale thick bullet proof barrier stretched across the width of the shed at the far end.

Alan covered Sam with his finger resting on the trigger of his Schmessier. Sam slung his submachine gun onto his shoulder and put his right hand behind his back and took out his Luger pistol from underneath his trouser waistband. He quickly cocked the weapon and flicked off the safety catch. Whenever Sam spotted any sign of life he fired a single bullet into the wounded Nazi's head, administering the coup de grace. He was very much aware that Leon wanted to salvage as many items of German uniform as possible in case they needed to disguise themselves as Nazi soldiers in the near future. Leon did not want blood, bones and brains ruining his precious uniforms. Sam was also very expeditious with his use of ammunition as they needed to save their ammunition for future missions, so he used a single shot Luger pistol to finish off the Germans, rather than the Schmessier which fired on automatic only.

"Clear!" Sam shouted when he was certain that every single Nazi stormtrooper was well and truly as dead as a dodo.

"All right, folks. You know the drill. Collect any weapons, ammunition and any equipment that we can use and store then in the Armoury with the rest of the gear. Strip the Huns and collect any uniforms that aren't too badly ripped or blood-soaked and dump them in the kitchen. We'll wash them later. Throw any uniforms that we can't use into the boiler furnace." Leon ordered. "Oh yes, remember to collect the identification tags."

"Mr Leon, what do you use the Hun's identification tags for?" Aurora asked.

"Forgive me, Aurora." Leon put his hand to his head. "I forgot that you're new to this game. I haven't thought it through yet, but I was thinking about possible psychological warfare."

"Psychological warfare?" Aurora asked with raised eyebrows.

"Yes, Aurora. We have the Hun's identification tags and their pay books that contain their home addresses. I thought about posting their pay books back to their mothers with their identification tags and their teeth enclosed."

"Their... their teeth?" Aurora asked.

"Yes, Aurora. The pigs shit them out after they've eaten the dead Huns. How else do you think that I keep my pigs supplied with a constant source of food?" Leon answered as if it was the most natural thing in the world.

Aurora's eyes bulged wide with horror. "Monstrous...!"

Leon shrugged his shoulders nonchalantly "Pigs have got to eat."

Anne was violently sick.

"A spot of fresh air perhaps, son?" Leon suggested.

Russ nodded his head, walked over to Anne, and guided her out of the shed's front door, holding her by the elbow.

"At last," von Clausewitz said to himself. "The farm." He started to walk down the road that led towards the farm house. Von Clausewitz looked over his shoulder. "Jesus Christ, lads! We're in the countryside on an Anti-Partisan search and destroy mission, not out for a Sunday stroll down Hereward High Street! So take your thumbs out of your arses, take your weapons off your shoulders and carry them in the ready position!" Von Clausewitz demonstrated by pulling the butt of his Schmessier machine gun tightly into his shoulder. He carried the submachine gun with one finger resting on the trigger guard, with his thumb ready to flick off the safety catch at a split second's notice. "This is hostile territory, lads! You're professional German soldiers, not Boy Scouts-act like it!" Von Clausewitz's eyes were red with rage at his men's casual attitude. They had become soft after seven months garrison duty in Hereward. The sooner that they invaded, Scotland the better.

Von Clausewitz used hand signals to order the squad to divide into their usual two fire teams. Charlie fire team walked in single file down the left hand side of the road, and Delta fire team mirrored them by walking down the right hand side of the road in single file.

Russ led Anne over to a large tractor tire. "Sit down, Anne, lower your head and put it between your legs. Now take nice, slow, steady breaths."

Anne followed Russ's instructions. Russ handed her a handkerchief, which she accepted gratefully. She wiped her mouth with it but was violently sick again. Russ just managed to grab her hair in time and hold her ponytail out of the way of the projectile vomit. Anne wiped her mouth for the second time.

"Was it like this the first time for you as well?" Anne asked.

"The 'first time?'" Russ asked in confusion.

"When you killed someone."

"Oh." Russ was silent for a moment before he answered. "The first time that I killed someone was at the Battle of Wake. Not a proper person, you understand, only a Hun. But yes, I was also violently sick, as was Bob. I killed some more Huns at Fairfax, but I wasn't sick afterwards. Bob and I were too busy trying to escape. Like Sam and Alan, we were some of the lucky few that managed to escape the massacre that occurred the next day. Since then I've killed so many Huns that I hardly give it any thought at all." Russ shrugged his shoulders. "It gets easier after the first one. Now I don't give it any more thought then I would to killing a rat. It got easier for me and it will get easier for you. I guarantee it."

"I... I hope so, Russ," Anne said. "Because I don't know if I could do that again. But really, Russ, feeding dead Huns to the pigs; is that strictly necessary?"

Russ put his hands on Anne's shoulders. "Listen, Anne. Those Nazi bastards killed your father and your mother, your uncle and your auntie, your cousin and her baby boy. They murdered your entire family. They got what was coming to them."

Anna nodded in agreement.

"And anyway," Russ continued, "after we've killed the Huns we do have a practical problem: what do we do with all of the bodies and the uniforms and equipment that we can't use? We have neither the time, the energy nor the inclination to bury the dead Huns. The solution is also extremely practical. We feed them all to the pigs; they will eat absolutely anything and everything, including bodies, uniforms and equipment, and leave no trace."

"Except for teeth."

"Except for teeth. For some reason the pig's digestive system can't cope with them and they shit them out."

Anne laughed.

Russ smiled. He was glad to see that Anne was beginning to recover her sense of humour.

"Russ, just do me one small favour?" Anne asked.

"Yes, Anne, what is it? Anything."

"Promise never to offer me any pork products from your farm?"

Russ stood to attention and gave the Scout salute as he solemnly gave his word. "I promise."

"Cross your heart and hope to die?" Anne stood up.

"Cross my heart and hope to die," Russ said.

Von Clausewitz spotted the "Mumford and Sons" lorry that had transported Blucher's squad to the farm, and also the captured British Army staff car which served as Monat's patrol car. Von Clausewitz's own lorry had also previously belonged to the same furniture removal company. Von Clausewitz shook his head with amusement as he imagined the ridiculous sight of the mighty German army being driven up north to take part in the invasion of Scotland, transported on furniture removal lorries. He was sure that the Scots would be absolutely quaking in their boots with fear (or laughter?) at the sight. His only consolation was that the Scots would probably be even worse equipped than the invaders were.

Von Clausewitz paused for a moment, with a puzzled expression on his face. He felt a familiar tingling in the pit of his stomach. Some thing was not quite right. Von Clausewitz used hand signals to order his men to halt, take cover, and take up a position of all round defence. His stormtroopers automatically lay down on the sunken road, with the last two men in both fire teams turning around to face the rear. The other soldiers faced to the left and right of the road like the legs of a giant centipede. They pulled their weapons tightly into their shoulders and carefully scanned their fields of fire with their fingers on the trigger and their thumbs on their safety catches.

Von Clausewitz's second in command walked up to him. "Trouble, Scharführer?" Rottenführer Schindler asked with raised eyebrows.

Von Clausewitz nodded. "Perhaps, Otto. I can see two people at the entrance to the shed, but no sign of the Obersturmführer and the rest of the patrol. Where are they?"

Schindler shrugged his shoulders. "The Obersturmführer and Scharführer Blucher are no doubt searching the buildings as we speak. They probably ordered the civilians to wait outside. Standard procedure."

"Maybe," von Clausewitz answered grimly. "But something's not right: I can feel it in my bones."

"Shall we watch and wait for five minutes, Scharführer?" Schindler suggested.

Von Clausewitz nodded. "Good idea, Otto. We'll wait for five minutes and see if any of our men come into view. But in the meantime, order the men to make ready for action: forward on my command."

"Yes, Scharführer," Schindler replied with a jackal's grin on his face. He was looking forward to seeing some action at last, even if it was only mopping up

209

partisans.

Von Clausewitz raised his binoculars to his eyes.

"Look, Russ: Aurora and Alan." Anne pointed. "Do you two lovebirds need a hand?"

Aurora and Alan both stopped pushing their loot-laden wheelbarrows in order to answer. In truth, they were glad of any excuse to stop working for a moment. Pushing wheelbarrows that were piled high with booty across a treacherous and slippery pig shit covered cobble stoned farm courtyard was hard work.

"I will treat that comment with the contempt that it deserves. If I wasn't so knackered I would retaliate with something suitably witty and cutting," Alan replied haughtily. "Luckily for you, I'm on my last legs; my arms feel as if they're going to fall off and I don't have the energy to reply."

Von Clausewitz watched the scene develop two hundred metres away. The rest of his squad were safe from view and safe from fire lying down in the sunken road.

"Two more civilians, Otto. A man and a woman." Von Clausewitz said in a low voice. "Correction: two girls and two boys in total. Where are the parents?"

"Probably with Obersturmführer Monat and Scharführer Blucher. It might be all perfectly innocent, Scharführer."

Von Clausewitz lowered his binoculars to speak to Schindler. "You might be right, Otto. I hope so. But there's still no sign of the patrol."

Chapter Fifteen

"Well, for what it's worth, I think that the two of you are doing a marvellous job." Russ said. "I don't think that these two star-crossed lovers need a hand, Anne. I'm sure that after they've loaded up the washing machine they'll find some excuse to disappear upstairs in order to have some quality time. I think you know what I'm talking about."

Anne laughed.

"And I am sure that your intentions towards Anne are as pure as the driven snow, Russ," Aurora said sarcastically.

"Touché!" Russ replied, but he could not help blushing with embarrassment.

"Everyone knows that your mind is as filthy as the pigs which you raise, Russ!" Aurora grabbed the nearest object that she could reach and hurled it at full force at Russ's head. "I just hope for Anne's sake that your body is not as filthy as your mind!"

Russ laughed and ducked his head.

"I hope that you insist that he has a shower when he takes off those dirty dungarees, Anne!" Aurora advised.

"Don't worry, Aurora; I will!" Anne replied with a mischievous wink.

Von Clausewitz's face drained of colour, and he dropped his binoculars onto his chest where they dangled around his neck. He turned to face Schindler.

"What is it, Karl? You look as if you've seen a ghost," Schindler said with concern.

Von Clausewitz nodded his head slowly. "I have, Otto; Monat and his men are dead. The girl threw a jackboot at her friends. A German Army jackboot."

Schindler stiffened to a position of attention. "What are your orders, Scharführer?"

Von Clausewitz snapped out of his momentary stupor and pulled himself together. He turned around to face his stormtroopers, the professional soldier once more. "Squad, listen in: the rest of the patrol are dead. partisans have killed them. There are four partisans two hundred yards to our front in front of a shed. Charlie fire team will cross over the fence onto the field on the left hand side of the road, and Delta fire team will cross over the fence on the right hand side of the road. Shake out into extended line. We will carry out a frontal assault on the shed with this road as our axis of advance. We need prisoners in order to find out what happened to our men. Don't fire until we're fired upon and only at my command. Advance at the double. Understood?"

"Understood," his men chorused.

"All right, let's go." Von Clausewitz nodded grimly. "Sieg Heil!"

Russ's brows furrowed in confusion.

"What is it?" Anne asked as she placed a hand on his arm.

"Both of the fences are shaking," Russ replied. "Look." He pointed at the two fences that ran parallel on either side of the road that led out of the farm.

"Pigs?" Anne asked.

Russ shook his head. "No! Germans! Take cover!"

At that precise moment a burst of machine gun fire cut Russ and Anne down where they stood.

Aurora stood rooted to the spot in horror with her hand to her mouth, oblivious to the rounds that ricocheted off the cobblestones at her feet. A thin stream of urine ran down her leg and formed a rapidly expanding pool on the cobblestones."Aurora! Come on!" Alan shouted as he grabbed her by the arm and pulled her into the farmhouse.

"But... Anne... Russ..." Aurora protested as Alan slammed the front door shut.

"They're both dead, Aurora, and we will be as well if we don't start fighting back. Quickly, grab a gun and start shooting."

"But from where, Alan?" Aurora asked as another volley of rounds slammed into the wall of the shed. "The weapons are in the shed."

"Christ, you're right," Alan replied. "Well, we better think of something quick, because we've got about thirty seconds until those Nazis reach us!"

Von Clausewitz led his men at the double towards the shed, with his Schmessier pulled tightly into his shoulder and with his finger resting on the trigger guard. "Otto, take Delta fire team and assault the farm house. Half your men through the front door and the other half through the back. I'll assault the shed with Charlie fire team."

"Yes, Scharführer!" Schindler replied. "You heard the Scharführer! Delta, follow me!" Schindler fired a burst of bullets at the farmhouse as his stormtroopers followed him at a run.

"We're under attack!" Leon shouted. "Quickly, Alice, break out the weapons! Sam and Bob, barricade the main door!" he ordered.

Sam and Bob both ran towards the front of the shed, making sure that they didn't run directly behind the shed door. Although the walls of the shed were made of concrete blocks the door was only made of corrugated iron, and was rapidly beginning to resemble the surface of a cheese grater. The rounds punched through the door as if it was made of paper.

"Sam! Start building a barricade made out of bales of hay! They'll act as a bulletproof barrier. When Dad returns with the weapons we'll kick the door open, return fire, and give the Huns a nasty shock!" Bob shouted.

"Quick thinking, Batman!" Sam replied. The boys swiftly built a barrier two hay bales thick and two hay bales high directly behind the door.

Schindler's fire team quickly reached the farmhouse. "Brandt, Polanski and me will go through the front; Schmitt and Mueller will go through the back, understood?"

"Yes, Corporal!" his men chorused.

"Let's go!" Schindler kicked open the front door, fired a short, sharp burst of rounds into the room, and backed out. Brandt swiftly threw a grenade into the room. "Grenade!" They waited for the grenade to explode before they charged straight in.

Alan fired one cartridge into Schindler's chest at point-blank range and another cartridge into Brandt's chest. Both men collapsed onto the floor of the kitchen. Polanski rapidly retreated out of the front door.

"Whatever you're going to do, do it quick, Aurora. They won't fall for the same trick twice," Alan said urgently as he reloaded Leon's shotgun with another two cartridges.

"How much time have we got?" Aurora asked.

"About five minutes."

Aurora picked up the phone and dialled desperately, "Please answer the phone…"

"Ready?" Leon asked.

"Yes, Dad," Bob answered as he held the MG 42 machine gun in a tight grip. Sam knelt beside him, tenderly cradling the belt of machine gun bullets in his hands.

As Leon pushed open the door, Bob squeezed the

trigger and swept the courtyard with a spray of rounds. Sam smiled as he saw a stormtrooper standing by the front door to the farmhouse fall to the ground and lie in a crumpled heap. Polanski was dead before he hit the ground.

A burst of rounds flew over the boys' heads and made Sam and Bob duck. A grenade sailed through the air and landed behind the boys. Leon picked it up and threw it out of the door. The grenade exploded in the courtyard, sending up a shower of shrapnel, pig shit and broken cobblestones. Another grenade swiftly followed the first, and Leon repeated the action.

"We're in a tight spot..." Bob said.

"Shut up and keep firing!" Leon shouted.

A stormtrooper stepped out from behind the lorry in the courtyard and threw a grenade. The grenade cart wheeled through the air and bounced off the front of the shed wall and exploded in the courtyard. Another stormtrooper stepped out to throw another grenade, but Bob cut him down with a brief burst of bullets. The German fell backwards and dropped the grenade, which exploded behind the lorry.

Sam smiled as he heard the cries of at least two men screaming out in pain and agony. "Good shooting, Bob!"

"Verdamnt!" Von Clausewitz swore furiously. This was not going according to plan. Four of his stormtroopers were already killed or wounded and he was rapidly running out of men, as well as ideas. Von Clausewitz punched his fist into the palm of his hand with frustration. He needed to try another strategy before his squad became combat ineffective.

The grenade blast stunned Aurora and knocked her off her feet onto the floor. If she had not been kneeling behind the sofa, she would've been ripped to shreds by the explosion. Two stormtroopers leapt into the living room and sprayed a burst of bullets into all four corners of the room. One of the stormtroopers spotted a body lying on the floor. He kicked the body in the leg and was rewarded with a groan of pain. The German spotted the shotgun lying beside the wounded Partisan and kicked it across the floor out of reach. The stormtrooper walked through to the kitchen and spotted the bodies of two of his comrades, Otto Schindler and Reinhardt Polanski.

"Partisan bastard," Schmitt snarled as his eyes clouded over with a thin mist of crimson fury. He stomped back through to the living room, kicked the Partisan with as much force as he could in the stomach, and raised his rifle to his shoulder.

"Eric!" the second soldier barked. "Remember what the Scharführer said: we need prisoners."

Schmitt slowly lowered the rifle as if he was awakening from a trance. "You lucky bastard." Schmitt kicked the prisoner again and the Partisan groaned painfully and curled up even tighter into a foetal position. He spat on the prisoner's face before he turned around to face Mueller.

Mueller's face suddenly lit up with undisguised delight. "Hello, hello, hello, what have we here?"

Schmitt smiled like a crocodile as Mueller dragged another prisoner to her feet. "Who said that every cloud has a silver lining, again?"

"How's Alice?" Sam asked desperately over his shoulder.

"She's all right, Sam," Leon answered calmly. "She got shot in the shoulder and I'm applying a field dressing."

"I'm... I'm all right, Sam, but I feel rather

woozy..." Alice slurred her words as she spoke.

"Alice, you've lost a lot of blood." Leon explained. "I'm going to carry you over to the side and lie you down against the wall of the shed, all right?"

"It... it hurts like hell." Alice winced between words.

Leon nodded. "I know that it does, Alice. But I saw enough shoulder wounds like this in the last war. It hurts like hell, but it's not serious. You're going to live, I promise you."

Alice smiled weakly and then promptly passed out. Leon tenderly picked her up and carefully carried her over to the side where he gently lay her down against the wall.

"Sam, she's going to be all right," Leon said confidently.

Sam nodded his head grimly.

"How much ammunition do we have left?" Bob asked between firing a burst of bullets.

"We've got one ammunition box of belted ammunition left, Bob," Sam answered.

"Well, that's not going to last forever," Bob said as he squeezed off another burst.

"Conserve your ammunition, son, and only fire at targets of opportunity. If the Huns start throwing grenades into the shed two at a time then we're done for," Leon said grimly. "I won't be able to throw them all out in time."

"So what's the plan, Dad?" Bob asked.

"I don't know, son. I'm still thinking," Leon admitted.

"Well, you'd better think faster because we're running out of options as well as ammunition," Sam said. "Hello, what's this?"

"A white flag." Leon answered. "Cease fire. The Huns want to talk."

Leon's face drained of colour as he watched two dirty and dishevelled figures shuffle out from behind the lorry with their hands held high in the air. He put his hand to his mouth in horror. "Aurora and Alan..." he said aloud.

"Partisans!" Von Clausewitz shouted. "Come out with your hands up or I will shoot your comrades! You have one minute to decide!"

Sam looked at Leon with wide bulging eyes. "What shall we do? We can't let them kill Alan and Aurora! We have to surrender! We have no choice!"

"We do have a choice, Sam! If we go out there, the Huns will kill us!" Bob argued.

Leon looked at both of the boys in turn. He knew that they were both right. He shook his head in resignation. "We're damned if we do, and damned if we don't..."

"Thirty seconds left, Englanders, and then I will execute the prisoners!"

Leon looked out into the courtyard and saw Aurora and Alan. His heart skipped a beat and a cold wave of panic swept over him. Where were Russ and Anne? He had presumed that they were with Aurora and Alan. If they were wounded, then he would have to tend to them as quickly as possible.

"It's over, lads; put down your weapons and step outside slowly with your hands in the air," Leon said with resignation.

"But, Dad...!" Bob protested.

"But nothing, Bob!" Leon said with fire in his eyes. "It's over! Your brother and Anne are missing! We must find them!" Leon snarled angrily.

Bob bowed his head in shame. He had completely

218

forgotten about his brother.

Leon held his hands up in the air and carefully climbed over the makeshift hay bale barricade. He was closely followed by his son and Sam.

Leon eyes bulged wide with a sudden cry of horror. "My son! My son!" He ran over to Russ and knelt beside him. He tried to staunch his son's wounds but there were too many bullet holes. Russ's eyes stared glassily into the distance. His life's blood had bled out of him a long time ago. Leon cradled his son's head in his lap, stroked his hair and cried rivers of tears. His entire body was wracked with grief and he sobbed unreservedly. Bob collapsed beside his father and tenderly held one of Russ's hands. Leon wrapped an arm around his sole surviving son and squeezed him tightly.

Sam walked over to Anne and knelt down beside her. She lay on her back, spreadeagled like a giant star fish. A line of bullet holes ran diagonally up her body from her left hip to her right shoulder. Sam gently put his fingertips on Anne's eyelids and tenderly closed her eyes.

Aurora and Alan stumbled over to their friends and sank down beside the bodies of their comrades. Tears ran freely down their blood and dirt encrusted faces.

"This is all very touching," von Clausewitz said as he walked up to the grieving partisans. "But what I want to know is: where is Obersturmführer Monat and the rest of the patrol?"

Leon stared up at him as if he was speaking a foreign language. If looks could kill, von Clausewitz would have dropped dead on the spot. Von Clausewitz was entirely nonplussed; the partisan was not the first man to have stared at him with such a look of pure hatred. He was not the first and von Clausewitz had no doubt that he would not be the last. They usually looked at him like that right before he shot them between the eyes.

"Your son?" Von Clausewitz pointed at Russ's body with his chin.

Leon could not trust himself to speak, but gave the barest of nods.

Von Clausewitz drew out his Luger pistol, cocked it, flicked off the safety catch and pointed it at Bob's head. "I'm sure that you think that losing one son in a day is quite enough. Where are Obersturmführer Monat and the rest of the patrol? I'm not a patient man, partisan. Don't force me to ask the same question again, or else you and your son will regret it."

The surviving members of von Clausewitz's squad had gathered around the prisoners. They were interested to discover how the drama would resolve itself.

Von Clausewitz looked up as a patrol car led a convoy of three lorries that trundled down the road leading to the farm. The stormtroopers all turned to watch as the vehicles came to a halt in the courtyard. Four men got out of the patrol car and started walking towards the stormtroopers. The three lorries also came to a halt, and a squad of fully armed soldiers leapt out of each vehicle. The platoon quickly formed up in the courtyard behind their officers and started to follow them towards the Germans. Von Clausewitz's brows furrowed in confusion. The new arrivals wore standard issue German Army field grey uniforms and were armed with German weapons, but... there was something not quite right. They looked too dark, for starters. The soldiers had not become that tanned under an English sun. Von Clausewitz started to get a familiar tingling feeling in the pit of his stomach.

"Reinforcements?" Von Clausewitz asked hopefully.

The officer in command shook his head. "Not really."

Von Clausewitz's face drained rapidly of colour as he spotted the shield on the side of the officer's helmet. Red, yellow, red, horizontal stripes - Spanish.

Oh shit.

"What do you want to do with him?" Lieutenant-Colonel Mendoza pointed his Schmessier machine gun at the prisoner.

Von Clausewitz was staring at the bodies of his men. His three surviving stormtroopers had been lined up against the wall of the shed and shot without ceremony.

"The Scharführer wanted to find out what happened to the rest of his patrol," Leon answered. "I'm going to show him."

Despite the fact that Mendoza had issued strict orders to his Legiónaries to keep what they had seen and done that day to themselves, word had spread throughout the Bandera like wildfire. The SS had attacked Lieutenant - Colonel Mendoza's daughter, Aurora, and although she had escaped injury the Nazis had in the process killed two of her friends. As a direct consequence the Legiónaries issued a fatwa against Hauptsturmführer von Stein in particular, and against the SS in general, as they had promised in their earlier ultimatum. As far as the Spaniards were concerned, all stormtroopers were now fair game. The Legiónaries were determined to extract their pound of flesh.

"The Spanish have declared war on the SS, General-Major," Hauptwachtmeister Bratge announced.

"Casualties?" Von Schnakenberg asked.

"Three stormtroopers were found dead this morning,

sir," Bratge answered.

"And you're sure that it was the Spanish who killed them and not the Resistance?"

"They were each found with a chorizo sausage stuffed in their mouths, sir. I'm no Sherlock Holmes, sir, but I think that the evidence is pretty conclusive."

Von Schnakenberg chuckled and shook his head with amusement. "Who said that the Spanish don't have a sense of humour?"

"Your orders, sir?" Bratge asked.

Von Schnakenberg steepled his fingers and thought for moment before he answered. "Double our Military Police patrols, but issue strict instructions that the patrols are not to interfere in any fracas between the Spaniards and the SS unless the lives of our own men or civilians are at risk. Clear?"

"Crystal clear, sir."

"The SS cooked up this mess; let them stew in their own juices."

"Let us remember before God,

    and commend to his sure keeping:

Anne Alexandra Mair and Russell Jonathan Leon who died for their country in this war;

And also those whom we knew, and those whose memory we treasure;

And all those who have lived and died in the service of our country.

They shall grow not old as we that are left grow old: age shall not weary them, nor the years condemn. At the going down of the sun and in the morning we will remember them." The Vicar read out the Act of Remembrance solemnly.

"We will remember them." The mourners repeated.

A schoolmate of Russell's played the Last Post on his bugle.

Russell Jonathan Leon was buried with full military honours on June 8th 1941. He was fifteen years old. Russ was laid to rest beside his mother's grave. Katherine Victoria Leon had been killed during the German attack on Hereward in September 1940. Anne Alexandra Mair was seventeen years old and she was laid to rest beside the graves of her mother and her father, her uncle and her auntie, her cousin, and her cousin's baby boy.

Chapter Sixteen

"What is the current casualty figure, Sturmbannführer Ulrich?" Brigadeführer Herold asked.

"Five dead, sir," Ulrich answered grimly.

"And Spanish casualties?"

"I don't know, sir," Ulrich shook his head as he answered. "The Spanish have commandeered a whole wing of a floor of Hereward Hospital, sir. The wing is heavily guarded around the clock by at least a platoon of Legiónaries and the only people allowed access are Spaniards or British medical personnel. I think that it's safe to assume that the Spaniards have suffered casualties of some sort or another. I very much doubt that our boys went meekly to their deaths; I'm confident that they put up a fight."

"Apparently they didn't put up enough of a fight, or else they wouldn't be six feet under. The whole situation is absolutely preposterous and totally unacceptable!" Herold thundered. "Who the hell do the Spanish think they are? This is a German town!" Herold's chest was heaving with rage. He looked as if he was about to burst a blood vessel. Herold slowly calmed down and sat back in his chair. "What is von Schnakenberg doing about this situation?"

"Nothing, sir," Ulrich answered bluntly.

"Nothing?"

"Nothing, sir," Ulrich answered. "Whenever any Army Military Police patrols see any trouble between our boys and the Spanish they make a swift exit, stage left. I think that General-Major von Schnakenberg has given the MPs strict instructions not to intervene."

"He's given them strict instructions not to go to the aid of fellow Germans?" Herold's eyes bulged wide in horrified disbelief.

"I don't think that the General-Major sees it quite in

224

those terms, Brigadeführer."

"What do you mean?"

Ulrich hesitated before he answered. "With all due respect, sir, you weren't here when Brigadeführer Schuster was in charge. A state of virtual civil war existed between us on the one hand and the Army and the paras on the other hand. More Germans were killed by each other than by the partisans," Ulrich explained matter-of-factly.

"The enemy of my enemy is my friend..." Herold stared off into the distance.

"Yes, sir."

"Well, if von Schnakenberg considers the Spaniards to be his friends and the SS to be his enemies, then we are well and truly screwed."

"What do you mean, sir?" Ulrich's brows furrowed with confusion.

Herold sighed. "By this time next week, Mendoza's men will not be the only Spaniards in Hereward. Franco has despatched the 1st Division of the Spanish Volunteer Legión to England to take part in the invasion of Scotland, and the entire Division will be based in Hereward."

Ulrich's face drained rapidly of colour until he was as white as a sheet. "Mein Gott...!" he said, with horror.

Herold nodded his head slowly. "You look exactly how I felt when I heard the news," Herold said grimly. "There will be eighteen thousand Legiónaries based in Hereward for approximately ten days before the invasion begins. How long do you think it will take for Mendoza's men to fill in the new boys with the current state of German-Spanish relations?"

"My God!" Ulrich exclaimed with his hand to his mouth. "There will be a massacre... there may well not be enough of us left alive to take part in the invasion of

Scotland..."

"My thoughts exactly, Ulrich." Herold nodded his head. "There are scarcely two thousand SS in the whole of Hereward. We don't stand a chance unless we even the odds a bit more."

"How do you intend to do that, sir?" Ulrich asked with the desperation of a drowning man gasping for air.

"We must bring the Army over to our side. Von Schnakenberg has about two thousand men in Hereward. The combined strength of four thousand Germans might be enough to convince the Spanish that it would not be a wise decision to declare an all out war against us. It would simply cost them too many casualties," Herold explained. "We must convince von Schnakenberg that the Spaniards, and not us, are the true enemy."

"But sir, General-Major von Schnakenberg has issued strict instructions that his MPs are not to intervene unless the Spaniards start to attack..." Ulrich was thinking faster than he could speak.

Herold said nothing. He waited for Ulrich's wheels of thought to stop turning around.

"Sir, you're not suggesting...?" Ulrich began to ask.

"I'm not suggesting what, Sturmbannführer?" Herold asked with a knowing smile.

"You're not suggesting... you're not suggesting that we carry out attacks on the Army and pin the blame on the Spanish?"

Herold shrugged his shoulders nonchalantly. "Why not? It's been tried before. We faked an attack on German border posts by Polish troops at the beginning of the War..."

"Except no one believed us, sir!" Ulrich interrupted. "The whole world knew that it was faked! If we try this stunt against the Army they will see through us and we will be in a world of hurt! Von Schnakenberg is not a fool, sir! We will be jumping from the frying pan into the fire, and we'll end up having to fight the Army as well as the Spanish!" Ulrich protested vehemently. "You will have to get someone else to do it, Brigadeführer, because I won't do it; I will not murder fellow German soldiers!"

"Are you refusing to obey a direct order from a superior officer?" Herold asked with raised eyebrows.

"Is this what this is, sir?" Ulrich asked. "Are you giving me a direct order to kill fellow German soldiers? Is that the order you want me to give to my men? Because if you are, then yes, I refuse. You'll have to get someone else to do your dirty work for you, sir, because I won't do it. You can demote me, you can send me back home in disgrace, you can even shoot me, I don't care; but I won't murder innocent German soldiers in order to carry out your Machiavellian plan, sir."

Herold stared at Ulrich as if he was looking at a mythical creature for the first time; a unicorn or a Minotaur, perhaps. Ulrich was literally dripping with sweat. Herold nodded with awe and amazement. At last he had found a man with a quality that was as rare as it was admirable: integrity. Herold smiled with newfound respect for Ulrich. Yes, he was convinced that Ulrich would sacrifice his life rather than sacrifice his honour and murder fellow German soldiers.

"At ease, Sturmbannführer." Herold chuckled with amusement. "I didn't give you a direct order; I was merely speaking my mind, testing the water, playing devil's advocate, if you will."

Ulrich's shoulders literally slumped with relief. He looked as if he was ready to collapse into a dishevelled and exhausted heap at any moment.

"I guess that we'll just have to think of a new plan to get the Spaniards off our backs…" Herold said.

"And by the way, Ulrich, I have some more good news…"

"Who else knows about the Führer's visit, sir?" Oberleutnant Nicky Alfonin asked.

"It would be more accurate to ask 'who doesn't know,' Nicky," General-Major von Schnakenberg answered. " The British, the Spanish, the SS and ourselves have been asked to provide one platoon each when the Führer inspects the Guard of Honour in Hereward Town Square on June 15th at three o' clock in the afternoon. Nicky, you will command our platoon Honour Guard."

Alfonin bowed graciously. "Thank you, sir, but Hereward Town Square?" Alfonin asked in disbelief. "Haven't they learned anything from the last time that they tried to hold a parade in Hereward Town Square? Have the deaths of the King and Queen slipped their minds? It's hardly the best omen…"

Von Schnakenberg shrugged his shoulders. "I did warn them, Nicky, but they just shrugged it off. They insisted that this time it would be different."

"How, sir?"

"This time the Führer's personal bodyguard will be ultimately responsible for his safety whilst the Führer is visiting Britain. His personal SS praetorian guards are flying over from Berlin to the Luftwaffe base at Duxford with him. They will supplement the local SS forces that will provide security in each of the places that the Führer visits - Hereward, Ely, Cambridge, Oxford, Bath and so on. Local SS forces will also provide security between the different venues that the Führer will visit. "

"So the entire operation will be an SS under taking from start to finish, sir?" Alfonin asked. "The Army will not be responsible for anything?"

Von Schnakenberg nodded his head. "That's right, Nicky. Brigadeführer Herold is to provide security whilst the Führer is in Hereward, which of course includes during the parade in the Square. Our orders are simply to provide an Honour Guard."

Alfonin gave a massive sigh of relief. "Well, I can't say that I'm sorry that we haven't been given the dubious honour of being responsible for providing security, sir. Security surrounding the visit will have more holes in it than a chunk of Swiss cheese." Alfonin said grimly. "I mean the British Fascist Militia is sure to be riddled with Free North spies, and the Spanish Legiónaries hate us as well. Edinburgh probably knows about the Führer's visit already. They're no doubt assembling an assassination team as we speak."

Von Schnakenberg nodded his head. "I would be if I was the British. Imagine if we discovered that we had a realistic chance to bump off Churchill? I did try to warn the powers that be that the British would send a hit squad to assassinate the Führer but they ignored my advice." He shrugged his shoulders nonchalantly. "As far as I'm concerned, I did my duty and honour has been served. From now on I will follow the example of Pontius Pilate and wash my hands off the whole sorry situation."

Brigadier Daylesford smiled in triumph like a man who had just won the lottery. "We have the complete Order of Battle of both Herold's Triple S Brigade and von Schnakenberg's Brigade. Dates, times, targets, everything."

"Are we sure that the information is reliable, sir?" Peter Ansett asked with raised eyebrows.

"As sure as we can be, Major." Ansett had been promoted to Major to give him a position of power and influence within the Special Operations Executive.

"The information has been verified by three separate independent sources."

"Excellent, sir. The question is whether or not this information will give us enough time to devise a defensive strategy to disrupt and destroy the German Invasion Plan."

Daylesford nodded. "Of course, that's the six million pound question. However, I'm certain that General Montgomery will be up to the job. After all, the Prime Minister has every confidence in his abilities."

"I wish that I shared your confidence, sir," Ansett said grimly. "It's just that all of our generals who have come up against the 'German Fox' have come a cropper."

Daylesford nodded his head. "I agree that Erwin Rommel is a formidable adversary, Major; but remember that Monty was the only one of our generals who was able to give the Jerries a bloody nose when they thrust through France, and it was that bloody nose which made the Jerries hesitate and their temporary loss of confidence allowed us to get most of our boys out at Dunkirk. If anyone can stop the Jerries, Monty can."

"Yes, sir."

Daylesford bared his teeth like a wolf. "And Pete, not only do we know the entire German plan for the invasion of Scotland on the east coast, we also know that Hitler will be paying a visit to Hereward and he will be travelling around England and Wales for a whole week before the invasion begins."

Ansett's eyes bulged wide with shock and surprise at the news. "Hitler's coming to Britain? When does he arrive?"

"The day after tomorrow."

"Jesus Christ! That doesn't give us much time,"

Ansett exclaimed.

"I know." Daylesford nodded his head. "The question is: can we get a team together in time to mount an operation?"

"We can't rely on Percy's unit?"

Daylesford shook his head. "No. They've taken heavy casualties recently and Percy has assured me that they are in no fit state to pull off a job of this size and significance by themselves. They need help. Can we give it to them?"

Ansett thought for a moment before he answered. "I've got two people in mind that would be perfect for the job."

Daylesford smiled, and put his hand on Ansett's shoulder. "Excellent, Pete. I knew that you wouldn't let me down. I want to brief them today; they leave tomorrow."

The three parachutes floated gently through the sky and came to rest within sight of the Drop Zone.

"Alice and Bob, put out the fires," Leon ordered. "Sam, you greet the nearest parachutist. Alan, you greet the furthest away parachutist. I'll collect the canister. Let's go!"

Alice and Bob doused the flames that the Reception Committee had set to signal the SOE plane carrying the parachutists. Sam and Alan hurried away with mounting excitement to meet the new arrivals.

Sam thought about the last time that they had met visitors from the Free North. They had welcomed Napoleon and his commandos to England less than two months ago, and every single one of them had been killed during their abortive attack on the convoy carrying Kaiser Eddie and the Wicked Witch to Hereward. Sam shook his head with sorrow as he thought of the tragic waste of life. He tried in vain to remember Napoleon's face, but he failed dismally. Sam shrugged his shoulders as he physically shook those feelings free. The important thing was that they had got the job done and the Resistance had accomplished the mission. Sam smiled as he remembered the look on the Puppet King's face as he had executed him. He wouldn't have traded that for all the tea in China. Napoleon and his commandos had not died in vain.

"Welcome to England, comrade." Sam shook the visitor's hand.

"Comrade?" The visitor's voice was raised in surprise. "Are you a Communist Resistance Group?"

Sam bristled at the tone of the question. "Does it matter?"

"No, of course not."

"Good." Sam nodded his head in the darkness. "Let's meet the others."

Every one quickly gathered around the dying embers of the bonfire.

"Welcome to England, gentlemen," Leon said warmly. "Follow me to the farm."

Leon led the way back to the farm in the pitch darkness. After a half an hour walk, they finally arrived at the farmhouse. "Bob, take first sentry duty," Leon ordered.

"Yes, Dad," Bob answered. He tucked his rifle into his shoulder, opened the door and walked outside, where he took up his sentry position facing up the road.

"You are not Communists?" Sam's visitor asked.

Leon looked at the visitor as if he had asked Leon if he wore ladies' underwear. "Does this look like a Collective Farm to you?" Leon chuckled "No, we're not Communists. But we're not Tories either. We're simple British patriots."

"Bloody Tories," Alan sneered. "If that spineless bunch of lily-livered custard-coloured cads had stood up to Hitler back in '33, as Churchill had warned, we wouldn't be in this mess in the first place."

"Damn straight," Sam agreed. He looked at the new arrival with a quizzical raised eyebrow. "But you're not British? You speak English with an accent."

The visitor nodded. "Correct. I'm from Gibraltar. Call me Greg. And this is Zed." Greg introduced his companion, who responded with a friendly smile.

"Zed?" Sam said with raised eyebrows. "What sort of a weird name is Zed? No offence."

Zed laughed. "None taken. My parents were missionaries and christened me Zachariah. Coincidentally, there was another Zachariah in my class at school. He was Zach and I was Zed."

Sam laughed "Zed it is. Call me Sam." Sam turned to face Zed's companion.

"Do you speak Spanish, Greg?"

Greg nodded. "Si, hablo Español. My mother is Spanish, my father is Gibraltarian."

"That's interesting," Alan interjected. "The Deputy House Master of Cromwell Boarding House speaks Spanish like a native as well. When I asked him about it he also said that he had been raised in Gibraltar before the War. Perhaps you know him?"

"What's his name?" Greg asked.

"John Baldwin."

"Short, fat, dark and rather ugly?"

Alan shook his head. "No, quite the opposite: tall, slim, fair and rather good-looking. All the girls fancy him."

"I'll vouch for that!" Alice answered. "Mr Baldwin looks like a Hollywood movie star."

Greg laughed and shook his head. "No, sorry. I don't know him. It must be another John Baldwin that I know."

"Pretty Boy is also a dirty fascist traitor, Al," Sam

said vehemently.

"Now, Sam. We don't know that." Alan defended his Deputy House Master.

"Al, he's a member of the Fascist Militia," Sam persisted.

"As am I, Sam," Alan replied.

"You're a member of the Fascist Militia?" Greg asked with wide eyes as his hand automatically grabbed the pistol grip of his revolver.

Alan laughed. "Only under orders. I'm in disguise."

"I'm glad to hear that, Alan. Or else I would be forced to shoot you," Greg said.

Alan laughed again. "Mr Baldwin doesn't get the chance to practise speaking Spanish very often. I think that it would be a good idea for you to meet him."

"I would like that a lot," Greg replied.

Alan yawned dramatically. "I don't know about you folks, but I'm completely knackered. I'm going to hit the sack. I'm next on sentry duty. I'm going to get some shut-eye before it's my shift."

"Good idea, Al," Leon said with an approving nod.

"I'm going to hit the sack as well," Sam said.

"And me," Alice echoed. "Good night, everyone." Alice walked over and gave Leon a hug and a peck on the cheek.

The youngsters disappeared upstairs, leaving the three men seated around the kitchen table and Bob outside on sentry duty.

Greg waited until the three teenagers had gone upstairs before he spoke. "I don't mean to be disrespectful, Mr Leon…"

"Please. Call me Archie," Leon interrupted.

Greg nodded his head. "I don't mean to be disrespectful, Archie, but I didn't expect your unit to include children."

"Include children?" Leon said with raised eyebrows.

"This unit is comprised entirely of children! I'm the only adult in it."

"You've got to be joking!" Zed exclaimed in disbelief.

Leon shook his head. "I wish that I was, but I'm not."

Greg shook his head in horror. "How are we supposed to accomplish this mission with a bunch of kids? We'll be like lambs to the slaughter!"

"Now, Greg, before you continue, let's just get one thing straight: those three kids alone have killed at least a hundred Jerries between them, and that's before I joined them."

"Before... before you joined them?" Zed asked in confusion. "I thought that you asked the kids to join you."

"Most adults think the very same thing," Leon answered. "Those three asked me to join them after they'd just wiped out a squad of SS stormtroopers and they needed some help to dispose of the bodies. Those three have killed more Germans than German measles!"

"Madre Dios!" Greg exclaimed.

"And you joined?" Zed asked.

"Of course!" Leon nodded his head. "I'd been scratching my head thinking about how I could start striking back at the Huns. Those Valkyries came up with the answer. My sons and I joined up with them and we've been fighting the Huns together ever since."

"Your sons?" Greg asked in confusion. "But I only saw Bob, where is your other...?"

Zed put his hand on Greg's arm to cut off his question.

"It's all right, Zed. I have two sons." Leon gave a massive sigh. "Correction: I had two sons. Russell was Bob's little brother. He was fifteen years old. The

Germans killed him." A tear slowly trickled down Leon's cheek.

"I'm... I'm sorry, Archie," Greg apologised.

Leon patted him on the arm. "It's all right, Greg. You didn't know. How could you?"

"When was he killed, Archie?" Zed asked.

"Last week," Leon answered. "We buried them last Saturday."

"I'm sorry for your loss, Archie." Greg paused before he asked the next question. "But you said them?" Greg asked.

Leon nodded. "Russ's girlfriend, Anne, was also killed. She was seventeen. She was the sole survivor of the massacre of Frampton-on-the-Ouse. She was buried beside the rest of her family who were killed in the massacre."

"Jesus Christ!" Greg exclaimed.

"Bloody German bastards!" Zed spat the words out with hatred.

Leon raised a clenched fist to his heart. "Russ's death is like a physical pain in my heart, a constant ache that doesn't go away. Every moment of every day I ask myself: what could I have done differently to have stopped the Germans from murdering my boy? This time last week my boy was still alive..." Leon's voice trailed away as he slumped further into his chair. His body was suddenly wracked with convulsions and tremors shook his shoulders as he wept uncontrollably.

"It's... it's all right, Archie." Zed wrapped an arm around his host's shoulders. "I also... I also lost one of my boys." He gulped. "My eldest son, Terry, was killed during the invasion last September. He was killed fighting against the Nazis in Wales. My youngest boy, Ray, is up in Scotland with the commandos."

"Did the aching ever fade away?" Leon asked as he wiped away his tears with the back of one of his hands.

"No," Zed answered grimly. "It never fades. I can still feel it as if it happened yesterday." Zed turned to look at Leon and placed both of his hands on his host's shoulders. "Hold onto your ache, Archie. Don't let it fade. Transform the feeling of love for your son into hate for the Germans: hate will keep you strong."

Leon nodded.

Greg pushed his chair back and stood up. "Tomorrow we will cut off the head of the Nazi snake and we will send Hitler back to hell, where he belongs!" Greg picked up his glass of port and raised it in a toast. "To tomorrow's mission, gentlemen: good hunting!"

Leon and Zed stood up and raised their glasses of port "Good hunting!" they chorused.

Chapter Seventeen

"So tell me, Sturmbannführer Ulrich: how are you enjoying your stay in England?"

"To be frank, mein Führer, I am not enjoying my stay in England at all," Ulrich answered bluntly. "It is hard to enjoy living in a place when the locals are constantly trying to kill you."

"I see," Adolf Hitler answered. "Thank you for being so honest with me. I was under the impression that England and Wales had been more or less pacified."

Ulrich shook his head grimly. "Far from it, sir. If this is England when it is 'pacified,' I dread to think what it would be like if it was unpacified. My Brigade has lost more men in the last nine months at the hands of the partisans then they did at the hands of the British Army during the entire Invasion."

"And yet you have survived all of those partisan attacks? I guess that's why they call you The Cat." Hitler smiled.

Ulrich shrugged his shoulders. "I've just been lucky, sir. But sooner or later my luck will run out."

"That's very pessimistic of you, Sturmbannführer." Hitler sat back in his leather upholstered seat.

Ulrich shook his head. "No, sir. I'm just being realistic. The trouble with being known as The Cat is that every Tom, Dick and Harry with a gun wants to be the last partisan to take away my tenth life."

Standartenführer Ernst Fraenkel, the SS Colonel in charge of Hitler's personal bodyguard, leaned forward from his seat beside the Führer. "I agree that Sturmbannführer Ulrich is being too pessimistic and I also think that he is being too modest, mein Führer." Fraenkel smiled. "When one of Napoleon's generals recommended another officer for promotion Napoleon said 'I know that he's clever, but is he lucky?' Luck counts for a lot, Ulrich, and the Gods of War are smiling on you, Sturmbannführer. May they continue to smile on you not just for your own sake, but for the sake of Germany."

"Hear, hear," Hitler said.

"Thank you, Standartenführer Fraenkel. Thank you, mein Führer," Ulrich said with a bow.

"Now tell me, Sturmbannführer, how do we pacify Britain?" Hitler asked with genuine interest. He sincerely wanted to discover what a fighting soldier thought of the current situation in England as opposed to the opinion of the legions of sycophantic bureaucrats in Berlin.

"The way I see it, sir, we have two options." Ulrich held up two fingers. " If we really want to bring peace to Britain we can either invade the Free North, capture or kill Churchill and the King and establish a Government of National Unity with Joyce as Prime Minister, or..."

"Yes?"

"We can leave."

"Leave?" Hitler reacted as if Ulrich had suggested that he resign his position as Führer.

"Yes, sir. Leave."

Hitler sat back on his seat. "Well, I tried that before, Sturmbannführer. I offered to leave the British alone." Hitler was obviously flustered as he smoothed his perfectly ironed trousers. "I assured the British that I did not covet a single square mile, foot or inch of their empire. On the contrary, I told them that the British Empire was a source of inspiration for me, not a source of jealousy. I told them that we would rule Russia the way that they ruled India. Surely there is no greater form of flattery than imitation? I said that I would leave Britain their empire and the world if Britain gave me a

239

free hand in Europe." Hitler paused before he continued. He clenched his fists on his knees and bared his teeth in anger. "And how did the British react to my generous offer? They turned me down and spat in my face," Hitler said bitterly. "Like I was the tinpot dictator of some Godforsaken Third World banana republic, instead of the leader of the most powerful country on the planet!" Hitler was literally frothing at the mouth with anger.

Ulrich waited for Hitler to regain his composure and self control before he began to speak quietly. "With respect, mein Führer, any student of history would have told you that there was never a snowball's chance in hell that the British would accept that offer. The British have never allowed any one single nation to become the dominant power in Europe - whether it was Phillip II, Napoleon or the Kaiser. It is in the British national interest to have all of the rival European powers, the French, the Spanish, the Russians and ourselves tearing at each other's throats here in Europe. In the meantime the British were busy conquering the rest of the world. I'm afraid that you have been poorly advised, mein Führer."

"So it would seem," Hitler said.

"And that is not all, sir." Ulrich continued. "As far as the British are concerned, it is not good enough that we simply leave Britain. The British will not rest until the status quo has been restored ante bellum…"

"What?" Hitler exclaimed in anger.

"With our frontiers restored to the borders agreed to as per the Treaty of Versailles…"

"What? That robber's peace? That diktat? Never!" Hitler looked as if he was about to burst a blood vessel. "Give up all of our conquests since 1938? Over my dead body!"

"I'm afraid that that's what it will take to restore

peace between ourselves and the British, mein Führer."

"Well, it's just as well that I decided to choose the first option, isn't it?" Hitler adjusted his lapels as he slowly calmed down and sat back on the leather seat. "I will raze Edinburgh to the ground when I capture it!" Hitler suddenly leapt forward in his seat. "I will destroy all of her buildings, her castle and her palaces, and I will bulldoze the rubble into the earth. I will sow the ground with salt so that nothing grows there for a thousand years. It will become a shooting offence to even mention the name Edinburgh! I will make Scipio's treatment of Carthage seem like a minor act of vandalism by comparison!" Hitler was building himself up to a crescendo. "And as for that Jew-loving Bolshevik war-monger Churchill; I will have him brought back to London in chains, I will have him hung like the common criminal that he is, at the Tower of London and I will have his head stuck on a spike at Traitor's Gate for the royal ravens to pluck out his eyeballs! And the King will be forced to watch the execution from his prison cell at the top of the White Tower!"

Ulrich did not reply. He was content to let Hitler rant and rave.

"Hello, we've stopped." Hitler leaned forward in his seat. "Driver, why have we stopped?"

"I don't know mein Führer," The SS Rottenführer driving the Silver Shadow Rolls Royce answered over his shoulder. "The whole convoy has ground to a halt, sir."

"With your permission, mein Führer, I will discover the cause for the delay," Ulrich suggested.

"By all means carry on, Sturmbannführer," Hitler replied.

Ulrich adjusted his helmet, straightened his tunic, and opened the door. Hitler absent mindedly drummed his fingers on the armrest and looked out of the window at the marshy Fens countryside whilst he waited for Ulrich to return.

The door opened and Ulrich popped his head through. "Animals, sir." Ulrich announced. "Animals are crossing the road ahead and we are waiting whilst they cross, sir."

"Animals? What kind of animals?" Hitler asked with interest. "Cows? Sheep?"

Ulrich shook his head. "No, sir. Pigs."

The explosion knocked Ulrich flat onto his back and the force of the blast sucked the air out of his lungs. He gingerly raised himself onto his elbows and peered through the billowing smoke towards the end of the convoy. The bridge that they had recently driven over had completely disappeared, and so had the armoured car that had served as the rear guard to the convoy.

"Mein Gott!" Ulrich exclaimed.

"What is it? What's going on?" Hitler asked through the open door.

"We're in a tight spot, mein Führer!" Ulrich explained.

"That's putting it rather lightly, Ulrich! We're under attack!" Fraenkel announced, as he grabbed his Schmessier machine gun and adjusted his helmet straps.

Leon ducked as a second explosion blew up the bridge at the front of the convoy. He stood up straight, shrugged off his cape, and fired a burst of rounds at each of the motorcycle scouts who had been knocked off their bikes by the force of the explosion and who lay stunned on the ground. Leon fired another burst of bullets into the front seats of the staff car that led the convoy, and another burst of rounds into the rear seat.

As the lifeless occupants slumped forwards he closed quickly on the next vehicle in the convoy, an armoured car that served as the advance guard. Leon cut down the commander, who was standing up in the turret, before he could react. Leon pushed the barrel of his Schmessier machine gun into the driver's hatch and emptied the rest of his magazine at point-blank range into the turret interior. He was rewarded with a chorus of screams. Leon stepped back, pulled the pin from a grenade, and posted it through the driver's hatch to finish off any survivors. The explosion abruptly cut off the crew's cries of pain.

Leon was changing his magazine and preparing to attack the next vehicle when he realised that the explosion had not only destroyed the bridge, but also the armoured personnel carrier which had been sitting on it. Leon smiled. So far everything was going according to plan. Now, where was Hitler hiding?

Hitler, Fraenkel and Ulrich crouched alongside the Rolls Royce as another burst of rounds thudded into the opposite side of the car. The driver and the bodyguard sitting beside him had not reacted as quickly as the passengers, and they both lay slumped forwards in the front seat. Ulrich watched as the surviving stormtroopers from the APC behind the Rolls Royce piled over the side of their burning vehicle. They crouched alongside their APC and looked to Fraenkel for orders.

"We're in a tight spot. How are we going to get out of here?" Ulrich asked.

Fraenkel looked behind them at the River Ouse that flowed parallel to the road towards the sea. "We can use the river to float downstream past the partisans."

"I can't swim," Hitler said.

Fraenkel's shoulders slumped as their last chance of

escape slipped out of his grasp.

"I've got an idea, mein Führer!" Ulrich eyes lit up with sudden inspiration.

"Scharführer!" Ulrich shouted across at the stormtroopers sheltering behind their burning APC. "Your vehicle is carrying standard issue amphibious river crossing equipment. Open the box at the side of your APC and take out the contents."

"Yes, Sturmbannführer." The SS sergeant did as he was told.

Ulrich nodded. "Good. Now pull the toggle."

The Scharführer followed his orders, and watched in wonder as the device self-inflated.

"You're an absolute genius, Ulrich! No wonder they call you The Cat!" Fraenkel said with genuine awe and admiration.

Ulrich shrugged his shoulders modestly. "Vorsprung durch technik, Standartenführer."

"I'll see that you get the Iron Cross First Class for this, Sturmbannführer!" Hitler grabbed his arm with a vicelike grip.

Another explosion racked the convoy.

"What was that?" Hitler asked.

"Land mines, sir." Ulrich answered. "The partisans are detonating them by remote control one at a time. They're trying to flush out any survivors and finish us off. We don't have much time."

"Then I need to buy you some time." Fraenkel stood up and pulled his Schmessier tightly into his shoulder. "Scharführer!" he shouted. "Are you ready to do your duty for your Führer and for your Fatherland?"

"Yes, sir!" the SS sergeant replied.

"Good! Prepare to assault the enemy position. Forward on my command! Understood?"

"Understood, sir!"

Ulrich watched as the half a dozen or so survivors of

the APC crew made sure that they had a full magazine of rounds, and checked that their grenades were close at hand.

"Standartenführer, you don't have to do this." Ulrich placed a hand on the Colonel's arm. "Let me go instead. I'll lead them."

Fraenkel gently took Ulrich's hand off his sleeve. "No, Sturmbannführer, the Gods of War are smiling on you once again. You came up with the idea to save the Führer. The body guard are my men and only I can lead them into their final battle. Besides, who wants to live for ever?" Fraenkel smiled. "Goodbye, Ulrich." The two men shook hands. "It's been an honour and a privilege to serve you, mein Führer." Fraenkel bowed.

"The honour has been all mine, Ernst. Your sacrifice will not be forgotten." The two men shook hands.

"Now, Sturmbannführer Ulrich: save the Führer!" Fraenkel ordered. "Get him out of here!"

"Yes, Standartenführer Fraenkel! Mein Führer, with your permission?" Ulrich stood up and held his Schmessier in one hand and the bright orange luminous inflatable dinghy in the other hand.

Bob Leon watched in disbelief as the half dozen or so stormtroopers burst from cover from where they had been sheltering behind a burning APC. They had barely run ten yards before he cut them down with one burst from his MG 42 machine gun. "Like lambs to the slaughter." Bob said in disbelief. "Stupid bastards. Why did they get up and run like that? If they'd stayed behind their APC they would have been safe and sound, and it would've been the devil of a job to deal with them."

"I don't know," Zed said. "Maybe their vehicle was about to explode and they preferred to die out in the open rather than be burned alive. Who knows?"

"Well, it certainly grabbed my attention," Bob remarked casually.

"Wait a minute!" Zed suddenly leapt to his feet. "Archie! Watch the river!" he shouted.

Leon carefully approached the broken bridge with his Schmessier tucked tightly into his shoulder. He could see Hitler's Rolls Royce clearly in front of him. Two bodies lay slumped in the front seats. Leon fired a short burst through the shattered windscreen to make sure that they were well and truly dead. The passenger door on the left hand side of the car was open. He couldn't be sure, but he didn't think that there were any bodies inside the passenger compartment. Damn! And he couldn't check either. He looked down at the fast flowing stream that separated him from the other side of the road. So near, and yet so far. The bridge had been blown up when Hitler's car had been on the wrong end of the bridge. Greg hadn't thought of that. No, that wasn't fair. It wasn't Greg's fault. Greg hadn't chosen the ambush sight; he had. The fault and the responsibility was all his. Damn and blast again! To have come all of this way for nothing! Wait a minute...Leon looked at the wreckage of the bridge and the destroyed APC below. Maybe he could use the wreckage to cross the river...

"We're doing fine, mein Führer..." Ulrich and Hitler lay flat on the bottom of their dinghy as the Ouse carried them rapidly down the river.

"I swear, Ulrich, if we get out of this I'm going to..."

"Not if, mein Führer; when," Ulrich interrupted. "We'll be home and dry in King's Lynn within half an hour, mein Führer. You mark my words..."

Hitler smiled. "Very well, Ulrich. When."

"You've got to be kidding me..." Leon was perched precariously on a piece of broken APC when he saw the dinghy floating down the river. He quickly unslung his Schmessier, nearly dropping it into the stream in the process, cocked it, flicked off the safety catch, and fired off a long burst of rounds.

Ulrich ducked as the rounds flew harmlessly overhead. He crouched up in the dinghy and fired a long burst of bullets in the direction of the attacker.

"It's all right, mein Führer. I think that I got him. Anyway, we're out of sight now, sir." Ulrich looked down in horror at the rapidly growing pool of blood in the bottom of his dinghy. "Mein Führer? Mein Führer!"

"Where's Dad?" Bob asked. "I haven't seen him since he started to cross the stream. He should've crossed by now. We should be able to see him on the other side."

Zed shrugged his shoulders. "We haven't seen him since the last two bursts of machine gun fire. He's probably searching the bodies trying to find Hitler and finishing off any wounded Jerries who still alive."

"Probably..." Bob knelt up and raised a pair of binoculars to his eyes. He scanned the wreckage of the ruined convoy and shook his head. "No. I still can't see him. Something's wrong. I can feel it in my bones."

"What's going on, Bob?" Sam shouted across. "The Huns will be here any minute. We have to bug out now!"

"I can't see my dad!" Bob replied.

Sam swore under his breath. "Your dad's a big lad, Bob. He can look after himself."

"We must bug out and head for the rendezvous point, Bob, as your dad ordered," Alan added. "When the convoy doesn't turn up on time the Huns are bound to send a patrol to investigate. If the convoy managed to send a contact report when they got ambushed there could be a patrol on its way as we speak. We need to bug out now!"

"He's right, Bob."

"Shut up, Greg!" Bob turned on him with teeth bared like a wolf and fire in his eyes. "I don't remember anyone putting you in charge. That's my dad out there; he wouldn't leave any of you behind, and I'm not leaving without him! You leave if you want to and I'll meet you at the rendezvous point."

"Come on, lads. Let's go," Alice said. "There's no talking sense into him. If Archie was here, he would order us to leave."

Alan, Sam and Greg got to their feet and gathered their equipment.

Bob shook his head at them with contempt and pulled his Schmessier into his shoulder. "Cover me, Zed," he ordered.

"You're not coming?" Greg asked.

Zed shook his head. "I'm staying with Bob. I'm going to help him find his father."

"Good luck, Zed. I'll see you at the rendezvous point," Greg said.

Zed nodded his head. He aimed his MG 42 machine gun towards the convoy and searched for any signs of life amongst the wreckage.

The burst of bullets cut Bob down where he stood.

"Enemy fighters! Take cover!" Greg shouted.

Zed looked up as two Messerschmitt 109 fighters swooped low over the ruined convoy. They started to turn around in a wide loop to come in for another pass.

"Cover me!" Zed shouted.

"You'll never make it!" Greg warned.

"I left Terry behind in Wales!" Zed shouted. "I'm not going to do it again!" Zed started running towards

248

Bob's lifeless body.

The Messerschmitts started their second attack run. Alan, Sam, Alice and Greg started firing all of their weapons in an attempt to throw up enough flak to put the pilots off their second pass.

Zed reached Bob and flung him onto his back in a fireman's lift. The first pilot's rounds over shot his target. The second pilot's didn't, and punched into the two partisans. Zed and Bob sunk to the ground, where they lay in a lifeless heap.

"Zed!" Greg shouted and started to run towards his friend.

"No!" Sam rugby-tackled him, and the two boys rolled Greg onto his back and pinned him down by his arms.

Alice grabbed the lapels of Greg's battledress and shook him. "Zed's dead, Greg! Zed's dead! We've got to get out of here, or else we will be as well!"

Greg nodded his head. He was numb with shock. Alan and Sam both pulled him to his feet and grabbed an arm each. The boys propelled him through the forest, with Alice leading the way with an MG 42 held at the hip.

A Navy patrol boat found the bullet-holed dinghy floating towards Kings Lynn. The crew's curious and confused questions and queries were instantly transformed into cries of consternation when they discovered the identity of the lifeless body that lay in the bottom of the boat. The speedboat raced towards King's Lynn at top speed, where a waiting ambulance transported the two patients to the local hospital. Sturmbannführer Ulrich had remained silent throughout the whole ordeal and he was sedated immediately upon arrival at the hospital. He slept the sleep of the damned for the next twenty four hours, without waking up once.

"Sturmbannführer Ulrich, Sturmbannführer Ulrich - you have a visitor, sir," a voice whispered in his ear.

"Wha-?" Ulrich slowly came around.

Adolf Hitler, the Führer of the Third Reich, stood in front of him with an outstretched hand and a Hollywood smile on his face.

"Mein Führer?" Ulrich's brows furrowed in confusion. "Mein Führer, I don't understand, I thought that you were…"

"Dead?" Adolf Hitler shook the dazed and confused Sturmbannführer's hand. "No wonder that you look as if you've seen a ghost!"

The Führer's assembled entourage laughed. Ulrich blinked as half a dozen bulbs flashed as the photographers took their photographs.

"It seems that you're not the only person who deserves the nickname The Cat!" Hitler smiled.

The crowd laughed dutifully. Ulrich noticed the reporters writing down every word that Hitler said.

Hitler straightened up his tunic. "I have come to honour a genuine German hero. Obersturmbannführer Ulrich saved my life and is the very finest example of the Third Reich fighting man. It is my honour and my privilege to award Obersturmbannführer Ulrich the Iron Cross First Class."

Ulrich was too stunned and shocked to react. His mouth hung open like a fish gasping for water as Hitler pinned the medal onto his hospital pyjamas. The camera bulbs flashed again, momentarily blinding him.

"Thank you, sir. Excuse me, mein Führer. Obersturmbannführer…?" Ulrich asked in confusion.

Hitler leaned towards him. "Yes, my boy; as a further token of my esteem and gratitude I have promoted you to Lieutenant-Colonel. You will command your own Regiment. Congratulations,

Obersturmbannführer Ulrich!"

There was another round of applause and more photographs as Hitler shook his hand.

"You mark my words: this young man is destined to achieve great things." Hitler announced as he pointed at Ulrich. "His future is written in the stars."

"Let's hear it for Obersturmbannführer Norbert Ulrich! The Führer's champion!" A voice shouted.

Hitler leaned in close and whispered in Ulrich's ear. "We'll talk later, Ulrich, in private once this travelling circus has left. Now, get some rest. That's an order!" Hitler smiled as he patted Ulrich's hand.

"As you command, mein Führer," Ulrich replied. "Heil Hitler!"

The sight of the wounded war hero with his Iron Cross First Class pinned to his striped hospital pyjamas executing a perfect textbook Hitler salute was too good a photo opportunity for the paparazzi to miss, and instigated another barrage of flashing camera bulbs.

"Heil Hitler!" The Führer replied before he swept out of the room, followed by his assembled crowd of admirers.

Ulrich looked down at the medal pinned on his chest in disbelief.

The sound of slow clapping suddenly dragged him out of his daydream. A figure had been standing silhouetted in front of the sun shined windows and now walked slowly towards the bed.

"Brigadeführer Herold!"

"I've got to hand it to you, Ulrich. I admit that I was rather sceptical at first, but you really do deserve to be called The Cat!" Herold shook his head in awe and wonder. "I don't know how you do it."

Ulrich shrugged his shoulders. "Just lucky, I guess, sir." He straightened up in his bed. "Any survivors form the convoy, sir?"

Herold shook his head sadly. "Just you and the Führer, Ulrich. Everyone else was killed. Over forty men in total."

"Mein Gott!" Ulrich put his hand up to his mouth in horror. "Any idea who carried out the attack, sir?"

Herold nodded. "We found two bodies in the marsh beside the road. Two men. Probably partisans."

Ulrich's brows furrowed. "Only two, sir? I think that I may have shot one of the attackers by the first bridge."

"That's possible, Ulrich. His body may have been swept away by the stream."

Ulrich was silent for a moment as he thought about the events of the last couple of days and how his circumstances had changed. For the better, he thought. He was now the Führer's champion and he was in effect untouchable. His future path was written in the stars.

"I must say, sir that the Führer appears to have made an excellent recovery." Ulrich shook his head slowly. "I could have sworn that the Führer was dead, sir. Funny how your mind plays tricks on you when you're under stress." Ulrich laughed. "Maybe I didn't take his pulse properly…"

"I would say that the Führer's recovery is nothing short of a miracle," Herold said cryptically.

"Hallelujah!" Ulrich smiled and waved his hands in the air like a Baptist preacher.

Herold said nothing.

Ulrich suddenly sat up in his bed. "That reminds me, sir. I must thank the Navy boat crew who rescued us and the ambulance crew who took us to the hospital."

Herold coughed into his hand. "I'm afraid that won't be possible, Ulrich."

"Why ever not, sir? Are they on leave? I'm sure that

the Führer can arrange for them to be recalled…"

"The Führer cannot arrange for them to be recalled from beyond the grave, Ulrich."

"What? I don't understand, sir."

"Partisans massacred a barrack room full of sleeping sailors last night here in King's Lynn. I'm afraid that your boat crew were amongst them. The Navy has gone completely crazy. Sailors have gone on the rampage, raping and pillaging across the Fens and have rounded up at least four hundred hostages from King's Lynn and the surrounding area. They will all be executed at dawn tomorrow."

Ulrich was too shocked and stunned to respond.

"And as for the ambulance crew? You can forget them too. The ambulance was found this morning over turned at the bottom of a steep hill. Brake failure. The two crew men were killed."

"Hos… hostages-?"

Herold shook his head dismissively. "No, they weren't real people, they weren't Germans. They were Hospital employees. British civilians."

Ulrich said nothing.

"I would imagine that that is what the Führer wants to talk to you about later. In private," Herold continued.

"Yes, sir," Ulrich replied as if he was sleep talking.

"Well, no rest for the wicked. I'd best be going." Herold smiled as he slapped his leather gloves into his hand. "Wars to win and partisans to kill and all that. You know how it is: busy, busy, busy. I'll see you around, Ulrich, get well soon. And by the way: congratulations, Obersturmbannführer! I've now got to wrack my brains in order to find you a regiment to command as per the Führer's orders!"

"Thank you, sir," Ulrich responded numbly.

Herold popped his head back into the room. "Oh yes, I nearly forgot: one word of advice, Ulrich…"

"Yes, sir?"

"You know what they say about shooting stars?"

"No, sir. What's that?"

"They may burn brightly, but sooner or later they fade away. Be careful, Ulrich. Watch your back."

Chapter Eighteen

An immaculately-clad SS Hauptsturmführer with recruitment poster good looks intercepted Herold in the corridor and flashed his pearly whites.

"Excuse me, Brigadeführer Herold. The Führer would like to speak with you."

Herold nodded. "Of course, Captain."

The Hauptsturmführer opened the door to the Hospital Waiting Room and ushered Herold in with clicked heels and a bow.

"My dear Fritz! How are you? You have no idea what a relief it is for me to see a friendly face." Hitler strolled over to Herold and shook his hand with genuine warmth and affection. "I am forever surrounded by sycophants and yes-men! I'm so glad that I can to speak to you before I leave for Cambridge this afternoon."

"This afternoon, mein Führer?" Herold asked with a raised eyebrow. "With all due respect, mein Führer, is that a wise decision? After all, you only narrowly survived an assassination attempt yesterday."

Hitler smiled. "I'm touched by your concern, Fritz. But look at me: I'm as fit as a fiddle! I've never felt better! These trials are sent to test us, Fritz, and yet again I have emerged unscathed from another assassination attempt with nothing more than frayed nerves and a few cuts and bruises. Once again the Lord has spared me to carry out his will! What further proof is needed that Gott mitt uns?"

"What further proof indeed, mein Führer?"

"Tell me, Fritz, how long have we known each other?" Hitler asked with a warm smile.

"We both joined the Nazi Party in 1919 and I was beside you when the Police opened fire on us during the Munich Beer Hall Putsch in '23." Herold smiled as

255

his eyes glazed over with nostalgia. "And then I commanded an SS Death Squad when we dealt with Rohm and his nest of treacherous SA vipers…"

"Why are the Spanish murdering my men in Hereward?" Hitler demanded abruptly.

"I… I don't understand, mein Führer…" Herold stammered.

Hitler suddenly slammed the table beside him with the palm of his hand. "Don't lie to me, Herold! Why are the Spanish murdering my men in the streets of your town?" Hitler emphasised the words 'my' and 'your' with venomous menace in his voice.

Herold's shoulders visibly slumped as he answered. There was no point bluffing. Hitler probably knew everything anyway. "The Spanish have a blood feud with one of my officers in particular and they have declared Holy War against the SS in general…"

"And you have no idea what is the reason for this vendetta?" Hitler asked with a raised eyebrow.

Herold shrugged his shoulders. "The vendetta started in Spain during the Civil War, mein Führer, at the Battle of Ebro between an Obersturmführer von Stein of the 4th SS Infantry regiment on attachment to the Condor Legión and a Captain Mendoza of the XVII Bandera of the Spanish Foreign Legión. Both of these men are now based in Hereward."

"What damned bad luck!" Hitler punched his clenched fist into his palm in frustration. "How did this happen?" He turned to face Herold. "Brigadeführer Herold, I don't know how this blood feud started, but I know how it will end: with a German victory!"

"Yes, mein Führer!" Herold bowed.

"I don't care how you do it, but I want you to solve this problem by the time that I return to Hereward on June 19th. If you can't solve this problem then I will find someone who can. Do I make myself clear?"

"Yes, mein Führer!"

"One other word of advice, Fritz - we first met in 1919, didn't we?"

"Yes, mein Führer."

"Well, I first met Rohm in 1914 and we served together throughout the war. He saved my life on several occasions and I did the same for him. We were blood brothers. And yet I ordered you to execute him when he failed me..."

Herold gulped, and a bead of sweat ran down his cheek.

"You and I met in 1919 after the War, Fritz. We are not blood brothers. Imagine what I will do to you if you fail me?"

"What happened, Alice?" Aurora asked as she placed a hand on her friend's arm.

"We failed, Aurora," Alice answered. "Look."

Alice showed Aurora the front page of "The Daily Telegraph" and began to read.

FÜHRER SURVIVES ASSASSINATION ATTEMPT

The Führer survived an assassination attempt when his convoy was attacked as he entered Hereward on June 15th. Over forty of the Führer's personal SS bodyguard, including their commander, Standartenführer Ernst Fraenkel, bravely sacrificed their lives in the course of courageously defending their beloved Führer from harm. Only one other SS officer, Sturmbannführer Norbert Ulrich, survived the attack, and the Führer has congratulated him for his cool head and courage under fire. The Führer has personally praised Sturmbannführer Ulrich for saving his life during the attack and has promoted Sturmbannführer Ulrich to Obersturmbannführer and has awarded him the Iron Cross First Class (see photo above)…"

"I swear to God, I don't know how he does it." Alice shook her head and she could not help herself from smiling. "Norbert is always in the right place at the right time…"

"No wonder they call him The Cat." Aurora said. She noticed her friend smiling. "How do you feel about the whole thing?"

Alice shrugged her shoulders. "I know that I shouldn't, but I can't help myself. I feel proud of Norbert in a strange way."

"Proud?" Aurora asked in disbelief.

"Yes, Aurora. Proud." Alice put her hand on her friend's arm. "I know that you might find this difficult to believe, Aurora, but Norbert is not a Nazi. If he had been born in England instead of in Germany he would be fighting the Nazis as hard as we are. The fact that he wears a Nazi uniform is no more than a stroke of bad luck and an accident of birth."

Aurora nodded her head slowly. "It's strange, Alice, but I could say exactly the same thing about my father…"

Alice picked up the newspaper once again, and continued reading:

"Two bodies were found at the scene and they are believed to be terrorists despatched by that despicable and deceitful Jew-loving Bolshevik war-mongerer Churchill to carry out this cunning and cowardly attack on our beloved Führer. It is very likely that more treacherous terrorists were involved in the attack, and SS and Wehrmacht units are scouring the countryside searching for these gangsters. Units of the British Union of Fascists Militia are assisting their Fascist comrades in their hunt for these enemies of peace…"

"Two terrorists?" Aurora interrupted. "Alice, I haven't seen Bob at school today, is he all right?"

Alice shook her head slowly as tears welled up in her eyes. "I'm afraid not. Bob's dead, Aurora, Bob's dead."

"No!" Aurora cried in anguish and raised her hand to her heart.

"And Archie as well, Aurora, and one of the parachutists from the Free North."

Aurora sobbed uncontrollably, and her whole body shook. Alice gathered her friend into her arms and hugged her tightly.

"Aurora, listen to me. Aurora." Alice raised Aurora's chin with her fingertips. "This isn't over. They haven't won. We can't allow them to win. Archie, Bob and Zed did not die in vain. We can't allow that to happen. Hitler will be in Hereward on the 19th of June until the 22nd, and possibly beyond that date. We can still kill him."

Aurora straightened up and wiped away her tears with the back of her hand.

"Then this time let's make sure that we do kill him."

Aurora's two Legiónary bodyguards watched the scene unfold from a discreet distance, with interest.

"Can you hear what they're talking about, Antonio?" The younger one asked.

Antonio shook his head. " No, Julio, but as I told the Colonel, I knew that being able to lip read was a skill that would come in useful one day…"

"So I want you to solve this problem once and for all, von Stein. I want you to stop the Spanish from attacking our men…"

"And just how am I supposed to do that, Brigadeführer?" von Stein asked with open palmed frustration.

"I don't care, von Stein!" Herold smashed his knuckled fists into the surface of his desk. "I don't care and I don't want to know. Just get it done because if you don't get it done by June 19th then you and I are both history."

"By June 19th? But sir, that only gives me three days," von Stein protested. He watched a thin line of blood drip from Herold's hand onto the desktop. The Brigadeführer did not seem to notice.

"Von Stein, the Führer has made it perfectly clear that if we cannot solve the problem then he will find someone who can. I don't think I need to spell out to you what will be the price of failure."

Von Stein gulped and a bead of sweat ran down his back. "No, sir."

"Good." Herold nodded. "Solve the problem by any means necessary, because if you don't then we will both be in front of a firing squad before you can say ready, aim, fire!"

"So what are you going to do, Antonio?" Julio asked. "Are you going to tell the Colonel?"

"I don't know what else I can do, Julio." Antonio idly toyed with the spoon in his coffee cup as he spoke. "I don't see that I have any choice. The Colonel chose you and I for this mission precisely because we both speak English and also because I can lip read English as well as Spanish. What is the point of putting us in this position if we don't use our skills?"

"But if you tell the Colonel, Aurora and Alice could well be in a hell of a lot of trouble. And anyway, the Resistance have not carried out any attacks against ourselves, only against the Germans, and are the

Germans not our enemies as well as the enemies of the Resistance?" Julio asked rhetorically.

"The enemy of my enemy is my friend?" Antonio asked with a raised eyebrow.

"My thoughts exactly," Julio nodded enthusiastically. "We are fighting the Germans and the Resistance are fighting the Germans as well. Does that not make us allies in practice, whether or not we accept that we are allies in theory?"

"Yes…" Antonio conceded.

"And if the Resistance killed Hitler, would that necessarily be a bad thing? Would it necessarily be bad for Spain, Europe or the World?" Julio persisted.

"God knows I hate the idea of the Caudillo going cap in hand to the victor's table begging for whatever scraps that Hitler deigns to throw to us," Antonio admitted. "If we want Gibraltar that badly then I say that we should simply take it - not beg Hitler to give it to us once they have defeated the British…"

"Speak of the devil," Julio whispered. "Hello girls, how are you this fine afternoon?"

"Aurora! Aurora!" Colonel Mendoza rushed from room to room with a drawn revolver as he searched for his daughter. He was closely followed by four heavily-armed Legiónaries. "Clear the house room by room and floor by floor!" Mendoza ordered.

He spotted the two bodies sitting in the kitchen. The Legiónaries sat slumped at the table with their heads resting on their chests. Mendoza grabbed hold of a handful of hair and pulled up the dead soldier's head. The Legiónary's face was a mess of blood, bones and brains. He had been executed at point-blank range with a bullet in the back of the head. The other Legiónary was in a similar state of ruin.

"Madre Dios…" Mendoza murmured. "Antonio and

Julio."

"Colonel!" a Legiónary shouted. "In the dining room!"

A tremor of terror ran up Mendoza's back from his coccyx to the nape of his neck. He entered the dining room and found two other Legiónaries sitting at the table with their faces buried in the plates of food in front of them. The soldiers had been killed at close range with a round in the back of the head as they both sat eating their lunch.

"Search... search the house for Aurora and Alice... they may still be here somewhere," Mendoza ordered. He had to lean on the dining room table to steady him because his hands were shaking so much.

"Sir..." A Legiónary handed him a piece of paper. " It was on the table, Colonel."

Mendoza read it with trembling hands:

WE HAVE YOUR DAUGHTER AND HER FRIEND. IF YOU WANT TO SEE THEM AGAIN THEN YOU WILL DO AS WE SAY. STOP ATTACKING US. FAILURE TO COMPLY WILL RESULT IN US RETURNING THE HOSTAGES TO YOU IN BITS. AWAIT FURTHER INSTRUCTIONS.

Mendoza read the words a second time and a third time as he tried to comprehend the implications of the message. He held the piece of paper at his side and rubbed his chin as he tried to figure out what to do.

"Sir, what are your orders?"

"What?" Mendoza replied as if he was in a trance.

"Colonel Mendoza, what are your orders?" The lance corporal asked.

Mendoza did not reply.

The lance corporal gently took the piece of paper out of Mendoza's hand. He read it once and then a second time to make sure that he clearly understood the message. "Colonel Mendoza, may I respectfully suggest that you ask the commanders of all units of the Division to comply with this demand?"

"What? Yes... good idea, Lance Corporal Lopez. Carry on."

"Very good, sir." Lopez saluted. "Galtieri and Banderas, you stay here with the Colonel. Cruz, you come with me."

But the message did not reach the rest of the Division in time. The next morning, two more stormtroopers were found dead on the streets of Hereward. A chorizo sausage was found stuffed into both soldiers' mouths.

"Are you sure that we have to do this?"

"I'm absolutely sure. He's failed to comply with the instructions. He must be made to understand that we are deadly serious. We can deliver the warning from Frampton to Hereward in fifteen minutes whilst it's still fresh."

"All right. Are you ready?"

"Yes. Do it."

"Can you remember who delivered the package?" Mendoza asked.

"Yes, Colonel," the captain of the guard answered. "An SS Hauptsturmführer, sir."

Von Stein, Mendoza thought to himself. His heart sank.

"He spoke surprisingly good Spanish, sir," the captain continued. "He asked me to give you this package personally."

"Open it, please," Mendoza ordered. His hands were shaking so much that he couldn't trust himself to open the bow.

263

"Certainly, Colonel." The captain opened the box and couldn't help stepping back and wrinkling his nose at the repulsive smell.

"Pass the box to me, please, Captain."

Mendoza accepted the box with trembling fingers and slowly unwrapped the bloody newspaper. He suddenly dropped the box as if it was red hot, and promptly passed out. Mendoza's head thudded onto the top of his desk before the startled captain could catch him. The captain tentatively looked inside the box. A delicately manicured severed finger lay within a nest of blood-soaked newspaper.

"Well done, Hauptsturmführer; whatever you've been doing, it's starting to work. None of our men were killed last night." Herold was grinning like a Cheshire cat as he stood up from behind his desk and shook von Stein's hand.

"Excuse me, Brigadeführer, but I don't know -"

"Come, come, my boy. No need to be so modest," Herold said as he wrapped a fatherly arm around his Prodigal Son's shoulders. "Listen, I don't want to know the details, just pass on my congratulations to your men on a job well done." Herold shepherded von Stein towards the door.

"Yes, sir," von Stein answered, with a bewildered expression on his face.

"Keep up the good work, Hauptsturmführer; we may yet come out of this with our heads still on our shoulders," Herold said optimistically.

YOU FAILED TO COMPLY WITH THE LAST INSTRUCTIONS AND AS A RESULT YOU HAVE BEEN PUNISHED. IF YOU FAIL AGAIN WE WILL CUT OFF MORE THAN YOUR DAUGHTER'S FINGERS. YOUR MISSION IS TO KILL HITLER.

COMPLETE THE MISSION BY 20TH JUNE OR THE HOSTAGES WILL SUFFER THE CONSEQUENCES.YOU HAVE BEEN WARNED.

Mendoza dropped the paper and collapsed onto the armchair. What the hell was going on? Why did the SS kidnappers want him to assassinate Hitler? Was there some sort of internal power struggle going on between Hitler and the SS? He shook his head in disbelief. It didn't matter. He didn't know, and he didn't care. It was purely academic. There was absolutely no chance in hell that he would be able to complete the mission. Aurora and Alice would be dead by this time tomorrow.

Chapter Nineteen

John Baldwin was busy packing his rucksack, when he heard a knock on the front door to his flat. He opened the door to find a small boy standing there.

"Yes, what is it, Kendall?"

"There's a German officer down stairs who wants to speak to you, sir," Kendall replied.

"Thank you, Kendall," Baldwin nodded. "Please tell him that I'll be right there."

As Kendall scurried off, Baldwin adjusted his St John's Old Boy tie and put on his favourite tweed jacket. He walked downstairs and opened the front door to Cromwell Boarding House.

A German officer stood in front of him as Kendall had described. Or at least he was dressed as a German officer, except for one significant difference: he wore a red, yellow and red horizontal shield on his right arm.

The officer flashed him a sunscreen advertisement smile. "El Bonito, I presume?"

"Excellent idea of yours to carry out a 'Fighting in a Built Up Area' exercise, Captain Baldwin!" Major Mason exclaimed as he tapped his swagger stick into his other hand. "The Colonel will be most pleased with your show of initiative, John."

"Thank you, sir," Baldwin bowed his head. "I thought that it might prove useful, seeing that we may well find ourselves fighting through Berwick-Upon-Tweed, sir."

"Sshhh!" Mason put his forefinger up to his lips dramatically. "Not so loud, John! On a need to know basis; the men don't need to know yet!"

"Yes, sir. Sorry, sir," Baldwin apologised. "With your permission, I will lead my company into Frampton and we will begin fortifying the village. I think that we will have fortified the village by noon, Major."

"Very good, Captain Baldwin, we will begin our assault at noon. Carry on."

"Thank you, sir." Baldwin saluted and walked off smartly.

Mason smiled. He always knew that it was a good idea to have recruited Baldwin into the Militia. There was far more to the young man than met the eye, and Mason would tell Colonel Griffiths that Baldwin was responsible for organising the F.I.B.U.A. exercise when the Colonel returned from the briefing.

Colonel Mendoza waited as the SS Military Policeman searched his briefcase. It was stuffed full of documents and Mendoza held it open as the policeman gave it the most cursory of inspections. There was a long line of officers waiting impatiently behind Mendoza, and the Invasion briefing was about to start. There would be hell to pay if any of the officers were delayed because of the jobs worthy examinations of an overzealous policeman.

"Thank you, sir," the MP said. "Please take a seat inside the Hall."Mendoza nodded and walked through into St John's Memorial Hall. The oak panelled walls bore the names of all of the Academy's teachers and past and present pupils who had been killed in the First World War and all of the various Imperial Police actions that British troops had fought in since. Mendoza noticed that the walls did not bear the names of those who had been killed in the more recent fighting. If Hitler succeeded with his plans to transform St John's into his official British residence there was a chance that the walls would bear the names of those killed in the present war; but they would be the names of German, not British, dead.

Mendoza carefully placed the briefcase beside his

feet and tested the strength of the chain that connected the briefcase to a handcuff around his left wrist. Yes, he was certain that there was no chance that he could become physically separated from his briefcase unless it was through his own decision. Mendoza pulled his collar away from his neck. He was painfully aware that he was sweating like a pig. He hoped that if anyone noticed they would put it down to the fact that it was an unusually hot day even for June. Mendoza was also genuinely nervous as he was going to present his plan detailing how the 1st LVE was going to relieve their SS comrades at the Beattie and Auchterlonie Bridges to none other than the Führer himself.

The convoy of requisitioned farm and furniture removal lorries carrying Baldwin's company of militiamen trundled up Frampton High Street towards the far end of the village. As the first lorry reached the top of the village the front wheel rolled on top of an anti-tank mine. The explosion tore off the wheel and ripped through the bottom of the cab, instantly killing the driver and his passenger. The force of the explosion flipped the lorry onto its left side, where it lay burning and smoking. The cries of the dead and dying men inside were abruptly cut short by the staccato sound of two MG 42 machine guns opening fire at point-blank range. After a brief burst of bullets to finish off any survivors the machine guns switched fire to the second lorry, where they shattered the windscreen, killed the driver and the passenger, and ripped into the rear compartment like a chainsaw.

Baldwin sat in the cab of the third lorry, momentarily paralysed with fear.

"Sir, what should we do?" his young driver asked frantically, with wide eyes of terror.

His words shocked Baldwin out of his temporary stupor. "We're under attack! Everyone out! Take cover in the houses!" he ordered.

His militiamen piled out of the back of the lorry as the MG 42s started to search for targets in the third lorry. Baldwin got out of the cabin just in time, as rounds shattered the windscreen. His driver was not as quick and he died with a look of complete and utter surprise and disbelief on his face before he could open the door.

The first militiaman reached a house, and as he turned the door handle the booby trap exploded and threw him back out into the middle of the road, where he landed in a burnt and bloody heap. His two companions who reached the door behind him were also thrown to the ground, and quickly bled to death before anyone could help them.

"Christ!" Baldwin's eyes bulged wide with horror. "Watch out! The houses are booby-trapped!" Baldwin warned his men as he looked around frantically searching for a familiar face. "Sergeant Cannon!"

"Yes, sir?"

"Where's Second Lieutenant Doxat?"

"Dead, sir," Cannon answered grimly.

Baldwin thought quickly before he spoke. "All right. Sergeant Cannon, you're in command of the Second Platoon."

"Very good, sir."

"Second Lieutenant Ball," Baldwin shouted as he spotted one of his young platoon commanders, "on my command you will take the Third Platoon and assault the enemy position, the house at the far end of the village, by executing a right-flanking attack - understood?"

"Yes... yes, sir," Ball replied nervously.

"Sergeant Cannon, on my command you will take

the Second Platoon and assault the enemy position, the house at the far end of the village, by executing a left-flanking attack, understood?"

"Yes, sir!" Cannon replied resolutely.

"The First Platoon is combat ineffective. I will command Company Headquarters and we will provide covering fire, understood?"

"Yes, sir!" Cannon and Ball chorused.

"Company Headquarters! On my command provide covering fire! Second and Third Platoons, on my command, assault the enemy position. Open fire!" Baldwin ordered.

"Here they come!" the first machine gunner said as the militiamen broke cover. He whooped like a Red Indian as he cut down the slowest three militiamen.

"We won't be able to hold them for long," the second machine gunner said. "It's time to bug out!"

"What about the girls?"

"We leave them as planned," the second machine gunner said as he shot another two militiamen. "Gotcha!"

"All right," the first machine gunner said. "Let's go!"

Sergeant Cannon was the first militia man to reach the house. He leaned against the wall with his mouth hanging open like a panting dog as he caught his breath. He wasn't as young as he used to be.

"Go!" he ordered. "No! Not through the door! It may be booby -!"

The young militia man kicked open the front door and instantly disappeared in a huge haze of smoke and fire.

By the time that Ball reached the house there was nothing left of Cannon and the Second Platoon but a pile of burnt and bloody bodies.

Ball bent over at the waist as he was violently sick. He quickly recovered and wiped his vomit smeared mouth on the sleeve of his filthy black battledress.

"Come on, lads," he said. "You know the drill. Let's do this by the numbers! Machine gunners!"

Two machine gunners stepped forwards and fired their Schmessiers through the open door, spraying the far corners of the living room. Another two militiamen then stepped forward and threw in two hand grenades. "Grenade!" they both shouted as they hurriedly backed out of the room. As soon as the grenades exploded the two machine gunners again stepped forward and fired into the room. "Clear!" they both shouted in unison.

"All right, lads!" Ball shouted. "You know the drill. We clear the house room by room, floor by floor! Let's go!"

Mendoza finished his presentation and sat down on his seat.

"Excellent presentation, Colonel."

"Thank you, Alfredo." Mendoza said with a smile. He looked at Major Alfredo Astray with genuine warmth and affection. They had served together since the Civil War began and Mendoza sincerely regretted that his actions were about to place his old friend firmly in the eye of the storm. But he couldn't see that he had any choice in the matter. There was no viable alternative to the path that he was about to follow.

"Sir! Sir!" Ball shouted from the top bedroom window. "Captain Baldwin! Come quickly!"

Baldwin stood up from his position behind a lorry. "What is it?"

"Come quickly, sir!" Ball said with a grim look on his sweat and smoke encrusted face. "We've freed two prisoners, sir!"

"Alfredo, come outside with me for a cigarette break," Mendoza said as he pulled out a cigarette case.

"But, Colonel Mendoza," Astray raised his eyebrows in confusion. "I don't smoke and neither do you."

"You'll start after what I tell you," Mendoza said as he wrapped an arm around the shoulders of his old friend, and guided him out of the Hall.

"Dirty bastards..." Baldwin said as he shook his head. "How could anyone do this?" He looked down at the two dirty and dishevelled girls that his men had recently rescued.

Ball had ordered his men to search the house for anything that they could find to cover the girls' nakedness. They were huddled together for warmth as well as for comfort with their arms wrapped around each other. Ball's men had managed to find a large double duvet that they delicately draped around the shivering girls' shoulders.

Ball guided Baldwin into another room by the elbow. He was glad to see that his men had formed a protective circle around the girls, as if to shield them from further harm. "We found each of them tied up... tied up to the four corners of a bed, sir." Ball found it physically difficult to speak. "They were each spread-eagled naked, sir. We found their torn and bloody underwear underneath the bed." Ball gulped.

"Those sadistic SS bastards cut off the dark haired one's finger, sir. I think that they've been... I think that they've been..." Ball couldn't finish the sentence. His eyes welled up and a large tear traced a track down his dirty cheek.

"It's all right, Tommy. It's all right." Baldwin put a

272

protective hand on the young officer's shoulder.

"It's enough to make you join the partisans!" Ball said furiously as he punched a fist into his other hand,

"That's enough, Tommy!" Baldwin warned with fire in his eyes. He whipped his head around to look through to the other bedroom to see if any of his militiamen had heard Ball's hasty words. "That's high treason you're talking!"

"High treason, sir? High treason against who, may I ask? Against Joyce's government? Joyce is only the prime minister because the Germans support him. Joyce is the German's creature, their slave, their plaything." Ball spat out the words with contempt. "And the Germans did this, sir! Germans cut off that poor girl's finger and Germans raped the girls! Those dirty German bastards! SS gear is strewn all over the house! Those Nazi bastards kidnapped these two girls and raped them for their own perverted pleasure! If we hadn't turned up in time they would probably have killed them!" Ball was talking as fast as a runaway train. "I'm not a Fascist, sir! I joined the Militia because I thought that it was the best way to bring peace to our country. And as for high treason, sir?" Ball snorted with derision. "Maybe I am a traitor, sir, because it looks like I've been fighting for the wrong side."

"I will choose to ignore that last outburst, Second Lieutenant Ball; you're tired and stressed out and you've been through a lot this morning. But I warn you not to express such sentiments in front of your men, and certainly not in front of the Colonel!" Baldwin said sternly. He thought before he spoke again. "We'll discuss your concerns later, Tommy. Have the girls said anything?" Baldwin asked.

Ball shook his head as he wiped his away his tearstained eyes with a blood smeared sleeve. "No, sir, they haven't said anything. They're too traumatised. The girls haven't even told me their names."

Baldwin shook his head. "They don't have to, Tommy. I know who they are. They're two of my students at St John's; Aurora Mendoza and Alice Roberts."

Ball put a hand to his mouth. "Alice Roberts? I went to school with her big brother, Angus. Well, Aurora's father must be worried sick. We must contact him and let him know that the girls are safe. God knows how long the girls have been missing!"

Baldwin clicked his fingers. "You're right, Tommy! The Huns have already looted Frampton. I very much doubt that we'll find a phone here. Quick, get the men back onto the lorries; we'll drive back to Hereward and I'll contact Colonel Mendoza from our barracks."

"Yes, sir." Ball saluted and hurried off to gather up his men.

But Baldwin did not manage to make the phone call in time.

Mendoza looked at his watch. It was five seconds to noon. "Alfredo, take cover!" he ordered.

"Wha-?" Astray asked in confusion.

At exactly twelve o' clock a seven and a half pound mortar round landed on the roof of the main school building. Simultaneously, Mendoza's briefcase exploded underneath the table where he had left it. The briefcase contained a one kilogram bomb fitted with a timed fuse, and when it exploded it killed or wounded everyone within a twenty five metre radius. For the next minute a further fifteen mortar rounds landed on the main school building, and shortly afterwards the entire building collapsed like a stack of cards.

"Cease fire!" Lance Corporal Lopez ordered. As his men secured the mortar, Lopez jumped out of the back of the lorry and walked around to the front where he climbed into the passenger cab. "All right, Cruz. Let's go," he ordered. Within five minutes the lorry had arrived back at the 1st LVE barracks. By ten past twelve the mortar had been returned to the Armoury without anyone noticing that it had ever left. By a quarter past twelve Lopez and his men were lining up in the lunch queue. No one had noticed that Lopez and his men had even left the base.

"Did it work?" Greg asked. He was sitting at a table in a dark corner of the 'Prince of Wales' pub, drinking a pint of Guinness.

Baldwin nodded. "I think so. Better than we expected." He took a sip of his Guinness. "By the time that we got back to Hereward the Huns were running around like a bunch of headless chickens."

"But did he manage to accomplish the mission?" Greg asked. Although there was no one sitting within earshot he was conscious that it was more prudent to talk carefully in code.

"I don't see how he can have failed," Baldwin answered. "The building looks as if it has been flattened by the hand of God himself. There's nothing left but a pile of ruins. The Fire Brigade are still searching for survivors but they haven't found anyone yet, and I doubt that they will. Colonel Griffiths and his second in command, Major Bennett, have not returned, and they are both officially posted as missing. I'm sure that they've both been killed."

"Who's been promoted to take his place?"

"Major Mason has been given temporary command. There simply isn't enough time to brief someone else on our Invasion mission. Anyway, I doubt that

275

Blackshirt Lieutenant-Colonels grow on trees."

"When do you leave?" Greg asked.

"Tomorrow." Baldwin took another sip of his beer.

"Well, be careful up there. The Battling Brits won't know that you're one of them. They'll take one look at your Blackshirt uniform and treat you as a dirty stinking Fascist traitor. If you're captured and you're lucky, you'll be shot as a traitor immediately; if you're unlucky you'll be tortured beforehand and then strung up by your balls from the nearest lamp post."

"I am aware of the risks, but thank you for pointing them out so graphically," Baldwin said dryly.

"You're welcome," Greg smiled sarcastically.

"Anyway, I don't intend to get captured. I intend to sabotage the invasion from within and then return to the Occupied South as a Fascist war hero as per orders."

"Well, good luck, compadre." Greg wiped his lips with his hand and stood up to leave. "I'll see you when you return, God willing. May the Holy Virgin look over you and guard and protect you, my friend." Greg kissed the talisman that he wore around his neck.

"Thank you, my friend. Adios, Ramón."

"Adios, El Bonito."

Mendoza saw the Militia officer standing outside his house and he felt an ice cold hand grip his heart. He willed himself to keep walking.

"Colonel Mendoza?" the young officer asked. "My name is Second-Lieutenant Ball of the 1st B.U.F. Militia. We have rescued your daughter, sir. Aurora and Alice are both alive."

Mendoza's legs buckled and he would have fallen to the ground if Astray had not caught him. "Where - where is she?"

"Inside, sir. My men are guarding her," Ball answered.

276

Mendoza rushed into his house. "Aurora!" he shouted.

"Papa!" Aurora leapt out of her seat and ran towards her father. When she reached him she launched herself off the ground into his arms. Mendoza caught her and gave her a gigantic bear hug, lifting her off the floor.

There wasn't a dry eye in the house as the half a dozen militiamen guarding the two girls wept unashamedly at the sight of the emotional reunion between father and daughter.

"You're... you're all right?" Mendoza asked with tear filled eyes as he stroked his daughter's dirty matted hair.

"I'm alive, Papa," Aurora answered resolutely.

Mendoza nodded his head with understanding. He could imagine what the SS kidnappers had probably done to the girls when they had been captives. "And your finger?"

"I'll live. I have nine spare," Aurora said stoically.

"Spoken like a true Spartan." Mendoza tenderly kissed her on her dirt encrusted forehead. "Alice!" Mendoza held out his arms and Alice tumbled into them. He held her closely as Alice hung on like a limpet. "I'll let Sam know immediately. Now, what do you girls want to do? Do you want to wash? Eat? Sleep?"

"A long hot bath, a change of clothes and a hot meal would be the first step, Papa."

Alice nodded.

"All right," Mendoza answered. "We'll talk when you feel that you're ready."

"Yes, Papa." Aurora kissed her father on the cheek and Alice followed her example. Both girls disappeared upstairs.

Mendoza waited until both of the girls had left the living room. "Major Astray?"

"Yes, Colonel?" Astray answered from a position of attention.

"Please could you organise a round-the-clock guard of platoon strength for myself and my daughter. I want a squad of Legiónaries guarding my daughter and myself at any one time. This is the second time that we've survived an SS attack; I don't think that we'll survive a third."

"Yes, Colonel." Astray saluted and went to the study to phone the barracks.

Mendoza turned to face Ball. "Second-Lieutenant Ball, I am indebted to you, sir, for finding and freeing my daughter." Mendoza bowed gracefully.

Ball bowed in turn. "It was my pleasure, sir. Any human being would have done the same."

"How did you find her?"

"We were carrying out a Fighting in a Built up Area exercise in Frampton -"

"The sight of the infamous massacre?" Mendoza interrupted.

"The very same." Ball nodded his head. "When one of our lorries ran over a land mine."

"Madre Dios!" Mendoza exclaimed.

"Yes, sir. Approximately sixty of my men were either killed or wounded in the ensuing ambush."

"My God!"

"But we found and freed the girls, sir, and that's all that matters," Ball said grimly.

"Well as I said, Second-Lieutenant Ball, I am forever in your debt. Did you manage to kill any of the kidnappers?"

"No, sir. But they were definitely SS. Both of the girls told us this and they left equipment lying all over the place. They must have abandoned their gear in their attempt to escape." Ball paused before he asked the next question. "If you don't mind me asking, sir, do

278

you know why the SS kidnapped your daughter?"

"I don't mind you asking at all. After all that you and your men have suffered you have the right to know," Mendoza said, matter-of-factly. "The SS and the XVII Bandera of the Spanish Foreign Legión have been conducting a blood feud which started three years ago during the Civil War. We are pursuing a vendetta against them."

Ball straightened up before he replied. "The SS killed and wounded sixty of my men, Colonel. The enemy of my enemy is my friend. The 1st Battalion of the B.U.F. Militia is also declaring a vendetta against the SS."

"May I count on your help and assistance against the SS when the opportunity arises?" Mendoza asked.

"You can count on it, Colonel."

The two men shook hands.

Chapter Twenty

Obersturmbannführer Ulrich looked at his watch for the tenth time in as many minutes. Five minutes to midnight. Five minutes until Operation Thor commenced. Ulrich shook his head in disbelief at the events of the last seventy-two hours. The Führer was in a critical condition in hospital, and it was widely whispered that it was fifty-fifty whether he would make it or not. He had only escaped certain death because he had been in a ground floor toilet when the mortar attack had taken place. The other members of his entourage had not been as lucky. Generaloberst Rommel, Brigadeführer Herold and General-Major von Schnakenberg had all been killed, as had their second in commands. The commanding officers of the Potsdam Grenadier Regiment, the Oberschutzen Jaeger Regiment and the 4th and 5th SS Infantry Regiments had also been killed, along with their second-in-commands. What had Monat said little more than two months ago? Yes, Ulrich smiled as he clicked his fingers, Monat did not think that Ulrich was fit to command the Triple S Brigade and he had been rather put out when Ulrich had agreed with him. But Monat was dead and he was still alive. And yet again he was the most senior officer in the Brigade, and the de facto commanding officer of the Triple S. Ulrich smiled. Every cloud did indeed have a silver lining.

"Five minutes, sir," the glider pilot announced over his shoulder.

"Five minutes, lads," Ulrich repeated to his seven stormtroopers. He was in command of one hundred and eighty men consisting of one hundred and fifty SS paratroopers and thirty SS engineers. The (DFS) 230A glider only carried eight troops and after the colossal losses that the Luftwaffe had suffered during the Battle for Crete, the air force had been forced to search high and low throughout their bases in Europe in order to find twenty-five gliders to transport Ulrich's strike force.

Ulrich thought about the last orders that Brigadeführer Herold had given him before he was killed: "Obersturmbannführer Ulrich, your mission is to seize the Beattie and Auchterlonie Bridges and the village of Robinson and hold until relieved." The mantra repeated itself in Ulrich's mind: hold until relieved...hold until relieved.

A sudden jolt abruptly interrupted Ulrich's daydream. "What was that, Captain?" he asked anxiously.

"Flak, sir," the glider pilot answered nonchalantly. He pointed ahead of the glider, where there was a sudden bright flash and a puff of smoke. The glider shook as the shock waves from the explosion reached them. "I used to be a bomber pilot, sir, before I was transferred to the Glider Squadron. The Tommies probably think that we're a group of bombers heading for Edinburgh. They often open fire on us as we cross over the border, but they rarely hit anything. Flak should be random and light, sir. Absolutely nothing to worry about," the pilot said confidently.

"I'm happy to hear that, Captain," Ulrich replied with relief.

The glider rocked from side to side as a flash and a puff of smoke appeared to the left of the glider, and then another flash and puff of smoke appeared to the right. Ulrich watched, open-mouthed with horror, as the next flak shell scored a direct hit on the glider to the left. The aeroplane instantly disintegrated into a thousand pieces and Ulrich's glider rocked and rolled violently from the vibrations from the blast, as the fuselage was hit by a shower of shrapnel that consisted

281

of pieces of plane and paratrooper. A body landed on the cockpit window with a massive thud and then slid off to fall away to the ground below. The window was splintered like a spider's web and looked as if someone had thrown a bucket of blood over it.

"This flak isn't random and light!" the pilot shouted.

A flak shell suddenly tore a massive hole in the left wing of the Junkers Ju 52 towing Ulrich's glider.

"Casting off!" the pilot shouted immediately, and released the towing cable without a second's hesitation. He had been on enough bombing raids to know when an aeroplane was going to crash and burn and he didn't want his glider to be dragged down with it.

The Ju 52's entire left wing tore off and the transport plane started to fall away, cartwheeling through the sky as it plummeted towards the ground. Ulrich breathed a sigh of relief as three parachutes billowed out from the Ju52 as the stricken aeroplane's crew bailed out.

"Making our approach!" the glider pilot shouted.

His co-pilot didn't reply. He sat with his head slumped forwards onto his chest as a thin trickle of blood dripped from his lifeless fingertips.

"Link arms!" Ulrich ordered. The paratroopers did as they were told and also raised their feet off the ground.

The glider dropped like a stone through a shower of flak and brightly-coloured tracer rounds, hit the ground, bounced once and skidded along the ground at one hundred and fifty kilometres per hour until it came to an abrupt stop.

Ulrich patted the pilot's shoulder. "Thank you, Captain. That was a fantastic piece of flying." But the Captain did not answer. He would not be answering anyone's questions ever again. The metal skid that ran along the bottom length of the glider had snapped on impact and had ricocheted through the cockpit window. The pilot was impaled through the chest to his chair, and stared with sightless eyes into the darkened distance in front of him.

"Everybody out!" Ulrich ordered.

The two paratroopers nearest to the door kicked it open, jumped out, and were immediately cut down by a fusillade of machine gun fire.

"Gott in himmel!" Ulrich fired a burst of bullets through the cockpit window and then knocked out the shattered pieces of glass with the barrel of his Schmessier. He crawled through the gap and jumped to the ground, where he took up a firing position. "Follow me!" he ordered. Ulrich fired short, sharp controlled bursts of rounds in the general direction of the British machine gun, as his men followed him out of the cockpit window and lay down around him like the hands of a clock in a position of all round defence.

Ulrich tried to get his bearings as his eyes gradually regained their night vision. It was difficult to see in the darkness through the haze of smoke that hovered over the battlefield. Brightly coloured British tracer rounds swept the ground as the machine gunners searched for German targets. There was the constant cacophony of grenades exploding, the yelling and screaming of men in pain, the bark of men bellowing orders and the runaway train crashing noise of gliders landing either under the control of their pilots or as they smashed out of the sky, burning to the ground.

Ulrich searched for a familiar landmark. "Mein Gott! I don't believe it!"

"What is it, sir?" one of his officers asked.

"Look!" Ulrich pointed.

"Mein Gott, sir! Beattie Bridge!"

"Yes! Despite the flak the pilot landed us right where he was supposed to!" Ulrich shouted above the noise of the raging battle. "Listen in, men! We're about one hundred metres from Beattie Bridge. We're going to carry out a squad attack on the enemy pillbox guarding the left hand side of the bridge! Stumpff: you, Kesselring and Brauchitsch will form Delta fire team and you will provide covering fire whilst myself, Halder and Blucher form Charlie fire team and assault the position. When we take cover we will provide covering fire whilst you assault the position and so on. Clear?"

"Clear, sir!" the stormtroopers replied.

"Sir?"

"Yes, Stumpff, what is it?" Ulrich asked, as he checked that he had a full magazine of rounds and a couple of hand grenades close at hand.

"Sir, is it wise to assault the enemy position? After all, we only have six men," Stumpff asked with a lowered voice.

"With six men or with sixty men, the numbers don't matter, Stumpff. Everyone else might well be dead for all we know. We attack with what we've got, as always. What counts here is not numbers, but surprise and daring!" Ulrich looked at his men. "Besides, do you want to live for ever?"

"No, sir!" his paratroopers answered with the light of battle burning fiercely in their eyes.

"Does that answer your question, Hauptsturmführer Stumpff?"

"Yes, sir!"

"Then let's go! Halder and Blucher, follow me!"

Hauptsturmführer von Stein steadied himself as the Ju 52 veered to the side again. A massive explosion lit up the sky as the transport plane immediately in front blew up. "Look out!" von Stein warned, as a stick of paratroopers floated into view in front of von Stein's

284

aeroplane.

"Up! Up! Up!" the pilot ordered, as he and his co-pilot used all of their strength to pull back on their controls. The Ju 52 responded slowly and started to climb steeply upwards. Von Stein held his breath as the aeroplane just missed clipping the parachute of the last soldier.

"What the hell is going on, pilot?" Von Stein demanded after the near miss.

"We're all supposed to fly at the same height, sir, to make sure that we don't hit any of our paratroopers. However, our barometric pressure altimeters aren't as accurate as we'd like them to be so it's difficult for everyone to fly at exactly the same height. Mein Gott!"

A burning Ju 52 suddenly appeared in front with its right wing on fire heading towards von Stein's plane on a collision course. "We're going to collide! Get out!" The pilot flicked the switch, signalling the green light to jump.

"Everybody out!" Von Stein ordered, and threw himself out of the aeroplane. As his parachute opened he looked behind him and watched open mouthed in horror as the two Ju52s collided. The aeroplanes exploded, sending burning pieces of wreckage hurtling through the sky. A piece of wing tore through a paratrooper and ripped him in half as if he was made of paper. Another piece of burning fuselage set a parachute on fire and sent the soldier screaming and hurtling to his death. Von Stein watched as a paratrooper floated helplessly towards a burning building. The soldier disappeared into the inferno with a last desperate cry for help before he exploded. He must have been carrying anti-tank grenades. Von Stein looked above him. He was alone. No one else had jumped out of his aeroplane.

Ulrich wiped the sweat from his dirty brow with a filthy hand, and raised himself slightly to look over the body of the dead paratrooper that he was using to provide cover from fire. The entire distance between himself and the pillbox was covered in a carpet of German bodies. He could have used the bodies of his fallen comrades as stepping stones to reach the bunker without touching the ground. Ulrich cursed. He had not realised that the innocent looking house to the right of the bridge had been transformed into a pillbox. The real house must have been demolished and replaced with a bunker that was disguised and camouflaged to look like the house that it had replaced. That rather significant development had not been noted and included in the briefing plan. Stumpff, Kesselring and Brauchitsch had paid for that intelligence oversight with their lives. They had been cut down as they made their first attack.

"What now, sir?" Halder asked desperately. "The Tommies are killing us!"

Ulrich spotted exactly what he was looking for amongst a pile of dead paratroopers. He turned to speak to his two surviving men. "I'm going to crawl towards the flamethrower and then I'm going to crawl towards the pillbox and burn those bastards alive. Then I'm going to fry the Tommies in the house next door. You two provide covering fire if the Tommies spot me. Understood?"

"Understood, sir. Good luck!" Halder wished. Ulrich nodded grimly. He stripped off his webbing and back pack to help him crawl easier. He checked that his Luger pistol had a full magazine and left behind his Schmessier, which was awkward to carry when crawling. Ulrich stuffed a couple of hand grenades into each of his jacket pockets. When he was ready he kissed the crucifix that hung around his neck and peered over the top of the dead paratrooper again. He needed to be definite about the direction in which he was going to crawl.

Ulrich started crawling slowly towards the pillbox in short bursts. He would crawl until there was a bright flash of light as an aeroplane blew up in the sky, or if an artillery or mortar round exploded on the ground. Ulrich would then stop crawling so that the Tommies would think that he was just another dead German. Eventually, he reached the flamethrower. He swore as he realised that the straps were hopelessly entangled and he wouldn't be able to physically separate the flamethrower from the body of the dead operator. Ulrich reached for the hilt of his SS dagger. Shit, it wasn't there. It must have fallen out somewhere. He looked around. There. He spotted a bayonet on a dead paratrooper's webbing belt. He slowly drew it out and started to saw the straps.

"There, Bert!"

"Where?"

"Over there! Lone Jerry, twenty five yards, at two o' clock!" The assistant machine gunner pointed. "A Hun pretending to be dead. He's been sneaking up on us, hiding amongst his dead mates!"

"Crafty devil!" Bert said with grudging admiration. "Well, let's help him join his dead mates, Ernie. Permanently!"

"Eric!" Blucher shouted. "The Tommies have spotted the Colonel!"

Halder watched as the British machine gunners opened fire on Ulrich, sending a sustained burst of rounds thudding into the bodies that provided him with his only cover from fire.

"We've got to give the Colonel a chance to get close to the pillbox! Give covering fire, Hans!" Halder ordered as he squeezed the trigger of his Schmessier.

Ulrich realised that the enemy machine gun had switched fire. He grabbed the flamethrower, jumped to his feet, and sprinted the last twenty-five metres to the bunker. He slammed his back against the front of the pillbox. Ulrich knelt down, adjusted the controls of the flamethrower, pushed the nozzle into the bunker aperture, and squeezed the trigger. He threw himself to the ground as flames shot out of the pillbox port. The British machine gunners were still screaming in agony as they staggered out of the bunker where they collapsed and lay in a burning and smouldering heap of cooking meat. Ulrich ran up to the next bunker, which was disguised as a house, before its occupants realised that their partner had been put out of action. He pushed the nozzle into the pillbox port and squeezed the trigger. Jets of flame shot into the bunker, setting the machine gunners on fire and triggering explosions as the ammunition blew up. The defenders also ran out and were cut down before they could run a dozen paces.

Ulrich dumped the flamethrower on the ground and shouted at the top of his voice, "The pillboxes have been destroyed! Everyone across the bridge! Let's go!"

Ulrich's orders were answered with a ragged cheer as paratroopers seemed to rise from the ground like Hydra's teeth, and started to fire and manoeuvre across the bridge, shooting their weapons from the hip.

Ulrich stumbled wearily across the carpet of corpses like a sleepwalker, to where he had left Halder and Blucher. "Thanks, boys. I couldn't have done it without you. I'll make sure that you get medals for this."

But Blucher and Halder wouldn't be receiving medals from anyone, unless it was awarded posthumously. Their glassy eyes stared up at Ulrich. He sank to his knees beside them and wept unashamedly. A thin stream of tears carved a wet path through his soot, dirt and blood-encrusted face. His men had sacrificed their lives in order to protect his.

"Right, lads, this is it," Oberleutnant Alfonin said. "We're going to go over the top and into the river any minute now. Remember your training. Row straight for the other side, and don't bunch up with the other boats: the Tommies will aim at two or three boats bunched up rather than one single boat on its own. Machine gunners provide covering fire when the Tommies open up; rowers remember to compensate for the river current as we practised." Alfonin looked at the circle of camouflaged young faces that surrounded him. Apart from his platoon sergeant, not a single one of his men was over twenty-one and they were petrified and absolutely scared out of their skins. "Remember that you are Potsdam Grenadiers, lads, Germany's finest. We are the tip of the spear and we are right where we deserve to be: in the position of honour, in the first wave." Alfonin paused as he let his words sink in. He could see a few of his young soldiers nodding their heads in agreement. "I know that General-Major von Schnakenberg is looking down on us from heaven as we speak, and I know that he wishes that he could be here with us." Alfonin could not help his eyes from moistening with tears at the thought of how the General had been cruelly snatched from them when the Regiment had needed him the most. Alfonin stood up from his kneeling position. "So let's make the General proud: for the General, the Regiment and Germany! Potsdam! Potsdam! Potsdam!"

Alfonin's platoon stood up as one man. "For the General, the Regiment and Germany! Potsdam! Potsdam! Potsdam!" his men echoed.

Alfonin smiled like a proud father. He looked at his watch as the artillery bombardment suddenly stopped. It was exactly six o'clock. "I'll see you on the other side. Let's go!" he ordered.

Alfonin grabbed hold of the rope that ran around the outside of the inflatable dinghy, and his men followed his example. "On my command, lift up!" Alfonin ordered. His men did as they were told. "Up and over the bank and into the river!" Alfonin ordered. Alfonin braced himself as he reached the top of the bank for a volley of machine gun rounds, and breathed a massive sigh of relief when the Tommies did not open fire. He sneaked a quick look across the river to the town. The entire north bank of the river was shrouded in a thick blanket of smoke and all of the houses appeared to be burning furiously. Berwick-upon-Tweed looked and smelled like a fiery inferno. Alfonin allowed himself a smile. Perhaps the Luftwaffe and the Artillery had managed to destroy the British machine gun and artillery positions after all.

Alfonin held onto the rope as the MG 42 machine gunner and his assistant climbed into the ten-man dinghy. They took up a position at the front of the boat and knelt up with their machine gun aimed at the opposite bank. Alfonin waited for the rest of his squad to climb into the dinghy, and then he climbed in last. He looked up and down the river. The twenty-four ten man dinghies of the first wave of Potsdam Grenadiers and Oberschutzen Jaegers were ready to row. As one unit, the entire first wave started to paddle across the river. Alfonin looked at his watch again. It was five minutes past six. The river crossing should take no more than half an hour. Alfonin looked behind him. The engineers were already starting to assemble their pontoon bridges. The plan was to build six bridges: three bridges would be for the infantry, and three bridges would be for the panzers and lorries. The engineers hoped to have the first bridges operational by nine o'clock, and at the pace that they were working Alfonin was confident that they would be able to meet their target. Alfonin scanned the opposite riverbank with his binoculars. Still no sign of any Tommies. Alfonin heard a flurry of splashing behind him as the second wave started paddling across the river. A quarter past six. The second wave was bang on time. He turned around to face the front. His men were rowing confidently in rhythm, and judging by the smiles some of them even seemed to be enjoying themselves. At twenty-five past six the dinghy was less than one hundred metres from the north bank.

"Right lads, remember the plan: our job is to secure the river bank. Second platoon will take up defensive positions facing towards the town with One platoon on our left and Three platoon on our right. The second wave will push through our position and clear the town. Clear?"

Before his men could reply a burst of machine gun bullets lacerated the front of the dinghy, instantly killing the machine gunner and his assistant. They toppled back into the boat as the next volley of rounds killed the half dozen men rowing in front of Alfonin.

"Take cover!" Alfonin shouted as he tried to burrow like a mole into the deck of the dinghy. The machine gun switched fire. Alfonin poked his head up. He was completely surrounded by dead men. His squad had been cut down at virtually point-blank range, and the boat was ankle-deep in blood. Nobody was rowing the boat; and Alfonin gradually realised that the river was taking the dinghy out to sea, and if he didn't act quickly he would soon find himself floating out to the North Sea. Alfonin quickly slid over the back of the dinghy and involuntarily sucked in his breath as the Baltic temperature of the water hit him. He started to push the boat towards the north bank. He ducked his head every time a volley of rounds came near him but he soon realised that the machine gunners were not wasting their bullets on boats full of dead and dying men. The Tommies had now switched fire to the second wave.

Alfonin eventually reached the north bank, where he pulled himself up onto a riverbank that was intricately interlaced with reels of barbed wire. He lay panting like a beached whale as he recovered his breath. Alfonin spotted several more figures lying on the bank, but most of them did not appear to be moving. He looked back across the river. Tracer rounds continued to track their targets as the machine gunners lined up on each dinghy in turn. The Tommies spent no more than half a dozen seconds drilling holes into each dinghy before they decided that it was time to switch fire to the next boat. The entire river was full of boats that were either sinking or drifting aimlessly as they were carried by the current out to sea. Barely a handful of boats were still rowing towards the north bank. Above the staccato sound of the machine guns firing Alfonin could hear a constant wail of pain, anger and despair as wounded men cried for help and for their mothers, as they drowned in their sinking dinghies.

Alfonin punched a fist into the palm of his other hand in impotent fury. Tears ran in rivers down his cheek as he watched his men, his Grenadiers, being massacred. All work on the pontoon bridges had also stopped abruptly. The bridges were barely ten metres long and they were covered in a thin film of dead and dying engineers who had been knocked down like so many skittles. "Grenadiers! Grenadiers!" he shouted at the men lying on the river bank. "Make your way to me!" he ordered.

Several figures slowly lurched to their feet and

started to stagger their way towards Alfonin.

"Be careful, lads!" Alfonin warned. "Watch out for land -!"

Too late one of the soldiers stepped on a land mine that exploded and sent him tumbling head over heels back down the steep river bank towards the Tweed. He toppled in and sank before any of his shocked comrades could react and save him.

"Use your bayonets and prod the ground for land mines!" Alfonin ordered.

Eventually half a dozen wet and weary, miserable and thoroughly bedraggled soldiers reached him.

"Grenadiers?" Alfonin asked.

"No, sir," The most alert soldier answered. "Jaegers, sir. We drifted downriver when our dinghy was hit."

"No matter," Alfonin said. "Any engineers?"

The men shook their heads.

"Anyone carrying explosives then?"

One of the Jaegers raised his hand.

"Excellent." Alfonin smiled like a wolf. "It's time for us to hit back and give the Tommies a taste of their own medicine. Let's get back into the war and even the score a little bit."

Chapter Twenty One

A runner arrived at Mendoza's slit trench. "Colonel Mendoza?"

"Yes, Stabsgefreiter." Mendoza noticed that the runner was a corporal, which was exactly Hitler's rank and occupation during the last War.

The corporal saluted. "Sir, the first three waves have failed to secure the north bank of the river. The Grenadiers and the Jaegers are no longer combat effective." The corporal waited for this unwelcome news to sink in.

"Do you know if anyone made it to the north bank?"

The corporal shook his head. "No, sir. The entire north bank of the river is covered in a thick blanket of smoke and fire. It's impossible to get an accurate situation report. We've heard nothing on the radio, nor have we seen any signal flares. We're assuming that they've been wiped out."

"I see," Mendoza said grimly. "What are my orders, Corporal?"

"The Artillery is going to commence firing at the north bank in ten minutes time at oh seven hundred hours, sir. They will also lay down a barrage of smoke to cover your river crossing, which you are also to commence at oh seven hundred hours. They will cease fire when you reach the other side, sir."

"Start firing at the other side?" Mendoza repeated in confusion. "But will the artillery not kill some of our own men?"

"Yes, Colonel." The corporal looked at Mendoza as if he was talking to the village idiot. "But we'll kill some of theirs as well. We do have another brigade in reserve, sir."

"Understood." Mendoza nodded his head.

"And then you are to proceed with your mission,

Colonel, push straight through Berwick, and relieve the paratroopers at Beattie, Robinson and Auchterlonie."

"Understood."

"Do you have any further questions, sir?" the corporal asked.

"No, Corporal. Thank you," Mendoza replied.

"Best of luck, sir." The corporal saluted and ran off.

"Keep paddling, men!" Mendoza shouted above the sound of the British machine guns as they searched blindly for targets through the thick smoke. "Fire at where the tracers are coming from!" Mendoza ordered. "Disrupt their aim!"

Mendoza looked around him. In contrast to the Grenadiers and the Jaegers, Mendoza had decided to launch all of his forty-eight dinghies at the same time. The entire regiment was crossing the Tweed at once. Mendoza reasoned that there were only a fixed number of machine gun posts and if he launched all of his boats at the same time then the British would not be able to spend as much time shooting at each individual dinghy. As a result, there was a veritable flotilla of boats rowing across the river. Mendoza could not help but be awed and impressed by the sight: this is what the armada must have looked like. The British machine gunners were firing blind on pre-arranged lines of fire, and they were hitting targets especially where adjacent machine guns fields of fire interlocked. However, the smoke was helping to camouflage their movement, and more dinghies were moving than were staying still or drifting aimlessly down the river. The British were firing mortars and artillery shells at the fleet and Mendoza and his men were soaked to the bone. Mendoza ducked as a high explosive round scored a direct hit on the boat beside him. The shell sent the unlucky Legiónaries flying high up in the sky, and

Mendoza and his men were showered with blood and body parts. Mendoza gritted his teeth. "Keep paddling, men!" Mendoza ordered. "We're nearly there!"

Mendoza allowed himself a smile. He started to think that they actually might make it to the other side. Mendoza suddenly wrinkled up his nose. What was that smell? It smelt familiar...

"Colonel! Look! The Inglese have set fire to the river!" a Legiónary shouted in alarm.

Mendoza looked behind him. A wall of flames suddenly shot up from the river into the air and engulfed the dinghy less than fifty metres behind him. The Legiónaries screamed in agony as their clothes caught fire. The soldiers jumped into the water to douse their burning clothes but the very river itself was on fire, and the Legiónaries were soon consumed by the flames.

"Madre Dios!" Mendoza said in horror with his hand on his mouth. "The Inglese have poured petrol into the river and they've set it on fire..."

Mendoza watched as the burning oil slick was carried down the river by the current. It caught up with and consumed all of the dinghies in its path. The Legiónaries in its way rowed frantically to escape, but to no avail. The oil slick moved faster than they could paddle. Tears ran down Mendoza's face as he listened helplessly to the sound of his men screaming, as they were burned alive. Mendoza looked at his men. They had all stopped rowing and were looking at the fiery inferno in fascinated horror.

"Legiónaries! Look to your front!" Mendoza ordered. "There's nothing that we can do to help our comrades. But we can help ourselves. If we stay on this river we will be burnt alive as well. We have a job to do and a mission to complete. Row for the north bank!"

As his Legiónaries started to row, Mendoza looked

to his left and his right. Barely a dozen boats had survived the fiery oil slick.

"Sitrep?" Ulrich demanded.

"We have captured both ends of the bridge, sir, but the British are continuing to launch constant counter-attacks," the young second lieutenant reported.

"What is our strength, von Mackensen?"

"Forty-five men, sir."

"Forty-five men out of one hundred and eighty?" Ulrich exclaimed in horror. "Well, I just hope that our reinforcements reach us pretty damned quick."

Von Mackensen coughed. "Sir, that figure includes paratrooper reinforcements. The paras are drifting into our position in dribs and drabs three or four men at a time..."

"Mein Gott!" Ulrich swore. "Any word from Robinson or the Auchterlonie Bridge, Untersturmführer?"

Von Mackensen shook his head. "No, sir. We haven't heard any word on the radio and we haven't been able to make any physical contact either with the platoons tasked to capture Robinson or with the platoons tasked to capture the Auchterlonie Bridge, sir," he reported. "However, there is the constant sound of small arms fire coming from Robinson, sir, so we can presume that at least some of our men are still alive and are trying to accomplish their missions."

"We're in a tight spot," Ulrich thought aloud.

"We're on our chin straps, sir." Von Mackensen nodded as he confirmed Ulrich's rather understated observation. "We are rapidly running out of ammunition, medical supplies, food and water, sir. Unless more reinforcements reach us soon it can only be a matter of time before the British crash through our defences and capture the bridge."

Ulrich nodded in agreement with von Mackensen's assessment of the situation.

"What are your orders, sir?" von Mackensen asked.

"Tell the men to salvage whatever equipment that they can from both our own and the enemy's dead and wounded. Tell the men that the infantry will have crossed the Tweed by now and that reinforcements are on the way. Tell the men that we need to hold on until the Spaniards relieve us," Ulrich said grimly.

"The Spanish, sir?" von Mackensen guffawed with derision. "I wouldn't pin all of our hopes on the Spaniards, sir. They hate us more than the Brits!"

Ulrich suddenly grabbed the startled young officer by his lapels with both hands and pulled him towards his sharp and snapping teeth. "If I hear you say that about the Spanish again, von Mackensen, I will personally shoot you in the face!" Ulrich growled. "The only thing that is keeping our boys going and stopping them from giving up and throwing in the towel is hope! If you take their hope away from them then you take away their only motivation for fighting and holding on. Whatever our differences are with the Spaniards, they are professional soldiers and they will carry out their mission or die in the attempt. We are also professional soldiers and we will do the same, Untersturmführer von Mackensen. Do I make myself clear?"

"Crystal clear, sir," the young officer replied sheepishly.

"Good." Ulrich released von Mackensen and straightened out his ruffled tunic. "Then we'll say no more of it. That will be all, Untersturmführer von Mackensen; carry on."

"Yes, sir." Von Mackensen saluted and scurried away with his tail between his legs.

"It's no good, sir. We can't get through to the bridge,"

the young corporal reported dejectedly.

Von Stein looked at the exhausted paratrooper. There were large black bags underneath his eyes and his face was covered in a mixture of soot, dirt, camouflage cream and blood.

"That's not good enough, Rottenführer," von Stein said angrily as he shook his head. "Tell Scharführer Mercer that he has to try again. My squad will provide covering fire."

"I'm afraid that won't be possible, sir."

"What do you mean that won't be possible, Rottenführer?" Von Stein demanded furiously. "Are you refusing to obey a direct order?"

"No, sir. Scharführer Mercer and his entire squad were wiped out in the last attack."

Von Stein was momentarily lost for words. He suddenly noticed the Luger pistol that he was holding in his hand. Von Stein realised with a shock of horror that he was preparing to execute the young corporal for refusing to carry out a direct order. He hadn't even been aware that he had taken the weapon out of its holster. Von Stein subtly flicked the safety catch back on and slipped the Luger back into its case. He hoped that the rottenführer had not noticed.

Von Stein turned around and looked at the tired and terrified faces of the young paratroopers who lay huddled together on either side of him, sheltering behind an abandoned bullet-riddled lorry. He turned to the front and put his hand on the young corporal's shoulder. "It's all right, Rottenführer; stand the men down for the time being. Get something to eat and drink. We'll need to think of another way to capture the bridge."

The corporal's shoulders sunk with relief as he repeated the orders to his squad. They took cover behind a burnt out car and as soon as they sat down the young paratroopers fell onto an exhausted sleep. Only the rottenführer remained awake, on guard in order to protect his men from attack.

He's a good leader, von Stein thought to himself with a smile. He looks after his men.

"What's going on here, Hauptsturmführer von Stein? Where are the rest of your men?"

Von Stein turned around and breathed out a massive sigh of relief.

"Sturmbannführer Schwarzenegger, sir! Talk about a sight for sore eyes! Am I glad to see you, sir!" He saluted, as the major did the same. At last, von Stein thought, he would be able to pass on the buck of capturing the bridge to someone else.

"Where are the rest of your men, Captain?"

"This is all that I have left, sir," von Stein answered matter of factly.

"A dozen men?"

"Yes, sir," von Stein nodded. "I did have about twenty men in total, but the rest were killed attacking the bridge." He pointed to the front. The one hundred metres between the lorry and the northern end of the Auchterlonie Bridge was covered in a matt of bodies. "Is this all that you have, sir?"

Schwarzenegger turned around and glanced at the half a dozen dirty and dishevelled, worse-for-wear-looking paratroopers crouching behind him. He shrugged his shoulders in resignation. "At one point I had managed to gather up a veritable army of about forty men - and then the airforce dropped a stick of bombs on me, and this is all that I have left."

"Which airforce, sir?" Von Stein asked.

Schwarzenegger shrugged off the question. "Luftwaffe or RAF, what difference does it make? Their bombs killed my boys, and here we are."

"Yes, sir."

"Why aren't you attacking the bridge?" Schwarzenegger asked.

"We've tried, sir and I've lost half of my men in the attempt. The problem is that we don't have any MG 42s, any flame throwers or any Bangalore torpedoes, sir," von Stein answered. "All we have are Schmessiers, rifles and hand grenades, sir. Every time that we've assaulted the enemy positions using a frontal attack the two pillboxes guarding the north entrance to the bridge have cut us to pieces, sir. We have to think of another tactic, sir."

"We don't have time to think of another tactic, von Stein," Schwarzenegger said icily. "You will just have to try again. You will have to attack the pillboxes again and you must be prepared to lose the other half of your men in the attempt. My men will provide covering fire." He pointed to his exhausted looking paratroopers.

Von Stein looked at his own paratroopers lying down beside him, who were listening intently to the exchange of words. They looked wide eyed with fear and horror at the thought of launching yet another futile attack on the pillboxes. They looked like rabbits caught in the headlamps of a speeding car.

"But, sir! We've tried that!" Von Stein protested. "A frontal attack won't work! We'll be cut down before we've run a dozen metres!" He looked at the faces of his frightened paratroopers. They were absolutely petrified. Von Stein looked into the young corporal's eyes.

"Hauptsturmführer von Stein, I'm giving you a direct order: I am ordering you to assault those pillboxes at once!"

Von Stein shook his head. "I won't do it, sir. It's a suicide mission. You'll be sending my men to their deaths. I may as well shoot them myself. We still have time to think of another plan."

"No we don't, von Stein," the major said with cruelly bared teeth that exposed his gums. "Time is a luxury that we simply can't afford." Schwarzenegger took out his Luger, cocked it, flicked off the safety catch and pointed the pistol at von Stein's head. "I won't ask you again. I'm going to count to three and then I'm going to blow your head off. One... two..."

The shot startled von Stein, who jumped out of his skin. He put his hands up to his face and searched for an entry and exit wound. I'm still alive, he thought to himself. He looked to his side. Schwarzenegger lay on his back with a shocked and surprised expression on his face, with a single bullet hole in the centre of his forehead.

"Anyone else got any objections to us resting here whilst the Captain thinks of another way to capture the bridge that doesn't involve getting us killed?"

All of the paratroopers, including the major's, shook their heads in relief.

"Good. I didn't think so."

"Thank you, Rottenführer...?"

"Rottenführer Barbie, Karl Barbie, sir."

"Well, thank you, Rottenführer Barbie, for saving my life," von Stein said gratefully.

"Don't mention it, sir," Barbie answered graciously. "And thank you, sir for saving my life by not agreeing to carry out the mad Major's crazy order. So we're quits now, sir. You owe me nothing. And anyway, I've always wondered what it would fell like to frag an officer, and now I know."

Alan ran the four hundred yards as if he was competing at the Olympic Games. Every few feet he passed dead or dying militiamen who he avoided as if they had the plague, running past them without slowing down, never mind stopping to help them. He remembered the last words that Captain Baldwin had said to A Company as they were about to cross the pontoon bridge: keep running, and don't stop for anything or anybody.

A salvo of half a dozen artillery rounds fell about one hundred yards in front of the running schoolboy. The middle two rounds landed slap bang in the middle of the pontoon bridge and exploded, sending a shower of wooden planks and the parts and pieces of a platoon of Blackshirts fifty metres into the air. Alan hugged the deck and took cover behind the body of a dead Militiaman as the debris fell back to earth.

"Come on, Mitchell!" a familiar voice shouted as a man grabbed him by the back of his webbing straps and dragged Alan onto his feet. "The artillery has found the range. It'll be only a matter of seconds before the Brits fire again! If you stay here, you'll die!"

Alan kept close behind Major Mason as his CO ran towards the jagged end of the ripped up pontoon bridge. Mason jumped into the river without hesitating, and swam for the other side of the ruined bridge. He climbed up onto the splintered decking and leaned down to haul Alan out of the water.

"Come on, Mitchell! I'll race you to Berwick! You should be able to beat an old man like me!" Mason shouted. "Last man there is a rotten egg!" Alan followed his teacher as Mason sprinted the last hundred yards at full speed.

When they reached the north bank of the Tweed they both collapsed in an exhausted heap. Alan looked up as he heard another salvo of artillery rounds flying through the sky. This time, four of the six shells landed on the pontoon bridge and blew it to smithereens. The entire structure broke free of its moorings and started to drift out of control along with the current. There was a wail of despair from the surviving militiamen as they realised that they were about to be swept out to the

North Sea.

"You see, Mitchell?" Mason panted. "What did I tell you?"

"Thank you, sir," Alan said as he finally recovered his breath.

"What for?" Mason asked with raised eyebrows.

"For saving my life, sir."

Mason waved his hand dismissively. "Don't mention it. I'm sure that you'd do the same for me."

Don't bet on it, Alan thought to himself.

"There it is, Alfredo. There's Beattie Bridge," Mendoza said as he lowered his binoculars and passed them over to his second-in-command. He looked at his wristwatch. "One pm. We're an hour late."

"Better late than never, sir. And for a while back there at the river, I thought that it was more likely to be never." Astray looked through the binoculars and then nodded his head. "It's about four hundred metres away. Shall I fire the signal gun and let the Germans know that we're coming in, Colonel?"

"Yes, Alfredo." Mendoza nodded his head. "How many men do we have left?"

Astray shrugged his shoulders. "About one hundred and twenty men roughly grouped into four platoons, sir."

"Madre Dios!" Mendoza swore. "One hundred and twenty men out of five hundred? How the hell did that happen?"

"We lost over half of our men at the river, Colonel, and the rest since," Astray answered.

Mendoza sighed in resignation. "All right. Alfredo, order the first two platoons to get over the bridge and take up defensive positions on the north side of the bridge and order the last two platoons to take up defensive positions on the south side of the bridge. I'll

304

meet you at the German headquarters, which I presume will be on the north side of the bridge. Get moving as soon as you see the flare's signal. Understood?"

"Understood, Jefe!"

"Good!" Mendoza squeezed his friend on the shoulder. "I'll see you on the other side of the bridge! Let's go!"

Astray grinned like a naughty schoolboy, saluted, and ran off to convey the command to the waiting Legiónaries.

Ulrich breathed a massive sigh of relief as he saw the three green flares explode in the sky in quick succession.

"Untersturmführer, pass the word along to the troops to hold their fire. Our relief force has arrived."

"Yes, sir." Von Mackensen smiled as he saluted, and ran off to pass on the welcome news to the waiting paras.

Herold's last words echoed through Ulrich's head. Hold until relieved... hold until relieved. Well, he had completed his side of the mission. The question was: had everyone else completed theirs?

"Obersturmbannführer Ulrich, I presume?" Mendoza said as he saluted the SS Colonel.

Ulrich clicked his heels together like a Prussian aristocrat and gave a slight bow. "At your service, Colonel Mendoza." He returned the salute.

"What's your sitrep, Obersturmbannführer?" Mendoza asked.

"We currently control both sides of the bridge and that's about all, Colonel," Ulrich answered grimly.

"No word from Auchterlonie Bridge or Robinson?"

Ulrich shook his head. "No, Colonel. I think that it's safe to assume that the mission to capture them has

305

failed. They are both very much still in enemy hands."

"Strength?" Mendoza asked as he took a cigar out of his tunic breast pocket. He chuckled as he noticed Ulrich watching him with bemusement. "It's an old tradition of mine, Obersturmbannführer, which I began in Morocco: I always smoke a cigar after I successfully complete a mission. Would you like one, Obersturmbannführer? Finest Cuban?"

"Thank you, Colonel," Ulrich said with a smile. "It's very kind of you." Ulrich accepted the cigar and sniffed it appreciatively. He cut off the end of both cigars with his bayonet and shared a lit match with Mendoza. "I have about thirty paratroopers left organised into roughly four weak and under strength squads, with two squads on each side of the river."

"Madre Dios!" Mendoza exclaimed with wide eyes. "And I thought that we had suffered heavy losses. I have about one hundred and twenty Legiónaries left. I've ordered them to dig in and reinforce your paras, Obersturmbannführer. If you'll excuse me I'll go and check that they're in the correct positions."

"Of course, Colonel. Please feel free to carry on. Make yourself at home. Mi casa su casa."

"Ah! You speak Italian!" Mendoza said with a toothpaste advertisement smile.

Ulrich laughed. "Only enough to make a fool of myself with the ladies!"

Mendoza chuckled. "I presume that you know that my daughter, Aurora is a good friend of your girlfriend, Alice?"

"Yes, I did know that, Colonel. I haven't spoken to Alice since I deployed up north a few days ago. I trust that Alice and Aurora are both well?"

Mendoza paused before he spoke. "Obersturmbannführer Ulrich, Aurora and Alice were both kidnapped."

306

"What?" Ulrich spat out his cigar and his face turned as white as a sheet. He held onto the side of the bridge to steady himself.

"It's all right. They're both safe." Mendoza put a reassuring hand on Ulrich's arm. "Fortunately, they were rescued." Mendoza watched Ulrich's reaction carefully. "You had no idea?"

"Absolutely none." Ulrich's eyes were wide with shock. "Nobody told me. What happened? Who rescued them?"

"A company of Fascist Militia happened to stumble across them on a training exercise. The kidnappers ambushed and killed about sixty Blackshirts before they successfully escaped. They abandoned the girls in their haste to get away."

Ulrich shook his head in awe. "I swear, Colonel, the Resistance are becoming more and more daring every day. First they killed the King, the Queen and the Prime Minister, and then they almost killed Hitler. I only just survived their ambush on the Führer by the skin of my teeth."

Mendoza shook his head. "It wasn't the Resistance, Obersturmbannführer. It was your lot; it was the SS."

"What?" Ulrich's eyes nearly bulged out of their sockets. "The SS? Kidnap Alice and Aurora? I don't believe it!"

Mendoza nodded his head. "I'm afraid so, Obersturmführer. Both Aurora and Alice identified their kidnappers as SS and the Blackshirts found SS equipment all over the kidnapper's hideout. The kidnappers were definitely SS all right. The kidnap was a continuation of the vendetta that we are pursuing with one of your officers, a Hauptsturmführer Manfred von Stein. Do you know him?"

"Von Stein? I should think that I know him." Ulrich raised his eyebrows. "He's the company commander of

307

one of my units, Charlie Company."

"Obersturmbannführer Ulrich, von Stein raped Alice and Aurora, cut off my daughter's finger, and threatened to return her to me bit by bloody bit. If the Militia had not rescued the girls I have no doubt that von Stein would have carried out his threat to mutilate and murder Aurora. Obersturmbannführer Ulrich, do you know where he is now?"

Ulrich was too shell-shocked to answer. One of his own men had raped his girlfriend? Ulrich simply could not digest the information. He had briefed von Stein and the other company commanders only the day before.

"Obersturmbannführer Ulrich, do you know where von Stein is now?" Mendoza asked again.

Ulrich shook his head and answered as if he was in a hypnotic trance. "I have absolutely no idea. His company was tasked to capture Auchterlonie Bridge. We've heard nothing from the Bridge or from the company which was tasked to capture Robinson. They could all well be dead for all we know." Ulrich's voice trailed off.

"No matter." Mendoza shrugged his shoulders. "As I said before, I better go and inspect the positions. By your leave, Obersturmbannführer." Mendoza bowed and left Ulrich standing dazed and confused, as his mind struggled to get to grips with the realisation that one of his own officers had kidnapped and raped his girlfriend.

"Well, that's set the cat amongst the pigeons." Mendoza said grimly as Astray joined him.

"Do you think that he knows anything, Colonel?" The major asked.

"Well, if he does, then that performance deserves an Oscar." Mendoza shook his head. "No, Alfredo; he doesn't know a thing. Unfortunately, it won't save him when the axe falls, which is a shame because he doesn't seem a bad fellow for a German."

"But, Colonel, you told me that the only good German is a -"

"I know what I told you, Alfredo," Mendoza said. "But I'm not a complete and utter bastard -"

"Oh yes you are, sir!" Astray interrupted cheekily.

"Oi!"Mendoza protested. "Less of your insubordination, Astray, or I'll have you reduced to the ranks so fast it will make your head spin!" Mendoza punched his old friend playfully on the arm. "It's just that I can recognise a fellow traveller when I see one."

"What do you mean by that, sir?"

"I get the funny feeling that Ulrich also thinks that he's fighting for the wrong side."

"Oh…"

Mendoza shrugged his shoulders in resignation. "Never mind; you can't make an omelette without breaking some eggs."

"A big Chinese fellow pulled me right over… a big Chinese fellow pulled me right over… You turned Indian, didn't you? You turned Indian, didn't you? Typical Italian, brings a knife to a gun fight… Typical Italian, brings a knife to a gun fight…"

"I think that we've heard enough of the ten o' clock broadcast, Jordan. You can switch back to the Militia channel now," Baldwin ordered.

"Yes, sir." Corporal Jordan chuckled as he switched channels. "Those BBC Radio Free North messages never fail to amuse me, Captain Baldwin. I can picture dozens of amateur Mata Haris and secretive Scarlet Pimpernels sitting around their radio sets listening intently for their special message. Do they not realise that that Jew-loving Bolshevik Churchill and his clique of war-mongering gangsters have lost the war?"

"Do you really think so, Jordan?" Baldwin asked.

Jordan guffawed. "I know so, sir. I fought as a Blackshirt in the East End of London against the Reds in the thirties, sir. I was as confident back then that Fascism would eventually triumph as I am now, sir. And here we are!" Jordan smiled like a wolf at lambing time.

" And here we are, indeed," Baldwin said.

"Anyway, sir," Jordan said. "I wonder what those messages do mean."

"Well, I know what 'you turned Indian, didn't you?' means for starters," Baldwin answered.

"What's that, sir?" Jordan wanted to join in the joke.

"This." Baldwin nodded.

Jordan fell straight onto his front with two giant bloody bullet exit wounds in the centre of his chest. Alan walked over to him, fired his silencer pistol twice more into the back of his head, and spat on the nape of his neck. "Dirty Fascist bastard."

The three red flares exploded high up in the pitch black sky.

"I wonder what those flares signal, Major. Perhaps another British assault?" von Mackensen asked. "A night attack, perhaps?"

"No, Untersturmführer." Astray shook his head sadly. "Those flares give the signal to execute Operation Glencoe."

"Operation Glencoe?" von Mackensen said with raised eyebrows. "What is that? A private Spanish operation?"

"In a manner of speaking, yes."

Von Mackensen felt as if he had been punched in the chest. He looked down to see a Legiónary dagger sticking in his heart. He futilely tried to grab the hilt, but missed. "You... you bastard."

"I'm sorry, my friend," Astray said with genuine sorrow. "You seem like a decent fellow... for a German."

But Astray's words of regret were wasted. Von Mackensen was dead before his body hit the ground.

Baldwin ran in short bursts through the back streets of Berwick-Upon-Tweed, with Alan hot on his heels. They were both acutely aware of the continued resistance of British diehards who were holding out in the hope of a successful British counter-attack to recapture the town. The pair took cover in doorways and behind blown up barricades, British lorries, and the burnt out carcasses of a couple of German Panzers.

"Captain Baldwin and runner coming in!" Baldwin shouted as he approached the Militia headquarters.

"Watch out for snipers, sir!" a voice warned in a thick Irish brogue. "Guard, covering fire!"

"Now, Alan!" The pair sprinted the last twenty yards as a hidden sniper tried to get a lead on them. They just made it as a lump of masonry exploded above their heads. The pair collapsed in an undignified heap inside the doorway. As Baldwin recovered his breath, he thought how ironic it would be if he had been killed by his own side. He smiled as he remembered how Ramón had warned him that this would be a better fate than that of being captured by the British.

"Thank you, Sergeant," Baldwin said with sincere gratitude.

"My pleasure, sir," the Irish sergeant answered with a smile.

"Captain Baldwin and Private Mitchell! What a pleasant surprise!" Mason welcomed the newcomers with a warm smile of genuine affection. "Tell me, what brings you to our neck of the woods? I doubt that

you're out on a stroll for the good of your health!"
Mason talked as if Baldwin had dropped in for a cup of
tea.

"You're right sir; I didn't run through the streets of
the town risking life and limb for the good of my
health. I came to ask you a vital question, Major."
Baldwin counted heads as he spoke: Mason, the
sergeant, a radio operator and three Militiamen.

"Oh yes, Captain?" Mason asked with raised
eyebrows. "It must be important for you to leave your
company headquarters."

Alan silently flicked off the safety catch of his
Schmessier machine gun and casually stood pointing it
in the direction of the sergeant and his four fellow
Fascists.

"It is, sir. You might say that the answer to this
question is a matter of life or death…"

"Now, I'm intrigued," Mason said with genuine
interest and curiosity. "What is this mysterious
question, John?"

"What is your favourite Shakespeare play, sir?"
Baldwin asked.

Alan saw the sergeant's eyebrow twitch. He knows
that there's something not quite right, Alan thought to
himself, as he aimed his machine gun at the Irishman.

"My favourite Shakespeare play?" Mason answered
with a furrowed brow. "Is this a joke?"

"No, sir. Far from it." Baldwin put his right hand
behind his back.

"Oh, I don't know… Julius Caesar?"

"Wrong answer." Baldwin shot him twice in the
chest with his silencer pistol. Mason timbered onto his
back like a lumber jacked tree.

Alan put first pressure on his trigger.

"The Scottish play - Macbeth!" the Irish sergeant
shouted.

Time seemed to stand still in the room.

"That was leaving it a little late, Sergeant. I almost shot you," Alan said with wide eyes.

The sergeant was breathing heavily. "You... you took me by surprise, that's all."

"What about these four, Sergeant?" Baldwin asked as he gestured with his pistol towards the remaining Militiamen.

"Trev's with me, sir. He's a sleeper as well." The sergeant gestured towards the radio operator.

"Err... the Scottish play - Macbeth." Trev stumbled the password.

"And these three, Sergeant...?"

"Sergeant O'Brien, sir," the Irish sergeant answered. "Tony's a convicted rapist and Mitch is a convicted murderer, sir. They only joined the Blackshirts to get out of prison, Captain. We'd be doing the Hangman a favour if we executed these two for him," O'Brien said matter-of-factly.

"Please, Sergeant...!" Tony fell to his knees and begged with upraised hands.

Mitch quickly followed suit and knelt praying, mumbling incoherently, with his face raised towards heaven.

Alan's nose twitched automatically as a sudden waft of ammonia assaulted his nostrils. He recognised the reason for that familiar smell. One or both of the criminals had pissed themselves.

Baldwin nodded. "And the corporal here?"

"Oh, Dave is a genuine dyed-in-the-wool Fascist, aren't you, Dave? Can't you tell by the toothbrush moustache, sir?"

"Bugger off, you dirty Fenian bastard!" the Corporal swore venomously. "I've never trusted the Irish! I always knew that you were a stinking traitor!"

O'Brien raised his eyebrows. "Isn't that rather like

313

the pot calling the kettle black?"

"Enough idle chit-chat," Baldwin said impatiently. "Sergeant O'Brien, if you wouldn't mind doing the honours?"

"Certainly, sir. It would be my pleasure." O'Brien cocked his Schmessier machine gun and flicked off the safety catch.

"Sergeant O'Brien, for the love of God, no…!"

"Mercy, please…!"

"I'll show you boys the same mercy that you showed your victims. May God have mercy on your souls, because I certainly don't?"

"No-!"

O'Brien opened fire.

The two criminals died begging on their knees whilst the Fascist died defiant to the last.

"What now, sir?" O'Brien didn't give the smoking corpses of his former comrades a second glance.

"Well, Sergeant O'Brien, I guess that proves that you're genuine," Baldwin said sardonically.

"True blue, sir." O'Brien nodded his head with a smile.

"Now we signal a general withdrawal and really throw a spanner in the works!"

"Lay on, MacDuff!" O'Brien said.

"Just one moment, sir," Alan said as he crossed the room to Mason's body.

"Alan, I shot Mason twice in the chest," Baldwin said with a hint of annoyance in his voice. "I think that I can safely assure you that he's dead."

Mason slowly opened his eyes. "Alan… what? What happened?" he asked, as if he had just woken up from a deep sleep.

"You see, Captain? I told you that he's not dead. We made the same mistake the first time. We shot him in the chest. You've got to shoot him in the head to make

314

sure that he's well and truly dead. Golden Boy here has more lives than a cat."

A firework exploded in Mason's head. "You... Sam! The St George's Day Massacre!"

Alan smiled like a lion before it devoured its prey. "You see, Major Mason. I told you that your amnesia wouldn't last forever and that you would remember what happened one day. Sam botched the job and I'm going to finish it. It's just a shame that you didn't remember before you saved my life today on the pontoon bridge."

"Why, you... why, you treacherous little bastard!" Mason spat out a globule of blood.

"I've been called worse." He pointed his pistol between Mason's eyes. "You know, it's a damned shame that you turned out to be a dirty, stinking traitor, because you were one of my favourite teachers. Oh well." Alan shrugged his shoulders nonchalantly.

"No, wait -!"

"This is for Colonel Hook."

Mason locked eyes with Alan, smiled grimly, and nodded his head.

"C'est la guerre."

THE END